- BOOK 2

SATY

KA

EYE OF BRAHMA

KEVIN MISSAL

FINGERPRINT!

Published 2024

FiNGERPRINT!
An imprint of Prakash Books India Pvt. Ltd

113/A, Darya Ganj,
New Delhi-110 002
Email: info@prakashbooks.com/sales@prakashbooks.com

Fingerprint Publishing
@FingerprintP
@fingerprintpublishingbooks
www.fingerprintpublishing.com

ISBN: 978 93 8836 915 2

THE STORY SO FAR . . .
DHARMAYODDHA KALKI: THE AVATAR OF VISHNU

NOTE: The book is divided into two parts and in which points of view of the characters intersect each other. For the reader's comprehension, the points of view have been separated.

PART 1 – THE BATTLE OF SHAMBALA
PART 2 – THE RISE OF KALI

THE BATTLE OF SHAMBALA

KALI'S POV

Kali, the young commander of a ragtag group of Tribal[1] outcasts, is seeking to seize Indragarh, the capital of Keekatpur province. The Tribals in his army comprise of Rakshas, Nagas, and Yakshas. The Tribals and the Manavs (the elite, human population) are enemies and Kali wants to bring them together and put an end to the socio-political ostracism of the Tribals. He defeats King Vedanta of Indragarh, spreading Tribals all over the northern part of the country, Illavarti. He begins to build his base in the capital city and live a free, dignified life. But his problems are just beginning.

After his triumph on the battlefield, he falls ill. Durukti, his overprotective sisters, is concerned for him. Kali begins to dream about his childhood and how he had lost his siblings in a fire, created as a result of the animosity between the Tribals. Durukti

[1] Non-Manav groups and clans in Illavarti.

learns from her handmaiden Symrin that there is a cure, known as the Soma, hidden in the caves adjoining Shambala, a village. It is considered a gift given by Lord Indra to the world, but is no one knows if it really exists. Durukti is unsure about the miracle drug's potency but still decides to leave for Shambala. And when an assassination attempt puts Kali's life in grave danger, she takes the army of Rakshas with her and reaches Shambala pronto.

KALKI'S POV

Kalki Hari, born to Sumati and Vishnuyath, and brother to Arjan, is a strong man who has powers greater than anyone around him. He resides in Shambala with his family. He falls in love with Lakshmi, who is a fellow resident in their sleepy little village, most famous for its self-sustained dairy economy. Kalki seeks to find out how he is so strong, until one day he returns to his dairy farm and finds his father has been kidnapped by Mlecchas.

With the help of Arjan, Lakshmi, and his strong friend Bala, Kalki begins to gather arms and resources. Kalki reaches Indragarh in order to take weapons from the armoury, and gets in trouble there. He returns in the nick of time, only to realize that Arjan and Bala have got themselves embroiled with Kripa, a drunkard who claims that he knows where the Mlecchas live.

Kalki saves the day but loses his father in the process. Before passing away, he tells Kalki who Kripa is. Later on, Kalki confronts Kripa, who tells Kalki that he (Kalki) is an Avatar of Vishnu. There have been many Avatars till now, but he is considered to be the last one. This explains the unnatural strength that courses through Kalki's veins and muscles. Kalki had ingested Soma indirectly when he was in his mother's womb, causing him to develop supernatural powers. Soma, the nectar of gods, can only work and show its true potency on the Dharm and the Adharm (the rough equivalents of good and bad in this narrative world) and help them to achieve their true forms. Kalki is Dharm.

Later, Kalki learns that Durukti has come with an army to their village, demanding access to the Soma. Fearing that the Soma would go in the hands of Adharm, thereby causing havoc, he tries to prevent it from happening by coaxing the villagers to come together and fight against the attack on their home and the mystical material contained therein.

The battle ensues. Kalki loses and Lakshmi dies. Kalki retaliates by attacking Durukti, who traps him in a cage and takes him to Indragarh, leaving Shambala in ruins. She has gained access to the Soma. Arjan, Kripa, and Bala plan to save Kalki.

THE RISE OF KALI

KALI'S POV

After ingesting the Soma, Kali starts recovering. He realizes there is a lot of political intrigue in the city and he begins to beat his enemies strategically. His careful strategizing involves playing on divided loyalties, making false promises, and backstabbing. He also begins to see visions that tell him to see his past and embrace his heritage of an Asura, an extinct race.

Kali is informed through Martanja (the Rakshas lieutenant in the city) that Durukti has taken a villager captive from Shambala. Kali finds out that Durukti has fallen for this villager. He gets jealous and physically assaults her. Kali then confronts this villager, who is Kalki, informing him that he will be tried on charges of sedition.

ARJAN'S POV

Arjan, Bala, and Kripa reach Indragarh where they take help from Padma and Ratri, who are related to the late Lakshmi. They begin to hatch plans and try to help Kalki escape from the heavily guarded prison. Kripa has an unusual idea. He wants to use the same Somas that had got them into trouble, and make bombs. He refers to these as *astras*.

Arjan, Bala, and Padma reach the location where the Somas and successfully take it, before they realize that the trials have begun. Kripa makes a *vimana* (a flying chariot) and swoops in with his comrades during the trial and helps Kalki escape. This daring and ingenious escape leaves an entire gallery of spectators spellbound.

Kalki ends up duelling Martanja. Though Martanja has ingested Soma (thanks to the devious chicanery of Kali) Kalki's manages to defeat him by tapping into his supernatural strength.

KALKI'S POV

Kalki and his gang return home only to learn that Kali has declared them fugitives. Kali also knows that they are living with none other than Ratri, who is a high level minister under the state administration. He burns down Ratri's house thinking he has killed everyone inside. Kalki and the others manage to escape. But Bala and Ratri had fallen for each other. Seeing Ratri in distress because of them, Bala chooses to return to save her. But tragically, both are killed by a wrathful Kali.

Meanwhile, Padma has been trying to find Vedanta's weakness since she wants revenge for her brothers. They had been killed by Vedanta. She finds his daughter and plans to assassinate her. However, Arjan stops her. The bell in the fort tolls and they try to escape. But a wounded Arjan is left behind as Padma manages to get away.

Feeling guilty for their own roles in the turn of events so far, Padma and Kripa leave with Kalki. Kalki has his own reasons to discredit them for their betrayal.

MANASA'S POV

Manasa is a side character in this story, but she plays a pivotal role later in the series. Manasa is the sister of Vasuki, the Naga king who believes Kuvera, the Yaksha chief, is in cahoots with Vedanta and is planning to overthrow Vasuki. Vasuki is assassinated by Kali, who

then forms an alliance with Kuvera and later overthrows Vedanta. Manasa wants revenge. Kali attempts to take her life but she manages to save herself. In the end, she plans to leave for her kingdom where she would gather her personal army and finish Kali off.

The book ends with Kali reigning supreme as the king of Indragarh and Durukti finding out that her handmaiden Symrin is working with someone sinister, who had planned all the events that had happened till now. This person has been using the Eye of Brahma which is a mysterious magical object.

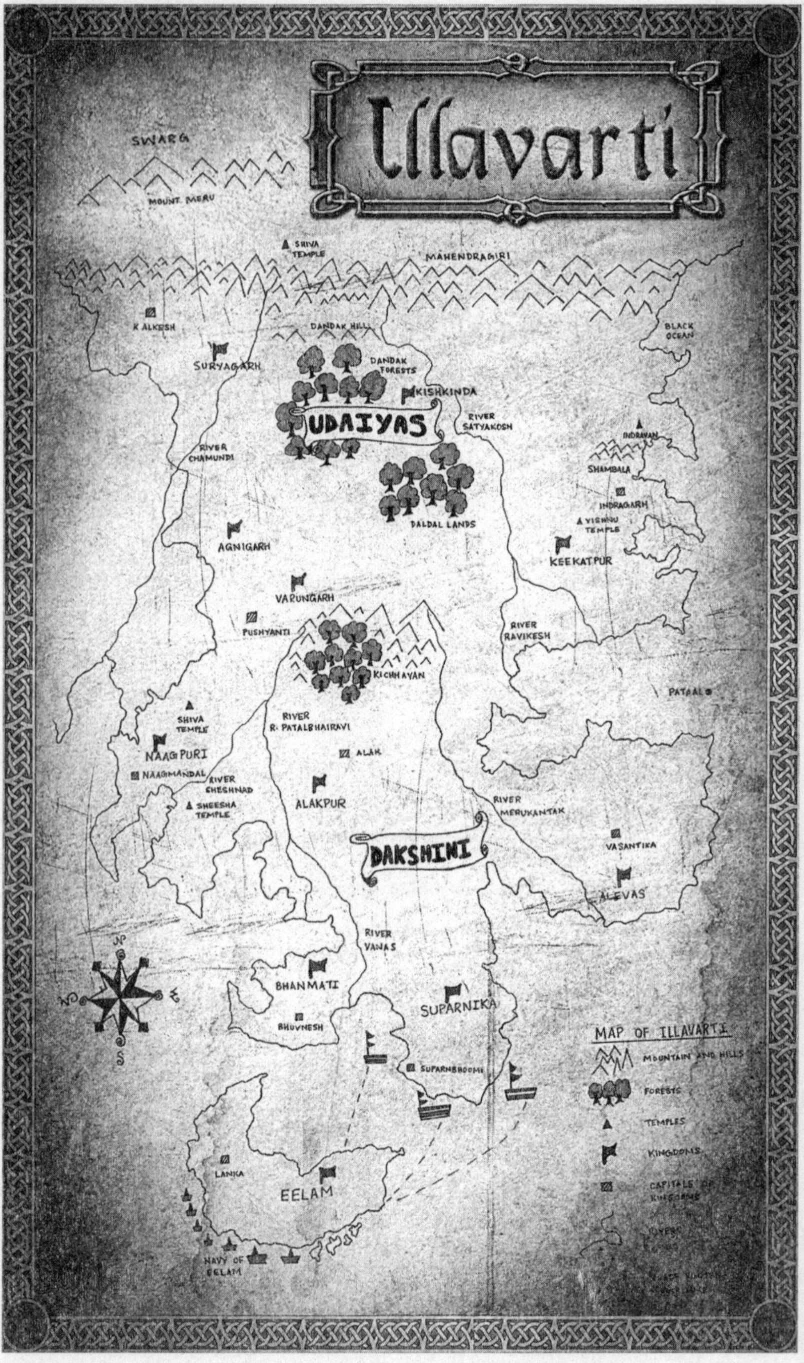
Illavarti
SWARG
MOUNT MERU
SHIVA TEMPLE
MAHENDRAGIRI
K ALKESH
DANDAK HILL
BLACK OCEAN
SURYAGARH
DANDAK FORESTS
KISHKINDA
UDAIYAS
RIVER SATYAKOSH
RIVER CHAMUNDI
INDRAVAN
SHAMBALA
INDRAGARH
VISHNU TEMPLE
DALDAL LANDS
AGNIGARH
KEEKATPUR
VARUNGARH
PUSHYANTI
RIVER RAVIKESH
KICHHAYAN
PATAAL
SHIVA TEMPLE
RIVER R. PATALBHAIRAVI
NAAGPURI
ALAK
NAAGMANDAL
RIVER SHESHNAD
ALAKPUR
SHEESHA TEMPLE
RIVER MERUKANTAK
VASANTIKA
DAKSHINI
ALEVAS
RIVER VANAS
N
E
S
BHANMATI
SUPARNIKA
BHUVNESH
SUPARNBHOOMI
LANKA
EELAM
NAVY OF EELAM
MAP OF ILLAVARTI
MOUNTAIN AND HILLS
FORESTS
TEMPLES
KINGDOMS
CAPITALS OF KINGDOMS

NOTE TO THE READER

This book has stemmed out of my love and fascination of Hindu mythology. I am a staunch believer of Lord Vishnu and his teachings have helped and guided me in life.

The events of the book bear resemblance to those in Ramayana, Mahabharata, and Kalki Purana, but it is a work of fiction and has been written for entertainment purposes only. You may find that most of the characters appear different from their mythological counterparts, but that is because I have taken creative liberty to fashion them to suit the story. The book is not a retelling but rather a reimagining of the Kalki Purana.

Some of my favourite movies have proven to be instrumental in inspiring me to write this book, such as The Empire Strikes Back (Star Wars Episode V), The Dark Knight, The Godfather Part II, A Storm of Swords, and Terminator 2: Judgement Day.

So here it is, the second book of the series. Thank you for picking it up. I hope you enjoy it.

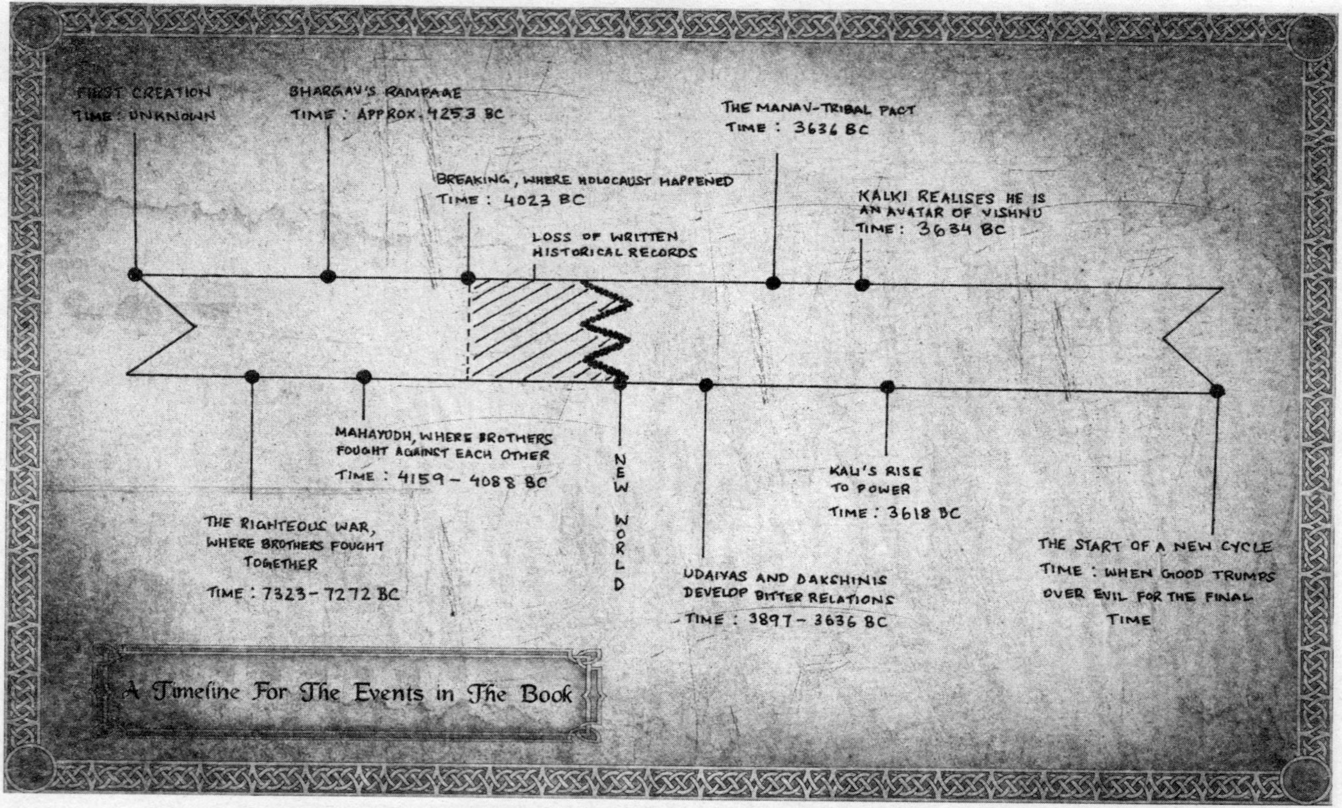

A Timeline For The Events in The Book

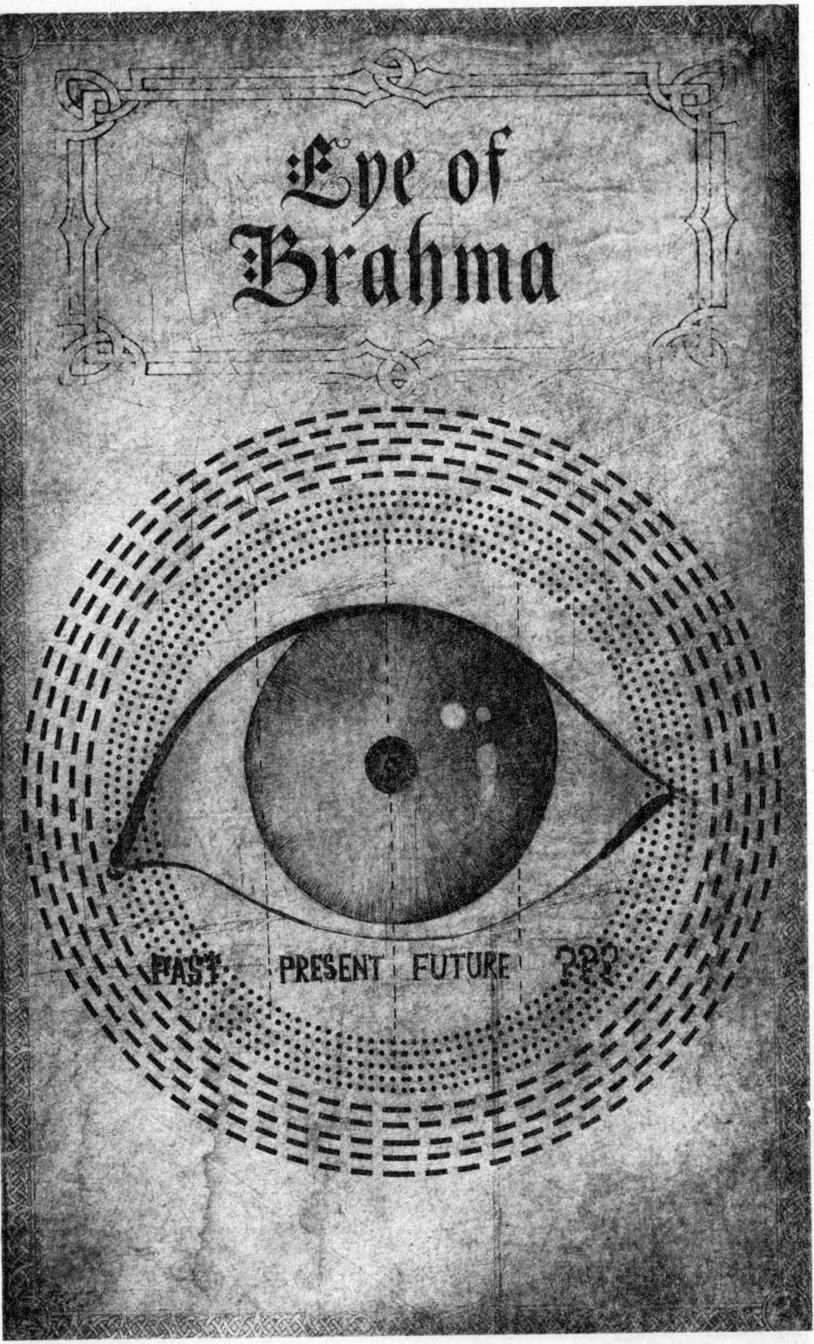
Eye of
Brahma
PAST
PRESENT
FUTURE
???

To my readers . . .

Prologue

Kalyug had ended. The war was over.

Sumati had been in the temple quarters for a while now.

It had been more than a year since she had received notes from her sons. They had stopped coming now. She was afraid, but she had faith that they were alive. She hoped they were safe. That they were content and they would come in time to see her.

Since the war occurred, not much had happened in Lord Bajrang's temple—the poor were sheltered and fed, a few orphans were taught while the priests kept babbling forever.

But faith in the institution was lost on the people. There were no more celebrations.

With each passing minute, Sumati was getting anxious. The most exciting part of her day would be midday, when the messenger would arrive and tell the people about the current events—who had perished and who had won on the battlefield.

And one day, casting a frightened look at the villagers, he had confirmed that Kalyug was ending.

Everything had come to a standstill, even the massive destruction on the battlefield.

The victors had not been decided yet.

No one, not even the messenger, knew who had won.

Sumati was afraid. In the era of Kalyug, countless lives would be claimed as was prophesied ages ago. Much of humanity would perish.

But she was only concerned for the safety of her sons. She would get up in the dead of the night, and pray for them. But her prayers stopped from that day—the day she was asked to come to the courtyard by the priest of the temple.

"Sumati ma, someone here has come to meet you."

Meet me?

The thought made her heart flutter in anticipation. She had had no visitors for the past year.

It couldn't be.

She hurtled forward, stumbling on her path, as she ran towards the temple dens, until she finally saw him.

He was standing—tall and firm, a few paces away from her. She momentarily paused in recognition. A parrot was perched on his shoulder, with a horse by his side.

The shadows *blinded* his face, but he was there finally and she recognized him without further ado.

Tears burst from her eyes as she rushed towards him and embraced him. Without even making eye contact, she started to trace each scar running through his upper body, borne by him over the past year—just so that he could protect his family.

She listened to his beating heart. It was faint. He was battered. And broken.

With his remaining strength, her son hugged her back, tight as he could. And then she pulled herself up from his embrace.

"Where is he?" she asked him. "Is he at the back? Does he really think he can surprise me?"

He started shivering in convulsing shock, as his head drooped down to finally meet his mother's eyes.

They were as cold as ice.

"No," she gasped, her hands covering her mouth in horror, "no, it can't be."

"I'm sorry," he said. "I couldn't protect him, Ma."

He tried to hug her again. She resisted with all her might, but she couldn't fight his strong arms anymore. And they enveloped her again.

No.

Her feeble ears were rooted to his chest. She was not ready to hear this.

She could not accept it. Every thought escaped her mind. All she could do was grope at silence.

What happened to the one who didn't return?

PART THREE

THE COUP AT INDRAGARH

1

He fell.

He couldn't see much amidst the falling rubble. Heavy rocks brushed against his arm, rupturing his skin, with numerous pebbles piercing his ankles and bloody knuckles. He heard the rush of water somewhere nearby. His trampled body rested to a halt now. Multiple gashes and wounds were inflicted on his body, with his tattered dhoti barely enveloping him.

Flexing his biceps, he made an effort to get up.

"KALKI!" Someone called out his name. It was a girl. *Damn wretched girl.* He didn't even want to talk to her, yet she called for him.

But then, it wasn't her fault. He himself fell off his horse from the slope of the mountain.

Kalki leaned against the rock, watching the overcast skies, so close yet so far from him. The voices echoed in the back, but he didn't care. He remained silent. He had been putting up with them for fifteen days, and right now, he just wished to be away from them. The fall, albeit a result of his clumsiness had made his wish come true. He watched the dank forests, foliage and the canopies, thick as a hive, just crowding the ground. He was up high, away from Indragarh and Shambala, where the entire nuisance had occurred.

"KALKI!" It was a man's voice.

Kripa. What a bloody mess he was! At least he didn't drink anymore.

"MAN!" Another voice appeared. This was not a familiar voice. And yet it sounded much closer.

His ears strained, his head cocked forward, as he looked at a small cave that led to the slope inside the mountains. From there, a head was peering at him, like a child.

"Man?"

Kalki narrowed his eyes. "Uh . . ." He looked at the back. He could see Kripa and Padma descending from the mountain with their horses. The uneven path was their problem. Kalki now hoped that they would reach him sooner. The creature had managed to appear in front of him in no time at all. His presence had an unsettling aura.

"Man?"

Kalki was frozen at his place. "Man, yes," he responded.

"Man," he nodded.

He turned around. Kalki realized he was wearing a lion skin over his head with whiskers coming out of his thin mouth. He had a strange furry neck that lined his chest. His chest was hairy as well. With his back strained, he had a convoluted frame, his arms and legs of the same length. His eyes were hungry, as if he would pounce at Kalki's throat at any moment. He walked on all fours like an animal. His wrists were crooked but when he stood straight, he towered over Kalki.

"Me Simha."

"Simha?" Kalki had definitely heard that name before.

"Darooda Simha." He clapped. With a manic smirk on his face, he said, "You, man," and started poking Kalki. His nails were so sharp that they pinched him.

"Darooda, eh?" Strange name, but then the man had whiskers. Kalki was surely in the wrong lands.

"Darooda." He began to jump, beating his chest and hooting.

"You don't need to be so excited, friend." Kalki mustered a grin. He had never liked Tribals. They had destroyed his village,

killed the love of his life, and left his friends to die. The Manavs irked him enough, but not so much as Tribals. And yet, here he was, standing in front of one, and trying to make friendly contact with him.

"Food?" Darooda asked. "Hungry?"

"Uh," Kalki was indeed hungry. By the gods, he had forgotten the last time he had eaten something. Apples perhaps, a few hours back, but they hadn't satiated his hunger.

"Mutton, inside."

"I don't eat meat, friend," Kalki said.

Darooda slumped in disappointment. "Meat good."

"I know." Kalki's gaze was unwavering.

"Come," he signalled at the cave, "food."

"I am waiting for my friends," he told Darooda, pointing at Padma and Kripa who had managed to appear on their horses at the right time. They had brought Kalki's as well.

"What on heavens were you thinking, mate? You are an Avatar! You are lucky you didn't die," Kripa scolded him.

Darooda instantly squealed and rushed back, staggering and scampering for safety towards the cave's edges. Kripa got down, grabbed the girdle of his horse, and patted twice on Kalki's back. "What's with him?"

"Darooda Simha."

"I asked what's with him, not who he is, mate" grunted Kripa.

"You should ask him yourself. Besides, your voice seems to have overpowered him."

Kripa scowled.

"All I know is that he is a Simha," Kalki added, while curiously watching the creature's mannerisms.

Simha. The name sounded so familiar yet he couldn't remember. "Where have I heard this?" Then he recalled. It was at the *gurukul* with Guru Vashishtha, when he had read about the ancient tribes.

Padma had reached down as well, gazing at the creature, and

freezing right in her tracks. She was a short woman, ugly and horrible. But then it was Kalki's anger that was making him see her in that manner. In reality, she was tall, slim, had a straight face with kohl-covered eyes and short, cropped silver hair with a noticeable jaded look. She was not one without peculiar habits.

"Looks like a Tribal to me," she said, trying to undermine her shock.

Kalki ignored her with a visible grimace. Padma noticed it, but chose not to retort. He had every right to hate her.

Because of her, Arjan had been kidnapped and might have been killed or worse, eaten. He didn't know what fate had been meted out to him by Kali. The very thought of it jolted a flash of anger and grief inside him. He was now overwhelmed with so many unfamiliar emotions.

"He is one of them. The Simhas," Kripa added jovially, "were once the unknowns, like the grand tribe of Suparns. They were proud beings and even had heroes amongst their ranks. Narsimha, as the legends say, defeated an Asura, when no one could. The Simhas, who are considered devotees of lions, wear their skin as protection and grow facial hair like a lion. Most of them went mad after the genocide. The survivors went missing."

"What led to their extinction?" Kalki asked.

"It was the battle with the Manavs, where the Tribals had lost. But this, again, is during the Mahayudh."

"Simhas are that ancient?" Padma asked, wondering about the war. That was way before their time, when the Ancients fought against each other. Back then, a plague had ravaged the land known as the Breaking, an aftermath to Mahayudh, as Kripa had stated earlier. Ancients had lived before Lord Govind and others like him. All of it was explained to Kalki, but that strengthened his suspicions even further. He wondered how old Kripa was. He had said that he was hundred years old, but the Mahayudh predated a century. Deep down, he knew it was not true. This was Kripas's version of events,

and he didn't trust him much. History was convoluted and he better not dwell on that now. Otherwise he'll end up believing a lie.

"Their lineage is quite old, mate," Kripa said. "They were warriors, worshippers of the sun, and now look at them. They have gone mad with time. This one must be a surviving descendant," he signalled at Darooda. "He has forgotten his proud heritage, and yet he exhibits the remnants of his bloodline's regality, ergh, the poor fellow."

Kalki asked, "How did they go mad?"

"During the Mahayudh, radiation was used—"

"Radiation?"

"Bombs," he snapped at Padma, glaring at her, "the one you took for your personal cause."

Kalki saw her hand slipping into her pouch, as if she was shielding them from Kripa's words. Perhaps she was still carrying them.

"They were used in heavy quantities, while the ones I gave you, lass, are pretty ordinary. They are damaging enough to a man, but not one to cause massive destruction," he clarified, noticing what she was doing.

"The ones used during the Mahayudh were horrible. The aftermath of the radiation was terrible, causing many to go crazy. Lands had become inhospitable. The kings had come after that, but none had survived. The survivors of the war had left for the mountains and died of starvation."

Kripa's version of the grim past spoken in a nonchalant tone was something Kalki was not really fond of. But after seeing enough bloodshed, he was used to it.

"What should we do then?" Kalki asked, concerned about Darooda. He figured that this creature must have seen enough evil for a lifetime.

"Do? We go north, as we were supposed to." Kripa reached for the horses, trying to manoeuver them to the opposite side, and go back to where they had come from.

"What about him?" He pointed at the creature.

"Let's stop here. It has started to rain," Padma intervened.

Kalki ignored the pellets, and Padma's existence.

"We go back!" Kripa said. "Mate, our mission is not helping bizarre creatures on our way, just so you know."

"Do you really have a heart or do you just want to let everyone die for your mission?" Kalki blurted.

"It's going to rain hard," Padma intervened again. She wanted to clear up the tense atmosphere. Kalki could hear the blazing, somersaulting clouds approaching. They had begun to make retching sounds.

Kalki had touched a nerve. Kripa balked. "What do you mean by that?"

"You know what I mean by that." Kalki's voice had a menacing tone. "Arjan told me something. Before he left, he told me about you."

"So, you have started to believe in hearsay." Kripa refused to budge.

The rain was now armed and was throwing bullets of drops at them. None of them deterred Kalki as he confronted Kripa with glaring, pale eyes.

"YOU TWO!" yelled Padma. "It's raining, we need shelter."

"We go through the rain," Kripa announced solemnly, "for it's not fire that we have to stay away from." His gaze wavered a little. Kripa sized himself up, an old man, with nerves pushing out of his fragile skin. With a stinking mouth and greasy hair, his body exuded the smell of blood and *suras.* But he had retained his nerves of steel.

Kalki shook his head. "No. We stay right here. We stay with Darooda," he gestured towards the creature, who had started fidgeting by now.

"I'm not staying with a madman!"

"Food," cawed Darooda, quietly from the corner.

Padma pushed both the men and holding their horses by the

girdles, dragged them towards the cave. "While you two imbeciles quarrel, I'll rest in the shelter. A pleasure to meet you, Darooda," she grinned at the bewildered hairy man as she entered the cave, finally getting out of Kalki's line of sight.

Kalki stayed rooted to his spot for a moment before he shrugged and said, "We both know you are more than what you show. I don't expect answers, Acharya. But I want to know if you still uphold your morality. I will not have innocent blood over me. I am important to you, which is why you keep me safe. But in time, I will find out why."

With that, he left the senile, old man in the rain. He'll surely not die of cold or rainwater illness. Kripa was an Immortal, blessed by the last Avatar.

Kalki had the power to make someone Immortal as well, but he didn't know how it worked. Endowing someone with immortality can be a gift or a curse and in this case, Kripa surely was cursed. He had gone mad like Darooda, but at least the Simha was kind and generous.

Shuko, his parrot sat down over his shoulder and began to caw, "Pisach! Pisach!" which Kalki didn't understand. He had sent his bird to sprawl its wings and locate any danger lurking in the vicinity. The foolish bird had ended up speaking gibberish and possibly alerting any threat trailing them.

Kalki entered the cave to find Padma standing at the entrance, frozen at her place. He looked at her pale, dilated pupils, lost into the distance. He knew something was amiss. He looked up. The cave, like any other mountain cave at this altitude, was filled with dirt, mud, and garbage strewn all over. And yet, unlike other caves, this one held people. Three people, seemingly alive, had their mouths gagged by dirty rags. Their knees were bruised and all of them were women—one bald, the second one had matted hair, and the third one had a strange inked pattern over her left eye in the shape of an arrow. Perhaps a Manav. Kalki couldn't figure it out.

"Food." Darooda Simha began to jump, clapping his hands, beating his chest.

"Them?" Kalki swallowed a lump in his throat.

"No," he shook his head as if Kalki had misunderstood him all this time. "*You.*"

2

Out of all the things in the world, Arjan had never believed himself to be a wrestler. And here he was, being shown as entertainment for the nobles and the aristocrats who were dining with the best of meat and wine, laughing with their women seated on their laps, and watching two hulking figures amidst Manavs and other races fighting each other.

Arjan realized he was next. With his hands chained, he watched the wrestlers, bound with the rest of the prisoners, as the contenders grabbed each other, their feet rooted to the ground, while trying to topple each other. One finally threw the other on the ground and broke his neck in an instant. This was a game where no one cared who lived and who died. Arjan breathed a sigh of relief. He didn't have to head out now and fight. He needed to wait, and learn from his would-be opponents.

The entire chamber was thronged with spectators. In the front, with his guards sat Kali. He had a satisfied expression on his face as an Apsara sat over his lap, with wine spilling from his glass, as he laughed and cheered. The nobles put bets, coins of unimaginable value were tossed and flipped towards the arena. All the nobles looked greasy and dishevelled.

Arjan felt like retching. All this drinking and whoring was happening in front of a huge Vishnu statue symbolizing purity. This sacred place was the outskirts of the city of Indra.

But none of this was Kali's concern. Gambling over life and death was the new routine now.

"Shh," a voice came from the back.

Arjan was standing in the middle of a huddle of sad, petrified faces. He carefully scanned all the topless, shackled men, wearing nothing but scorched loins. They were barefoot, had bloody bruises, and their backs were being flogged by a leash made of tiger skin. Master Reddy, their jailor and trainer, was leading them. Arjan hadn't learn a lot from him. His body was not ripped, unlike the other wrestlers, and his height was relatively short as well. Though he was incharge of the prisoners, they never took him seriously.

Arjan turned to see a boy, perhaps a little older, with wide eyes. Bangs covered his forehead, and he was a little plump unlike the others. Arjan was confused as to who fed him, since in the prison, the prisoners only got some potatoes and milk that smelled like the sweat of a hag's breast.

"My name is Vikram," he said. "How do you do, fella?"

Seriously?

"I had seen you out there, on the flying thingy, during my trial."

Arjan hesitated to take the conversation forward.

"Didn't get a pardon. I was flogged and sent down here for a few more years." He grinned as he tried to explain his situation. "But that was a wonderful sight. How did you operate that, fella? Need to know. Sooner or later, I'll get out and find meself a nice barn where I'm gonna work out my latest inventions."

"I hate to be blunt but we are looking at our potential deaths and you are worrying about the flying thingy?" Arjan interjected his enthusiasm.

"Oh, they just intend to scare us." The chains rattled as Vikram waved his hand, dismissing what Arjan had said. "They will only

show the best fights while the rest of us just dawdle and train. We don't have to go to the arena. No one wants to see a boring, one-sided match, you know."

"Things will change soon," Arjan said, gritting his teeth. He could feel it. Ever since Kali had assumed the throne, the Nagas had mysteriously vanished overnight, and the Manavs had been appointed jailers and officers in the prison. He even held power over his predecessor's fort. If it had been up to Vedanta, Arjan would have been executed for trespassing into the royal grounds with the silver-haired girl in tow. But he had been brought in front of Kali, and the new king had different plans for him.

The fight had ended and Kali came forward, declaring the winner. The announcement met with applause and hoots from the side who had bet on him. The fair-skinned champion had a stern, straight face with broad, dark features and a set of angry, stubborn eyes black as charcoal. He was handsome, but something about him churned Arjan's stomach which he dismissed. The last thing he wanted was to fancy a fighter he would end up battling to death. But he knew that in a duel with the champion, Arjan would be smashed to a pulp, his head would burst, and he'll be nothing but a crushed carcass, just like the potatoes for his daily ration.

The champion went by the name of Rudra, which was one of Lord Shiva's names.

"Our best fighter," Kali spoke in a sleek voice. "No one can beat him, and none ever will." He held out Rudra's arm up into the air. "You feast with me today, boy," he said and slapped Rudra's back proudly, who nodded with a grunt before moving towards the horde of wannabe wrestlers. Arjan was one of them.

Arjan kept praying. He didn't want Kali's slithering golden eyes to find him amidst the crowd. But then, Kali walked up, passing and patting the wrestlers' arms as he said, "All of you are going to be trained—to fight, to continue the legacy of the great Lord Jarasandha, to keep his spirit alive!" There was great jubilation

in the crowd. Lord Jarasandha was the megalomaniac emperor of Udaiyas. Being an Ancient, he had ruled before the Breaking, even before the Mahayudh. He had died horribly, courtesy to Lord Govind who with Vrikodara's help had set up a wrestling match. Jarasandha was an Asura, a race that was now extinct. He couldn't die because he had been drunk on Soma, or that's what Kripa had told him while they were travelling towards Indragarh. Kripa had talked about these stories of Mahayudh as if he had lived through it. One of the Ancients was an ancestor of Arjan, though he didn't know who.

Jarasandha was finally killed when his body was sliced into two parts and thrown on opposite sides. Confused, he couldn't form himself again, dying of blood loss and a prolonged state of mutilation.

When he had listened to this story for the first time, Arjan had gasped for breath, letting out a nervous laugh. The nature of Jarasandha's death was too fantastical for his sound mind. None of these things happened. But then he had seen Kalki. He had seen his brother in action.

Kali stopped at Arjan's side. He glared at him, his eyes narrowing and widening in recognition. Arjan could feel his breath, but he showed no fear or anger for that was exactly what Kali wanted—Arjan to react. He controlled his impulses.

"You," he grabbed Arjan's shoulder, pulling him from the crowd.

Arjan was forcibly taken away and put in the midst of raving gamblers. With their tongues lolling, they were scampering and shouting at him, spilling their drinks while amorously engaging with their women. Arjan was helpless, his hands were still bound. He couldn't understand why he was being pushed into the arena when he wasn't even trained. He was just another prisoner. Rudra stood still, watching Arjan with a look of disdain.

"You are weak!"

"Why are we sending off an amateur? Train him first!"

"He doesn't even have muscles! Throw him out!"

All the spectators started yelling.

Kali grabbed Arjan by the shoulder, locking him in his grasp. For a king, Kali was strong; his biceps were thicker than Arjan's.

"Why don't we have a little fun, eh?" Kali grinned. "Why don't we let Rudra, our star, fight with someone untrained? Someone who has yet to rise through the ranks."

Arjan's heartbeat rose.

No.

Master Reddy, the stout, snarky man with betel leaves in his mouth came forward, trudging carefully. "My lord, the boy has no idea how to defend himself. It won't be a fair fight."

Kali looked at him as if he had made an ill-timed joke. "What about it? We need a change in the competition. This is about survival, not fairness!"

Everyone began to clap and hoot.

"But my lord, I have others Rudra can compete with. Others who are fit and fine." He paused, frightened. "Let me train him first and you can then do what you want to do with him."

Kali came to Master Reddy, who immediately backed off. "Leave!" he coldly rasped and the jailer slowly scurried towards the back. Arjan had nothing against the man. He desperately sought his help; he needed the jailer to defend him.

People clapped loudly, laughing. Arjan couldn't see Vedanta or Kuvera amongst them, but then the audience only had nobles, merchants, and a few foreigners, including some senior officials.

"Let's have a bet," yelled Kali to the people. "Who do you think will WIN?"

Everyone took Rudra's name. In fact, Rudra sniggered at the question, glaring at Arjan who chose to remain silent and impassive. Deep in thought, he began to think of a few strategies to defeat Rudra, recollecting all the instances from Rudra's previous fights. Rudra always locked the enemy under his deadly grip, grabbed his opponent's neck, and then twisted it. Sometimes, he would force

the body to plummet down on the ground, let the mud sweep in, and then break the bones one by one. Horrible as it sounded, those were the things Arjan could recall at that time, as his head slowly swivelled towards Vikram gulping in tension.

The plump man had previously told Arjan that only the best fighters enter the arena. *Ah damn well.* Arjan knew Kali would take his revenge for stealing his Soma and burning the entire stock. If one thought about it, Kali was being generous in not just feeding Arjan to the lions. But then, the first look of Rudra was no less than a hungry lion approaching its prey. Arjan was shivering with nervousness as he knew he was going to bid farewell to his life.

The Manav guards came forward, unlocking Arjan's chains and then tossing him on the ground. Arjan felt the mud slapping his face, as he looked at the chamber, the recess he was in, under the open, bloody sky. The entire place was small. The logs had been kept over the pedestals for the audience to sit and cheer the fighters as they marched to their gruesome deaths. The arena was situated away from the actual fort, Rajgirh. This was in the outskirts of the city. Ideally, a king would never make the effort of being a part of such an establishment. But Kali had travelled all the way from Indragarh to see this spectacle. His smooth demeanour outlined with his fascination for torture, it was hardly surprising that he had desired to witness it.

Arjan stood up, cracking his knuckles and taking his battle pose. Rudra was in front of him, grunting, with a playful smile dancing over his lips. Arjan glanced at Kali who was seated behind his favourite guards, Koko and Vikoko. Kali rubbed the top of his nose and then with a sweep of his arm signalled the fight to start.

The trumpet's sound shook everything in the arena. Everything went blank for Arjan and when his visual senses came into focus, he was pushed violently and rammed to the ground by a basilisk of a man. His back brushed harshly against the ground. The enormous surge of pain made his eyes tear up.

Horror seized Arjan as Rudra tried to grab his neck. Arjan dodged him, deflecting his bulky arms with his hands. Whenever Rudra would come forward, Arjan would sweep his hand and knock it aside. Rudra saw an opening in his stance and finally wrapped his legs around Arjan's, coiling them tightly, and turned his upper body on the other side while twisting Arjan's hand at the back. Rudra leaned forward casually as he began to nibble his ear, and he whispered, "Liking it much?"

Arjan arched his brows, confused. Gathering his strength, he used his body weight and pushed himself from the ground. Rudra staggered. The crowd stopped jeering for a second as Rudra regained his balance, brushing off his left shoulder as if a flea had landed on him.

"You are good," Rudra grinned, "but your strength's lacking. To survive, I have to kill you!"

Arjan's feet remained frozen as Rudra rushed towards him like a raging bull. He lurched at the impact, but gained his composure soon. His hands clenched into a fist to counteract Rudra's mighty punch.

As of now, this was not wrestling.

Rudra released a flurry of blows at Arjan, as he felt each bone in his body shattering. His joints splintered to the point where his listless torso was dropped on the ground. Rudra sat on his chest, his heavy, thick thighs upon his badly beaten trunk.

"Sorry friend. There is no escape for you."

And there was no escape surely. When Arjan tried to fidget, Rudra punched him in the face, leaving him with a bloody, broken nose. Arjan thought he had seen the worst in Shambala when he had eaten some poisonous berries, but his battered bones and bloody face had proved him wrong. He choked on his own blood. The pain kept escalating in his ears, the beating of his heart increased to the point that it became difficult for him to see properly.

Rudra, with his two hands, began to choke him. Arjan, already

gasping for breath, tried with all his might to get him off, but it didn't work. He began to see dark spots, the air in him withering away as darkness welcomed him at last.

3

The entirety of Udaiyas was on the far left now. Manasa was sailing through the simmering river, towards the east of Illavarti. She was on a small boat that was being rowed by a Naga. He had blue eyes, of which the left one was glassy. He broke into a banter about how he got into the whole rowing business and how most of the well-to-do princes and princesses would take the route from the central entrance that led to Naagmandal, which was the capital of Naagpuri.

"Only the merchants and farmers climb aboard my humble abode. But my lady, you are the king's own sister. You are royalty personified!" the boatman emphasized gleefully as he rowed.

Manasa rebuffed his praise. She didn't want to direct too much attention to herself while she travelled to the centre of the city. She expected to be escorted from this boat to a real, lavish one. A transport fit for royalty. But then, that was all valid and agreeable before Lord Vasuki, the King of Nagas, also known as Naagraaj, took an entire army of Nagas and stationed it at Indragarh, the land of Manavs. While Vasuki was away, the ministers had expressed their anger about the whole situation. But Manasa had managed to deal with them single-handedly. They were still under her thumb. Kadru, her cousin, had eventually replaced Manasa during her time in Udaiyas, helping Vasuki accomplish his duty in the foreign lands.

But given the current situation, with their king dead, she didn't want to direct any unwanted attention on herself. She knew what she had to do—meet Sambhavi, Vasuki's wife, console her and her children, and tell them about Vasuki's fate. She would promise them that no harm would come to them, and then leave for Kadru's domain where she would assemble her army. She didn't want the ministers to get involved, nor have the slightest inkling about her intentions.

Her return was sudden. And everything would have to be done in secret.

If her appearance was made public, it wouldn't take long for the ministers to figure out the truth. She would ensure no usurper got his hand on the throne of the Naagraaj.

The successor was yet to be decided. In mind, Manasa had chosen Shakti, the eldest of Vasuki's sons. With Kadru's approval, she could get the influential ministers on her side. And then, she would be able to leave for Indragarh.

It was a shameful thing to admit, but Kadru, with a much lesser time in the court, had a better rapport with the ministers than Manasa had ever had. But then, Manasa was temperamental and adamant. She believed her word was gospel and the ministers didn't like that.

As she entered from the back entrance, she took a long look at the lush greenery around the soapstone, granite complexes. They looked more beautiful than before. The smell of fruits and vegetables engulfed her, the sound of birds and the blacksmiths shaping their weapons made her recognize her home once again. She saw the silhouettes of the farmers weeding out their fields, standing upon thick foams of mud. Her gaze moved towards the clear lake as she gaped at the entire Naagmandal being drenched in water. No one could travel on foot to come here. To travel to the inward city, one would have to travel via the waterways for far distances. They would have to take a boat ride, big or small,

depending one one's class. There were no long roads and winded paths. There were no rocky platforms. All of it was lush green grass and fields, trimmed, looking exactly like mini-islands huddled around each other. The main complex was made of pure granite and stood with inscriptions written in Nubian—their native language carved on their rock structures, some towering and the others tiny, like a conical hat on top.

As she entered the royal courtside, many people noticed her. Some even gasped. She hid her face under a shawl as she reached the north side entrance, finally looking at the *pur*. The pur was the official name given to the city's complex soapstone houses.

Manasa stepped off. She tried to pay the boatsman but he retreated his hand. "I don't want any money, my lady. It was a pleasure to be your travel companion. I will cherish this for my whole life."

But Manasa urged him to take the fare, to which the boatman said he would give it away in Lord Sheesha's temple. Manasa nodded. The apparent loss of a royal guardian had humbled her. It was a new experience for her.

She began to look for Sambhavi's pur, but was unable to find it. She stepped on the mush ground, walking several steps at a rapid pace as the Naga guards looked at her. They came to her at a moment's notice.

"My lady," they said, bowing to her.

Things had already started to go wrong. That's exactly what she was trying to avoid. But then the central entrance would have been worse for a silent approach. The ministers lolled around right in the open.

Then, everyone in the country would have known of her return.

"Where is Lady Sambhavi's pur?" she hissed.

The guards, dumbfounded, looked at each other. "My lady, don't you know?"

Manasa shook her head. The guards lowered their heads in

unison. They took her where Sambhavi's pur was supposed to be. What lay in front of her was a half broken complex, shattered ruins from the top, and the door crumbling under a huge basilisk of a burden, too narrow to move through. The workers were trying to make sense of the wreckage, while the guards had sealed the area shut.

"What happened here?" She didn't want to know, but she couldn't turn away without an answer.

She was gradually falling into hopelessness. As if a boulder had smashed her heart and it had escaped into nothingness, deep in a void.

"My lady," one of them began in the Nubian language, thick and coarse in its accent, "Lady Sambhavi's house was, um . . . raided by a few Suparns who . . ."

She didn't want to hear it. *Suparns? That's odd.* Suparns never visited Naagmandal.

She knew the only person who had the answer to this predicament.

Situated in the biggest pur in Naagmandal was Vasuki's domain, which was close to Lord Sheesha's temple, where the auspicious Naagmani was. It was a sacred place where most meetings, decisions which would impact the nation, were taken.

Manasa barged inside. As she came near the golden-fleeced pur, she was stopped by the front guards. She removed the shawl covering her face and the rushing guards faltered.

"Our apologies, my lady," they said.

With wide, kohl-smeared, raging eyes, Manasa made her way inside. Large statues, portraits of the earlier Naagraj had been built parallel to each other. Takshak, the first Naagraj's sculpture could be seen right at the beginning. The statue of another Vasuki, not the previous king, had been put up as well. In the culture of the Nagas, Manasa was well-aware that they prided themselves on their legacies. Similar names were passed down through multiple

generations. The fabled Manasa, the one who predated her, was now a myth in their city.

The entire corridor was lined with jewels, rubies, coppers, and the high ceiling had been built with gold and platinum, glimmering and reflecting in her clouded, rage-filled eyes. She reached the council room as every guard backed out of her way. They didn't even dare to obstruct her path. They were shocked, even horrified, to see her. Some frowned at her sight for she had forsaken them for a foreign alliance. Her bold move was widely loathed by the citizens. The Tribal Truce, though supported by Vasuki and aided by Kali, had met with apprehension from the people of Naagpuri. They didn't want any truce, they just wanted self-sustenance which they were still vying for. With their king effectively removed, they were devoid of proper leadership. Well, except to look up to an injured woman who was a distant relative of the previous king.

Not drawing attention to herself was not an option anymore. As she opened the ornate gates and stormed inside, she found the long-drawn table coiled with snake images. The robed councilmen were sitting on their long, arched chairs talking, and in the far end, at the top seat was Kadru.

She had long braided onyx hair, green eyes instead of blue, because of which some people thought she wasn't a Naga. But Manasa didn't care. Kadru was her childhood friend, and a loving cousin whom she had unhestitatingly promoted through the ranks. Just because she didn't have her colours right, doesn't mean she would be discounted of her rights. Manasa could understand that because she herself was physically lacking.

All the ministers stared at Manasa and Kadru. She was in her battle armour with linings of inked snake designs reaching out to her arms. A heavy, awkward silence began to seep in as a wide-eyed Manasa stared at Kadru, as if she wanted her to come forward and say something, or even the ministers to stand up at her presence, but no one did.

"The meeting is adjourned, we will discuss the strategy later." Kadru banged on the table, a customary practice, before walking towards Manasa as the ministers quickly exited through the other door, like thieves, whilst passing quick, concerned glances at Manasa.

As they left, Manasa noticed a minister who was ogling at her—Jamun the vile. A fat, reckless, rich brat of a pseudo-ruler who controlled much of the territories in Naagpuri.

Kadru came forward, her eyes cold. "What are you doing here?"

Narrowing her gaze, Manasa couldn't believe the words that had come out of her cousin. "What's wrong with me being here? This is my kingdom."

Kadru shook her head. "You were supposed to be at Indragarh, were you not?"

"Yes," she nodded.

"Let me ask you again. Why are you here?"

There was an unsettling feeling that jolted Manasa. She didn't want to tell Kadru what had happened, how the truce they had sought for so long had backfired, and that she, no, both of them, had to escape.

She remained speechless.

"We heard about Vasuki." Kadru's brows furrowed. She was looking straight at Manasa.

Manasa was dumbfounded. "You did?"

"Yes." Kadru sighed. "You could have sent a note informing me that you were coming. Why didn't—"

"WHY didn't you send me a note about Sambhavi?"

There was a flash of anger in Kadru's eyes for a second. She just took a deep breath and gestured towards the chair in front of her as she sat back down. She had a troubled expression on her face. "I'm sorry. I'm just very exhausted."

"Vasuki died protecting us. Now, his family has suffered the same fate."

"You don't understand," Kadru looked at Manasa, "we are at war."

"Why?"

"Because of VASUKI!" she yelled. Manasa's eyes widened in shock. No matter how much she loved Kadru, she was young and she wouldn't dare raise her voice against Manasa.

"I am sorry, *di*," she reverted to the honorific she always used for addressing Manasa, "I should have told you about Aunt Sambhavi. But I was afraid of telling you the truth. It scared me. The Truce, well it was a horrible idea. Not only it did it create a hole within the city, but it also ended up opening an unmonitored gateway to the Suparns."

"Maruda," Manasa whispered.

"Yes, Maruda." Kadru was referring to the Suparn Chief of Command, Maruda, the descendant of Garuda. They had been embroiled in a cold war with the Nagas. Suparns had not been involved in the Truce as they were considered 'uncontrollable' by Kali.

"Maruda found an opportunity to attack us since we had no king. He went straight for Vasuki's family. He slaughtered them. His rage knows no limit. His attacks have been vicious and constant. We have been trying to deflect his attacks, rebuild our defences, but now, we are out of resources and men. Most of our army has been sent to Udaiyas by Vasuki."

Kadru began to weep, covering her face with her hands. Like the big sister she was, Manasa came forward, grabbed her head, and hugged her tight. Her jewel-studded clothes were wet, but it didn't matter to her, for she realized how horrible Vasuki's decision had been. At that time, vanity had played a part. Joining a cause against Manavs had been fun and respectful, but now it had destroyed Vasuki's family and his empire.

"The ministers have decided to drop you off from the council," Kadru said.

Ah, thus the coldness. But it was to be expected.

"Who will be the Naagraj then?"

"They tell me I should lead them, but I can't. I can't take this burden up anymore." She looked up, teary-eyed. "Challenge them, di. Try to swing a handful of the ministers towards your side . . . get us help. Save us." She cried, "I-I can't handle this, di. It's too much. I cannot lead my people to their downfall."

Manasa had to think fast. She knew she didn't have a lot of say in the present government right now. Any move on her part would be frowned upon. Her voice had no audience. With Vasuki's death, Manasa knew the ministers wouldn't follow her anymore. Also, Manasa couldn't topple their leadership by hiring assassins, for they were the heads of some of the greatest purs in the Naagmandal, providing food, fresh water, and soldiers. They were sponsors to the crown. And the crown was on the head of a poor child.

"We will find a way, darling." She patted her cousin's head, trying to comfort her as she began to plan a few things for the future.

She was wrong. She had thought she would come in, get an army, and attack Kali. But no, she would have to solve the civil issues that were brewing in her own city first.

And she had to solve them without letting anyone know her true objective.

There was another war waiting for all of them, once this was over.

But before she could exact her revenge, Maruda must die.

4

Arjan was alive.

Lord Kali wouldn't let Arjan die in an easy, cheap fashion. He would ensure Arjan suffered enough, till the point where he would beg him for death. He still wouldn't kill him. His death was inevitable. But it had to be painful. He had to inflict more hurt. This was clearly a personal grudge, for the scum had broken in and destroyed the one thing that had kept him alive. If Arjan was let out, he would surely become a major threat to him.

There was something about torturing people on the brink of death—it was not giving them the satisfaction of letting go, of being released from their material bodies. Lord Kali ensured they wouldn't die under his watch. Taking their last breath was not an option. Lord Kali had tortured his prisoners and had slowly started to develop a taste for it. He had started to enjoy the act of killing.

Without giving much thought to the unconscious Arjan who was now being hauled to the infirmary, Lord Kali made way to his fort over his chariot. Koko and Vikoko stood next to him, with their hands clasped strongly on their swords' handles, waiting for any suspicious movement around so they could attack in an instant.

Koko and Vikoko weren't originally pledged to Lord Kali. They were supposed to protect another king—Parikshit, the last king of the Kuru dynasty, and the last great king of Udaiyas—before it

had been divided into smaller kingdoms like Indragarh. They were meant to protect him until he met an unforeseen end.

Lord Kali had vague memories of Parikshit. He didn't think about his friend a lot. It made him wonder how the death of close ones impacted one so much. He faintly recalled when he had taken an entire expedition to settle a score with a man he had hated at the time. It wasn't just the fact that his barn had been burnt with his siblings inside, Parikshit's death also churned strong feelings inside him. Grief choked him. He tried to stay strong. Friendship was always an opportunity to be your better self and in time, Lord Kali had become someone more than he used to be—from a simpleton who had no knowledge of royal affairs to the man who had ascended the throne. But deep down, he knew he still missed his family terribly.

He tried to focus on his present objective. In his daily affairs, he had learnt to please his officials. It was important to busy them with trivial matters like wrestling and gambling for them to enjoy and support their lord without any opposition. They were all Vedanta's men. The only way to sway them from the honourable but pompous Vedanta to his side, was by bringing them to the ground and giving them what they want in full fervour.

Vedanta didn't like the vices in the city. In fact, why would he? He was a religious person. But Lord Kali didn't care about morality anymore, especially in the current times. He understood that this demeanour would ensure his survival in the political intrigue that was soon to come. He knew the hunger for the throne rested inside these bloodthirsty courts.

The chariot was met by the glares of people who had initially sided with Vedanta. They looked up at him. Some grimaced, while others folded their hands in fear and begged for mercy. Lord Kali witnessed the poverty and the horror that had struck the city. Surely, the inclusion of Tribals to his knowledge had crippled the city administration.

"Stop," he commanded the charioteer.

The man looked up at him, and reined the horses without a question.

"My lord," a meek voice from the back appeared. It wasn't any of his twin guards, but another guard who always accompanied him—Pradm, the commander of the Rakshas. "What happened?"

Pradm had a huge gash that rounded around his torso. He had purple eyes and his hands were folded in supplication. Currently, Pradm was thinking of Raktapa. For quite some time he had been lying to him about how everything was fine, while ensuring that Raktapa ruled, dined and revelled in Agnigarh with his iron fist over Lord Samrat, the former king of Agnigarh.

Lord Kali scanned around, glancing over the poor side of the city. The royal end, the south, was bedecked with beautiful buildings, lavish alleys, and shops by merchants with high-rise bazaars and exquisite fruits. But here, there was an atmosphere of sickness and filth. Many wore shawls that were scorched under the sun, some coughed, and everyone entered their small complexes, broken and shattered beyond repair.

Lord Kali had not done anything for them. Yet.

He recalled how when he was young, Durukti had had a conversation with him.

"So you plan to be a king?"

"Well, something like that." He grinned. They had been sitting inside a stable while it was raining. At that moment, many of the beggars rushed inside their shed. They were amongst the many that had fully drenched in rainwater.

"What do you plan to change if you become the king?" squeaked a young Durukti, the idea clearly amusing her.

At that time, Kali had had no clear intention to be the king. He never thought he would be one. He began to say, "I would make palaces and I would make a statue of mine whom people can worship. I'll have the best of armies, the best of the navy fleets . . ."

"And do they have a place in your vision?" Durukti signalled at a family

who had found cover in the shed, covered in one blanket as they hugged and shivered. "O King, what would you do for these people?"

Kali couldn't believe a kid like Durukti had thought of something so important while he had overlooked it in a flash of pride. He felt guilty. "Yes. I'll, uh . . ."

"Wasn't the king supposed to be kind, give the poor shelter, help them when they are in need, protect them from an adversary? Or are those oaths plain promises?"

Kali believed it was all the books she had got from the street vendors that had got her thinking. "A kingdom is as great as its people. Without the people, there is no kingdom," he said to himself, believing no statue should exist if its real-life counterpart was not respected.

"Yes, you are right," he grasped her hair, kissing the top of her head. "I will make sure they don't have to find a shelter like that. I'll build a great city for everyone to live lavishly on their own terms."

"Now that's a kingdom I would love to stay in," Durukti said, grinning childishly.

There was magic in their struggle. All the time that he had lived outside in the wild, protecting himself and his sister, there was magic, for without struggle there is no success. He cherished his position more than ever as he stood on the platform, away from his shelter, followed by his guards. He walked to the corner, as people began to surround him, crowding him, as if he was the most popular theatre actor in the kingdom.

The Rakshas guards led by Pradm and the Manav guards led by Koko and Vikoko immediately began to create barriers to prevent the people from coming too close to Lord Kali.

Lord Kali sat in the corner; there was a slight pedestal where he could rest his back on. He looked at the clear sky.

It was the right time.

"I have come here . . ." he found his words and repeated, "I have come here to help you all. Please, one by one, come to me. Tell me what you want."

And so it began, when each villager scampered to the front, begging for his audience. Not for gold, but for food. Lord Kali had no food on him, but he had coins he had earned from the arena bets. He handed half of the sum to the women with the two embroidered linen pouches. Upon sighting the amount, they fainted. Lord Kali smiled with a childish glee. One couldn't deny the pleasing effect of doing nice things. It made you feel better. Much better than being violent. It gave you a slight and quick boost inside your chest. Although being violent had its own perks.

"My lord," an old man appeared, "I don't have a place to live in. I have sought refuge in the streets, even slept on them. I don't want to trouble you, but then, what do I do?"

Lord Kali arched his brows, trying to find an immediate solution to the old man's plight. Without a moment's hesitation, he took off his crown and handed it to him. "Barter this at the bazaar and you'll receive enough amount to buy yourself a fort," he said, laughing as the old man remained stunned.

"No, my lord. I cannot accept that."

Lord Kali stopped smiling. Glaring at the man, he said, "Would you say no to your king?"

The old man took it, overwhelmed with gratitude. He put it up for everyone to see, as his cracking voice proclaimed, "The great Kali! Our KING!"

Other voices joined with the old man's, trembling in awe of their king.

Lord Kali knew the ramifications of his actions. He knew that inculcating fear in others could make you powerful. But occasionally, love could make people respect you.

"My lord," a woman's voice brought him back from his reverie.

A frail woman appeared with a girl on her side, her face covered and her head down in a respectful gesture. "She has been harassed and humiliated by a moneylender. We had taken a loan from him

to buy some food. But we couldn't pay him back. We tried, my lord. But he wouldn't go empty-handed. He demanded I offer my daughter to him. And he forced himself on her."

She broke down, crying. In a flash, Lord Kali's expression changed.

Vile memories stirred inside him—which were often dismissed, forgotten. The very memories instilled a vengeful aura in him.

Lord Kali turned to Koko and Pradm, while Vikoko remained on the other side. "I thought there were no moneylenders operating in this area."

"Some rich landlords act like that, my lord, in the outskirts of the city," Pradm responded. Koko nodded in agreement.

Lord Kali said to Pradm, "Send five of your men with this woman." He looked intently at the lady and said, "I want you to point out the moneylender. Consider the loan cleared. We will ensure he pays for his crimes." He watched the girl on the woman's side. "Child, do not worry. You stay strong," he pulled out his rings studded with rubies, "and take this as a token of my apology for overlooking such matters. The last thing I want is a woman to be ill-treated."

He paused. He knew it was hypocritical of him to show compassion now. He had physically hurt Durukti once. The incident had slighted his pride.

But when angered, does a man still retain his morality?

The girl took it with eager hands and Lord Kali noticed how young she was. Her mother bowed again in respect, but the girl ran towards Lord Kali and embraced him. Vikoko was alarmed but Lord Kali signalled her to not do anything while the girl embraced him tearfully and then left without a word, with her mother.

After five hours when the sunlight had dimmed, Lord Kali realized there were so many more people in wait. He was exhausted. Facing the people, he asked, "I see you have suffered a lot. Why didn't you come see me before? Why wait till now?"

One of them answered, "My lord, we didn't know you would answer us. We didn't expect a king would come to our rescue."

Kali bit his lip in annoyance.

"Where would you go then?" Kali asked.

"To Lord Vishnu's statue; we prayed to him for all our miseries. King Vedanta had ordered us to not come to his court. Instead, he had asked us to go to the temple where our wishes would come true."

Kali clenched his hand into a fist. "And? Did they ever?"

Many shook their heads.

"It's false!" someone said.

"Stop talking about Lord Vishnu like that," someone else cried out. The voice died out in a mumble.

"A real god listens and helps," Lord Kali began, snapping back at them. "You, my fellow countrymen, have been ridiculed by false gods into believing they will help us when they are made of nothing but stones and granite." He looked up at the malicious statue of Lord Vishnu which stood high over the ground, far off, but still visible. It was the most prominent landmark of the entire city.

"Promise me, no, promise yourself, that you won't resort to god's grace anymore. "You don't have to worship them anymore. Come to me." He gazed at the statue in disgust.

"This idea of your former godly king has to be demolished for good."

5

The sparrows chirped and the mist was coated around the high dusk mountains. Kalki realized he had to do something fast, as Darooda approached with big, watery eyes, watching him in fascination.

"You eat them?" asked Kalki, glancing at the three strangers Darooda had managed to kidnap for food.

"Me?" Darooda's hoarse voice quipped with surprise. "Me, no. They will."

They? Who?

Kalki couldn't understand what Darooda was saying. Coupled with this frustration was the fact that he couldn't decipher what Shuko's constant battering of "Pisach! Pisach!" meant. Sometimes the bird could really get on Kalki's nerves with its incessant squawking.

He had to think fast about how to help the hostages. They looked poorly rested. One of them had matted hair, another had an inked face, and third one was bald. To Kalki's surprise, he had never seen anyone like her. Shaven heads often reminded him of Kali.

The thought of him makes me angry.

That wretched evil man had slaughtered his friend Bala, who Kalki was supposed to protect, and Ratri had got caught in the ensuing mess. She didn't deserve it.

None of them did.

And yet here he was on his way to meet a man who he was supposed to blindly trust, but was now confined in a cave with a raving rarity of a Tribal who hooted and jumped as Kalki stood dumbfounded.

"You need to leave them," Padma whispered. Nevertheless, he came forward, but his arm was firmly grabbed by her.

He shot her a look of contempt.

"Let's leave," she whispered.

Kalki couldn't act like that. He wouldn't leave without saving the strangers. He jerked his arm out from her grasp and advanced towards Darooda with an intimidating snarl. Darooda howled, forcing Kalki to recoil in surprise, while he reached out and grabbed a spear from the back with a swift movement.

"You, here," he signalled Kalki to sit down.

Kalki had had enough of this. "I don't want to hurt you, Darooda," he muttered.

"No, hurt, me hurt you." He arched his brows.

Ugh. I need to show him then.

Kalki, in an offensive stride, lunged forward. He heard the yelps of the Tribal who instantly regained his composure, as if he had anticipated it, while Padma gasped in surprise. Kalki grabbed the spear and as he touched it, he realized it was fiery hot, like lava. He instantly let go of the blade. He wanted to break it. But that strategy was out of the window. He couldn't shatter something so hot. Kalki was then jabbed on his shoulder with the spear, and was violently pinned against the wall.

Darooda growled at Kalki, his incisors popping out of his drooling mouth. At that very instant, Padma leapt from her position, pulled out her two daggers in the process as she clambered on Darooda's back. Darooda struggled as he tried to shirk her off. Kalki pushed himself back up from the ground, using his head to pummel right at the centre of Darooda's chest. He staggered back in pain, as he realized Darooda's skin was hard. He tried to hit Darooda in the

same spot, and collapsed on the ground, as blurriness crowded his eyes. *How could this vile creature be so tough-skinned?*

Kalki coughed in pain, and shifted around to see a little of what Padma was trying to do. She had locked her arms around Darooda's neck and was trying her best to pierce his skin with her blades, but whenever she hit, Darooda deflected it with his huge claw-like hand, until he finally used his force and slammed her flat on to the wall. Padma coughed up blood as she struggled to retain her consciousness. Darooda pummelled her against the sharp rocks and Padma fell on the ground, senseless.

Now, Darooda came forward with the spear in his hand, ready to stab her when Kalki saw the shadow of a figure appear at the cave entrance.

"Simha!" he yelled.

It was Kripa armed with a blade with a serrated edge.

Darooda turned in surprise. Without further thought, he went for Kripa. Both were locked in fierce combat. A dazed Kalki, with his battered feet and arms, struggled to get up. He shook his head violently as he crawled towards Padma. No matter how much he hated her, she was his comrade that he had to protect. Kalki came to her and flicked her face, trying to wake her up while Kripa was immersed in a battle with Darooda. Rather than going for the kill, Kripa was intent on dodging Darooda's attacks, as he rolled over with superior acrobatic finesse. For a man as old as he was, Kripa had surprised Kalki with his agility and combat skills, which could have only been gained through experience.

Padma opened her eyes, only to see Kalki looking down at her with concern. He didn't say anything. Padma blinked for a moment, staring at him. "What just happened?"

Clenching his teeth, Kalki ignored her. He limped towards the strangers and opened the straps gagging their mouths. As he did, he saw Kripa being tossed on the ground, as he skid on the mud with a sharp snap, like the breaking of a twig.

"Ugh, this doesn't feel nice, mate." Kripa sighed in pain as he struggled to get back up.

Growling, Darooda Simha paced himself and sprinted towards Kripa with full force, and landed a blow on Kripa's torso. Kripa's howl resounded in the cave. Darooda hit him continuously with pure rage. Kalki tried to stop the berserker by grabbing him by the torso and throwing him to the other end.

This was it. He was tired, having sustained enough injuries from the brawl. Kalki raced forward while Darooda rampaged ahead. Both began to deliver blows unto each other, fists of fury smashing into each other, as they tried to break each other's bones, whilst barely maintaining their balance. Kalki had just about managed to regain his composure as he came face-to-face with the beast, gazing deep into the furious eyes of a Simha.

"Come on!" yelled Kalki.

He wished he hadn't taunted him.

Darooda, with a surprising dexterity, twisted his legs up in the air, and landed consecutive kicks on Kalki. He then tilted to the side and with a quick jolt, landed a devastating punch on his face.

And at that moment, darkness and blood overwhelmed Kalki's eyes.

Kalki opened his eyes, finally realizing he was back where he had been a while ago. But time had passed and he had his arms tied up from behind by multiple ropes, which were directly connected to his legs. He knew that if he moved, his legs would be strained. Escape was not an option anymore. Darooda was smart. He could gauge his intelligence from the fist fight they had had. Darooda had understood that Kalki had the strength to break the rope, which was why he had furiously knotted it and bound it to his legs. On his side was Kripa with a bruised cheek, and a smug and sullen Padma.

Kalki swivelled his head to see the strangers, who were still captives, blankly staring at him. Their faces were blank, almost as if they were saying, *Yeah, that didn't work out well for you, did it?*

Darooda was nowhere to be seen. The stench of something rotten had started to engulf their senses. A slight breeze entered the small opening in the cave as it coalesced and fluttered calmly over Kalki's face. It was much-needed fresh air.

"I told you we should have left the moment we saw them." Padma gritted her teeth.

"This didn't go according to the plan," Kalki spat in frustration. "Where is he?"

"Gone out to fetch more of us, I believe?" Kripa's nonchalance was irritating Kalki.

"What about the horses? Did he kill them?"

Kripa laughed. "Kill them? Simhas don't kill animals. They worship them."

"Why does he have a lion skin on his head then?"

Kripa went into a confused daze. "Um, I don't think I am wrong here. But I am pretty sure he is letting them be."

"How will we leave for Mahendragiri now?"

"Mate, I'm the last person to whom you should ask this question. Am I not in the same situation? Have some pity on me." Kripa turned to face the convicts. "Hello there! Might we ask how you all got here?"

The strangers didn't even flinch.

"That helps a lot, Kripa. Demanding answers from people who can't speak."

"At least our mouths are open. Just don't bore me to death with your chit-chat." Kripa grinned.

"Yeah, yeah," Kalki dully nodded. Being huddled together as captives was one thing, but being held captive with Kripa was a different matter altogether, especially when a certain someone spoke a lot of horseshit.

"How is he so strong?" Padma asked Kripa.

Kripa looked at her as if it was stupid to even ask the question. "He's a Simha. You have no idea how strong these Tribals are. Their physiology is superior in every way."

"That doesn't answer my question." Padma shook her head in dismay.

Kripa snorted. "Well, throughout the ages, these majestic Tribals have been bred for bloodshed and violence, so that might somewhat answer your question."

"Thank god, it's only one of them."

Kalki was angry that regardless of his insurmountable strength, he had not been able to defeat a raging Simha. Maybe he had to just accept the fact that he wasn't strong enough. Not yet, at the very least.

Kalki realized Shuko had escaped when he had been fighting with Darooda. He whistled and hoped he would come. He whistled harder, quicker, louder, and the parrot appeared. He flapped inside the cave, and perched on Kalki's shoulder.

"Look at the proud one. At least one of us is not trapped," Kripa gleefully said.

"Pisach! Pisach!" The words were gibberish and before Kripa could speak again, Kalki signalled at his tied arms.

"Open," he said to Shuko. "Bite," he motioned at his hands.

Shuko flapped his wings and reached down, and with his sharp beak began to tear the knots apart. As the rope splintered and the last strands were undone, he freed his hands from the restraints. Kalki, grinning, patted Shuko as he went for his legs, opening the remaining restraints at ease.

"Fast, fast, the shadows," Kripa hissed under his breath.

Kalki swivelled his head and from the entrance of the dark caves, the moonlight allowed Kalki to see a shadow appear. He hadn't realized it was dark outside now. For how long had he fainted? By the gods, he had to be fast. The shadow materialized,

and it was none other than the huge Simha. He was crouching with bumbling hands and arms around his gigantic body. Kalki hurriedly undid the knots on Kripa and then started opening Padma's.

"I'll rescue the others," he said as Padma looked at him questionably.

"You could have just ignored me," Padma gritted her teeth as Kripa helped Kalki free the others.

"Okay, we don't need another fight now," Kripa silenced them.

Kalki snapped back, "I wish I could, but you are travelling with us."

"There's a reason why I'm doing it."

"Perhaps to get us in trouble?" Kalki frowned.

"Your brother made me promise to help you!" she exclaimed.

Kalki shot her a glance, confused. *Arjan made her promise? A stranger like her?*

Padma averted her eyes and crouched towards the three women, in an attempt to open their bounds. They began to untie their knots.

Kalki did so as well, gritting his teeth. He undid the restraints for the bald-headed girl. He noticed that she had big, brown eyes just like Lakshmi. For a moment, he found her full lips and aquiline nose extremely attractive. She had a face that anyone would love to just stare at, like a canvas of beautiful scenery.

"Uh," Kalki blushed, until he realized she was saying something to him.

"Hello!" She slapped him hard.

"Yes, yes, I'm sorry," Kalki sighed, trying to grasp the situation.

"There are more!"

"What?"

He felt a pat on his shoulder. It was Kripa. In haste, Kalki turned around to look at the cave entrance.

There are more.

Kalki realized what the bald-headed girl meant. Standing at the

entrance, there was Darooda Simha with two comrades hunched together by his side. Shuko looked at them once, and wasted no time in flying away to ensure his safety.

"Food," Darooda grinned, his sharp incisors glinting in the frightening moonlight.

6

"Aw, come on, learn to fight," Kalki prodded.

Arjan shrugged. "I'm not a fighter, Kalki. You know that more than anyone." He firmly grasped his book in response.

"Stop being such a wimp." Kalki instanlyt lurched at him, but ended up twisting his foot and tripping on the floor; his chin suffered a bruise.

Putting his book on the ground, Arjan bent to pick him up. They were in Shambala, in the farm that they owned. Skies met the green fields, foliage, bushes and shrubs, all held up and folded around in a warped reality. The scent of mangoes and olives and the sound of soft whistling wind with the chirp of the sparrows let Arjan wonder that Shambala, out of all the villages of Keekatpur, was a peaceful place, and not home to warriors.

And yet, Kalki was like that, born in the wrong land. Perhaps.

Arjan dusted his dhoti off and helped Kalki to stand up. "So much for being a wimp."

"Shut up." Kalki flared his nostrils. "I can't believe you don't fight. Fighting is exhilarating. If it were up to me, I would fight all the time. I'll find someone manlier to spar with. Where is Bala?" He grimaced at Arjan and left.

Arjan did feel out of place. Sometimes he wanted to be Kalki's sparring partner since he often felt left out from Bala and Kalki's adventure plans. He liked to travel as well, but violence was not an inborn trait that he had. Arjan sat on the ground, tossing away his book in frustration.

He wanted to have the same adrenaline rush like Kalki, the superhuman drive that he had. He wanted to, but he knew he could not ever match him. Besides, he had never liked fighting.

"I presume you didn't plan on throwing it away." His book was handed back to him.

He looked at it and then turned up to see his father, Vishnuyath, smiling warmly at him.

"Papa." Arjan smiled as Vishnuyath sat next to him on the ground.

"He ran away again, eh?" Vishnuyath bobbed his head in disagreement. "I'm telling you, your brother is not at all serious about the household. I told him particularly to stay here."

"He's meeting Bala."

"Oh! That barbarian!" scowled his father. "Anyhow, why are you in such a dull mood?"

Arjan lowered his eyes. "Why am I not a fighter, Papa?"

"Why do you want to be a fighter?"

"I want to be but I can't. I don't like it."

"Doesn't that answer your question?"

"Yeah, I know, but um . . ." Arjan blinked hard. He was confused. "I want to be manly, you know. I want to fight. I want to have rippling muscles. I want to be an untamed force in battle. What will all these books help me with? Nothing! I won't have any practical knowledge. I will be just stuck in my home, reading all the time."

Slowly Vishnuyath wrapped his arms around Arjan. "Well you shouldn't really care to be violent, son. Don't we already have enough of it? We need readers . . . knowledgeable people who could guide us in the right direction."

Arjan shook his head. "But how does reading add to that?"

"I don't think you understood my point. It teaches you about the little things, the kind things, and the brave things." He paused. "Never forget real strength is not here," he touched Arjan's flaccid muscles, tickling him in the process to which Arjan giggled. "It's here," he signalled at Arjan's head, where his brain was. "You can have all the strength in this world, son, but if you don't know how to use it, what is the point of it?"

"But all the fighters in the stories are heroes, the ones who battle in the forefront of the army, the fables. Isn't that what the stories tell us?"

"Never forget the Pandavs wouldn't have survived without the intelligence of Lord Govind to win the Mahayudh." His father smiled; there was a certain charm and warmth to the way he pulled up his lips. "Fighters change the outcome of a battle, but a reader can change someone's world by his knowledge."

Arjan woke up with a jolt, sweating profusely as he stared into the pitch black nothingness in front of him. He turned his head frantically, his neck throbbing in pain as he looked up to see iron bars from where the moonlight had slipped through, letting it dance over the ground. Scampering about in his cell, he felt a sense of elation as he recalled how he had been dreaming about the conversation he had had with his father when he was young. And how everything had changed. He had decided not to be a fighter like Kalki and here he was, thrust into the lion's den, living the life of a wrestler.

"Psst!" He heard a sound.

Arjan slowly moved to the iron bars. On the other side stood the plump, fat-faced Vikram was staring at Arjan, wide-eyed.

"Sorry fella, how are you doing? I heard you were in a pretty darn bad condition."

Arjan would know. He had been knocked out by Rudra and the next thing he had seen was his cell. After being treated in the infirmary, he had been thrown into the cell again where he had begun to have lucid dreams. The dream, though was so alive and vivid, he could still feel the fragments of Shambala ebbing from his thoughts. Perhaps it was the influence of the drugs and the leaves that he had been forced to eat to recover. They were making him delusional.

"I didn't know they'll let a newbie like you out there. That never happens."

Arjan glumly nodded. *Yeah, you sure didn't know, fat-face.*

"I just want to apologize for giving you false hope, fella."

Arjan waved him off. "You aren't the first one."

"The champion, Rudra was congratulated though."

Of course he was!

"Where is he now?" Arjan asked, gritting his teeth in anger.

"In his cell, of course, fella."

"He was congratulated by the king. He even feasted with him but was then thrown back in this gutter?" Arjan guffawed.

"Short-lived happiness I suppose, heh," Vikram grunted as he laughed.

Arjan couldn't help but grin at the way Vikram was—the one adorable boy you always have in your gurukul class who everyone bullies, but you end up liking him in the end.

"You never went out into the field?" Arjan asked him about the arena. Professional wrestlers participated in different matches which was a different form of entertainment altogether, but surprisingly not frequent. Wrestling in Indragarh had become a popular sport for the wrong reasons. The system exploited the prisoners to flourish the gambling business. Most of it had been conducted under Vedanta's nose who hadn't given it much thought or perhaps hadn't known, but Kali had made it mainstream to the public. He had put the show out in the open, inviting more nobles, ministers, and Apsaras to add glamour to the show. It was quite a clever tactic, now that Arjan thought about it.

"Truth be told ya, I want to. I really do, heh," he grunted again. "It's just that, my weight, you know. No one cares to throw me out there."

"Never volunteered?"

"Doesn't matter." He frowned, getting embarassed. "Even if I did, they will overlook me. Truth to be told ya, no one wants to see a fat wrestler fighting to the death. They want to bet on the strong ones, you know."

Arjan wouldn't know. He wasn't a strong one and yet Kali had thrown him out there. It was a matter of personal vendetta.

"Why have you been locked inside?"

"Ah well, my father was a criminal," said Vikram.

"So?" Arjan didn't understand.

"Oh, you don't know? The sins of the father are passed down to the sons."

Arjan detested the very idea of it. "But there's no rule."

"Ah yes, there isn't, but um . . . you know, fella, it's a strange world. Even if there are no official rules per se, there are some internal ones that these officials follow, who make up their own stuff to huddle people together like sheep."

"Who was your father?"

"None of that really matters, fella," Vikram shook his head. "He was a minister, did treason, you know."

"Treason, you say," Arjan mumbled.

"There's been a great number of revolts, you know, fella, before all these Tribal thingies," Vikram raised his voice as if he was announcing something, but realized what he had done. He kept his voice low now in an attempt to not let the other prisoners hear their conversation. "One of them concerned with the idea of democracy, give power to the people, hee-yah, one thing is about it fella, it's a beautiful thought, even though it might never be real, isn't it?"

"Seems like it. Kings are a dying breed causing more harm than good."

"Now Vedanta, our dear old king was an honourable man, but an idea of democracy, naw, naw." He was speaking to himself more than to Arjan now. "He killed my father and made sure his young son didn't exact vengeance. So he put me in here, thought the democratic influence on me would be far too risky in the near future. Many were imprisoned along with me—three soldiers, friends of my father who were Dakshinis, my younger brothers, and a sister as well. They were then killed. Vedanta ensured no one from that revolt lived to tell the tale, felt that each one of them had seeped into an infectious democratic idea and it would build up like a tumour, infecting the entire state with undesirable ideas. Detestable fella, eh?"

"Why did he let you live?"

"I didn't seem much of a threat," he quipped with pride. "I was even fatter then, so much so that I couldn't walk properly. He pitied me. He felt that killing me wouldn't do much good since I anyway didn't have the strength to to attack him, and he's right. Even if I'm out there, I won't be able to take my revenge," he said matter-of-factly.

Arjan recalled how Kalki had taken revenge by killing Keshav Nand, the head of the Mlecchas, who had killed his father. One man is willing to shed blood, another sits in the jail and rants.

There are all kinds of people in the world.

"How did your father rope in a Dakshini?"

"You know how," he smiled, "they were friends, almost like family. The eldest and my father were buddies, you know, fella. They wanted similar things, but I tell you, I had my suspicions about them."

"Why?"

"Aw . . . well they were Dakshinis, of course, and they were of royal heritage."

"Royal?"

"Family of King Vibhisana, I should say, fella, cousins or something, don't know much. They left for Udaiyas for . . . well, you know all that jibberish from the south."

Arjan nodded. Vikram's tale was getting interesting, but at that moment the candles were lit and the soldiers entered with cuffs and bonds. The iron cages were opened as soldiers entered every cell, even Arjan's. They pinned him against the brick wall, as his hands were tied behind.

With Vikram behind him, he was dragged outside. He followed the other prisoners as they walked in a line.

"Must be the practice for the good old sport."

Arjan sighed. His bones ached and he wanted to sleep. But it was night and night was when they practised the most. Arjan was

thrown on the field now. The chains were opened so he, like the other prisoners, could begin practising. Looking at the barriers above the prison walls, Arjan recalled his escape through sticky situations while trying to find a way to free the trapped Kalki. Though now, Kalki won't be here. Arjan was alone and the very thought of no one coming for him, let alone knowing he was alive, made him sick in the stomach and burned his eyes with tears. He wanted to go home and he wanted to cry and hope his mother would come and take care of him. There was no one to send her notes anymore. She must be worried sick. How would she survive while knowing that one of her sons was in prison while the other was either dead or was out there in the wild, fighting every day to stay alive?

Master Reddy began to line them up, commanded them to jog around the place. Arjan did all of that. Then, they were asked to arm themselves with maces, which they were supposed to use as per their body weight and swing them to gauge their arm strength. As Arjan did all of that with Vikram, he turned to see Rudra. He was walking towards Arjan.

Arjan ignored him while Rudra stood there for a while.

"What I did was a show, kid," he said. His voice had a cutting edge of hoarseness to it—a thick, grave, salty air. An air of regality surrounded him and yet here he was, a mere prisoner. "You are not going to stay furious with me, are you?"

Arjan clenched his jaw.

"You are smart. You knew how to unlock my grip and work your way out. It was difficult taming you and believe me, I never had the intention of hurting you." Rudra winked at Arjan.

Arjan sighed. The moonlight was harsh, unforgivable, even the wind seeped with coldness inside Arjan, but with the amount of exercise he was doing, it yielded some warmth in him.

"I was glad Lord Kali stopped me. It's not my fault. I have been at it for years now, so I knew what to do to defeat you."

Arjan flared his nostrils and with sweat trickling from his face,

looked impassively at the stubborn, persistent man in irritation. "What do you want?"

"Business," he said. Arjan noticed that Rudra had a dusky complexion and his face and neck were glistening due to the sweat from the exercise.

By the gods, I need to stop looking at him that way.

"Business? Of what?"

"I'm looking for strong men on my team, and uh, you are obviously a candidate who I would appreciate working with," he said with a charming, disarming grin. Rudra continued, "Lord Kali hates you. That means you did something to piss him off in the gutters. That means you have the biggest motive out here. You want to escape."

"Business of what?" Arjan prompted again.

Rudra came close, the smell of his sweat made Arjan feel a lot of things inside his stomach as he avoided any unwarranted contact with him. Rudra whispered, "Business of escaping this godforsaken place, kid. All of us have had enough. I have been gathering men for weeks. All that's left is to figure out how we are going to escape."

Arjan narrowed his eyes, but before he could say anything, the loud noise of Master Reddy interfered their moment of secrecy.

"What are you two pimpleheads doing out there together!" he yelled.

"Sorry, Master," bowed Rudra innocently and turned to Arjan, almost irresistibly. "I'll see you around. Think about it," he winked, brushing his hand calmly over Arjan's hand as he left.

Arjan stood there for a moment, contemplating over what had just happened. He was yet again included into a plan that involved an *escape.*

And this time, he didn't have his brother to look out for.

7

Manasa had pledged that the only place she would stay in will be where Sambhavi had died. She had to build the walls, put the ceiling back up again, and have the outside area cleaned. Manasa didn't talk to the carpenters, for they were at the lowest rung of the caste system, but she was hoping that she would get to hear their conversations. She might learn more about the Suparn attacks that way.

And none bore her the answer she wanted.

She sat on the chair, looking at the complex that held the family blood, the same family she had longed to visit and hug and laugh with. There were little things in life that one must cherish before they wither. Manasa shed tears, wiping them off as carpenters walked in front of her. She didn't want her vanity to be lost, to show that she was weak. She was the king's sister. She was the heir apparent to the power of this entire city.

There was no one now she could trust except for poor Kadru. There was no one to love, no one to care and protect. She didn't even have a lover on her side, but then she had never fancied having one after her short marriage. The thought of love always bugged her, messed up her thoughts. She never did care, but she liked the idea of companionship, now most of all, when she wished to depend on someone, to trust someone wilfully. Vasuki, the younger

brother, always used to look up to Manasa for help. His absence was now clearly felt.

At least, they all are together.

The thought comforted her.

Manasa swivelled her head, facing the carpenter who was putting up the window. He had paused in between and was staring at her blankly.

She raised her brows, eyes widening. She knew she had a way of looking at an individual that could frighten them. "What is the problem, worm?" she spoke even though she shouldn't have. "Rather than glaring at me, worry about fixing this pur up." She had venom in her tone, but then she realized she shouldn't have taken her anger out on a poor man. She should calm down and think about her future prospects in this city. She had to eventually lead an army, defeat Kali, drive him to the point till he wept and begged for his life. The very idea of him resigned at her feet made Manasa grin with delight. She wanted all of that.

And that was when her mind began to be clouded with intense plotting. She was visited by a shadow that formed into flesh. The figure appeared at the gates and entered inside the pur. He was in his loose white robes that hung over his topless frame, tall and great with a fair-skinned body, and black hair pulled at the back.

Manasa saw Nanda and felt so many things at once. He was her ex-husband, but more so, he was a vengeful ex-husband. He was a vile man who had left her for a young girl, but then, Manasa didn't have the greatest feelings for him in return. But seeing him after so many years brought back memories, flushing a whirlpool of emotions inside her. She had to calm them down and look at him unperturbed, as if he didn't bring any complication to the situation she was in at present.

"I heard you were back." His voice was paper thin, the sleekest Manasa had ever heard unlike the rest of Nagas who had huskier

accents. "I'm glad," he said and gave her a warm smile which Manasa dismissed.

"What are you doing here?"

"Ouch, calm down, woman." Nanda walked over to the other side. "I apologize for what happened to Lady Sambhavi. The poor woman didn't deserve this. But it's good you are helping rebuild her house in her honour."

Manasa stood up. "What do you want, Nanda?"

"I am here to see you."

Nanda was not the most influential person in the Naga society thus making people wonder how the king's sister fell for him. Very few people were aware of his ability to pull strings in the shadows. He was a merchant, a traveller, and a charmer. He would sleep and whore and sell. He was a criminal, by some standards, but he had left all of that when he had married Manasa only to return back to it when he got bored of his daily life. And now, she had no idea what he was up to. For all she knew, he was here trying to do business with her or with someone else, and she was the bait.

"No, you weren't. You want something from me."

"You always thought of me as a detestable man. But no. I just want to make sure you are all right."

Manasa sighed. "Well, I'm fine. You can leave."

"You don't care to know what happened to Sambhavi, right?"

Manasa furrowed her brows, cocking her head forward with curiosity. "She was attacked by Suparns, right?"

"Ah well." He came close, the scent of tulips and liquor mixing well with him, as his newly-shaven face gave her a glimpse to the past she had had with him. "Have the people of Udaiyas made you so gullible that you believe what you hear?"

"What do you mean?" She paused. "She wasn't attacked by them?"

"Oh, she was. Sadly, I witnessed the aftermath when they were escaping in the middle of the night. I even sent you a note."

"Then why didn't I get it?"

"Exactly, why didn't you?" He frowned. "Don't you think it's awfully strange that out of all the purs the Suparns could have attacked, they went for Vasuki's family?"

"Kadru said they wanted to hurt Vasuki."

"Hurt a dead man? Um, that's awfully redundant; the poor woman had no intention of taking revenge."

"What are you implying?"

He was serious. The way he looked at her, it was as if his eyes could pierce her soul. "There's a camp close by, a bunch of Suparns have taken refuge there. I know the camp head well; we did business together over gooseskin. I can take you there and we can see how the story unfolds."

"So, you don't know yourself?"

"I don't know the whole story but I do know there is something wrong with the council and a sword is dangling over your cousin. If she moves or even fidgets, she will be silenced forever." Nanda clenched his jaw. "It's on you to decide now."

Manasa gave him a reluctant nod. "If this is some conspiracy to trap me and assassinate me, I'll make sure to kill you first," she said, and raised her hand in anticipation.

Instead of hurting her back with words, Nanda grabbed the fingers tightly, a smirk besmirching his face. "I don't know if you believe me or not, but as of this moment, I'm the only one you can trust in Naagpuri."

She was weak and exhausted. Her hand ached from the wound that she had received by an arrow. Her paralyzed hand made her feel vulnerable. *What if I'm attacked and can't defend myself?* Nanda could not be trusted. He did business with the worst of the criminals.

But here he was, claiming to be on her side.

She didn't want to go with him. But did she really have a choice?

8

It was different.

Without the crown, the glory, and the vanity, Vedanta felt naked. He had been thrown and tossed in the midst of his streets while watchers stalked him, with the intention of hunting him and lashing at him. He had been forced to give up the one thing he had been fighting for for so long and that had been the crown. He wanted to be the king of the strongest city of Udaiyas, but he couldn't now. He had let his people down.

Why?

Kali had found his weakness—his innocent little girl of thirteen, who played with wooden figures that she made herself.

And whenever Vedanta thought about his daughter, tears brimmed in his eyes. The very thought of her leaving this world grieved him, the kind which he couldn't handle. His wife had died in peace but he was in disarray. And now he didn't want Urvashi to leave him as well and for that, Vedanta was fine with leaving his throne, for now. He was ready to not let his vanity consume him and cause his daughter harm.

He recalled the dreadful day when he had been stripped of his powers.

"You can't do this to me," Vedanta said when Kali proposed the new option of giving away the crown to someone worthier. He had come to Vedanta's fort and demanded that in his office.

"Well, I can and I must." Kali shrugged his shoulders. "Don't you understand, your highness, you are a threat to me?" He had a way with his words, a loose accent that Vedanta was not fond of. "You and Kuvera . . . you both conspired against me. And I can't have that."

Vedanta had no idea how Kali had found out about it, but since he had recovered from the illness that had struck him, it had made him quicker in execution, and wiser. He had his ravens to spy on people.

"A price must be paid. I would've killed you but I can't make your daughter an orphan. Also, killing you wouldn't really please me. I don't prefer unnecessary bloodshed."

Bah! It was horseshit.

"I didn't conspire—"

"We can speak and meander around. You say you didn't do anything, I heard something else. You wanted to get rid of Vasuki, kill his general, and then he retaliated, which is why I might have been attacked, perhaps; I don't know, but then I ensured he received his proper dues. And so will his sister. He was about to do something nasty, but I protected the city from the wrath of a degenerative Tribal. Don't you think you owe something to me now?"

"You were the one to bring him here."

"La la," he played with his hands amusingly, as if listening to flutes in his mind. "I don't care if you conspired with him or not. You, my lord, are not needed here. And besides, I can't take the risk."

"Why aren't you punishing Kuvera?"

"Oh, I will." He grinned. "But in time."

"I wouldn't give away my crown." Vedanta stayed firm on his decision. "You have taken enough from me. Leave. Now."

Kali narrowed his eyes. And that was when a thud broke their dispute. Vedanta's eyes followed the sound which had come from near the door where a curtain had been draped. A pair of eyes was peering at them, a familiar pair of eyes.

No.

"Leave Urvashi," Vedanta ordered. She had been eavesdropping.

"No, no, please, come, come in, child," Kali interfered, standing instantly.

From the curtains appeared his darling, the apple of his eye, with curly hair and a rosy face, holding a wooden figure. She had a set of dangerous eyes stuck on Kali, as if she would do something reckless.

"My name is Kali." Kali bent down and offered his hand. "What's your name?"

Urvashi looked at Vedanta for approval. He reluctantly nodded.

"Urvashi," she said, her voice stern.

"Ah, like father like daughter, eh?" Kali's gave her a perfectly senile grin. "Attitude runs in the family, perhaps."

"Leave, Kali."

Kali stood, squaring his shoulders. "You have a lovely daughter here. You should think about her, you know. My offer was made out of kindness and respect that I have for you." He shot a glance at Urvashi. "Don't mistake my kindness for my weakness." And he left, storming out.

"What was that about, Father?" she asked.

Vedanta walked close to the potted plant he had kept in his office. "Nothing."

"It wasn't nothing, Father. That was a threat."

Vedanta glanced at her. Impressive. She understood subtlety in her age.

"I know."

"What will we do about it?" She blinked. Her eyes were watery. "We must fight."

"We must think." Vedanta sighed. "And think fast."

Between that day and this day, things had changed. His mind didn't revolt at the idea of someone else being on the throne anymore, if it meant securing Urvashi from the ensuing chaos. But his daughter was furious. She hated not being the princess anymore, not having the same respect. She didn't realize there were more important things in this world than just being a king.

Vedanta had been on his chariot with four guardsmen on their

horses surrounding him. The rider of the chariot reined the stallions that neighed at each lash.

Vedanta had a thali in his hand to worship Lord Vishnu's idol in Indragarh. He went there every weekend, praying and kneeling, worshipping and singing to his glory. Urvashi was dragged, even though she wasn't a believer. She found Lord Shiva much better in all aspects.

But today, her mood was different. She was pissed at the people she saw on the street. They looked at her with ease—no fear, no respect in their eyes. They simply didn't care.

"You are a nobody now," Urvashi whispered, perhaps hoping to slight her father.

"A title doesn't matter."

"You should fight back."

"I'm planning on it."

"You've been planning for a long time now, Father!" she growled.

Vedanta had a contentious look in his eyes. "We can't just attack the king of the city. He's the head of Keekatpur, king of Indragarh. We need to have a solid plan."

"I suppose that you just don't care."

"I do, child. I just don't want to take a risky step and endanger your life because of it."

"What about your dwarf friend?"

Does she know about my meetings with him? No, that's not possible.

"He's not my friend."

"He must have something in mind."

And surprisingly, Kuvera didn't. Vedanta had gone, first thing, to meet Kuvera to ask him to gather some resources and attack Kali's fort, but he had been declined. Kuvera was too afraid now to do anything after what having seen what Kali was capable of. He had a quick way of getting rid of major threats and Kuvera didn't want to create unnecessary problems for himself.

That was when the chariot jerked.

"What happened?"

"My lord, there are people in front, blocking the path."

"Get rid of them!"

"They are too many."

Vedanta got off his chariot. People had thronged around the temple. Pradm's men were controlling the crowd, preventing them from coming near the idol.

With his guards and his daughter, Vedanta reached to the centre, breaking away from the people who had gathered. His soldiers were strong enough to create a pathway in this beehive. And once he reached the middle, he could see the gate of the temple. Guards had lined up around the temple while Koko and Vikoko rode the horses from a distance. And right there in the middle was Kali, sitting casually on a colourful mat as he ordered his generals to move forward.

And Vedanta realized why. Koko and Vikoko and the rest of their men had tied ropes to the idol of Lord Vishnu. The men were clutching the ends of those ropes.

They were about to pull and rip it apart.

"Kali! What on heavens are you doing?"

Kali turned, as if amused by all of it, as he narrowed his eyes. "Oh, if it isn't our previous king."

Most of the people who hadn't noticed Vedanta earlier were now grimacing. Some were even snickering, but he ignored them.

"What are you doing?"

"Oh! I apologize for all of this; it'll just take a while."

"What will take a while?"

"Oh, that."

Kali clapped his hands. Vedanta swivelled his head as he saw Koko and Vikoko with the other guards. They began to scale the statue. The ropes tightened as they circled around the statue. It began to move and topple, and finally collapsed on the ground as the idol, made of marble and soapstone, crushed and cracked into a thousand pieces when it made contact with the floor.

Vedanta was frozen at his place, seeing the one thing that he had believed in for so long being torn apart by the man claiming to be king. His eyes darted towards the imposter king who was now approaching him.

For a moment, Vedanta wanted to send out his men and murder the heretic but he regained his composure when Urvashi tightened her grasp around his wrist.

"You shouldn't have done that." Tears were streaming down his eyes.

Kali shrugged. "The people of this city should understand to not worship false gods anymore."

"Then who should they worship?"

"Their work, their passion, whatever that makes them who they are. Not some idols where they put money in and hope blindly."

"The priests won't leave you unscathed."

"Irony?" He grinned. "I am the lord of the city now, Vedanta. It is time to accept a few changes." And with that Kali walked to the crushed idol, grabbing the heavy head of Lord Vishnu that had been carved by Vedanta's forefathers. "This is your god. Puny. One who doesn't take care of his people doesn't deserve the status of a god. Remember, these are mere stones that can be destroyed."

And with that, Kali began to squeeze the head until the head crushed even more under his arms. Vedanta was shocked by Kali's strength as the head turned into dust. Kali tossed the remnants, wiping the marble dust from his palms.

Vedanta was still unable to understand what had just happened. He had not been only robbed of a title, but his beliefs as well. He looked at Urvashi who was returning her gaze at him. And she nodded, signalling Vedanta to do what had to be done.

9

Kalki had always believed that his death would be gloriously epic. Death by being eaten alive was something he had never expected.

Darooda Simha and his comrades were now discussing with each other. And by definition of discussion, they were thumping their chests and hooting at each other. By the faint knowledge of what they spoke to one another, Kalki could make out through the grumbling that the other hulked creature was called Purab Simha.

Kalki had been restrained with multiple bamboo ropes and tossed away in the corner just to ensure he wouldn't escape. Padma watched him with cold eyes, while Kripa whistled away in boredom as if being held captive was not a new thing for him. The bald woman, along with her two friends, paid no heed to Kalki. His confidence was shrinking with each passing moment.

"So, how long until we are fresh meat?" whispered Padma.

There, she had said it. She had voiced out what everyone was thinking, and dreading at that moment.

"I don't think so, lass. None of us are dying here," mumbled Kripa. "I mean, it doesn't make sense for them to trap us here and then eat us."

Kalki had a frown on his face. He tried to say something but all that came out was an unintelligent groan due to his mouth being wrapped up.

"Yeah, mate?" Kripa swivelled his head towards Kalki. "Remember, these are your failings when you try to be a hero, you know. There's a reason why I'm taking you to meet Bhargav Ram. You try to be a hero, but you end up looking like a blumbering idiot. You have no idea how the Simhas' strength works and you just went for it. Without a proper strategy. You must realize lions always come in a herd."

Padma narrowed her eyes. "That doesn't make sense, old man. They come alone. Wolves come in a pack. Lions *always* come alone."

Kripa's mouth twisted in a grimace. "Yeah, whatever. Now to answer both your questions, Simhas aren't exactly cannibals. I mean they eat animal meat, but they never eat humans."

"So, what are they?" Padma blinked.

Kripa just realized something and Kalki could notice his uneven reaction. "Ah, you won't like the answer . . ."

That was when Kripa got interrupted. Darooda Simha and his friends came over and dragged the sulking Kalki to the side as he resisted with all his might. Then they did the same with all the captives, one by one.

The Simhas tied their legs and dragged them out of the cave to hook them onto the horses—*Kalki's horses.* Kalki couldn't believe what was happening. The harsh sun was beating down on their faces. Darooda sat on the horse while his friends did the same with the rest. Padma and Kripa were tied to the second horse, and the bald-headed girl with her friends was tied to the third.

They are taking us somewhere. But where?

Darooda excitedly beat his chest as they moved on. Kalki had to face the onslaught of pebbles, stones, and the dust, as his face rubbed against the surface.

It can't be worse than this.

Kalki could feel he was somewhere he wasn't supposed to be. The surface had now turned into pastures with leaves and twigs pricking his skin. Though it was a welcome sight after the dust. His friends were groaning. Kalki felt like resting in his bed and slumbering for just about forever, but he couldn't afford that luxury.

He could hear the mumbles of Darooda while he closed his eyes and thought about Narsimha—the majestic lord of the Simhas who had lived before the Mahayudh, before the Breaking, before Lord Raghav. He dwelt on the fifth Avatar, whom he had learnt about in the gurukul.

Kripa was right. He was not ready to fight. The only option was to learn how to defeat a Simha from another Simha.

He began to use his Channelling powers, trying to gather his focus as much as he could, while being distracted by the occasional thud from hitting into rocks and dirt. His hair had turned greasy, but he didn't care. The extraneous distractions evaporated and he let go of the reality that he was living in. His arms slowly began to loosen up and he opened his eyes.

He was in a forest.

It reminded him of the outskirts of Shambala—the lush greenery and the whisper of the birds. There was also the smell of oranges and apples.

Kalki turned to see a strange, fair-skinned man. He was as tall as Kalki, and had a lion-skinned fur over his entire body. Long nails were protruding on his fingers, and upon a closer look, Kalki realized they weren't nails but claws. They had been fashioned out of blades and wood in such a way that they seemed wearable.

He could not help but be enthralled by the ingenious invention.

Kalki had known from Bhargav Ram, during one of his Channelling sessions, that he could use the power of Channelling and converse with the memories of the other Avatars. But they would be limited and wouldn't go far. There was little time. Kalki had to ask Lord Narsimha now.

"My lord," Kalki began, "I need your help."

Lord Narsimha turned and Kalki saw his heavy beard that covered his face. His beady eyes reminded Kalki of a lion. He had hair over his chest. The way he watched Kalki, the aura around him was making Kalki's knees go weak.

"What do you want?" he asked.

Kalki thought of the question—how to kill a Simha? Now that seemed stupid to ask from the Simha legend.

"I have been kidnapped by your kind."

"Must be a good reason for it," he guffawed.

He was quite civilized for a Simha, which made Kalki realize what they had become now. But his sarcasm was something that Kalki didn't appreciate.

"How do I defeat the worshippers of the lion?"

"You cannot. We are indestructible."

Perhaps, the image of Lord Narsimha is of the past—full of pomp and self-confidence. Kalki knew that Narsimha was unaware of their eventual fate. The Simhas were eventually trampled and destroyed. Kalki had to ask for the solution in a different way.

"I know about you, Nar." Kalki came forward, his chest heaving. "You saved Prahlad from his own father."

Narsimha's eyes softened at the name of 'Prahlad'.

"You helped an Asura's son. Why would you do that?"

He closed his eyes, sighing. "Because I believe the sins of a father do not follow posterity." He paused, eyeing Kalki with deep interest. "It's always amusing when I think about how I ended up defeating Hiranyakashipu."

"How did you do it?"

"By anticipating his behavioural patterns. To defeat your enemy, you must first think like your enemy."

And then the image dissolved. He was back, his head grazing the ground and his mouth filling with dirt. He turned around to

see that he was in a forest, with little to no sunlight. They were enveloped in darkness.

To defeat your enemy, you must first think like your enemy.

He knew what he had to do.

He began to convulse and mumble and groan as much as he could. Darooda stopped his horse and looked quizzically at Kalki. He got down from the horse and walked over to Kalki as the current Avatar kept fidgeting in the place, toppling, letting the leaves brush against his nose harshly.

Darooda knelt and took off the wrap-around from Kalki's mouth. "Big man, what?" he questioned.

Kalki knew what he had to do. He began speaking gibberish, hooting, mumbling, and shouting to distract Darooda, and then he improvised. Darooda responded to it enthusiastically because this was Darooda's way of communication. It made Darooda feel that Kalki was the same kind.

"What are you doing?" Kripa yelled.

Kalki wanted to shut him up. He kept hooting and soon it was followed by Darooda grinning and hooting back at him. Even Darooda's friends began to behave the same way.

Kalki showed his grip where he was tied, asking him to open it. Darooda grinned, nodding, and began to use his nails to tear it apart.

Very good.

Kalki made faces. He showed his gritted teeth and beat his chest, while he lay upside down from the horse. He had to find the opportunity to now grab Darooda's feet and topple him. As soon as his hands were free, he was going to untie his legs help his companions out and attack the other two Simhas.

While all the planning was being rushed in his mind, Kalki realized that Darooda had turned silent, as if he had just realized something. Kalki's blood went cold as Darooda's dead eyes watched Kalki for a moment before he collapsed on the ground.

And that was when his plan began to falter as Kalki's sight fell on a simple dart that had pierced Darooda's back. Soon, two other darts were stuck across the other two Simhas who fell from their horses.

What in the heavens?

Kalki pushed himself forward as he began to untie the knot that bound him to the horse and finally when he did so, he heard footsteps—silent and scary. He turned around, but tripped in the process. Strange-inked men emerged from the shadows with just rags covering their bodies—they had long hair till their knees, and were armed with flutes which were being used to spit the darts.

Soon, he found other kind of individuals jumping over the branches and logs of the trees, travelling like monkeys.

Kalki slowly moved towards Kripa who was just grinning to himself. "Simhas were never cannibals. They were scavengers. They got what they could and gave it to someone in return for weapons or whatever they required."

"So who are they?" Kalki's eyes widened, his pupils dilating. He didn't like the smell that came from these inked men.

"The ones Simhas were employed to."

"Why did they kill them if they were their employees?"

"I suppose, mate, they had served their purpose."

"Who are *they*?" Kalki gritted his teeth. The men were circling them now, baring their yellow teeth.

"Oh, they?" Kripa gulped while Padma rolled her eyes, exhausted from the time Kripa took in responding. "They are . . . well . . . they are called Pisach."

"Pisach?" Kalki had heard the name somewhere. They were uncivilized creatures that lived close to the cremation grounds. That's what the teachers at gurukul had taught him, but then seeing them right in front of him wasn't exactly pleasant.

"Yes. And one more thing."

"Yeah?" Kalki was running through several ideas to fight these

Pisach now, but he had no weapons. He fidgeted in anticipation of the darts that might be shot at them any moment.

"They are definitely cannibals."

It made sense now why Darooda had referred to Kalki and his companions as food. They were not food to him, but to the Pisach. Kalki flared his nostrils as he looked at the Pisach, and was close to surrendering again . . . this time to be eaten for sure.

10

Jamun was a vile, vile man.

As Manasa waited in the dimmest of nights for Nanda to bring his boat, she thought of Jamun. She had glanced at him leaving the council chambers when she had gone to meet Kadru. Kadru had been talking to Jamun, surely out of necessity since Jamun was an influential sponsor for the army. He fed and clothed them, and provided money for weapons as well. Kadru had to entertain Jamun. He had become an important part of the council.

That only complicated things more.

If Jamun had been cunning enough to trap a snake like Kadru, she would have to do whatever she could to stop him. And Jamun had hated Vasuki, which meant he had hated Manasa. Her father and Jamun's father had been rivals. The rivalry had ended when the former had killed the latter's army. It was a settlement, but a dirty one. Surely, the battle had been concluded with a truce, but revenge is always at the back of the mind and is ready to bite you with poison the moment you turn away.

Jamun's father had gotten his revenge by killing Manasa's father. Before Vasuki and Manasa fought through the ranks to get the throne back, this was still a precarious situation. Once Vasuki ascended the throne, Jamun had been allowed to live.

Vasuki, however, had beheaded Jamun's father right in front of his son.

Since then, Jamun remained cordial and political while hiding his true ambitions.

"We should have killed him," Manasa said to Vasuki. "One day, he would return to end us all."

"If we remain strong, he won't. Jamun is in no way related to the bloodshed his father started," Vasuki responded.

"But what if he does? We killed his father . . ."

"Nagas don't believe in emotions, my dear." Vasuki had a perfect grin, his blue eyes shimmering against the lake that was in front of them. "If they did, you would be weeping right now for Father, but you aren't. You are thinking of murdering someone. And the turmoil doesn't show on your face."

Manasa thought for a while. "We have to keep Jamun busy then. Content, yes. We cannot show ourselves as weak. This may be a bad political move and it'll worsen if we don't have a strong hold on the situation."

"Don't worry. We will never go weak. And it's not a bad political move because we need Jamun and his money. He holds more money than the bloody treasury—pros of having an ancestor who had built the Sheesha temple. That's the place he gets all his wealth from." Vasuki rolled his eyes.

"Do not worry, it'll be fine."

Manasa's mind raced back to the present. And she smirked. It had been foolish of Vasuki to let Jamun live. She will have to constantly watch her back now.

The boat arrived and she saw him in all his glory. Nanda stood tall and firm with his jet black hair and the charming wisp of a smile. He had brought a wooden cane with him. The boat was made of rigid papyrus reeds, with two men using oars to steer it towards the place where Manasa was standing.

"Well, you look classy," Nanda grinned.

Manasa shrugged, stepping on the boat when she slipped a little only to be held by Nanda. She grimaced and went in a corner,

feeling like a klutz already. The boatmen began to steer, while Nanda came forward and sat next to Manasa.

"It's an all-night journey. I hope you don't ignore me throughout our journey, my love. There's no one to talk to anyway."

"You have no right to call me me 'your love', Nanda." Manasa flared her nostrils at the idiot. "You lost that privilege a long time ago."

Nanda sighed. "You have always been difficult."

She surely had been, but her husband used to be a man of crime. She had tried to sober him, get him away from the Suras and the gambling, but he had eventually found trouble. It had been the last straw when he had cheated on her. She didn't know who the other woman was, but she didn't care. He had done it and that was all that had mattered.

"I hope I don't get killed during this journey."

"You won't. I'll protect you." Nanda seemed sincere.

"I would end up protecting you, believe me." Manasa scoffed.

"What's your problem?"

"Nothing."

"Oh, please."

Manasa turned her head to see the moon and the stars. Even though the night was romantic, nothing else was. She was with the most unromantic person.

"Who is the chief of that Suparn camp?"

"Maruda."

She turned instantly, gritting her teeth. "Maruda?" She had recently learnt a lot about Maruda. "What is he doing so close to the camp?"

"That's what we are going to find out."

"You did business with Maruda over gooseskin?"

"What can I say? These birds love it!"

Maruda had been okay with doing business with a Naga?

The only reason why the Suparns had been staunch rivals of the

Nagas was because of their fight over an exotic plant. She brushed away her wandering thoughts. The more she mulled over the strained history, the more she would be detracted from her mission. The battle had been going on for so long that reconciliation didn't seem like a solution anymore.

"Maruda is the man who killed my brother's family."

"Ah well, we are going to figure out why."

"What if he sees me and kills me as well?"

"He won't."

"How are you so sure?"

He played with his lips. "Because he owes me. He still hasn't paid for the gooseskin, you know." He smirked.

"It's not funny. He can kill you and the payment is done."

"It's not that simple. The Suparn tribe could be vengeful, even crazy but its people are not backstabbers."

She was going straight into the heart of trouble and she didn't like it.

"Ah, Manasa?"

"Hmmm?"

"Since the night is so lovely, I have a confession to make."

"Confession?" She turned to face him, surprised. "What sort of confession are we looking at?" Even though she didn't want to take this conversation forward, she was leaning forward, wondering whathe was about to reveal. There was something about Nanda; he had a way of getting inside your skin and cozying there.

"A really honest one," he responded.

"Tell me."

"See, I think this is the right time to tell you."

"Go on."

"I am, uh . . ."

"You are getting married again to that wench?"

"That's what I want to talk about."

Her heart sunk and she didn't know why. Her heart shouldn't sink, since she didn't love Nanda anymore. "Okay . . ."

"There was never any other girl."

"What do you mean?"

"It was a lie."

"You told me to my face that you wanted to end things because you liked someone younger and I was an old woman you couldn't take care of."

"It was all a lie. You are the most beautiful old woman I know." He chuckled softly. "And it was a lie to get rid of you."

"Why did you want to get rid of me?"

"Because of your brother. He forced me to."

Is this one of his lies? She really looked at him, hoping to find a hint of insincerity but found none. "I don't believe you."

"You don't have to. I hid this truth for the sake of your brother. You must believe I have never been a good man, right? I mean I always pledged myself to doing something absurdly ridiculous. Then, I found you. I was having the most wonderful time of my life with you, and then your brother stepped in. He wanted my help." He sighed, trying to recall, choosing his words carefully. "He was leaving for Kali's campaign against the Manavs and he chose me to do something stupid—he told me to loot Lord Sheesha's temple."

Manasa couldn't believe what she was hearing. Surely Vasuki wasn't always the most religious person but telling her husband to loot a temple was just preposterous.

"There's a reason why he had tasked me with this job. He wanted to take away whatever little power Jamun had. So I took some of my men and went there one night. Apparently, Jamun knew about the attack. And he guarded the place all night. We fought and we lost, and we scampered back. I did all of this for Vasuki's happiness and also because of the money. I told him I lost my men and I wanted some coins for compensation. He refused. He said he would destroy my life by putting me in prison if I ever ask for

money or utter a word about it. He was so frantic that he even told me to leave Naagpuri which meant leaving you, because he thought I'll be a threat to him if I stayed here. f the word had gotten out about him ordering an attack on the temple, it would have lead to a rebellion. He didn't kill me, perhaps, because I was your husband, but there was bad blood already. I wanted to kill him. Unable to take it anymore, I left the place to have a new beginning."

"You left because of my brother's conniving plans?"

"Yes."

"There was no other girl?"

"None whatsoever. Hell, I've never liked anyone after you. It was always you, Manasa. Always. And because of your stupid brother, we had been forced to separate."

Manasa didn't know what to feel, but she had a sudden urge to slap him. She looked at him for a few seconds, and then smacked him right across his cheek. "You broke my heart again."

"What?" He massaged his cheek in confusion. "I thought you'll like me more after this."

"No, I hate you more. You lied to me. That's worse. At least, I respected you for telling me you loved someone else. You were a cheater. Now you are a liar."

He looked at Manasa incredulously. "You know, I will never understand you, Manasa. Never. I pour my heart . . ."

"You lived fearing that my brother could destroy you. But if you had really loved me, you would have fought back."

"He was the king of Nagas."

"Well, not anymore, and that's why you told me. You are such a loser!" She smacked him again on the shoulder.

"Ouch, it hurts."

"It's supposed to!" Manasa added angrily. "That's why I'm hitting you, you idiot!"

An awkward silence steered in the conversation while Manasa looked away. The clear water reflected the blue sky. A gentle breeze

was flowing, rustling the leaves on the trees surrounding them. The silence was broken by the boatmen. They were humming a tune. Manasa closed her eyes, humming with them.

She didn't want to face the pathetic man. She didn't even want to talk to him anymore. Argh! She hated him more than anything right now . . . but deep down, she still loved him. And that made her feel even more miserable.

Thinking about him would only lead to further crisis, so she looked closely at the boatmen now. Something was off about them. Manasa noticed their knives. They had serpents carved over their hilts—the same design that the soldiers of Naagmandal had on their weapons.

"Listen." She turned to face Nanda.

"Now what?"

"Where did you get these two?"

"They are farmers."

"No, they are not," she whispered.

"What do you mean?"

And that was when one of the boatmen dropped the oar and pulled out the knife.

Instantly, Nanda lurched in front of Manasa, letting the knife pierce his skin. Manasa didn't retort. She was stunned for a moment. The other boatman made his move. She pulled out a small knife and threw it at the second one as it cleanly sliced his throat, pouring out a gush of blood.

She saw Nanda pulling out the knife from his stomach and plunging it in the belly of the other boatman.

The boatman didn't resist much and collapsed for a few seconds. But then he stood up, and Nanda fell back, feeling weak as ever. Manasa could see how pale he had turned.

She headbutted the boatman who was coming towards Nanda. He was trying to gather his remaining strength. Rather than attempting to shield himself, he pulled the dagger out and blood splattered across his torso.

She knelt down and grabbed the boatman's throat, narrowing her gaze. "Who sent you here?"

The assassin smiled. "You shouldn't care, woman! You are ancient . . ." he began coughing.

"Never call me old. I'm very sensitive about that subject." She pressed his throat even tighter. "You know I've become quite handy when it comes to torturing idiots like you. So tell me now and you will be forgiven."

"You do not have the power to forgive me. You and your accomplice shall be wiped by the council."

The council? They ordered the assassinations! That meant they knew that she was going to meet Maruda. They didn't want her to meet him.

"How do they know about our destination?"

He smiled. It was a self-satisfied grin. "They know your every move."

"You speak in riddles and you are just irritating me now." She took the knife that the assassin had tossed aside and stabbed him again. And again. And finally, after three stabs, the assassin lost his slowly ebbing life.

She stood in a pool of blood amongst two corpses and one injured Naga. She walked over to Nanda who was coughing and leaning against the boat. She sat beside him, letting him keep his head on her chest. She then tore off the end part of her gown and wrapped it around his gash.

"I saved you . . . ugh . . . that counts for something, right?" Nanda said, struggling with words.

"Shut up, you." Manasa patted him on the head. It had been quite long since she had held Nanda so closely.

She looked at the river. The current was steady and the boat could move without the help of oars. But reaching their destination might take a little longer than estimated. Though she also knew that she couldn't leave Nanda. He would probably fall sleep and if he slept, he would die. She needed to keep him awake.

"I hope Maruda has the first aid to help you get back on your feet."

"I don't care."

Manasa narrowed her eyes. "Why?"

"Because if I die tonight, I will die as I intended—in the arms of the woman I love."

Manasa couldn't help but fluster at what he just spoke. *Always the petty romantic!* His head was down and he couldn't see her, but she couldn't help smiling to herself. She liked it. Even though she would never admit this to him.

She had liked everything about the night except for the fact that the two assassins hired by the council had tried to kill her.

"The council is making sure we don't find the truth. I'm just worried about Kadru."

Nanda didn't say anything. Though after a pause, he began, "It's not the council. The council are a bunch of straightforward scholars and sponsors who live upon the people's goodwill. It's bloody Jamun. He wants you dead for what you did to his father."

"What is our plan then? We know it is Jamun who is doing all of it. What should we do?"

"We convince Maruda to work for us rather than for him."

"That's why we are going to meet him? You knew it all along, didn't you? That it was Jamun?"

"Guilty!" He grinned.

She wanted to smack him again. But then the night was old and so were they. Old and bruised. Not the best time to smack him. *I'll do it some other time.*

Initially, she had wanted to take Maruda out of her way. But now, a pact with him was necessary. Or else, she would perish before she could have her revenge.

She woke up to the sound of swords being pulled out of their sheaths. This sound was nostalgic. It reminded her of her father, who used to do this all the time to prepare himself for combat—quickly and readily. If the sheath wasn't knitted well or the sword won't come out well, he would tell his weaponsmith to craft it again.

And that was it—the sound. She woke up. It was day and there were no owls hooting, but sparrows flew in the sky. She had slept and she had no idea for how long. She saw Nanda on her side, his face white as a sheet, his eyes closed.

No . . . no . . . I hope he hasn't died.

She saw his gash and it had darkened. She tried to sway him, when he broke out of his sleep, blinking and looking at her.

"You scared me," she whispered, finally breathing a sigh of relief.

"I'm scared too," he sheepishly said.

She couldn't understand why, when he asked her to look in the front. She now knew where the metallic clangs had originated from. Five Suparns were standing on the boat, one of them pricking the dead Nagas with his sword. Their armour had a flying bird as their emblem. And they had quivers designed like wings. They were so bright and brown-coloured, they looked like that they had golden skin. She turned to see if she was close to the land, if the boat had docked by itself, or perhaps the Suparns had seen the firelights and pulled them closer to their side of the land. There was no clear answer.

"Ah well, what do we have here? A criminal and a washed-out queen," one of the Suparns said. "Give me one good reason why we shouldn't slaughter your pretty faces right now."

11

Arjan hadn't thought about the escape plan that he had discussed with Rudra until Vikram asked him about it after their training.

"Are we escaping, fella?"

Arjan didn't know whether he should tell the fat boy or just keep quiet.

"You don't need to be silent, fella. I heard about it. The word is out. Rudra is planning it with Harsha."

Harsha? Arjan hadn't known about that. He had seen Harsha and he was anything but like his name. Harsha seemed sweet when spoken politely to but he was a mammoth—a giant, worse than Rudra. Rudra was tall and sleek, able to justify his serpentine moves with his fit body; Harsha was the opposite. He didn't move much and others couldn't move him without his consent. He would just stand there and if someone would come in front of him, he'll just smack them on their faces. Rudra was the brains and, one could say, Harsha was the brawns behind all of it.

Wrestling in the prison was just a word no one believed in, really. Sure, it was called wrestling and many a times Arjan had to train to fight, but all it was, was cheap entertainment. *It depends on what the audience wants.* Sometimes, they just wanted to see some petty bloodshed and the idea of blood just twisted the insides of Arjan's stomach.

He had seen enough blood in the battle of Shambala and he had been sure he won't have to see it anymore, but he had been wrong. Every day, something or the other was broken in his body and his nose was now smashed. He had to wear a bandage around his face and some might say with the scar and this contraption, he looked quite dangerous, and not a boy from a village.

"He doesn't like ya much, fella," Vikram said. "Don't know why, though."

"Harsha?"

"Yeah."

"Why doesn't he like me?"

"I don't know; mistrust probably."

Arjan rolled his eyes. "How did you know about the plan?"

"Oh, everyone does. They all want to escape. Word on the street is that we will flee during one of our night practice sessions."

"Do you know when they'll do it?"

"Oh hell! If I knew, I'll be ready, fella, but I don't know. They are being quite secretive about it."

Arjan nodded. Vikram was in the dark, so was Arjan. He was not interested in carrying out the conversation anymore. He turned over and lay his head close to the ground as he thought about the escape. *Was it idiotic to even escape or was it sheer genius?* Sure, it would be lovely to escape from here and go out and find Kalki or go to Bajrang's temple and meet his mother. He could think of endless things to do once he got out of this wretched place. The idea of escape slowly began to form well. He had done it once and he could do it again. He was ready.

And that was when the footsteps became clear. It was night and through the rails, he could see the dark skies devoid of stars. *Who would come at this time?*

Arjan turned and also saw other inmates breaking from their slumber. They finally realized that a Manav soldier had come, armed

with a spear. There was another person who accompanied him and they stopped right in front of Arjan's cell.

"What is the meaning of this?"

They opened the cell and without even asking, roughly pulled him out. Knobbing the spear right at his spine, they made sure he walked silently.

"What are you doing? Where am I going?" Arjan cried.

But none of his words were responded to. He walked in confusion to find other inmates sticking themselves close to the cell gates to watch Arjan—some with suspicion and some with pity. He even got a chance to exchange glances with Rudra, who blinked with a worrisome expression.

"Where am I headed?" he asked the Manav soldier again, whispering this time, his voice defeated.

"To Lord Kali's quarters," the soldier responded with a raspy breath.

Arjan realized that Kali's room didn't resonate with the person he was. It looked quite ordinary—it was devoid of any devil horns and thorns and fire. They all joked about it in prison, about how Kali epitomizes the idea of evil. Everyone hated Kali in some way or the other. Kali's room was quite simple—with hardbound books, a table, a chair, fire lamps that lighted the place up, and nice granite flooring. A window was at the back from where the prison could be seen.

Fortunately, the prison and Kali's fort were close by so Arjan didn't have to walk much.

Kali was sitting on a chair, whistling as he read a book. He had gone bald and he had the same wispy golden eyes that pierced through the darkness. Shadows danced over his chalky skin and there was a hint of beauty about him that indicated that he was once

a handsome man, but there was no trace of his old self anymore. He looked a dilapidated version of himself.

The soldiers left Arjan and didn't care to bind his hands since they knew that Kali could singlehandedly beat Arjan with ease—now that he had gotten hold of the Somas and could use it to overpower him.

"Where is your crown?" Arjan asked.

He smiled. "I gave it away to a man in need. A hermit, perhaps." He had a way of speaking, as if he was amusing himself with each word he spouted.

"Why am I here?"

"You are so direct." He manically watched him. "I wanted to ask you something, and that's why I called you."

Arjan gritted his teeth. What would he want to ask a prisoner like him? Though Arjan had noticed that Kali had always taken interest in him for some reason—perhaps because Arjan was Kalki's brother, the man Kali hated.

"Do you think I've gone mad?" he ended with a husky laughter to his own question.

And he's asking me if he's mad. Arjan wanted to roll his eyes, but surely it would look disrespectful. He remained silent, though it didn't mean he had no answer to the question. He did. Kali surely had gone mad, but his madness wasn't exactly a day's affair. It was escalating. Slowly.

"You can speak your mind. I've already tortured you enough, boy." His eyes softened. "I just want to know the answer from a third party."

"I believe then . . ." Arjan gulped down his nervousness, "you were always mad. You just chose to show it now."

"And why is that?"

"Why would you show it now, you mean?"

"Yes."

"I suppose because you stopped caring."

He clapped his hands instantly. "Absolutely! You are right. I stopped caring. For some reason, the Somas really made me want to not pay attention to someone else, as if they all were underneath me."

"I understand."

"You know, Arjan, even though I do things that might seem extreme to other people, I still feel kind of unhappy. No one knows what I went through. No one knows why I behave the way I behave. They choose to see me now, the way I am, but they don't see who I was. I wasn't always like this. You are a brother to someone. I was a brother as well." His eyes wandered in the empty space as he thought deeply about what he was going to say, choosing his words carefully.

"I was a bad brother because I couldn't save him. He was a few months old, the only other boy amongst my siblings. I had a few siblings, all were girls and he was the one boy who I couldn't save. Do you know why he was burnt to death?"

"No, I don't know."

"Because of Tribal conflicts. There was a battle, unimportant as it may seem, between two Tribals. My entire village was razed to the ground and many Manavs died there. And all I could do was escape with Durukti. I left my siblings to die. Do you know why? Because of petty Tribal politics. We are all uncivilized monsters, destroyers. We are not ready to be governed by each other. We need someone to show the way. That's why we believe in the puny religion—something to look up to." He paused, taking a deep breath. "And that's why I rose from being an orphan to a king, because you see, I wanted to make sure nothing like this would ever happen again. That no child, mother, or father would live to see their loved ones conquered by death because of politics. And I tried my best. I thought the Tribals could live amongst each other, but that also didn't happen. They began to consume each other and I had to be the king, the sole ruler, because you see . . . we need

someone supreme ruling over us or we will end up eating each other alive."

Gods, he makes sense.

"How do you know you are fit to be the supreme power?"

Kali's eyes glistened with dread. "If not me, then who else?" He paused, but did not give Arjan a chance to reply. "And with the kingship comes a certain price—making the council happy. They are the people who help maintain order in the city. How does one make them happy? By giving them some blood and violence, a form of entertainment. That's why I began training prisoners for wrestling. Do you think I enjoy putting this sport up?"

"I don't know."

"Well, I don't. I'll be honest. I hate it but people enjoy this sort of entertainment and I'm not wrong to give them that."

"At the expense of a human life?"

"Oh come on, you are all killers and kidnappers and betrayers and it's not like I'm picking up civilians from the streets to fight," he scoffed. "I say all of this, Arjan, because I have a plan. No matter how crazy and unpredictable I can be, I always have a plan to sustain my life a little longer. So, when I hear . . ." Kali walked and stood dangerously close to Arjan, so close that Arjan could feel Kali's breath on his face, "that a bunch of idiotic prisoners are planning an escape, I feel it's a threat to my plans."

Arjan's blood ran cold. *He does he know?* The word is getting out, Vikram had said. *Gods save us. Kali has his spies within the prisoners?*

"I don't know what you are talking about."

"Sheesh, I think you do know, but it's all right. I know you won't partake in it since you won't be stupid enough to do it again. You'll fail miserably as I hold the administration of the prison under my thumb."

Arjan nodded in dread.

"Who are they?" His face turned placid, his voice callous. "I know you know the names, so just give them to me."

"I said I don't know what you are talking about."

Kali sighed. "What if I grant you freedom from the prison in return for this information?"

Arjan's eyes lit up with shock. *Will he really*? He was just thinking a few moments back how he would like to go everywhere once he left this place.

"Ah yes, I got your attention, didn't I? Well, tell me then and I shall approve your release."

Arjan gulped. This was a tough moment. Could he trust Kali in helping him leave or could he not?

He thought about Rudra, Vikram, and hell, even Harsha. Slowly and faintly, Arjan wiped the sweat that trickled down his face as he said what he should have a while back. "You are wrong. There is no escape at work."

Arjan had been in the courtyard, yet again practising his wrestling moves but also learning the ways of a javelin. The day was mighty and the sunshine struck hard on his back.

He had been genuinely petrified last night when he had lied in front of Kali, as his golden eyes had sunk into Arjan's soul to identify the truth. But he hadn't budged.

He felt relieved and while he practised his javelin, he saw Rudra walking up to him, noticing the gaze of Master Reddy who was on the other side of the field. Rudra began to stretch his muscular arms and crunch his tight stomach, letting his chest convulse with sweat and energy. Again, Arjan felt things he shouldn't be feeling in such a situation. And so, he tried to ignore Rudra, in every way possible.

"Arjan?" Rudra's soft voice called out.

"Yeah?"

"Where were you taken last night?"

"To Kali."

Arjan was not looking at Rudra, so as to not act suspicious in front of Master Reddy. They were practising their respective routines, but it was all a front for their conversation.

"What did he want?"

"To know if there is a revolt being planned in the prison."

Rudra stopped with his spear and turned. "I hope you didn't say anything."

"Of course, I didn't." Arjan was hurt because Rudra had suspected him of ratting everyone out. "He even offered me freedom, but I refused. If we go, we all go, not just me."

Arjan realized that Rudra was grinning from ear to ear. "Thanks, Arjan. I guess you're not just a handsome man, but also a true friend."

Arjan blushed. Gods, the worst thing that could happen is him being flustered in front of a man like Rudra. But he kept quiet and gave a meek nod. "I don't know what 'handsome' plays a role in this."

"I was just trying to fit in a compliment somewhere." Rudra smiled, though it faltered as he continued. "You must know that Harsha is telling others you are Lord Kali's spy who's feeding everyone information."

"Me? That's stupid."

"I know, I trust you, but others don't. I'll try to convince them by telling them what you just told me."

Arjan appreciated the gesture and Rudra's hand parted from him, as he walked away only to realize everyone had stopped practising. They were looking up. Walking in the field with a bunch of soldiers was Kali. He had a devious grin on his face. Master Reddy, at the sight of his king, instantly bowed and told other prisoners to bow as well. His appearance in the prison was so swift and unexpected that Arjan couldn't even see from where he had arrived. Arjan bowed as well, his head down, but he peered from the corner of his eye.

"At ease," Kali gestured. "I'm glad you all are taking your sport in great spirit." He was bored; it was the monotonous voice that made it too evident. "I've just come here because, well . . . I have got some unfortunate news for you all."

Everyone looked strained. Arjan shared a glance with Vikram who had come skipping over to his side.

"I have learnt from my recent gatherings of information that you all are planning to escape. What is wrong? Did I do something? Is the food bad? Is the accommodation not comfortable for you? Maybe you don't want to battle with each other so much. I understand your skepticism; I do." He began walking through the lines where all the inmates were kneeling down. "I want you all to be away from this life."

Arjan didn't understand who Kali was pointing at until he realized that he was right behind him. All inmates raised their heads and looked at Arjan. Kali grabbed Arjan by the head and pulled him up. That hurt, but not too much. Arjan withstood it like he withstood most of the pain he had suffered till now in his life.

"Because he ratted you all out. I know everything about what you all are up to. And he gave the information to me. And it's just fun, because now you all will suffer the consequences." He patted Arjan on the back as Arjan's feet began to grow cold as he blankly looked at Kali. He couldn't understand what was happening. "Thank you, boy. You helped me out yesterday. Everyone! Because of him, your plan is sabotaged. And now as a punishment to all, including him, since he was part of it initially as well, you will all combat to death. Absolute hardcore wrestling, I must say. So yes, thank you and think twice before you mess with me again!" He patted Arjan again before leaving the premises.

Arjan was befuddled and he realized what Kali had just done. He had put the blame on Arjan. This will make him the prime target in prison. Now as he glanced at the disappointed eyes of Rudra and

the angry eyes of Harsha, he knew he was in a lot of trouble. *What a sadistic madman!*

Since he was untrained, Arjan realized he could be pretty much dead by the next match he was going to be in.

12

The scarred man . . . the fire . . .

That's what she kept thinking, scribbling down in her notebook. Durukti had realized what Kali hadn't—a conspiracy was brewing around everyone, perpetrated by a man who people should be afraid of, but was unfortunately unknown to all.

Symrin was just a pawn for that scarred man, a fiddle that'll be knocked away once her duty was fulfilled. But it also meant that Symrin, who she had simply adored, was a cheater, a liar, and a horrible person. Though all the hatred Durukti had for her had to concealed, otherwise Symrin would run away and the truth will be lost.

Who is this scarred man? She tried to recall all the conversations, all the history that she had learnt over a period of time. She tried to wonder while she constantly ignored Symrin, whenever she could—sometimes saying she's busy, sometimes dismissing her, but it was always for a valid reason so Symrin wouldn't think Durukti was doing all of it on purpose.

The scarred man was around here, ensuring that everything began and ended at the right moment. He was the one who was orchestrating each and every single move to cause a domino effect. He wanted Kalki out and he wanted Kali ill.

Durukti recalled the conversation she had had with Kali when he had been ill. He had told her about a dream he had had—the dream or a nightmare, as one may call it which had showed that the reason behind the fire in the village was not the Tribal conflict. It had been a one-man job . . . a tall man with a scar over his forehead.

Could this person, who Symrin was talking to, be the same person?

And what was the Eye of Brahma? Durukti had overheard Symrin telling someone about it, but she had no idea of what it was.

The only way to know more about what Symrin was up to, was to track her movements.

And that was what she was doing. For days, Durukti had made sure to keep her distance, hiding herself in a black cloak and staying out of sight while following Symrin. Most of the time, Symrin would take a quick turn and when Durukti would follow, there won't be anyone—or when Symrin disappeared, a boy would be there instead of her. It was like Symrin knew magic, like she could shapeshift if she felt someone was following her. Symrin always managed to dodge Durukti's gaze, one way or the other, and Durukti had been unable to find out where Symrin was going all the time.

Today though, Durukti made sure that she was quite far from Symrin, hiding behind a different fabric cloak and doing things on the side, while peering from the corners. She didn't even have guards to support her. She was ready to take a leap of faith with it and just like that, Symrin didn't change direction. When she did turn, it was her and no one else. She didn't shapeshift, perhaps because Durukti was being careful about it.

Symrin strolled across the marketplace and close to the ravines of the city, passing along the mud houses. She had now reached a building that was Ratri's library, now helmed by a few other Manavs. Vedanta took care of it mostly, which meant he wasn't around, but his men were.

Durukti saw Symrin entering the library and Durukti entered as well, checking herself in. The library was grand in every sense

and had become better than the last time. It had bronze staircases and golden tapestry, paintings by the local painters, and the musty fragrance of paper which was aromatically sensual for Durukti.

She watched Symrin move up and leave for the end aisle, upstairs. Durukti followed but rather than being in Symrin's aisle, she went opposite only to see her pull out a book after discussing with the librarian. Durukti could hear a little of what she was saying to her.

"Thank you for ordering this book for me."

"It came after much difficulty. It was out of print."

The book was hardbound but rather scorched at the corners. For one hour then, Durukti saw Symrin read it cover to cover and finally when she was done with it, she kept it back from where she had pulled it out.

As Symrin descended, her eyes fell over to Durukti, who instantly covered her face and began to search books in her aisle, avoiding eye contact. She wished Symrin hadn't seen her. When Durukti looked from the corner of her eye, she saw that Symrin had vanished.

Instantly, Durukti walked to the book Symrin had pulled out. She held it open, dropped it on the table, and started flipping the pages. It talked about ancient artifacts in detail—the Sword of Shiva, the Scythe of Yama . . . they were all weapons in some way or the other with scribbled illustrations in black and white, giving a very ancient feel to it. She finally flipped over to find a strange eye symbol on which four Shards of glass had been designed, all joining together to form the design of one eye that had long lashes.

At the top was written The Eye of Brahma.

Each Shard represented something or the other. The first Shard represented Past. The middle one said Present. The third one said Future. And the fourth one was the most interesting. It didn't say anything. It was left incomplete.

"The Eye of Brahma . . ." she spoke to herself, reading it, "lets

you watch the world in all the four ways, as Lord Brahma sees it." And she read ahead.

In the beginning of Illavarti when mankind was less in number, animals were more, darkness didn't exist, and hope filled the world—there was a tribe that included all the other tribes. That tribe was headed by Lord Brahma. They were pious, devoid of temptations and restlessness. They were eternally happy. They all were in love with each other. Lord Brahma, the leader of that group, chose to use his powers for good, protecting his people. But that led him to battle the Demon Kashyapa—the leader of the Daityas, creatures of the underworld. They began to terrorize Lord Brahma and his race. Finally, Kashyapa won and took over Illavarti causing Brahma to lose his governance over his people, who were then divided into five major tribes—Nagas, Rakshas, Gandharvas, Yakshas, Manavs. Brahma lost and chose to leave for heaven, but made sure that like him, future generations would not face this problem of impending doom. He asked Lord Shiva to cut off one of his heads. When Lord Shiva used his sword to do so, Lord Brahma's head turned into four Shards. The Eye was a gift for mankind. Named the Eye of Brahma, it has been lost ever since and those who find it, are said to be of divine importance themselves. The Shards represent the past, present, future, and—

The rest of the page was blank. She stopped reading. *This just doesn't make sense. It's absolutely stupid.* This was just a myth. Durukti began to think that there must be some scientific reasoning behind all of it. But then, she had seen what Symrin could do and how the scarred man had once used a shining image of himself to communicate with her—that was in the territory of magic.

Not all things in this world need reasoning behind it.

Durukti closed the book. Who could she trust to share this information with? She wanted to talk to Kalki. But he was not here. A gut-wrenching worry soaked her. She just wondered what he was doing. Hell, if he was even alive.

Arjan . . . Kalki's brother . . .

He was in prison. He seemed dependable. She could share it with him, but then, trapped in the four walls, he might not know much.

What if I help him escape and we can go together to Kalki?

But where will she find him? She didn't even know if Kalki was alive. No. It seemed far-fetched. She wanted to see that boy's face and feel the warmth in her heart again, like a flustered girl.

"You do realize you don't do quite well in concealing your identity, Lady Durukti," a voice softly chided from the back.

Durukti turned to face the ponytailed girl of thirteen staring back at her with her almond eyes and a cherub face, wearing a lovely gown and clinging to a simple doll.

It was Urvashi, Vedanta's daughter.

"What are you doing here?"

"This is a library. What do you think?" She winked playfully.

Durukti felt stupid. "What do you want, Urvashi?"

"I'm quite curious as to why the king's sister is looking into her handmaiden's practices. So much to gossip!" Urvashi clapped her hands, a glint of mischief in her eyes. "Quite fascinating, isn't it?"

She had said the word 'king' as if it was derogatory and it was valid to say it like that because Kali had practically stolen the throne from Vedanta. Though, regardless of that, Durukti had no contempt towards her.

"I must apologize for Kali's behaviour . . ."

"It's not your fault. Just like the sins committed by my father, which I do not have to worry about." She smiled. "We are our own individuals and we will be the sum of our failures and our choices will define us. No other person can state it for us, you know."

"Absolutely right," she exclaimed. She hadn't expected such wisdom from a thirteen-year-old.

"You should be careful with your handmaiden."

She arched her brows. "Why?"

"Well for one, she is a Vidhyadhara."

Of course! Vidhyadharas were magicians trained in the art of disguises and illusions. *That's why she had been able to disguise herself as a blind astrologer when Kali had been attacked.*

"How did you know?"

"Oh, because I read about them. And also, because I saw her change her shape while you were busy hiding yourself. She suspects foulplay, you know."

"Well, she better."

"Might I know why you are following her?"

Durukti noticed the curiosity in the girl and just shrugged. "It shouldn't matter to you."

"Oh well, you are right, Lady Durukti, but you must not underestimate a person like me. I can be quite the help around here."

"Why would you want to help me?"

"Because I'm bored. I need some amusement for myself."

Durukti sighed. "You are funny . . ."

"You want something out of her, right?"

Durukti narrowed her eyes. "And how did you know that?"

"It's evident. You can't ask her straight thus you are following her. You think there is something sinister going on. Otherwise you could have used your power as the crown's sister to end your handmaiden's life who is practically a nobody. That means, your handmaiden has a grip on you and you need a way to do it in such a way that your brother doesn't find out. It makes me wonder . . . why don't you tell your sweet brother?" The question was laced with pure sarcasm.

Durukti nodded. "Because it's a personal matter." *And I don't trust him.*

"It's all right." She paused. "But if you want my help, do let me know." And she began to turn around.

Durukti coughed, "In what way can you help?"

Urvashi swivelled her head to face Durukti and pulled up the corners of her lips. "I know exactly how to make your handmaiden speak more than she would want to."

"How?"

"Oh, you'll see."

Durukti had thought of Arjan as an ally in this mission. But she had just found an unexpected one. Someone quite young, and who would later turn out to be quite powerful.

13

Vedanta had thought that he knew what was best for the city he once used to rule. The iota of religion that Vedanta had managed to seep in was leaving. He had no idea about the other cities of Indragarh, but Indragarh itself had been damaged enough in all spectrums. And he had vowed to finish this tyranny of the so-called King Kali.

He had thought long and hard, wondering what could be the best way to do it. He thought of possible strategies, read books, and tried to find solutions from the emperors who had ruled before him. But the problem was, none of it showed how one could beat someone empowered by the Somas, which made him think—could he use it to fight Kali?

No, that's adulterating myself to substances.

He didn't want to be Kali, but to defeat him, he had to become someone like him, perhaps. Even if he thought of going down this path, where will he find more Somas? The stock had been destroyed. Perhaps Kali had hidden some of it. Did he have more?

Vedanta was getting restless and he had to take the crown back. He had a few soldiers who still respected him, cared for him, and looked up to him. He also had his daughter who he had to take care of.

To get the city back, the current king must die. A coup must arise.

And for that, he had to hire more soldiers, and bribe them. But money was an issue and he knew money could only be taken from only one man—Kuvera.

Vedanta travelled on his horse with two of his soldiers behind as the city watched him. He was moving towards Kuvera's fort and as he shared glances with the cityfolk, he couldn't help but remember the time few individuals had dared to stand against him. The rebellion had happened a long time ago, before Urvashi's birth, when he was with his wife. He was hot in blood, but yet afraid. Fear was always there within him, once he had inherited the throne from his father. He didn't want anyone to take it away—the helm, the crown. He was so insecure that he had all the people in the rebellion killed. King Vibhisana had assisted these traitors. His father, Vibhishana the first, had ruled one of the greatest cities in Dakshini—Lanka.

Vibhishana was also the cousin of Raktapa. When Vedanta had defeated Vibhisana and killed his family, Vibhisana had sworn revenge, but nothing had happened. Vibhisana had lacked the courage to keep his word. Thus, Vedanta could understand why Raktapa had been so eager to join Kali's campaign. He had wanted Vedanta to fall for hurting Vibhisana.

Did Vedanta regret all of it? Surely, he did. He was a changed man now. He had a daughter so he could understand what Vibhisana had been through. And if Vedanta could ever get a chance to plead for forgiveness from the Dakshini king, he would. But not now. Now, he had graver issues to deal with.

He reached Kuvera's fort which was just like what he had expected it to be—everything from the floor to the ceiling was adorned with pure gold. The place smelled of fruits, and the accompanying sounds were of dancers in skimpily-clad clothes who entertained Kuvera's ministers.

Vedanta dismounted from the horse and walked forward, his

one hand over the hilt of his sword. Passing the dancers and the ministers, he climbed the staircases to see the dwarf-like Yakshas glaring at him. Yakshas could be categorized in one simple line—they were small and ugly. He was unattractive but huge, and so were his sons—Nalakuvera and Manigriva. Unlike Kuvera, Vedanta had heard a lot of good things about them. They were charming, handsome, and fierce when needed.

Vedanta entered Kuvera's quarters and he found him sitting on a mini-throne eating grapes given by an Apsara. It was the classic act of living a life filled with gluttony and indulgence.

"Ah," Kuvera mused, shushing the Apsara who walked away in an instant. "Please come in." He directed his hand at a cushion to sit, to which Vedanta refused.

"We need to do something about Kali."

"You surely are an idiot, my lord."

"Excuse me?" Vedanta growled.

"You shouldn't have come to meet me in broad daylight. Lord Kali has grown smarter with his spy network now. He will know."

"Let him." Vedanta announced as loudly as he could, his voice booming across the room. "I had given my crown for my daughter but I won't let him take my beliefs away. He's destroying each temple, every shrine in the city, taking people's beliefs."

"Fortunately, not mine."

Vedanta gritted his teeth. "I don't care about yours. You are worshipped as a god amongst your men. You have a different, primitive religion than mine."

"Ah well, yes." Kuvera grinned and Vedanta noticed the purple lining across his throat as if his clothes were choking him. But Kuvera showed no haste and he looked comfortable. "Not primitive, advanced is the word. Have you come here to belittle me?"

"I would like your help."

"I would advise you to watch your manners then, my lord,"

he gestured with his hand, chuckling softly. "How do you plan to defeat Lord Kali, might I ask?"

"I shall take away his army. He might be strong by that bloody liquid, but he cannot defeat an army."

"Do you have your loyalists?"

"Yes, there are those who believe in me and there are those who don't, whom I shall pay."

"Bribes? Well, I never expected that from an honourable man like you."

"These are desperate times."

"And since the treasury is under Lord Kali, you need money from me."

Vedanta nodded glumly. "In our prior participation, I had helped you kill Vasuki, even helped—"

"You do not need to justify your alliance with me. To be honest, I need Lord Kali to go as much as you do. But he's grown smarter and madder. If he sees us betraying him, he shall not even hesitate to kill us," he thoughtfully mused. "But also, he's handling his government well. The grain prices have been reduced, the tax rate has been lowered, he's giving away money in charity and building houses in the poverty-stricken places. Yes, the endowments he would be getting from the idols will go away since he's destroying them—"

Vedanta snapped. "I don't care what he's doing. I ruled better than him, any day. I believed in traditions which our forefathers left us with."

"And who says these traditions were right?"

Vedanta went silent.

Kuvera smiled. "I had two sons—Nalakuvera and Manigriva."

"I know."

"No, you don't. I just received the news that Manigriva has been killed."

Vedanta arched his brows. "I'm sorry for—"

"Tsk, it's okay. He was never my favourite. And imagine who killed him? Nalakuvera. His brother. Heh." He clapped his hand in laughter. "It was a petty feud over an Apsara. You see, Manigriva was the honourable one, doing things out of duty and love. He was emotional. He cared while Nalakuvera was mad, frantic, and unpredictable. Manigriva's so-called honour killed him. You see where I'm getting at? We don't live in times where good, honourable men triumph. And if they do in the rarest of instances, they lose something in the process."

Vedanta could understand that he was being equated with Manigriva and Kali with Nalakuvera. But Vedanta was older, wiser. He had seen wars and crushed all rebellions. Manigriva had not had his experience. "I'm not as honourable as you think I am."

"All right. Good. Then you must do something for me and in return, I shall fund your coup."

"What do you want?"

"Kill Pradm. He's a thorn in my plans."

Pradm? He was the Rakshas general of Kali's army. *He would have to die eventually but why did Kuvera want him to die?* Something didn't add up, but questions beget insecurity and Vedanta couldn't show Kuvera that.

"It's good for you, my lord. He's the one who's destroying the shrines under Lord Kali's order. Relieve the executor from his work. And you have my support. Easy."

Vedanta nodded.

"You seem confused."

"I thought you'll ask something else."

"Of course not. People still trust you. Your soldiers still love you because they believe you are a great man and no matter what, you shall never go against your morales. You show me you can take down Pradm, I will believe that you have the capability of killing Lord Kali, that you still have guts."

Capability? Of course, I have the bloody capability. With a stomp, he walked away from Kuvera's chambers, wondering how he was going to kill a brawny, fierce Rakshas.

14

Padma had never thought that in her journey of living the life of a ferocious assassin in the city of Indragarh, she would become a rebel and end up babysitting a so-called saviour. Kalki was anything but a hero. He was an idiot, first of all, rude, disrespectful and worse—he was just plain irritating, always whining, always coming up with stupid plans that made no sense.

There was a reason why the Pisach had appeared out of nowhere. It was because Kalki had made so much noise with his mouth that it had alerted the Pisach. They wouldn't have come up if he hadn't caused a ruckus. While they were being dragged with the horses, she had been cutting down her restraints with her pocket knife. She had been *this* close to escaping but the saviour chose to use his pea-brain at the worst possible moment.

And now here they were, inked Tribals surrounding them, jumping from one tree to another, and the ones who were on the ground had their darts aimed at them. With the slightest of movement, they would surely shoot them down.

Padma knew that the Pisach wouldn't kill them. They would toy around with them and then eat them, but not kill them instantly. Pisach were the bottom feeders of the society, the illiterates, the dark and dusty. They were looters and rapists, but they also followed a system. They must have hired the Simhas to get them more humans

because Pisach believed they facilitated the soon-to-be dead to the afterlife. With the help of their brethren, they could deliver people from their wretched lives. In short, they were a cannibalistic cult.

And Padma, Kripa, and Kalki were just about to meet their head chief.

They travelled inside the trenches of the jungle to see the ground was turning murky. Leaves were going scarce but the dense canopies hid the little sunlight the place had. And soon, her eyes fell on the dark path that lay ahead of her. Grotesquely beautiful she could call it, as she saw the entire ground was swamp—deep, dark, and dingy. It smelled and mosquitoes swarmed all over it. Frogs crept around it. The only sound she could hear were the crazy syllables made by the Pisach. She knew what they talked like—their language was same as their own except they were speaking in reverse. It was confusing. *I wonder how they all learned this language.*

Over the swamp were huts and nets that covered the distances between each tree. The huts were long and elongated, some camouflaged under the canopy. They were made of wood and reed. The branches were tough as well. The nets were carved in such a way that they acted like paths. There were ladders that helped one to go out, but neither the hostages nor the Pisach needed a ladder. They were able to jump from one place to another, barefoot.

Though the scary part was the vines. When one hut was far off and the net wasn't there, Padma saw them using long vines to travel—like monkeys.

"Where the hell are we?" Padma quietly said, only to get a response from Kripa.

"It's called Daldal Lands. Where no man walks and if they do walk, they never return."

Padma narrowed her gaze to look at Kripa questionably when Kalki asked him, "You make things as you go, right?"

"Sometimes, mate." Kripa grinned.

Padma was then told to travel by the ladder. She climbed up

and reached the nets and carefully walked over them until she finally reached a hut that had a solid green surface made of branches, woods, and leaves. Kalki was behind her and they all were standing in a line when the Pisach knocked on the door of the hut.

It opened.

Standing close to it was a fairly-sized Pisach who nodded at Padma and then gestured them to enter. Padma did, followed by the other captives. She didn't even know who the bald-headed girl was, who had been travelling with them, though she looked a lot like an Apsara—exceptionally beautiful. But she had no hair which made Padma wonder if she was an Apsara in the first place.

The room of the hut was incensed with candles, the sound of light drums played by the Pisachis—the female counterpart to Pisach—could be heard. In the middle, cross-legged, a dark-skinned Pisach sat, his arms outstretched, his eyes closed, and he had a piercing right across his nostrils. He had his hair tied up in the top, oiled well. And the worst part was, he had a necklace made of human skulls, disturbingly enough one of the skull was of a child.

"Their god," whispered Kripa. "Or their current god; it keeps changing."

"What do they believe in?" Kalki asked rather loudly. Padma just felt like smacking him on the head.

"They believe that the strongest is the fittest and should survive. If two Pisach fight and one loses, the defeated must be killed as it is considered a 'dishonour' to lose a duel."

"They duel? Where the hell do they duel?" Padma scoffed.

"SILENCE!" the leader of the Pisach roared loudly.

Padma was swept with a chill she had only experienced when she had been about to kill Urvashi, but had refrained. It was a chill that comes after a realization and right now, it surely was a realization of dread.

Worse, the leader of the Pisach spoke in their language.

He opened his eyes and Padma realized they were bloodshot.

A smile crept over his face as he began, "How indecent. You speak in my territory . . . without my permission. Who is the leader of this group?"

The bald-headed girl came forward. "It's not a group. We are different sets."

"Ah, interesting." His voice had a wheezing sound to it as if his throat had an infection. "Not many women here dare to speak and here you are blabbering away."

The bald-headed girl gritted her teeth and Padma could feel the tension right now. In fact, she had hated the statement as well. Illavarti was still primitive and unlike Nagas, who were not patriarchial, every other tribe was rooted in orthodox ways in some way or the other.

"What is your name, dear?"

"Ratna . . . Maru."

The leader hissed. "And who are your friends?"

Ratna looked at the matted girl. "That's Smrit." And then she looked at the inked girl. "And this is Aina."

"And you?" His red eyes turned over to Padma.

"Padma, and that's Kripa and Kalki."

The leader nodded. "You all seem exhausted and worried. I welcome you to my abode. Please get some rest." He paused. "Also, I apologize. I seem to have forgotten to introduce myself. I am Brahmaputraksh."

At that time, Kripa nudged Padma. Padma shot him a glance, mouthing *what*. But Kripa remained fixated on the leader as if he had instantly recalled who this Brahmaputraksh was. He was being quite courteous. But then, something felt off about this whole thing. They were cannibals and yet they were behaving normally.

Padma ignored Kripa and they began to move when Brahmaputraksh called out, "Just wait."

They all froze.

"We have a little game that we play when we receive our guests.

It's a game of survival. Since you are of two teams, three each, we would love it if you could get ready for some duelling."

"What?" Padma said.

"It's a tradition we follow. Whoever wins will get to live another day." His smile widened and Padma noticed a worm slowly wheezing out of his gums which he instantly ate. He didn't look so courteous, after all. Rather, he seemed disturbing to even glance at. "Our first duel will be with you," he pointed at Aina, "and you."

He pointed at Padma.

15

Urvashi thought about a lot of things—but she wasn't allowed to execute any of them.

Always under the protective arms of her father, Lady Urvashi had been homeschooled, home-trained in the arts of warfare—swordsmanship or horse riding—with prominent military tacticians. She didn't have a lot of friends and the one she had forged a bond with had been her guru who had turned out to be a Vidhyadhara. The guru hadn't told anyone except Lady Urvashi, for Vedanta was xenophobic and didn't want anyone but a Manav to train his daughter.

Lady Urvashi, on the other hand, didn't care. She didn't mind if her guru was a part of an extinct tribe.

She loved learning, books, and most of all, she loved magic. She loved it to the point of being obsessed with it. She could never be a Vidhyadhara but that didn't mean she couldn't perform External Magic.

Vidhyadharas were magicians. They looked like Manavs and were ordinary men and women, though they could conjure magic tricks of their own. It could be as simple as creating things out of nothing, travelling to faraway places, and using control over elements of nature. They could do it in two ways—External Magic and Internal Magic. Internal Magic was the elemental form of

magic—using fire, water, earth, and wind. Her guru had taught her that each Vidhyadhara has a fragment of Indra, Vayu, Varun, and Agni, with which they could use their powers but not to a godly extent; they could slightly tap into it. External Magic relied on using an object that held magical properties, like an amulet or a bracelet.

Urvashi, being a Manav, could have control over External Magic and her guru had taught her something diabolical after she had urged him to. He had taught her how to hurt people without physically touching them. Urvashi had thought that that was impossible, but she got her proof soon.

And when she saw Lady Durukti, the docile sister of Lord Kali, frantic and in need of help, Urvashi knew she could give a pretty good hand with her problem. Also, her guru had left to improve upon his craft and she was all alone. She couldn't practice the magic. Thus, she could apply it in the best manner possible through Lady Durukti.

"I only have one request," she said to Durukti as they entered her chamber. "Do not mention any of this to my father."

"Don't worry, I won't." Durukti nodded with disbelief.

Sometimes, Urvashi envied Lady Durukti for being a beauty. It was just so effortless for her while Urvashi had to spend time to add shine to her hair and powder her face. Of course, Urvashi was young and still in the growing stage, but she knew she wanted to grow up and look like Lady Durukti—with her ravine, black hair, full eyes, small mouth, and an angular jawline. She was everything that Urvashi wanted to be. And thank the gods, she had found Lady Durukti in the place which she frequented.

"Also, this doesn't change the fact that your brother and my father hate each other. We are not friends. I'm bored and you need help." Urvashi stated her intentions, though her voice was soft and childlike, and didn't match the intended command.

"I know, I understand." Durukti nodded again. It was like she

didn't care much about her warnings. Like she was still treating her like a child.

Well, I'll prove her wrong.

"All right, I would like you to do something for me." Urvashi began to fumble in the bag, as she pulled up a wooden figurine.

"What is that?"

"This is a wooden figure that I carved. My father thinks it's a hobby, and it is, but it is also a way to connect to a person. You can hurt them with this."

"For a young girl, you are quite a menace."

Urvashi blushed. "Oh thank you very much, madam." She paused. "Now I want you to go to Symrin and distract her, while I pluck a hair from her head."

"Hair? Are you sure?" Durukti's face contorted.

"Oh yes, because then we need to tie her hair around this figurine."

"Then what happens?"

"You'll see."

Durukti glumly nodded. "I hope this works, girl."

"Or what?"

"Or . . ." Durukti was speechless. "It'll be a waste of my time. That's it." And with that, she stormed out of the room.

Urvashi followed Lady Durukti while she studied the little architectural foliage of the entire fort. Lord Kali hadn't done much to the fort in terms of upgrading it, but he had managed to amp up his guards in number. He seemed paranoid since each new corridor had been stationed with two to three guards.

As they reached the final door, Durukti stopped and took a deep breath.

"You know, I heard you had raided Shambala. Why are you so scared of a mere handmaiden?"

"She's a Vidhyadhara," Durukti whispered. "And I'm a woman of science. I don't know how to deal with someone who dabbles with magic."

Urvashi patted her on the shoulder. "Magic and science, as history has told, go along with each other."

Durukti softly smiled before she knocked on the door. "I'll distract her while you . . . what will you do again?"

"Don't worry about my plan."

Before Durukti could protest, the door opened, revealing Symrin. She was not as beautiful as Lady Durukti, and she had a large forehead which was offly irritating about her. Also, she had six fingers in one of her hands. The extra one was protruding, like some creature. Urvashi had heard about these defects and if this defect would have been found in the Rakshas tribe, she would have found her home in the gutters.

Not that Urvashi promoted this kind of behaviour.

"My lady." Symrin bowed.

"What were you doing?" Durukti asked, retaining a blank expression on her face.

Oh, she's playing well.

"My lady, I was sewing some of my torn clothes."

"All right," Durukti snapped loudly, which made no sense to Urvashi. There was an awkward silence. Urvashi realized that it was time for her to pitch in the conversation.

"You know, we were planning to go to the market and buy some fresh apples and the . . ." Urvashi abruptly trailed off. She looked at Symrin's hair and exclaimed, "Oh dear!"

"What?" Symrin was confused, touching her hair in the process.

"What is that?" Urvashi pointed at her hair.

"Nothing, what?" Symrin ruffled her hair even more now.

"Dear, dear, that must be so disheartening. Hold on, let me check." Urvashi came forward and grabbed a strand of hair, plucking it right off her head.

Symrin moaned in the process. "What was that about?" She eyed Urvashi with suspicion. "My lady, what is it that you meant?"

"I saw a white hair, it's all right now."

"How is that possible?"

"Bye!" Urvashi waved at her. Without glancing back, she grabbed Durukti's arm and took her away from Symrin.

"What about the trip to the bazaar?"

But Urvashi didn't bother to respond to that.

They were back in Durukti's quarters and Urvashi slyly sat over the bed. With her lip protruding in full focus, she began to wrap the thin hair around the wooden figurine.

"You were good," Durukti remarked, clearly impressed with her spontaneity.

"I know." Urvashi smiled.

"What do you plan to do with the doll?"

"It's not a doll. It's Symrin." She had tied the hair properly now and showed it to Durukti.

"Symrin?"

"Oh yes, this doll is Symrin now. The wood is not ordinary wood. It contains magical properties. My guru gave it to me, to use it to make dolls out of them and then use it as I saw fit. You see, if I do anything to the doll, the actual person will be impacted."

Durukti held the doll with an inquisitive face. "Interesting. Are you sure it works?"

"I tried it on one of my servants. They weren't happy about it."

"So, I prick, poke and stab . . . what if I break the doll?"

"The person will be broken as well."

"This is black magic, right?"

"Yep."

"What kind of guru did you have?"

Urvashi flustered. "Um, I shouldn't have told you this but since you are a Tribal yourself, I didn't think before revealing my secret. Let's come back to the matter at hand."

"How will this doll help me get the truth out?"

"You can just torture someone into doing your bidding." Urvashi clapped excitedly. "Can I see when you do it?"

"Torture? How are you even Vedanta's daughter?"

Urvashi sighed. It had often been said to her that she was mean, that she had a dark streak. She would never admit it to anybody, but she had never been afraid of bloodshed. But then again, she wasn't a bad person and she would never hurt anyone intentionally. Lady Durukti had made the choice to hurt Symrin as much as she wanted, making her the torturer. Thus, this absolved Urvashi from her supposed crime.

Urvashi's penchant for cruel and dark things didn't stem out of her mother's sudden death, but it had had its part to play. After her mother's passing, she had secluded herself from everyone, engaging in cruel acts against the local horses, and even the soldiers. She would stab the animals in anger and then run away. Since she was the king's daughter, she had never been punished. She had calmed down a lot since then. There were a lot of feelings, emotions that she felt she should have, but she didn't care. The only emotions she now had were towards her father. Rest of the people were dolls and toys to play with.

"I still don't believe you, you know." Durukti's tongue lolled inside the cheek of her mouth, something Urvashi noticed that she did a lot.

"I am telling you the truth. This only works when you are in close proximity."

"How close are we talking about?"

Urvashi cheekily grinned. "Let's test it out!"

Urvashi had knocked on the door of Symrin and instantly rushed away from the scene to the farthest corner where Durukti

was. They stood together, hidden at the end of the corridor, shrouded in the darkness. The door opened and Symrin came out, looking left and right, hoping to see the person who had knocked.

"Now watch." Urvashi licked her lips as she took the doll and with her metal hairpin, she pricked its abdomen. And she did it so much that it pierced hard into the wood.

"Ouch," the sound didn't come from Symrin.

It was from Durukti.

"Wait, what?" A confused Urvashi turned to see Durukti reel back over the floor, her tunic turning red from a wound at the very point that Urvashi had punctured the doll.

Instantly realizing what had happened, Urvashi pulled out the pin and tossed it on the other side, sitting down on the floor and grabbing Durukti's head. She was worried, befuddled. "I'll call the aid, don't worry. I don't know how this is . . ." and she was left out of words when she saw Durukti's pale face. Blood was draining away from it. She had been careful. Magic was never supposed to work on the wrong target. But it had happened. She began to make a move when she realized that the hair thing wasn't working. Perhaps because the magic had been reversed. But it could have been reversed only if Symrin had known that the hair had been taken from her. The only way this could have happened was if Symrin too had Durukti's hair at her disposal.

Binding magic was quite a complicated affair, but in short, Symrin had played them. Symrin had realized that her hair had been plucked for the ritual and she had reversed the effect towards Durukti. But when did Symrin get Durukti's hair? Though it was no surprise. They were practically together all the time. She could have taken them at any time.

And in the middle of her thought process, Urvashi realized a shadow had turned up, dimming the light. Urvashi turned to see Symrin at the back, cross-armed. She had a disarming grin on her face. Now, she looked like a witch.

"Well, well . . . since you two have found out everything, it's time I end you both." And with sparks around her fingertips, Urvashi realized that Symrin was using Internal Magic.

Escape was out of the question. They were about to die.

16

Finally, he would get the chance to kill a Rakshas.

Vedanta was prepared. He had worn his tuni and his bronze armour with the symbol of lightning emblazoned on it. He prayed to the power of Vajra, Lord Indra's bolt, asking for his blessings. He was ready. The axe was holstered, the sword was sheathed, the boots were tightened, but he was worried.

He didn't know why. Sitting on the bed, he swallowed a lump in his throat.

By Lord Indra, I should not be afraid.

And yet he was. It hurt him to realize he had to do such things in the name of honour and justice, to take back what was rightfully his. He should have done this earlier, but now, these were desperate times.

They hurt my beliefs. And I shall hurt them now.

He looked at his plants and noticed something. In all past few chaotic days while he had been planning and plotting on how to hurt Pradm, he had forgotten to water them or tell his servants to do so. And the plants seemed off—dead leaves lay there, some withered from the roots. He touched them gently, almost wondering if the plants were trying to communicate something . . . that he was withering like them.

No.

Vedanta straightened. He decided he would come back later and bring a set of new potted plants to put in the porch of his room. He called out to his maidservant who instantly rushed in. She was wearing a long, dry gown, almost raggedy, and a clothed headwear that was wrapped around her bald head.

"Where's Urvashi?" Vedanta asked.

The maidservant shook her head. "She went to the library and has not returned yet."

"Are the soldiers with her?"

"Yes, my lord."

"If she returns before me, tell her . . . take her to a safe location, the lair, underground with food and clothes and stay there until my messenger comes to get you. Either he comes or I do. Don't move before either of us arrive at the location."

The maidservant nodded.

"What are you planning to do, my lord, if you don't mind me asking?"

He didn't mind her asking, but he closed his eyes and pictured his wife. If only she wouldn't have passed away due to illness, things would be far simpler. There would be someone to take care of Urvashi if something happened to him. But no. Things will never be simpler. And he had to act now.

He didn't say anything. But he knew what he was doing. He was waging a war against a king, the very thing some people had done to him a long time ago.

They had failed. But if he failed, then everything else will.

Vedanta had roped in a few of Yaksha archers from Lord Kuvera. Kuvera had gladly given them to him. He was on his horse with almost more than a dozen of his personal soldiers—trusted

ones. He could have done it discreetly, but no, he wanted to do it in public and show his might, in honour of his people.

He passed the bazaar and made way to the shrine where Pradm was supposedly stationed according to the scouting reports he had received. When he reached, he did find the shrine of Lord Indra's abode—his carrier, Airavarta, who used to help him travel from one place to another. Unlike others, Lord Indra didn't travel on foot or on horse, but on his elephant who had the ability to fly. Vedanta believed in the scriptures and how they were told, though many said Airavarta was an advanced form of a vimana, which were flying machines fuelled by Soma. But that was just nonsense.

He saw Pradm who was speaking to some of his men. He was wearing a saffron coloured cloth wrapped around the body. His armour was glinting in the light and a flimsy sword hung on his belt. Other Rakshas were hammering away, breaking apart the shrine. People had already begun to gather to see the spectacle and Vedanta was feeling more confident than he should have. He was going to enjoy this. He had more men than Pradm, and Pradm in comparison to Vedanta looked weak.

"Infidel!" Vedanta called out the Rakshas General.

Pradm turned, confused, watching the army in surprise. Even his men stopped hammering and looked at Vedanta. Somewhere deep down, Vedanta felt triumph and he cast his fears aside.

"What is the meaning of this, Lord Vedanta?"

Even for a Rakshas, Pradm was quite decent. Rakshas were uncouth, foul-mouthed, rowdy creatures, like Martanja. He was a menace wherever he went.

"This is a rebellion against the actions performed by you and Kali," Vedanta announced, dismounting from his horse.

Vedanta peered across the skies. The rooftops of the tall buildings were lined up with Yakshas archers, ready to hit if Pradm tried to do something funny.

"You are out of your mind. Go back to your home."

Vedanta shook his head.

Pradm laughed to himself as if he was witnessing some joke and then he pulled out his sword. Vedanta did as well, gesturing the archers to not hit him.

It was a duel between him and Pradm.

Not even Vedanta's soldiers intervened. They were just roaring and clapping for their true, honourable king.

Pradm came forward with his sword, dashing it, while Vedanta dodged it, deflecting metal with metal and hitting it right across the knee. He grabbed Pradm from the waist and then pushed him forward, using his sword to parry, only to be deflected by Pradm.

"You cannot defeat me. I'm from the great Rakshas tribe."

"Watch me."

The public was stunned and all the noise in the background had gone silent for Vedanta. That's what he had learnt in the swordplaying practices when he was young—*just focus on your opponent and you will only hear your opponent's movements.*

And that's what happened. Each step Pradm took, Vedanta noticed it, calculated his countermove, and then dodged the incoming attack. And finally with one quick step, he sliced through Pradm's torso, and with another swift action, stabbed him in the eye. Blood spilled all over as Pradm fell on the ground.

Standing on top of him, Vedanta pulled out the sword and lifted it high up. Some men from the crowd beamed. His men roared with laughter and were clapping.

The other Rakshas didn't interfere in the rejoicing moment of Vedanta as he came to them, walking slowly. "I shall not kill you for a king doesn't harm the innocent. Go to Kali and tell him that Vedanta is coming for his head."

The Rakshas were confused, especially when Vedanta noticed blood trickling out of his body. He turned to see an arrow had pierced him in the back, which he hadn't realized in a purge of happiness. He pulled that arrow out and looked up.

The Yakshas had shot him down.

And then the storm of arrows descended on him.

Some tore through Vedanta's men and their horses as they collapsed. Some tried to defend themselves from the onslaught, but with the consecutive attacks, defense was out of the question. In a fit of rage, Vedanta cried out in fury as a volley of arrows was shot at him—four arrows simultaneously pierced him.

He fell on the ground, dust swirling around him, his sword slipping from his grasp. As he looked up, he saw his men, bloody and sprawled dead on the floor. The survivors were crying in pain. There was a stampede in the public, and people were still trying to understand what was happening.

And in the darkness that ensued, from the corner of his eye, he saw a large, golden chariot upon which sat Kali, a few paces away from all the destruction. With his soldiers flanked on each side, he was doing nothing but watching the mass slaughter. Enjoying the bloody spectacle.

And on Kali's side, standing firmly, and beaming with confidence, was Kuvera.

17

It was a long walk.

After coming to the shore, opposite to the river, the Suparns made them walk all the way. Manasa didn't give much thought to it as they were escorted to the military camp, with swords being pointed at them, in case they decided to attack. But Manasa didn't have the slightest intention to attack them. What she wanted to know was why would the Suparns vow to destroy Vasuki's bloodline? This was clearly not a one-sided battle. Multiple forces were at work. If her brother's family hadn't been killed as collateral damage by the Suparns, she would have tried to form an alliance with them.

Not that she had a choice anymore.

She couldn't help but remember how it all had started. The two tribes, the Nagas and the Suparns, used to be partners—they had found a river where marshes of Somalata plants used to grow. These plants produced a liquid that could be harnessed and used for various purposes. Since it had originated from the caves that joined the river, it had gone to Suparns because it had been in their region, but they were happy to share the minerals and ores of Somalata with the Nagas to have a fruitful relationship with them.

Suparns began to use their Soma for purposes of burning them and then using them for flight—artificial wings made out of metal and feathers and doused in Soma. That helped them to undertake

long flights in the air and gave them an advantage in their military capabilities against other Dakshinis, especially the Rakshas and Vanars. The Nagas wanted Somas for their health and well-being, though they used it sparingly, for it came expensive to them from the Suparns. They called these Somas 'Amrit' or 'Naagmani' since they believed Lord Sheesha had gifted them from his throat to the Nagas.

Manasa thought about the conversation she had had with Padma back in Indragarh. How she had lied to her, saying that the Nagas had no Soma left. Truth was that they had had some of it stored in Lord Sheesha's temple. Though now they had nothing. The temple had been raided during the Suparn attack.

Problems started occurring when Amrit started running out of stock and the Suparns stopped the trade. They decided it would be beneficial to have the rest for themselves. They chose to sever relations with the Nagas over this and that angered the Nagas since they believed Suparns were hindering the nectar of Lord Sheesha. Thus began the war between the two. It started off with small battles and then grew into a full-scale war.

Vasuki had stopped caring about the Soma. He had chosen to be a part of Kali's campaign. Udaiyas seemed more of an interesting world to him. Manasa's stance was also similar. It didn't matter much to her either, but there was something odd about all of this. The reason the war began between the Nagas and the Suparns was because of Manasa and Vasuki's father, who had been ill and had wanted the Soma to recover. Things went sideways from then on. After having the Soma once, he grew deranged and had to be taken down by his own men. That had proved to the people that the Amrit could make you mad. Manasa didn't dispute this fact since she had noticed that whoever used Soma, went on a spiralling effect of fever, dementia, and acted like a whack.

Amrit was never supposed to be for humans and even if it was, Nagas were better off without it.

They had reached the camp. It was in the middle of a thick

jungle—there was swirling smoke and fire, smell of roasted snakes and worms wafted around, soldiers in their tunics and their dhotis walked around without the slightest of caution, tents of red and golden colours had been set up and flags had been set up on the boundaries. Eagles had been etched on the flags. Some people roared and sang together while others sat in silence, sharpening their swords. Some were even training.

The Suparns were taking Manasa and Nanda to the centre of the entire camp and as they moved, her blue eyes and her black hair were noticed by the golden-haired Suparns who began to whistle and make kissing noises. Nanda was getting uncomfortable.

"You are not welcome, sister."

"Sister? She's too much of a wench to be someone's sister."

"Look at those. I shall just bite them off."

All these words were spit by the Suparns who sat on logs comfortably. They all had battle scars and looked weary for the day.

"Shut up!" a pale-faced Nanda protested.

Manasa patted him on the shoulder. "It's okay."

Nanda nodded as he held on to the medical leaves that were wrapped around his chest, covered in paste and ointment. They entered a huge tent that was hammered to the ground by thick iron nails. The flaps were multicoloured—bronze and red—and inside there were platters of grapes, apples, papayas, and wines of different colours, of a delicious amber and brown. A carpet had been spread on the ground over which Manasa saw a strange, slim man with wild, bushy hair that flew in the wind. He had strange glitter-like golden paint over the top of his eyes and a scrawny beard on his slender face.

"Nanda! Ah, what a pleasant surprise." Maruda grinned and stood up, offering his hand to the injured man.

And before Nanda could say anything, he just collapsed on the ground. Manasa came forward to help him.

"Oh! By the wings of Garuda, you are sick. Take him to the

infirmary and make sure he's fine. Give him whatever he wants and bring him back to me. I need him alive since he owes me big time."

His men nodded, grabbing Nanda and taking him out of the tent.

Owed Maruda? I thought it was the other way around.

"And who you might be, lady?" Maruda looked at her with a bored and exhausted expression. He went over to the wine table and poured himself one glass. "How can I be of service to you?" And then his eyes noticed Manasa's gloved and limped hand. "Hold on . . . ah, if it isn't Vasuki's sister? The infamous broken hand. Tell me something, Nanda was your husband, right? How did you, you know, do it with one hand not working?" He stifled a laugh which only made Manasa furious.

But she made sure to control her temper because she was in his domain and she had no army to back her right now.

"We came here because we needed your help." She paused. "I know you killed my brother's family. You slaughtered his sons. But our matter is greater than personal conflict."

Maruda shrugged as he walked to the carpet and plopped himself down on the comfortable cushions. "Honestly, he brought it on himself. I didn't want his sons to come and take revenge in the distant future. I was just being careful, though I forgot there is always his sister who could do the same. Well, I'm glad you are here. You have made my job easier." He laughed.

Manasa wanted to pulverize him.

"I'm serious, Maruda. I am not here to seek revenge. I'm here to question you."

"Question me what?"

"Why is a Suparn camp close to Naagpuri?"

Maruda stopped smiling. "We were welcomed."

"What is going on? Do you work for Jamun?"

"And how does it matter to you?"

"I want to know what's going on."

Maruda thought for a moment. "You know, you came with my friend, Nanda, so I shall reveal a little bit, but only a bit since I know so much only. I'm just a simple executor. Lord Tarakshya is the one who commands us. Your minister and him, they had some deal going on for the so-called betterment of the people."

Lord Tarakshya was the king of the Suparns. Manasa had heard a lot of things about him—he could eat a hundred snakes at a time, though that was stupid and unbelievable. And he was regal and handsome. His father had been the one waging wars against Manasa's father and the war between the two of them had eventually caused conflict between Tarakshya and Vasuki, until Vasuki stopped fighting and left his kingdom to join Lord Kali's conquest.

"What kind of deal?"

"Let bygones be bygones."

"And what does that mean?"

"Lord Tarakshya wanted revenge for his father's death at the hands of the Nagas. Your minister felt it was only fair that his progeny be allowed to exact that revenge, but before anything could happen, Vasuki dropped dead. So his family was left and that led to their . . . you know what happened then."

Jamun was the one who had let the Suparns infiltrate their land and kill Vasuki's family under Kadru's nose, which only made Manasa more worried for her niece.

"It was a gift by your minister, an offering of truce. They sent boats and let the army watch while Vasuki's family was slaughtered and his house was burnt down. It was a sad affair. I *had* to do it." He didn't look remorseful at all.

Manasa tightened her fist. She was feeling so many things right now, but she chose to hide her emotions. If she attacked him now, she would be killed by his men.

"But, we were just planning to leave and, and you two had to show up. Rogues! Bah!" He clapped his hand excitedly. "Always

a bit of enjoyment when conflict arises. Weren't you part of your dead brother's conquest in the bloody part of this country?"

"Yes," she nodded, almost fighting back her tears. Her eyes had welled up. "What does Tarakshya want now and how do the Nagas fit in this picture?"

"All we want is to live in harmony as the reason for bad blood is now mostly over."

"Don't the Nagas want reserves of your exotic plants?"

"Oh no, consider it selflessness on our part to initiate harmony after decades of war. Or hasn't it been made clear to you yet?"

Something felt off. She could feel it in her bones.

"Now bugger away, lady, to your trader friend, and ensure he is in good health. We don't have all day, we need to make arrangements for the party and all, you know."

Her ears perked up. "Party?"

"Yeah, a feast by Lord Tarakshya inviting the elite of the Nagas to his chambers as a sign of a new beginning. The minister was damn pushy about it, I tell you. Perhaps he has realized the worth of the Suparns, the Golden Eagles, the Descendents of Lord Garuda."

No, not really, you idiot. The party is of course just bogus. There is something more to it.

"Well, thank you so much for telling me."

Maruda shrugged. "Yeah, yeah, of course. Just leave now."

"I hope I can count on your protection within these grounds."

"I'm a Suparn, not a snake . . . I mean, maybe it's time to start respecting snakes since we have a feast with them. I'm not a Manav nor am I a Yaksha. I don't go behind someone's back and stab him. I would love to, of course, but no. Though we would be having a different conversation right now if Lord Tarakshya had ordered me to kill you. Tend to your husband now. Off you go!" He laid his head back in frustration.

Manasa did leave. But not without a plan in her head.

When Nanda woke up, Manasa was the first one to make him drink the hot soup. She then tended to him by using wet rags to regulate his temperature. His gash was still not cured, but it looked better. Veins were not protruding at the very least and the wound had been sutured.

"I'm sorry. Did I pass out?"

Manasa waded her fingers through his hair, nodding to herself. Nanda was definitely a very handsome man, someone fit enough to be with Manasa—big eyes, smart mouth, long ears, and hair that was softer than the fabric she was wearing. She never really had any experience with men because they were all imbeciles. But Nanda . . . he was different. The man was an imbecile but he was not someone with a shrewd heart.

"No problem, so here's the story."

Manasa told him everything till the party scenario, whispering as the infirmary had female Suparn nurses who were watching them, on the lookout for anything suspicious. They were in a secluded tent but it had too many open flaps for anyone to enter and the soldiers outside were already gawking at them.

"A feast?"

"Yes."

"That doesn't make sense."

"Vasuki's family was bait. Jamun made them believe that they were ready for a truce. Jamun showed Tarakshya a way. He would give anything and Tarakshya must have asked for Vasuki's family as payment, which Jamun didn't hesitate to let go. There's something wrong about this scenario. Jamun wants something from Tarakshya, and that's why he has consented to a feast at their city."

"So he could infiltrate the base and get what he needs."

"Perhaps he needs the Somalata," Manasa sighed. "Or to

know more about their designs, how many soldiers they have, bannermen, their architecture and what-not. Study it, scout it, and then when you know everything about the opponent, attack and conquer their kingdom—the eternal dream of a Naga. After all, the last time the Nagas had been in Suparnika had been hundreds of years ago. I hear that they have guarded themselves quite well. Suparns are the most secretive tribe. They only indulge in foreign affairs if they are messed with. They cover themselves with dome-like walls that prevents any army from barging in. One can only enter if invited. This was not the case a century ago. Tarakshya, who had modelled it, had realized that he didn't need to trade with other cities. Everything was available within short distances from their city. Thus, the news about Somalata, the Amrit, it didn't spread like wildfire because the Suparns had kept it to themselves and the Nagas didn't want anyone else to know. Otherwise other tribes would have come and fought for it. It is all safely stocked in their city. Yet some of it is in Indragarh, which piques my interest. That means, there might be other caves, plants hidden elsewhere which the Nagas don't know about."

Nanda nodded. "But what if . . . what if it's just a feast?"

"Oh god, don't act like the eagle men here. They are famous for being idiots. We are not. This is politics. Jamun would not do anything just to have a good time. He will be here for a reason. And I dread when I think about it."

Nanda looked at her intently. "All right, I agree with you. So, what's the plan? We know the game, so what do we do now?"

"Believe it or not, we need the Suparns right now to just gauge Jamun's actions."

"But they won't trust us," Nanda remarked.

Manasa smiled. "I know. And I have a plan for that. We kidnap Jamun with the help of Kadru, make him speak in front of Maruda, and get him and his people executed. Once he's dealt with, we will have the city back and also we will have Tarakshya's trust to which

in return we will ask for a one-time supply of Amrit. We will use it for our army, make them stronger." She could picture riding with the Suparns and Nagas to Indragarh and just grabbing Kali's throat, massacring his men and inhumanely torturing him.

"That sounds quite easy when you say it but Jamun is the most powerful person in Naagpuri right now." He paused. "And you really want Suparns in your army?"

"They might be stupid, but they are good at what they do—fighting and flying."

"Rightly said." He clenched his jaw. "All right, let's execute this crazy idea of yours, my lady."

Manasa couldn't help grinning and just came forward, kissing Nanda on the cheek. Embarassed by what she had done, she sat back. "Uh, sorry."

"Please, don't be. In fact, if you want to, you can do it again. I won't mind at all."

Manasa rolled her eyes playfully. "Shut up."

"No, seriously. I really want it. I think my wound is starting to heal because of this."

She ignored him. "What kind of deal do you have with Maruda? He could have killed us, but he didn't. He's treating you like a fellowman and he also says you owe him. I don't get it."

Nanda softly scratched his chin. "If I begin telling you about what Maruda and I owe to each other, it'll take us a long time."

Manasa laughed and Nanda did too. A good plan and a good partner, with a cool breeze around them, made them forget their dire situation for a moment.

Let's hope to Lord Sheesha it sure damn works.

18

Urvashi woke up to find herself in a dingy room. It wasn't like the ones she had stayed in, in her entire life—there were pipes and furnaces, leaking soiled water, moss over the floor, the smell of a dead rat engulfed her nostrils, and she could hear the drumming and the humming from the floor above.

I am in the underbelly of the city where the coal miners work.

And yet there were no miners around. Instead, she was with Lady Durukti who was massaging her head, mumbling to herself. Their gowns had dirt and black soot spattered all over them.

Father would be worried.

"Where are we?" Durukti looked around. "What happened?"

She doesn't remember!

"What is the last thing you remember?" Urvashi asked.

"I don't know." She looked clueless. "Who are you?"

Oh no.

Urvashi wiped the sweat from her face and tried to get up when she found Symrin coming towards them, out of nowhere. She was worried and frantic. "My lady! My lady!" she called out to Durukti.

"Symrin?"

Symrin sat beside them and held Durukti's hand. "My lady, what are you doing here? Why are you with Vedanta's daughter?"

"I . . . I . . . Urvashi?" Durukti was still massaging her head. "No, I don't know."

"We heard rumours that she had kidnapped you."

Urvashi stood up, gritting her teeth. *This is just stupid.* She knew now that Symrin was playing her hand. She must have replaced Durukti's recent memories with fake ones. She must have also tried it on Urvashi, but Urvashi had a bracelet hidden under her gloved hands that charmed off any spell.

"Kidnapped me?" Durukti looked at Urvashi, horrified.

"Of course, and that is why I was knocked out like her." Urvashi sarcastically said. "Lady Durukti, Symrin is playing games. She doesn't want you to remember what happened. Symrin is a witch, a Vidhyadhara who's manipulating you. Please do not hasten in making decisions. She brought us here—"

Symrin snapped in between. "No, my lady. She's lying. Believe me, I have been your trusted advisor for a long time." There was a hint of confusion in Symrin's eyes. She hadn't anticipated this. Urvashi remembered what had happened. Her spell had failed.

Durukti nodded. "I need some time."

"Of course, my lady. We should leave this wretched place Urvashi has brought us to." Symrin grabbed Durukti's palm.

Urvashi knew why Symrin had brought them here in the first place. If her plan had gone awry, she could easily dispose both of them, burn them amidst the black reserves of coal and no one would know. Till now the plan was working. Urvashi had to turn the tables. Immediately.

"We must tell Lord Kali about Lady Urvashi's indecent nature, and he shall imprison her." She paused, mustering more words to make a case against Urvashi. "We need to rush since Lady Urvashi might hurt us again."

"Of course." Durukti slowly nodded. "We should go."

Wrapping her arms around Durukti, Symrin guided her to the door. She glanced back at Urvashi with a venomous stare.

"But hold on," Durukti stopped in her place, turning to Symrin. "If I was kidnapped by Urvashi, why did you come alone to rescue me? Where are the guards, the soldiers? More importantly . . . where is Kali?"

Symrin was speechless.

Yes. Thank the heavens. Lady Durukti is catching on.

"No, they are right ahead . . . they are . . ." Symrin fumbled nervously until her face went placid, as if she couldn't care less about anything now. "All right, time to end you both."

Durukti shook her head. She was still recalling things, Urvashi could notice it, and there was confidence in her voice now. "No, it is you who will perish. You work for someone. Who is it?"

"Enough with the questions." Symrin closed her eyes and Urvashi knew that she was conjuring magic for a nasty purpose.

Urvashi instantly tore her bracelet and when Symrin, with a spark of elemental energy, used fire from the furnace to attack Durukti, the bracelet came in between, causing the spell to break.

"How in the . . ." she turned towards Urvashi with a furious face. "You know too much. How is it possible?"

"I have been trained well."

"By whom? You are not a Vidhyadhara."

"Yes, but I know their ways."

"Still, you are no match for me." She began to conjure fire again.

Urvashi saw Durukti reaching out for some coal lumps and throwing them at Symrin. One of them missed while the other hit her straight on the head. Symrin groaned, confused about whom to attack first and then she did the unthinkable. She thrust her hands forward, her fingers sparkled with fire energy as she directed both her hands towards Urvashi and Durukti.

"You shall both die now."

Urvashi instantly went for the grill that was kept inside the furnace, burning bright. With the help of her solid gloves, she

picked it up. It was hot, but not too much. Urvashi turned to Durukti and she nodded back at her. Durukti took the lump of coal in her fist, while Symrin had closed her eyes as the fireballs grew in her palms.

Durukti instantly tossed the coal lump at Symrin, breaking her concentration. In anger, she directed the fire towards Durukti only. Urvashi came forward, her eyes closing in brutal acceptance as she stabbed Symrin in the back with the hot grill. It went through her, skewering her bones and flesh, tearing them apart and passing on to the other end.

Durukti dodged the fire directed at her, though some of it burnt her gown.

Symrin fell on the ground, her energy sparkling from her fingers, but nothing happened. She took deep breaths as Durukti came forward.

"Should we take her to the court?" Urvashi asked.

"No. She's the root of all my problems. She made my brother ill and attempted his assassination," Durukti announced, fearless. "And worse, she tried to take my memory away."

Durukti grabbed Symrin by the throat as Urvashi saw her piercing her nails in her skin. Symrin flailed helplessly. She dragged her across the room and tossed her close to the fire. Durukti then pulled out the grill from her to which Symrin screamed in pain.

"Who was that man you were communicating with? The scarred man?"

Urvashi didn't understand a word of what was going on, but it had an intriguing air to it. Plus, it was getting too hot here and she was breathless. But Urvashi didn't mind. She liked Durukti's flames of anger running ablaze. It reminded her of her own self.

"He is the harbinger of change," Symrin replied, coughing bile and blood.

"Why do you want the Eye of Brahma?"

"It's lost and separated, and no one knows where it is. My

master had it once, only the Third Shard, the one which showed the future, but only for a short amount of time."

"I know the First Shard shows the past, the Second Shard shows the present, the Third Shard shows the future. What does the Fourth Shard do? TELL ME!"

Symrin was panting, struggling to breathe. "I removed the information. I didn't want anyone to know, but now it doesn't matter."

"What does it DO?"

"It shows you the probable outcome to a particular action of yours. It shows outcomes to your actions which you haven't performed yet. In that way, you would always take the best path because you'll know which choice needs to be made."

"But isn't that similar to the Third Shard?"

"The Third Shard only shows the future. It doesn't show how your choices determine your fate. Fate is a tricky thing . . . In this case, your choices determine your fate and thus, this particular . . ." she coughed, "this particular thing is bound to happen. There is no way to change it. The future is intangible." She paused, thoughtfully musing to herself. "I just thought if I could find it, I could use my energies to locate it and please him . . . please him." She repeated it again and again, as if lamenting her failure in her mission.

"You love him. That's why you did all of it. He's not just your master."

Symrin nodded. "He's my soulmate."

Urvashi could hear Durukti's voice calming at that statement. "Who is he? Please tell me."

"If I do," Urvashi saw Symrin turning, her teeth tinged with blood as she giggled manically, "all we did, all that we have planned, will be worthless." She paused for a moment before murmuring in resignation, "You cannot change your fate."

And then Symrin pushed herself frantically inside the furnace, her head burning in the boiling fire as Durukti stepped back in horror. Urvashi couldn't bear the sight and they hugged each other

as they saw Symrin's flesh dissolving, her bare, broken bones visible to her two enemies.

Urvashi led Durukti outside, wondering about the information she had received from Symrin and how much Durukti knew about it. The scarred man? The Eye of Brahma? This was information beyond the ordinary. As they left the underground cells, they realized they were in the middle of a half-empty street, the dawn was almost near, and the skies had a scarlet thread, cutting right across the overcast clouds. Wind was sharp and the sound of sudden footsteps of the civilians irritated Urvashi.

"Who would have thought . . . two princesses fighting witches and travelling without their entourage behind them?" Urvashi grinned to herself.

"We don't need men or soldiers to handle us." Durukti winked at her.

"You know I shouldn't ask you about what happened down there—"

"Don't." Durukti shook her head. "It has turned out to be a deeper mess than I had imagined. And I don't want to get into it. I pity her, you know. She never received what she longed for. I don't want you to get into this mess, Urvashi. I don't want to lose my friend," she smiled at Urvashi, "because I intend to be in her company for a long, long time."

"You can have my company, if you don't piss me off."

They both laughed as the city in front of them gleamed brilliantly. They walked forward, hiding their faces so that no one would recognize them, until Urvashi realized that all the people were running in the same direction. She narrowed her eyes and instead of going back to her fort, she made way to the crowd that had assembled, with Durukti on her side.

"Was there any carnival today?"

"I presume not," Durukti responded.

They walked in the midst of the crowd, holding each other's hands, and followed the people to see what was happening. Wooden barricades had been put in front while guards stood over the pedestal where announcements were made. And then, Urvashi saw Lord Kali. Lord Kuvera was sitting at the back, with a bored expression.

And she saw someone else.

Her father.

He wasn't standing. Rather, he was kneeling on the ground, his hands bound, his entire front naked. Urvashi could see dark, maligning scars that ran across his back. His hair was greasy and his beard bloody.

No. This is not happening.

Urvashi glanced at Durukti and she began to move to protect him, but Durukti grabbed her hand. She calmly whispered, "Don't. If you go as well, Kali will kill you."

"The crimes of the betrayers shall be answered in face of the public. Lord Vedanta, the former king of Indragarh, went against the crown and for those who go against the crown, they shall be met with one fate." Lord Kali, in his shining golden robe, unsheathed his sword and laid it close to Vedanta's neck. "Lord Vedanta rebelled against me and killed an officer of the court. General Pradm, from the Rakshas regiment met a harsh end. In most cases, an executor would be doing what I'm doing right now, but I choose to do it myself since the king himself must pass the sentence and execute it."

Urvashi was stunned, frozen. *Please don't.*

"Do you apologize?" Kali asked Vedanta as the public booed in unison. "Apologize and I shall let you live."

"May Lord Indra's Vajra . . ." his sentence was cut off as Lord Kali sliced his head, beheading it from his body.

The head popped and dropped from the pedestal, hidden behind the guards who covered the pedestal. Blood sprayed from the body as it motionlessly fell over to the side.

No.

Urvashi almost fainted.

"We are leaving," said Durukti through her gritted teeth. She looked at Urvashi with concern. "He will come after you now. You need to be safe."

Urvashi was motionless.

Her hands drooped down, away from Durukti's palms. In pain. Anger. Betrayal.

19

Padma prepared herself for the duel.

She hated the fact that she had to duel someone she didn't know—mostly she killed people based on contracts, not out of personal vendetta. Vedanta's soldiers had to die because they had killed her brothers. And she will do her utmost to defend herself from anyone who was a threat to her. There was a reason behind the kill. Always.

In this situation, she was being forced to commit the same act under the command of a creature. Brahmaputraksh was not human. He was a deranged creature—who wilfully spoke Padma's language, but was also very primitive in his style of walking, with half-bent and slouched shoulders. His skin was dark, just like the Rakshas, and he had red lips smeared wide over his face, probably cherry or worse . . . blood.

Padma was in her own hut with Kalki and Kripa on her side, while Aina was on the other end of the hut with Ratna Maru and Smrit. They were whispering and their language was what caught Padma's attention. They were not Manavs. They were Apsaras. *But they don't look like their kind.*

A sense of relief washed over her since Apsaras were easy to kill. Hell, they weren't even the warrior kind. They were seductresses often employed at brothels to please the rich merchants and kings.

They couldn't fight. Nowhere in history had there ever been a record of an Apsara fighting in a battle. They were always kept in the inner quarters to please the men, or in some instances, women.

Brahmaputraksh let them choose their weapons and Padma asked for her two daggers that had been taken by Darooda Simha, back in the cave. When rummaging through the rucksack of Darooda, they had found those daggers—saffron-hilted with a crazy, studded with a gleaming gem. She swung them in the air, practising for the fight.

"Anything else I should know about these beings?" she asked.

Kripa shrugged. "Only that if you die, lass, they'll eat you."

Padma rolled her eyes at the thought of her body being ripped by a dozen Pisach. "I don't understand why they make people duel. Why don't they easily consume them?"

"I wish I knew. Perhaps it's a fun sport for them. To eat the weaker kind and reward the stronger one with the spoils of the battle and to live another day. You see those skulls that Brahmaputraksh wore?"

Padma nodded, so did Kalki. Padma gave him a contemptuous look. *The so-called saviour.* But he couldn't proclaim it now, not especially when someone else was fighting the battles. *Ugh.*

"These skulls signify the people he has killed to come to this position. They believe the strongest shall rule them and if not, they will be eaten, for they are good for nothing but food. That's why there aren't a lot of Pisach out here in the world. They keep eating each other. Kind of poetic, eh?" He giggled nervously.

"Why did you nudge me back then when you heard his name?" Padma was in no mood to joke. She never joked, now that she thought about it. Sadly, she couldn't even remember the last time she had smiled. Not the snarky, sarcastic smile she had for Kalki's stupidity, but genuine laughter. *Oh, it has been ages.*

"Because Brahmaputraksh is someone I've heard of. Back when I was trying to stop the spread of Soma and I was down there

at Suparnika, disguised as a traveller to burn down their Somalata plants, I had heard rumours about Brahmaputraksh. He was a Suparn whose family had been burnt down by the Nagas during one of their teensy battles." He frowned at the thought. "And he went mad. Killed a bunch of Suparns for not doing their duty. Since the Suparns were quite the majestic kind, they exiled him. I suppose he ended up here. Ugh, you should have seen how he killed the men—guts out, lungs eaten up, faces scarred . . ."

Kalki shook his head. "That's enough, old man."

"All right."

"Did you burn the Somalata plants?"

"Some of them. The Suparns won't let them out of their sight."

Kalki intervened. "I don't understand what was the use of the immortality you have, the endowment you received. Here you stand and the Somas stay exactly where they are. It seems like you practically did nothing to stop the spread of the Somas."

"Hey! I did, all right. It's just . . ." he got awkward, "I kind of got tired of failing."

Kripa grew pensive. Kalki decided to change the subject.

"You know, sometimes I wonder . . . what if we are wrong and it's not Kali? What if it's someone else and we are just targeting the wrong guy?"

Kripa looked uncertain. Padma had learnt enough about the prophecy—Somas, Dharm, Adharm, Endowments, the Breaking. She knew exactly what Kalki was talking about, since Kripa had explained to her when they were ascending the hills.

"Mate, Kali fits the poster of the ultimate bad guy."

Kalki furrowed his brows. "I sure hope so."

"Can anyone be a Pisach? I mean, if they fight their way up to the ladder." The idea seemed interesting.

"Yes. Unlike other tribes where you are born into a certain role, Pisach and Apsaras are two tribes which are achieved and not ascribed," Kripa affirmed.

"They seem quite the same as the Rakshas."

Kripa shook his head. "Oh, I wish. Rakshas are military men, sort of crazy, but they follow a code. They fight for a cause while the Pisach don't. They are just dense maniacs and one must stay away from them as much as possible. Which makes me question, have built your strength throughout our journey?" He grinned at Kalki.

Kalki snorted.

Padma let out a guffaw. Her tension eased a bit. That is when she noticed a Pisach entering the tent, with the same ragged loins, nail jewellery around his neck, and dirty, messy hair. He stomped his feet.

"I think it's time." Kalki looked at her.

Padma looked back at him. At that moment, she could see he was afraid for her as well. *Wait . . . is he . . . worried? I thought he hated me.*

"Just don't get killed, all right?" He awkwardly patted her on the shoulder. The gesture made her happy, though she would never admit it to anybody.

Padma nodded, and avoided his gaze as she walked to the exit and moved towards the net which was in between two trees. The net was being used as the arena. She realized it was going to be quite tough for her to move fast. She had good footwork when it came to duelling, but that advantage won't be of much use now.

She stepped over to the net when she realized her spectators were several Pisach. They had climbed over the vines and were hanging from them. Some even hung upside down. They all hooted and howled as Padma rocked the net, desperately trying to control her balance.

Aina jumped on the net and cradled her body, straighteing her posture. She had a strange weapon—a dagger axe. On one end, it was an axe with a jutted blade protruding and glimmering. On the other end, it was conical and the dagger blade was coming out, sharp.

Brahmaputraksh stood at the other end of the net, on a bridge that towered over the two trees, a few paces away from the net since all of the area was covered with vines, canopies, foliage, marshes, and branches. He spoke in a weird lingo and everyone went silent. And then he clapped his hands which made everyone loudly chatter.

Padma looked at Kripa and Kalki who had clenched faces, while Ratna Maru and Smrit were quite calm.

And then, Aina came forward swishing her axe towards Padma's face. She instantly fell back, her foot getting caught in the space of the net and her sandle slipped and fell down in the swamp. Padma just realized there was a swamp beneath them and it was the best way to die in there, lest she be defeated.

Aina didn't care. Her moves were swift and she was calculating the space between the nets as she attacked again. But this time, Padma deflected her axe by one dagger and with another she slashed her knees. At that moment, the hooting grew and Aina fell.

And as Padma bought herself time, she tried to pull her foot out of the net, but it was just twisting more into a knot and she was getting worried. *I won't be able to fight like this.*

Aina, bleeding now, still went for the attack and Padma tried to roll over, but her foot hindered her from doing so. Aina disarmed her by taking one of her weapons. Taking her dagger, she smashed it hard on Padma's shoulder, almost stabbing her. But Padma stopped her by using her other dagger and with her free foot she plunged a kick in Aina's abdomen. Aina fell back, groaning in pain.

Padma went for the dagger which was in the corner. Reaching out to it in anger, Aina walked over it calmly and just kicked it away from the net. It fell in the swamp, drowning with a plomp.

"Now that was a coward's move."

Aina shrugged. She had some weird ink over her face and Padma realized it wasn't just any ink—it was a brand given to Apsaras by their owners. Most owners don't do it since it spoils

their faces, though some do it to show ownership over their property. And by the looks of it, she was quite frustrated from being owned by someone.

"I know you are an Apsara," Padma tried to distract her. The Pisach hooted in the background. "I know someone owned you and I'm sorry."

"I don't care if you are sorry. I intend to survive. That's all that matters."

"I know. I have been taught the same thing." Padma was buying time, thinking of ideas. "Ever since I was young, ever since I lost my family, I had been taught to kill. Things changed when I met this individual who taught me that there's more than just killing. There's life and life is greater than anything." And in that brief moment, she admitted to herself that she missed Arjan.

"It doesn't matter what you say, girl. Either you live or I do."

"I'm glad you were liberated from the clutches of a man." Padma came up with a move she could use. "That's why I'm sorry for what I'm gonna do."

Aina narrowed her gaze in confusion. Padma instantly turned to the farthest corner of the net, grabbed it and turned the net upside down. Aina slipped from it, collapsing deep in the swamp, while Padma didn't, since her foot was caught in the net and she hung upside down, but with a grin. Though she wasn't able to ignore the wails and cries of Aina as she tried to save herself by swimming in the swamp. Her effort was in vain as she started drowning.

She saw Brahmaputraksh grinning as he clapped. The Pisach who were hanging from the vines tied those vines back up and jumped in the swamp only to pull Aina up.

Aina was grateful for her rescue. She spluttered water from her mouth. There was a sense of relief before Aina realized that her clothes were being torn by the Pisach in mid-air, her skin was being scratched, and her head was being sucked and eaten by the cannibal.

Padma rested her eyes and took some water from the bucket the Pisach had given her. She washed her face in a hurry. She felt responsible for what had just happened. The image of the Pisach eating Aina alive was replaying in her mind. It was a dishonourable way to go, but it turned out to be worse since the killing was inhumane. In fact, everyone had turned their faces except Ratna, who had watched it intently.

She was in the hut again and her feet ached and her stomach lurched with disgust. "I lost my sandles," she spoke to herself, her eyes half closed.

"You did a smart thing, lass."

"I feel horrible." Padma shook her head. Though she knew why she was feeling horrible. She never looked at her victims after slicing their throats. She didn't have to see the aftermath, but here, she had had to face the consequence of her actions.

"Well, you should," Kripa shrugged. "But at least, you live to tell the tale."

Brahmaputraksh had announced that the next battle would be between Kalki and Ratna Maru. But after witnessing Aina's death, Kalki had turned white since he knew what fate awaited the loser. He knelt down, asking Kripa to do the same. Kripa retorted, "My knees hurt. I'm old, don't forget that."

"Shut up. We need to escape."

"You don't say?" Padma remarked.

Kalki clenched his fist. "We need a way out, otherwise we can . . . well . . . we will keep dancing on their fingers. That's not who we are."

"All right," Kripa agreed.

Padma did too.

"We have one day to figure it out. I will Channel the past Avatars to know about it more—my strength. I need to learn how

to use my strength better. If I'm the Avatar, I should start behaving like one."

Padma nodded. Finally, he was embracing his role. *Thank god.*

"I will be on the lookout and make sure Ratna doesn't kill you during your sleep." Kripa nudged Kalki only to see that Ratna was watching them sitting in the other corner with Smrit on her side, dozing over her shoulder.

"Yeah, you do that." Kalki turned to Padma now.

"Me? I think I will rest a little." She massaged her feet, groaning.

Padma could see that Kalki had just frowned at that. But she was hurting and she didn't care if he minded her resting. And yet, instead of making a snarky comment or a rude remark, Kalki pulled out his slippers and handed them to her. When Padma didn't take them, he softly slipped them under her feet. Her feet didn't feel anything, but her stomach lurched even more for some reason.

"Good work." He had a steady face, almost genuine.

"Thank you," said Padma. She was confused. *Why is he being nice all of a sudden? Is it because he thought I was going to die? Well, he better!*

"I'm glad you are alive."

All Padma could do was nod at that moment. Kalki left the corner and sat at the other end of the hut for his Channelling session, closing his eyes, and letting his core connect to the spiritual plane. Kripa then whispered to her, "Don't worry, lass. I won't tell."

"What?" Padma narrowed her gaze.

"That you just blushed at his gesture."

Padma widened her eyes as she rubbed her hot cheeks in embarrassment.

20

Arjan had thought that he had come to know how to wrestle after being in the prison for such a long time. But when he saw Harsha strangling someone by just hauling him up the ground and then releasing the dead meat, Arjan knew that he had thought wrong.

I'm going to die a horrible, horrible death.

Master Reddy had given up hope on Arjan and concentrated on the other wrestlers, while Arjan practised by himself.

After the dreadful day with Kali when he had portrayed Arjan as the mole in the group, everyone eyed him with suspicion. In fact, Rudra hadn't spoken to him as well which was kind of a disappointment for Arjan. Vikram had eventually come up to him and said, "I know you didn't say anything."

"Thank you." Arjan sighed as he strengthened his upper body by trying to stand on his arms. Over the past few months, he had gotten quite tough. Vikram had helped him with the sessions.

"But there is a high chance you would die in the competition. I know it's deliberate. I don't know why Lord Kali hates you so much."

"I kind of burnt down his treasures." Arjan nervously chuckled to himself at the thought. Truth be told, he would have gotten angry if someone would have done the same to him.

Vikram awkwardly nodded. Arjan continued with his practice, choosing to go to a separate place where there was a dummy. He began to practice with the dummy stuck to a wooden rod and he caught it from behind, hit it in the legs, and tried to grab it by the neck when he heard a voice from the back.

"That's not how you do it."

Arjan turned to see the gleaming body of Rudra, standing tall and firm in front of him. Arjan turned away, ignoring him.

"If you practice like this, they will skin you alive in the arena."

"Why do you care?" Arjan mumbled to himself.

"What did you just say?"

Arjan could feel the anger pulsating from Rudra. He came in front of Arjan and grabbed his hand. "I've been trying to save your ass for so many days. Harsha had planned to take you down at lunchtime, but I have been holding him back."

"Really?"

"Yeah, really."

Arjan looked down, parting his hands from him. "Why would you do that?"

"Because I car—" he stopped, gulping down his anger. "I know you didn't do it and that Lord Kali is pitting us against each other. He really hates you."

"Yes, thank you for believing in me."

"But just because I believe in you, doesn't mean Harsha will. He has readied himself to challenge you in the competition and break you in front of Lord Kali and become his favourite fighter."

Since when does Harsha care about being good in Kali's eyes?

"Everyone wants that. But I can't see you go down in the process. If you train like this, you will be surely killed."

Arjan nodded. "What's your plan?"

"Let me train you. At least, you can fend him off and tire him out. That big, fat man has everything but stamina. And even if you have nothing, you can count on your stamina. So, it works both ways."

"You don't care if Harsha dies?"

Rudra came forward, standing tall in front of Arjan. He was almost as tall as Kalki, or perhaps taller. "I just don't want you to die."

Arjan lowered his eyes, mustering up the courage to ask what he had wanted to ask Rudra for a while. "Why . . . um . . . why are you here in prison?"

At this, Rudra's eyes narrowed and his forehead creased. "Well, if you train well and beat me, I shall tell you."

Arjan smiled. He was expecting a harsher reply. "Let's go with it then."

The training was excruciating to say the least. They practised in a corner, away from the other prisoners, and seeing Rudra as an active participant Master Reddy didn't even care to interfere. In a few days, Rudra taught Arjan about the various complications faced by a wrestler and how Arjan must build his core strength.

"It's not about the muscles." He patted his arms, flexing his biceps. "I mean they do look massive but that's not all. Wrestling is all in here." Rudra pointed to his head. "Mind games. You need to anticipate what your opponent is going to do and then counter them. It's about being quick. Be decisive." And when he said it, he moved like a python, grabbing him from the back and locking his head with his arms. Arjan felt breathless for a moment. "With this move, you can suffocate your opponent, though not in a life-threatening way. Harsha may be strong, but if he can't breathe, he can't fight." Rudra released Arjan.

"Great. What else can I do to win against a giant like Harsha?"

"I'll show you. Pass between my legs and from the back, grab my throat and make sure you choke this little thing here," he pointed at the larynx.

"Come on, try it. I won't defend myself."

Arjan went between his legs and then grabbed him from the back.

"Okay. Now, whenever you grab someone's neck, make sure you also grab their forehead or at least their arm, so they don't try to get the upper hand on you. And now to play dirty, you can just poke Harsha in the eye."

"Won't that be a rule breaker?"

"It doesn't matter if you break rules. You need to be alive, so cheat, if you must."

Arjan left Rudra and stood opposite to him.

"Now when you begin a fight, always dodge him, since he can easily toss you off. Since this match will be to the death, he won't just toss you up. He would break your bones if he catches you. To prevent that, you need to tire him out." Rudra came forward, albeit slowly, and Arjan quickly went around him. Rudra turned and Arjan did the same thing.

In a flash, Rudra stormed towards him.

Arjan's heartbeat increased, as the practice just became serious. With a quick leap, he somersaulted in the corner causing Rudra to miss him.

"Very good, Arjan." Rudra smiled. "You are quick. Have you battled before?"

Oh, you have no idea.

"Here and there." Arjan smiled. He was profusely sweating now.

Arjan practised a little more as Rudra helped him strengthen his arms, his waist, and his legs, telling him exercises that'll work best for him. He also taught Arjan how to break someone's neck cleanly, especially ways to deal with Harsha's big neck.

"We shall practice more tomorrow."

Arjan nodded and Rudra began to leave since the practice hour was getting over and the guards were telling all of them to go to their cells. "You didn't tell me why you are here."

Rudra turned, thoughtfully musing over it.

"Did you kill someone?"

"Uh, no. I loved someone."

Arjan could understand the pain that Rudra had behind his eyes.

"I was a carpenter and uh . . . he . . . he was a noble's son."

Wow.

Arjan didn't really like the fact that Rudra's heart had been broken and he had been thrown in jail because of it, but he was also glad that Rudra liked men. *Well, I'm relieved.*

"What happened then?"

"Someone caught us and Lord Vedanta had a strict policy of no love between men so he uh . . . he couldn't let the minister's son take the fall, so he made me take the blame after a lot of flogging."

"Lord Vedanta was surely the worst ruler. Period."

"It's not that . . . uh . . . Lord Vedanta put me here. But my so-called lover didn't do anything to stop it. After all, if I was wrong, he was wrong as well."

Arjan agreed. They stood in an awkward silence and Rudra left the scene. Amidst all that hard exterior, the dry humour, was a sensitive man. Arjan wanted to say something more, but he couldn't. That's how he always was—left in the middle whenever he wanted to say something because he was not courageous enough to speak his heart out.

You were not wrong, Rudra. You were not wrong.

Arjan was half asleep when he woke up to the sound of sobbing. He realized it was morning and it was just another day except for the weeping sounds that were coming from the next cell. He saw Vikram whimpering, rubbing his nails together. Tears were streaming down his face.

Sighing, Arjan crawled close to the adjoining cell as they were separated by a grilled wall. Vikram turned to see him, wiping the

tears. Seeing this big ball of fat and fur, Arjan kind of pitied him—red-faced, double chin, hardly a body for a wrestler, and yet he was here, stuck in some prison for what his father had done.

"What happened?"

"I did a bad thing, fella."

Arjan arched his brows. "What?"

"I . . . I feel bad for doing it, if it helps."

"What did you do?"

"I . . ." he was choking, wiping his tears.

"You can say."

"Yeah, I . . . uh . . . I kind of ratted you all out." He shook his head, regretting the words, but speaking quietly so no one else in the entire corridor would hear it. "Lord Kali called me in the middle of the night, said there were rumours and he . . . uh . . . he promised me freedom if I told him the truth."

"And you confirmed it."

He nodded his head. He had shut his eyes. Perhaps he was embarrassed, unable to look Arjan in the eye.

"I didn't know he w-would blame it on you, fella."

And yet he did.

"I so apologize, ya," he paused, "that's why . . . that's why I went to Lord Kali and told him he shouldn't do this to you. He said he'll look over it."

Arjan thought of this decision of Vikram as stupid, but he didn't say anything. "Don't worry about it," he responded. "What's done is done and we need to get out of the mess."

"I want to leave this place so much, ya. I want to." And then his eyes met Arjan's. "Believe me, it's like I have been here in this bloody prison since I was a wee-bit tall. My childhood was spent here. I have been here for so long that I have lost my ability to think about freedom, to think about myself. I don't even know who I am. Am I a person? If I am, what are my passions, my hobbies, my quirks? I . . . uh . . ." he kept rubbing his nails as if

he was trying to push his nervous energy towards them. "I don't know. I just don't know."

You live so long in isolation in such a way that you don't know yourself anymore. How unfortunate. At least Arjan had an identity. He was a reader, and a poet sometimes. He wanted to travel, though not in an adventurous way but more in a way of escaping the world and knowing the realities of the different tribes, and yet here he was, tied up like a pigeon.

"I'm here to figure it out with you."

Vikram wiped the last of his tears from his eyes. He was calm now. "Thank you. You are a true friend. But please don't tell anyone. You are still protected by Rudra. I am not with anyone."

"I won't." Arjan slid his hand through the space in the grill and kept it on Vikram's, saying, "And you have me, I'll protect you, as much as I can."

"Only a wee-bit little."

They both chuckled.

As Vikram sniffled, the corridor doors opened and the soldiers entered. Arjan heard the cells being opened and the prisoners being escorted outside. Arjan and Vikram were thrown in a line.

"What is this for, fella?" Vikram asked the soldier who was walking adjacent to them.

"The wrestling match starts today."

"What?" Arjan's voice came out as a whimper.

"Oh yeah," the soldier patted him harshly on the back. "Let's see if you can survive that."

The entire arena was filling up with people and it wasn't like the one in Kali's fort. This was a specially made *akhada* with poles that showed different flags of the tribes. It had Kali sitting in the front row with Lady Durukti on his side. She didn't look happy.

The prisoners were put in the corner of the field and Arjan realized all the sand here was red rather than golden. The sun was orange and the arena was dark in colour. It already gave him the creeps. The hair at the back of his neck stood up. He couldn't even feel his legs and felt a bit like retching out of fear.

Rudra came forward to meet Arjan as his eyes slowly focused on Harsha who was stretching himself.

"Don't worry, you can do it. Just keep dodging. Tire him out and you will win."

"What if I faint before him?"

Rudra frowned. "Please don't."

Easier said than done.

Arjan licked his lips as he came in the arena, looking at everyone in the crowd, wondering if anyone from Shambala was there. Deep inside, he wished Kalki was here to have his back. He picked up the sand and let it slip from his fingers to feel how hot it was.

"We are here," Kali began loudly, "to commemorate and enjoy one of the greatest and the most amazing fight this kingdom has ever seen. Initiated by King Jarasandha, I shall continue it. And I have bet it all on the one I know will win."

He's lying.

"He has promised to win this competition and defeat anyone, big or small. The toughest of the lot!"

And at that, everyone snickered and scoffed.

"And he will prove you wrong, no doubt. Arjan, my dear boy, are you ready?" Even though warmth encased his voice, he was just enjoying the moment like a pure sadist.

Arjan nodded glumly.

"All righty. To fight him . . ."

At that moment, Harsha raised his voice. "I CHALLENGE HIM!"

Everyone began clapping. They wanted to see Arjan beaten to a pulp. Even Kali looked happy. He clapped while Lady Durukti sat there, stern-faced.

"Very good, we already have an opponent for our champion but um . . ." Kali frowned, "too easy, eh?" He turned to Durukti to question. "Na, too boring as well . . ."

He doesn't want Harsha to fight me? Harsha looked confused as well.

"You!" He pointed at one of the wrestlers. "I want you on the field."

Arjan swivelled his head to see, wishing Kali was not pointing at Rudra. His face lost all colour when he saw who Kali was pointing at.

Vikram.

21

Arjan was stunned for a moment. He stood there, his palms sweaty as he stared at Vikram and then at Kali.

This is not happening.

Vikram was frozen at his spot. He was wearing a long tunic on his body which the guards came forward and tore apart. In a wrestler's rag, he looked like a chubby baby, a newborn who has been fed enough.

It was never about killing me. Arjan's heart sunk deeper.

Vikram bumbled forward awkwardly being pushed by the soldiers as the public began to boo him. And for the first time, Arjan saw the chances of winning the match.

Vikram stood there in front of Arjan, looking meek, and amidst all hoots and boos which Arjan ignored, he could smell Vikram's fear.

It is either him or me.

Arjan knew. To survive he had to kill Vikram . . . with his own bare hands. He glanced at Rudra who was nervous, biting the top of his thumb, though he had a triumphant curve of a smile. Rudra didn't know Vikram like Arjan did. And Rudra knew that Vikram can easily be beaten.

It was never about killing me. It was about making me the killer.

Arjan had had it with Kali. The man was grinning as Arjan looked at him, pursing his lips. "I won't fight," Arjan protested. At that, the public instantly booed, but Arjan didn't care. "You are doing it on purpose. I know. And I won't do it." Vikram had gone to Kali to absolve Arjan of his crimes. *He must have realized we are friends.*

"Sure, I understand." Kali just clapped his hands.

Manav soldiers appeared from the corner with their spears pointing at Arjan and Vikram.

"If you don't, feel free to drop dead," Kali proclaimed.

Lady Durukti stood up to protest but Kali gave her a look, as if daring her to speak. She sat down, her eyes downcast. Kali turned to Arjan again.

"Arjan," a familiar voice spoke from the back.

Arjan turned to see Vikram, who was not weeping but had a determined look on his face. "Let's do it." He leaned forward and stuck his upper body in the wrong posture. Even Arjan, who didn't know much about wrestling, knew it was the wrong way to stand. "Otherwise they will kill ya. My time is done here and I would rather die by your hands."

"But I don't want—"

The spears came forward, almost poking Arjan.

"It's all about making choices, fella. I know you are . . . you are confused. But it's about doing the right thing."

"How is killing you the right thing, Vikram?"

"Because you'll be putting me out of my misery and you'll be living another day. My purpose was . . . done when I came to this prison, but I know your purpose is greater than this. I know ya will do wonders. So, let's do it."

Arjan nodded, getting ready. The crowd cheered. Vikram dashed in the front and Arjan grabbed him by the neck as he plummeted into him with full force. Though Vikram was fat, he had good strength and he would have toppled Arjan if Arjan hadn't

maintained his balance on the ground. Then with a quick snap, he turned to his back, his hands grabbing Vikram's torso, and with a slight shift he tossed him, throwing Vikram's body up in the air. Vikram was difficult to lift, but Arjan used all his strength.

The red dust swirled around them and Vikram lay there, not even fighting anymore, but panting.

"Do it," he whispered.

Arjan grabbed him by the neck, tears almost trickling down his eyes, his breath steadying. He put Vikram's neck in a headlock as Vikram protested. Arjan closed his eyes as he heard the final words being whispered to him by Vikram, "It was . . . nice . . . knowing . . . ya . . . fella."

And with a sharp twist to the throat, Arjan lost his only good friend, his life ebbing away in gratefulness.

No one clapped for the fight had been short and one-sided. Arjan stood up wiping the red sand from his knees. He glanced at Vikram's corpse as it laid there peacefully with a slight smile over his chubby face.

"It was great knowing you too, friend."

I know ya will do wonders.

Oh, I will. I will not let your death be in vain.

He turned to glare at Kali. Arjan had never felt angrier in his life.

I am tired of him playing with me.

"You got what you wanted. I won the battle." Arjan was feeling a lot of things right now. He recalled how Vikram had sobbed in the morning. It just wrecked him to think that he had killed his friend with his own hands. "And now I want something."

"You are in no position—"

"I CHALLENGE YOU, KALI!" Arjan yelled.

At that moment everyone in the crowd gasped, even Durukti stood up from her seat. Kali, for a moment, was confused. Arjan saw a hint of nervousness in him before that same, confident smile appeared.

"I can break you in so many parts, you have no idea." Kali laughed. "No, I'm glad. I accept the challenge." His smile faded with a feverish look in his eye. "We will do it two days from now. RIGHT HERE!"

Arjan nodded, walking back as he looked at Rudra who just ignored his glance.

I might just have agreed to my death.

Arjan knew that Kali had ingested the Soma. The only person who might be strong enough to beat Kali was none other than Kalki, and Kalki was either dead or was out there in the hills, perhaps learning about his true powers.

Arjan had no idea about how Kali should be tackled.

While going back, Rudra had commented, "You had saved your ass but you had to mess with him." Grunting his disappointment, he had left for his cell.

Arjan shook his head, rubbing his palms together as he sat in his cell, looking at the ceiling. And he slept after a while. The next morning, he went for practice and he kept wondering how he would be able to defeat Kali. Rudra didn't know what to teach him for everyone knew how powerful he was. Rumours had started flying around.

"I hear he can raise the dead."

"He can kill a person with just his finger."

They were outlandish claims but then this was prison and not many had the time to really ponder over the truth to such claims.

After a while, Arjan realized he couldn't kill Kali. Challenging Kali had seemed the right thing to do at the time, but he could see now that he had been hasty.

As the practice got over and he felt numb going back to his cell, he was approached by a soldier.

"Lady Durukti demands your presence."

Ugh. Now what?

Though Arjan had hated Durukti in the beginning when she had wrecked Shambala, Kalki had later on explained that Durukti was not completely bad. It was Martanja's men who had ensured the destruction ensued. Still, she was the person who had led the forces and Arjan didn't like her.

What does she want now?

The soldier took Arjan to the farthest corners and into a room, just opposite to his cell block. It was not yet another cell, but an empty room where Durukti was standing in a beautiful dress. *If she hadn't led an attack on my village, would we have been friends?* Arjan recalled how he had taught Padma about forgiveness. Perhaps it was time to practice what he preached.

"I'm sorry for what happened." Durukti lowered her eyes.

"It's not your fault." Arjan had a metal clasp that tied his hands while a soldier stood in the back.

Durukti dismissed the soldier who walked away into the darkness. There was little light in the room.

"No, about Shambala. I shouldn't have done that. Soma has practically turned my brother into a monster. You should know that I am collecting funds and will be devoting them to Shambala's reconstruction."

An apology? And she is planning to help in the reconstruction?

Arjan nodded. "I can't say I forgive you for what you did, but at least you regret it. You called me here for this?"

"I . . . uh . . ." she paused. "I was afraid of meeting you but when I saw you yesterday, I had to. You are going to fight Kali tomorrow and I . . . I don't know what to do. Can I help in some way?"

Help? Is this one of Kali's tricks?

"Why should I trust you?"

"Because Kalki did."

Arjan clenched his jaw. "Yes, he did. He did, of course." He repeated the words, mulling over them. "I need your help in releasing the prisoners who are tied up here."

"But they are criminals."

"They are good people. I know. I have seen them and they are all tied up here for the wrong reasons. Lord Vedanta was an unjust ruler. Just because a king feels a rule is broken, doesn't mean the rule is actually broken. In fact, did the rule ever exist on logical terms or did the king create it to frame them?" Arjan made her understand the philosophy of it all.

"I will think about it." Durukti was still confused.

"That's one of my demands. And I also want one more thing."

"Yes?"

Arjan sighed. "I want the Soma."

"Soma?" Her eyes widened in shock. "No, no, please!"

"I need to have it. That's the only way I will survive tomorrow's match."

"But you burnt it all."

"You are Kali's sister. You know him more than anyone. And you know he would always keep a backup for himself. He might be having some of it. Find it and give it to me by tonight or tomorrow morning."

Durukti's eyes shimmered. "What if . . . what if you go mad after taking it, just like him?"

Arjan had no answer for this. Kripa had made him understand that Soma might lead a man to do some wacky things and one must have it in the right dosage, otherwise they could be corrupted. Only the Dharm and Adharm shall be strengthened and they shall be able to use the effects of Soma the way they are supposed to and not let Soma control them.

"I would only require a small dosage, something to charge me up."

"You are basically telling me you will kill my brother if you get as strong as him."

Arjan shook his head. "I am not like your brother. I would surely imprison him, but not kill him. I do not needlessly kill people."

Durukti nodded. "I promise to try—for you, for my redemption, and for Kalki."

Arjan smiled at her and she returned it. As he turned around to leave, she asked from behind, "Is he all right?"

"Who?"

"Kalki."

"I don't know. I'm in the dark as much as you are."

There was a sliver of worry over her face. "I hope he returns soon."

"If he does return, he will."

"Yes, I hope so too." And she left the room.

22

Durukti was hesitating. She didn't want to enter Kali's room.

She was about to do something against Kali. Till now, she had been internally protesting against him, but now she was about to act on it. And if she was successful and Arjan defeated Kali in combat, Kali would be in jail. And Durukti would finally get time to teach Kali where he was going wrong—forcing people to do things was not the way to do it.

But then, she flustered. *Hadn't she done the same when she had attacked Shambala?*

Durukti saw Kali doing some paperwork as her eyes scanned the room. It was precise, ordinary, little bits scattered here and there with papers and folders—otherwise everything was set up well. He looked worried as he scribbled with his quill, dropping the ink in the process.

"Ah, my dear sister," he called out of her. "To what do I owe this generous pleasure?" Even though his voice was warm, he was busy writing and did not even look at her.

"How did you know it was me?"

"I'm your brother. I know when you are around."

At that her heart sank. *Does he know about Symrin? God, I hope not.*

"How is everything?" Kali asked.

"I just came here because so much has happened."

"Oh yes—the city needs to be fixed. We have a good amount of army which we clearly don't need but we don't have enough food supplies." He looked up, chewing the end of his quill. "What was that place you attacked a few months back?"

"Shambala."

"Oh yes." He wrote it down. "These small villages are revolting. The city folk are all right with the changes but the villagers, oh no, they want to fight." He kept mumbling.

"I was talking about how you beheaded their last king in public and how you accepted a challenge for a wrestling match with a commoner."

Kali stopped scribbling and when he looked up, his golden eyes glinted sharply. There was something in them, a manic energy, when Kali pulled up the corners of his lips. "How's Urvashi?"

Durukti's heartbeat rose though her expression didn't change.

"Uh . . . how would I know?"

"Well, since we ransacked Vedanta's house and we found no one but his maidservants . . . I wonder where Urvashi ran off to. Have you seen her?"

Durukti shook her head. She clearly wasn't going to tell Kali that she had hidden the daughter of the last king in her room, making her sleep under the bed at night. Durukti had no choice. If Urvashi was found, she will be mutilated. Urvashi often complained about having to stay in her father's killer's palace, and Durukti knew that a few days more and Urvashi will escape.

"I have enlisted Vedanta's maidservants at our service. We needed them to clean the place. Check up on them, all right?"

"Why did you pick a fight with a commoner?"

"Arjan? Ah . . ." He furrowed his brows. "Well, you seem interested. Surely, he's not a commoner for you." His voice got wheezy as he stood up from his chair. "His brother was your lover, wasn't he?"

"No, he wasn't." Durukti sighed. "I have told you so many times . . ."

"Just because you two didn't do anything, doesn't mean you didn't want to." Kali smiled. "And it's all right. He's dead, after all. It doesn't matter."

Durukti nodded, realizing that she hadn't told Arjan about the fact that Kalki may have been killed in a fire that Kali had caused. She wanted to believe he was still out there, hoping he would return one day. But if he didn't, Arjan was the only one who could stop Kali.

"Arjan is a toy I love to play with, like a whining baby who can't do anything, but you could do a lot of things to him. I love to exercise my power over him, break his beliefs, bring his morals down, break his soul. It's like . . ." his smile vanished, "something inside me tells me to do all of this, sister. They want me to hurt him but not kill him, to change him but not stab him. Is it too confusing?"

"You hear voices?"

"Ever since I drank that bloody Soma," he patted his belt at that moment and Durukti realized why.

The Soma is there.

"It's making me think too much. Making me . . . ugh . . ." He scratched his bald head. "Anyway, I shouldn't bore you with the details."

Durukti walked to him and knelt next to his chair, looking up in his eyes. They had the same iris colour. "No, my dear brother, please let me know your pain. We need to fight this together."

There was a genuine look on his face, the same look he used to have before he had had Soma, when he used to have compassion. "I . . . uh . . . these voices, they tell me to embrace my heritage, but what is my heritage?"

"Asura?"

"I don't want to go back to that dead island." He rolled his eyes.

"Perhaps facing those fears can help you fight these voices."

"And leave the city to the god of riches, Kuvera? Oh no. He'll burn down every last hint of my existence from this city. The only reason I've tied him to the leash is because I've promised him to get Naagpuri, but honestly between you and me, I'm more inclined towards the Suparns, for they have an abundance of Somalata plants that we can use. But it is said that only if the Suparns allow can one enter their city, otherwise it's impossible to do so. And I don't want to kill this city by going to the Dakshinis. It's almost stupid to think the Suparns don't use the Somas to make themselves strong but use it to fly. Bah! They have always been the secluded bunch, quarrelling with the Nagas all the time."

"They must have figured it out that Soma isn't good for your mental health and should be used on an object rather than on a person."

"What are you implying, my dear sister?" He paused, laughing. "I'm just messing around. All of this information, I learnt it from Vasuki's diary," he pointed at a brown-coloured notebook. "He wrote extensively about Suparns and their system and the civil war between Nagas and Suparns."

She shrugged. Durukti spoke comforting words to him as her hand slipped towards his belt where she saw a lopsided pouch and she was this close to touching the fabric of it when someone knocked. She pulled her hand back and stood up along with Kali.

"Come in."

Koko and Vikoko opened the doors from outside, letting a strange, short man enter. He had a bulbous nose, a thick upper mouth, and long ears with frizzy hair that he hid a little with his turban. He also wore a shawl that covered half of his body and on his lower half, he was wearing a strange dhoti.

"Yes?" Kali narrowed his gaze.

"I'm Captain Aruna," he bowed, "from General Taar's camp."

"Taar? Who the hell is he?" Kali paused. "Hold on, I know you. You are a Vanar."

Aruna looked similar to Kali and Durukti. But then his bulbous face, with a thick tuft of hair around it which one would say looked like a beard, was a dead giveaway to his race. But they didn't have moustaches. They worshipped the monkeys and believed they were the superior beings of Illavarti since the Vanars had fought with Lord Raghav against Lord Dushasan.

"I'm surprised." Kali sat back on his chair. "A Vanar has come and when I had come to Lord Bajrang, he was very adamant he wouldn't join my campaign. He even called me . . . well . . . mad to do such a thing."

Aruna didn't smile. He sat on the chair and said, "I'm not here from the court of Bajrang, the infidel. I'm here from General Taar's camp, a revolutionary in spirit."

"I do not understand your monkey politics, my dear friend." Kali laughed.

"It's a long story of betrayals and fighting and what-not. But we have a strong leader and we have a strong cause. And we want to join forces with you." Aruna looked up at Durukti. "Can we speak in private though?"

Durukti began to move when Kali caught her hand.

"No, I would love it if she stays here. She's my sister."

"Ah, my apologies then." Aruna had a refined way of speaking, almost aristocratic. "I have travelled from the outskirts of Dandak to meet you. General Taar sends his regards." From under the shawl, he pulled out a sheathed sword. "A token of friendship."

Kali was impressed. Durukti noticed this as he picked up the sword and studied the inscriptions over it. "What does it say?"

"Fate favours the brave."

He sheathed it back. "You have my attention now. How can I be of service?"

Aruna was glad, almost pulling up a little smile. "My lord, we

want to join forces with you and become a part of your campaign, as I have said. And we also know you had a fallout with the Nagas. You need a powerful—"

"Yeah, it doesn't matter." Kali waved his hand nonchalantly. "What matters is that Lord Bajrang apparently has a hold on you."

"We want you to help us get rid of him from the throne."

"Just so you could join me?" he coughed, laughing loudly. "Let me get this straight. You are ready to join forces with me if I send my men to the borders of Dandak to fight your little battles with Bajrang?"

"Not just join forces," Aruna was calm even though Durukti was offended the way Kali explained the situation. "But to give you something powerful in return."

"And what would that be?"

From under the shawl, he pulled out a scroll and whipped it open, over which a was a design that Durukti had already seen.

Her blood ran cold when she saw the inscription of the Eye of Brahma, divided into four parts, albeit more detailed. It had a lot of information compared to the one in the book that she had read.

"What is this?" Kali's voice turned grave.

"The Eye of Brahma—no one knows how it came to be, there are tales that Lord Brahma handed it to us, but I do not believe it. We were researching and a long time back, the time when Lord Indra walked the land of Illavarti, he had hired a bunch of physicists at his disposal. He was a man of science, Lord Indra. With the help of the physicists and the Somalata plants that he had grown here, he had been able to create four Shards. Each Shard represents something—the past, the present, the future, and the alternate reality."

"Alternate reality?"

"It shows the outcome of your actions before you act on them."

Kali nodded. "Interesting," he looked up at Aruna, "and you think Bajrang has this?"

"Not all four, unfortunately, but this one," he pointed at the middle Shard which showed the present, "it has the capability of making you see whatever impending battles or revolts you are facing, right now. You can see each move of your enemies and plan things accordingly."

"What if it doesn't work?"

"I have seen it work, my lord. The reason Bajrang didn't join forces with you back then was because he had seen what you were doing that time—shaking hands with Nagas and Yakshas, and Bajrang hated that."

"So, he sees everything."

"Whatever is limited to his knowledge."

"That's something I can use." Kali turned to Durukti for an acknowledgement, who quietly nodded back at him. "So, to make it simple, you want my soldiers with you to fight your cause, get the throne of Dandak, and in return, you shall give me your support and this Shard?"

Aruna nodded.

"What if you decide to keep my army and the Shard, and then choose to betray me?"

Aruna shook his head. "You, out of all people know, when a Vanar promises, he keeps his oath."

"Yeah but, we live in a world where anything can happen." Kali shrugged. "What about the other three Shards?"

"No one knows where they are," Aruna dismissed. "Uh, I can understand your skepticism, Lord Kali, but—"

Kali waved his hand in dismissal. "See, I don't care if you betray me because I'll instruct my soldiers to slaughter you the moment you turn your back on me. But I'm just . . . you have made me curious, Captain. I am quite interested in this Eye of Brahma."

"I'm glad."

"You can take two thousand men of mine."

"But my lord, we need five—"

Kali shook his head. "No, you need only two. If you bring me this, I will supply five thousand more to guard your Dandak well and please your general. You can tell Koko to fetch you the army."

Aruna reluctantly nodded. "Yes, my lord." And he stood up and left the room.

Durukti was silent as Kali played with the scroll and then the sword.

"Do you believe that the Eye of Brahma really exists?"

"I don't know, brother."

Kali shook his head. "I wouldn't have believed it as well if he would have come a few months back, but now I do after I have learnt about the Soma. There is certainly some magic out there in the world, I'm sure."

Durukti nodded. She had seen enough magic in the world by fighting Symrin. The thought made her shiver. "Anyway, I should leave."

Kali nodded, returning back to his work.

"You are doing a good job, brother. Talk to me when you can. I am here for you."

"Hmmm . . ."

Durukti came forward and hugged Kali, putting her head on his shoulder, wrapping her arms around him. "Be safe."

Kali smiled, patting her back. "Don't be so gushy about it now, shoo," he playfully chided.

Durukti smiled and left the room as she faced Koko and Vikoko, Kali's guards standing outside like diligent armymen. She walked away from them as she pulled out the pouch she was hiding in her tight-fisted palms. She had taken it from Kali when she had hugged him.

She opened the pouch where the blue fossil-like stones glimmered. There were only two of them.

23

He was not a perfect man. But he was my father.

It had been a few days since she had hidden herself in Lady Durukti's house, ordered to not go anywhere. And Lady Durukti was right. If Urvashi had gone out, a Rakshas or a Yaksha would have caught her. Lord Kali was quite serious about catching Urvashi. He had planned to put to her on trial, just like her father. Though trials were a sham in this city.

She thought about Vedanta, reminiscing the days she had spent with him. She remembered the time her mother had died. Vedanta, who had always been distant, had held her tight and clasped his hands in hers that day. He had been supportive. After that, he had made sure to come every night to tell stories or talk about people, letting Urvashi know that she was an integral part of his life. Vedanta had confessed to Urvashi about how he had been disappointed when she had been born. He had wanted a son. *Forgive me, my dear. I was a bad father.*

It had been two days since Vedanta's beheading. Urvashi was growing restless. She saw new servants entering her room. She hid under the bed when they appeared, but then she found out that the new servant was the same one Vedanta had had, who had tended to Urvashi. She skit out of the bed and surprised the servant.

"My lady!" she exclaimed.

"Shush!" Urvashi closed the door behind.

"What are you doing in Lady Durukti's room?"

"Hiding. She's helping me to stay alive."

"Oh, what a wonderful lady."

"Why are you here?" Urvashi arched her brows.

"Lord Kali has employed us. Are you all right, my lady?"

"What do you think?" Urvashi wiped the dust off her face.

"I apologize for Lord Vedanta's passing . . ."

"Passing? Say it like it was. Beheading."

"You were there?" the servant shrieked.

Urvashi nodded, wiping her sweaty forehead. "I need to leave. Is there any keep my father left behind? What has happened to the fort?"

"It has become an armoury, my lady."

Urvashi gritted her teeth. *That despicable Kali!* And she was in his sister's room. What are the chances she would backstab her like Kali had done to her father?

"My lady, I have something." The servant pulled it out from the apron. "I found it in Lord Vedanta's room before the soldiers came to escort us. It was addressed to you, a letter."

"And you have been carrying it around?" Urvashi took it, studying the envelope carefully.

"Never found a safe place to keep it other than with me. It might have some important information and I didn't want to hand it to the usurpers."

Urvashi smiled. "You did a good job."

"Do you trust Lady Durukti?"

"I don't trust anyone, to be honest." She sliced the envelope.

"What do you intend to do?"

Urvashi softly smiled at the maid. "I'll let you know. Do not worry. I know one thing for sure. I shall take my father's throne." She paused. "Do not tell anyone of my presence."

The maid was reassured. Urvashi sat down on the bed as the maid left the room and she began reading the letter.

Dear Urvashi,

What I am about to do can bring about some change in the way we have lived so far. But if I don't survive, I want you to know that I always wanted you to be happy, content. The times spent with you have been the greatest and I choose to go with those memories rather than the ones I have spent as a king. A king can always be dethroned in front of his people. I hope I am doing the right thing. I do not know. My fingers shiver as I write this for I feel I might not return from where I go. But I hope when you read this, you form your own resolution. Become stronger. You must realize my death could also be an opportunity for you to fight for the throne. Fight for what's rightfully yours. You are a queen by birthright. Finally, you can act like one.

Love Always,

Daddy

Urvashi didn't shed tears. She felt her chest contracting. And then she lowered her eyes, folded the letter, and kept it clasped in her arms.

Urvashi was thinking about how to escape when the door opened again and she hid herself under the bed only to realize it was Lady Durukti. She was wearing a nose ring and a large, shiny diamond necklace. For some reason, she looked unsettled, thoughtful. She was holding and rubbing a pouch in her hand.

"What's wrong?" Urvashi asked.

"Have you had your food?"

"Yes, I had a maid from my fort to help me."

"Yes, Kali had enlisted them."

Urvashi's blood boiled thinking about Kali being in the same premises as her. If only she could go there and cut him up, but Durukti had warned her from doing anything stupid. Lord Kali went with his guards everywhere.

"What's there in your hand?"

"Nothing." Durukti kept it in the drawer at that moment to which Urvashi just felt odd. Durukti was hiding something perhaps, but she shifted her attention when Durukti continued, "I met Arjan. I hope you remember him."

Urvashi did. For being with Durukti meant conversing about these things. Durukti shared a lot of her insecurities with her. She had tried to convince Urvashi that Kali was not a bad man. She even talked about Kalki and Arjan, though Urvashi could never picture them since she had never met them. But they at least sounded better than Kali.

"What did he say?"

"He wanted . . . um . . . he wanted me to help him escape."

"Help him?"

"I mean, the prisoners. All of them."

Urvashi arched her brows. "That sounds ridiculous. It'll be a riot . . ." and the thought of it just ignited a spark in her mind. *It'll indeed be a riot.* And that'll put a dent in Kali's regime and she could take him out with their support. There must be more than a hundred prisoners as of now. The idea just kept growing to the point that her fingers danced and she was getting excited about it.

"I know, it'll be, and I'm just thinking it'll change everything. But he says they are innocent. And they are mostly those your father had thrown in without sufficient evidence."

"If he did throw them in, there must be a good reason behind it."

"Not according to Arjan."

Whatever. It doesn't matter to me. What matters is, will they help?

There's honour among thieves, as the saying goes and they might just be Urvashi's chance to get Lord Kali off the throne.

But Urvashi had no intention of telling Durukti all this.

"I need to contemplate more about this."

"Sure."

Durukti went to bed as Urvashi laid her mattress on the ground. She turned overand started thinking. After a while, she could hear Durukti snoring. She slowly went over to the drawer and opened it up to see the pouch in which she found some blue stones.

What the hell are these?

Urvashi tightened the pouch and placed it back inside. She wrapped the shawl around her that belonged to Durukti and covered her face completely. With one last glance at Durukti, she took her leave from the room. Her eyes were fixed on one goal as she walked the corridors of the fort searching for her maid.

Because she knew what she had to do.

She had to find her bag of all those illusionary tricks that her guru had given her and she had to free those prisoners.

Did she have a better plan?

No.

Would the plan work?

She would find out soon.

24

Manasa hadn't slept at all while going back. They returned by the same boat and by this time, Nanda had regained his strength even though he groaned with each row he made with the oar. Manasa's one hand was absolutely useless, so she had to pummel the waves of the river with her free hand, forcing her muscles to contract in sharp pain.

The were an uncomfortable silence between them.

"I wonder what Vibhishana is up to these days," said Manasa.

"Lord Vibhisana has no control over his subjects," Nanda growled as the wind blew on his face.

Manasa understood what Nanda was talking about. In Illavarti, the land was divided in two parts—Udaiyas consisted of Indragarh, Varunagarh, Suryagarh, Agnigarh, and now Dandak. The other side, the lower half of it was called Dakshini which consisted of Suparnika, Naagpuri, Eelam, and Bhanmati where Lord Vibhishana lived. He was the only Manav chieftain of the Dakshinis. Vibhisana was the sole ruler and but still refrained from interfering in the council proceedings of these places. He was rich and abundantly gifted in grain and water, and he didn't need to rely on anyone. The only other peaceful ruler in Udaiyas was Vedanta. Though Vibhishan had often had conflicts with Vedanta over their ideologies, he had a begrudging respect for the man.

"He has no control over anything," Manasa responded, as her muscles grew exhausted from the rowing and they finally reached the shores of Naagpuri after a few hours. "I've known him since I was a child. My father had sent me and Vasuki out there to be trained with Vibhisana. He was a child back then. We had loads of fun, but he was in fact a quiet kid. He still keeps to himself."

Nanda rolled his eyes. They had reached Naagpuri at sundown and the place was littered with sapphire-coloured fire lights. They had an ingredient plucked from their own grass reserves that they mixed with the candle waxes to produce the colour of the skies that they worshipped.

"What should we do now?" Manasa asked Nanda.

"Before we meet Kadru, you come with me, and I'll get a few mercenaries I know around the corner to help us and be on constant guard."

"Sure," Manasa nodded. "And do you know these mercenaries as well as you know Maruda?"

Nanda grinned.

Manasa wiped her face clean with the water as she was cooped a small inn. Nanda had managed to get them a room here. The manager owed him.

That man owes to everyone and everyone owes to him.

She would never understand Nanda. He was so many things at once. And as she went over to the bed and laid herself down, closing her eyes, waiting for Nanda to return from his meeting with those mercenaries, she began to picture them together.

If there is no other woman, should I be with him?

It had not been his fault, but Vasuki's. And she almost felt bad for him. She began to think whether this plan would work or not,

or whether she'll be free enough to control Naagpuri, get favours from Tarakshya, and win the throne of Indragarh from Kali, defeat him and then . . .

Do what?

She hadn't thought about what she would do after this. It was her revenge plan for basically destroying her army, killing her brother . . . but after achieving the goal, she might just return back to Naagpuri, be with Nanda perhaps, and start a family. That sounded like a plan and a smile came over her face at the thought. Nanda was surely a sore in a person's life, but for her, he was someone she had taken a liking to. And he was helpful. He was just there for her sake, whenever she wanted.

She studied the intricate designs of the room. The Naagpuri inns weren't exactly peachy—the décor was just bad, the floorbeds were tainted, the beds were more like mattresses on the ground with a little elevation from the wooden platform, the ceiling had a slight, casual tapestry, there were firelights across the room, blue reflections, and Manasa's dark shadows danced as she moved inch by inch. She hated being here, but it was a good hiding place, better than being in her own place where Jamun would be waiting for her.

Everyone wants their own revenge.

Why was Jamun taking so much time to start his vendetta? Could he see that the city was weak and just jumped at the chance? Did he learn about Vasuki's death and that made him want to assume the throne? There were so many questions that Manasa had. She had no idea what Jamun was thinking. The man had no morals. He had gone behind Kadru's back and let people murder a family.

Oh, how cheerful I used to be!

Even though Vasuki wasn't perfect, she missed him. She missed those days she had spent with him. Since they were children, he had always teased her but also looked up to his big sister, always asking her for advice.

I couldn't even save my baby brother.

She didn't cry, but she did feel her head shrinking, her gut feeling weird. And that was when the door opened and she was startled, jumping up only to realize it was Nanda. He had a straw bag with him from which he pulled out some loaves of bread and a curry to share. Manasa hungrily wolfed it down as she was famished. Nanda sat opposite to her on a cushion and just looked at her for a while before Manasa asked, "What is it?"

"I've talked to the mercenaries. They are ready to do it for a sum of money. I've paid them as well."

"You had money?"

"Of course. I don't go around without it."

"How's your rib?"

He touched his wound. "It hurts."

"I never thanked you for saving me."

"You don't have to. I could see it."

Manasa smiled, and before she could begin the discussion about her and Nanda, Nanda pulled out a strange locket from the bag. "I want you to have this."

"Where did you hide this?"

"I was carrying it around." He handed it to her.

Manasa held it in her palms, looking at the sheen of the locket. It was a big glass amulet attached to a ribbon.

"What is this?"

"Got it from a trader when I was travelling before I heard about you coming here, I don't know." Nanda frowned. "Thought it'll look nice on you so I bought it."

"It's going to hinder me when I fight."

"Fight? You aren't fighting. Why do you think I hired the mercenaries? I don't want us to die."

"You want to fight a war from afar?"

"I want us to be safe, that's all. That's what I want."

Manasa shook her head. "We are going right now to Kadru

and then we are barging inside Jamun's house and taking his head with us."

"The other ministers wouldn't be happy."

"Once I'm in power, I wouldn't care what they think about."

Nanda chuckled. "That's so you."

"Also, uh . . ." Manasa sighed, "I wanted to tell you that after this is over, after we stop Jamun from basically ruining Naagpuri, we should talk about us."

Nanda was stunned for a moment. His brows went up and he gasped. "Are you serious?"

"I thought about it and it . . . well . . . it feels right."

"Yeah, sure." Nanda couldn't stop grinning.

"Stop smiling."

"Oh no, I won't, darling."

Manasa hit his shoulder playfully.

"My sources say he is in Naagmandal," Nanda spoke.

Manasa nodded. These sources might be the mercenaries who were out there asking around. They arrived at the little island of Naagmandal. The houses that stood here were owned by the important ministers. Initially, Vasuki had bought a house there too, but after his death it had been sold off.

"Also, you must know," Nanda said, as they walked towards the main entrance of Naagmandal, "I have alerted Vibhisana about the thing we are going to do."

Manasa shot him a look. "Why?"

"He wouldn't interfere. I know him. I just thought if this fails—"

"It won't fail and we don't need his help."

Manasa was stringent about it and as she reached the gates, the guards tried to question her but the mercenaries, who were

more than a dozen, grabbed them, pumelled them to the ground, and tossed them on the floor. Manasa opened the long, bronze gates and walked on the corridor, her each step making a crackling noise as all the guards in Naagmandal were alarmed. Seeing Manasa with her own little army, the guards hesitated to make a move as the mercenaries raved around looking for a worthy challenge.

She finally reached the main place where the long table was and the fire lamps were lit. In the middle, she saw Kadru looking over some papers. Her men got alarmed on seeing Manasa, but they eased up when Kadru waved them off.

"What is this, cousin?"

"This is desperation." Manasa walked over as she scanned the entire hall of the council. It was empty and the doors to each end of the hall were locked. She looked up the staircases and the balcony which was isolated. "There is a traitor amongst us."

"I don't understand."

"Jamun is the one who is planning a treatise with the Suparns for some reason and he was the reason behind Vasuki's family's death."

Kadru was confused. "But how's that possible? He was always there with me and he has been instrumental in rebuilding this city."

"No, he's not. He's planning to join hands with the bloody Suparns, my dear, so that he can get Amrit for himself and his men."

Kadru nodded her head. "I understand. Amrit? You mean the Somalata?"

Manasa nodded.

"Why is he doing that?"

"Taking revenge for what my father did to his father, perhaps."

Kadru sighed. "Sister, I'll be honest." Her voice was quiet. "I . . ."

And that's when the doors opened. Jamun entered with Naga soliders around him, a smile encased over his face. The soldiers that

were inside the room pulled out their swords and pointed them towards their mercenaries and Nanda.

Manasa was confused, her fingers shivering.

"He didn't do it because of a petty revenge." Kadru completed her sentence. "He did it because he worshipped your father, but unlike him you and your brother never wanted the Somas and wanted to stay away from the Suparns. Guess what?" A malicious grin swept her face. "We don't want that. We want to suck the Suparns dry for they have what belongs to us, gifted to us by the great Lord Sheesha. We decided to acquire it even if it meant giving them the first win, which was Vasuki's family."

"You . . ." Manasa gasped in horror, turning back, pulling out her dagger from the sheath. "You were part of this?"

"It was my plan, my dear sister, to send those assassins. Jamun doesn't like much bloodshed."

Jamun shrugged at that statement as if it wasn't true.

"I didn't want any complications and there were none. I wouldn't have harmed you at all if you had been in Indragarh. But no! You had to come to the South, damage us, our big, grand plan of taking back what's rightfully ours."

Manasa attacked Kadru, lurching from her place with the dagger. Kadru countered with a punch quicker than Manasa's stab. She fell back. Nanda yelled in horror, but Jamun's men shot an arrow right across his knee as he collapsed on the ground.

"Husband and wife, planning their deaths together. How poetic." Kadru came over to Manasa, knelt down, and stared at her. "You shall be executed, both of you, for interfering and talking to Maruda about us. After all, he was an idiot to welcome you, but hey, that's all right."

"The reason . . ." Manasa sighed, panting, "Vasuki didn't fight for Amrit was because he had seen our father going mad because of it. He had seen what it did to people when they had it."

"It's because they didn't know how to use it. And now we do."

And with that, Kadru punched Manasa in the gut as she lost consciousness, her worlds slowly colliding, both in dreams and reality.

25

Urvashi knew her way around her fort. With the help of her maid, Shivani, who had delivered her the letter, Urvashi had been able to leave Lord Kali's fort undetected and had now reached hers. Shivani had covered Urvashi's face with a shawl. Kali's men were still looking for her.

Guards stood at the front gate, so they decided to enter from the back. Shivani hoisted Urvashi, so that she could jump over the wall.

Shivani had told Urvashi that all things from their rooms had been kept in the storage room. While the papers and clothes had been burnt, other personal belongings had been stored.

Urvashi tiptoed on the dark corridors of the fort. There was a door ahead for the servants to enter and exit. Surprisingly, the armoury didn't have any soldiers on the ground floor, though when Urvashi did descend to the storage room area, she found two soldiers inside, talking.

She knew she had to distract them in some way or the other. She crept down and then turned to the nearest wall, carefully peering from the corner. They were chatting about the daily affairs of the disorganized state system.

Urvashi sighed. She had to do something. She closed her eyes, thinking about whatever her guru had taught her.

If you have no magical object that I've given you, the best thing to do is to act on your own. Trust your judgement.

Urvashi nodded to herself, and then she began to cry. Clutching her stomach, she fell on the ground. The two guards got alarmed and rushed to her.

"Oh dear, who is she?"

"Isn't she Vedanta's daughter?" said the other one, confused. "How did she . . . is she injured?"

Urvashi had her back to them.

"Girl, you fine?"

They came forward. One of them put his hand over her shoulder. At that moment, Urvashi turned, pulled the sword from the soldier's sheath and stabbed him in the stomach. Blood sprayed over her face which she wiped clean. The other soldier was stunned for a moment before he took out his sword, but then Urvashi kicked his knee. He knelt and groaned. She pointed the sword at his throat, puncturing it slowly.

"That's for betraying my father."

She had always liked the idea of killing people and the guru had liked her feistiness. She had learnt how to kill in her early days as a trainee when her guru had taught her quick, specific methods to defend herself in times of crisis. He had wanted to show her that she could use magic for the right reasons, that it will come in handy when she was in danger. And she needed her skills now.

She took the storage room keys from the guard's pocket and walked towards it, unlocking it. Finding herself in a tiny room, she began to search for her stuff, hoping it wasn't burnt. She had kept it in a turquoise-coloured bag made of tweed. Finally, after searching for some time, she found the stuff that belonged to her, including all the dolls she had carved with her knife along with some Charm. Charm was a powder that could be used to hypnotize people. Urvashi knew exactly how she was going to use it.

She packed her bag and dangled it on her shoulder as she made her way out.

She knew where she had to go now.

Next stop: Prison.

26

Lady Durukti was waiting in the same room again, with the same soldier standing outside to protect her. She saw shadows moving on the wall. It was Arjan, walking towards his cell.

"You are back." He had a smile on his emaciated face.

He looks beat.

Physically, Arjan was ripped, muscular like a wrestler. The bags under his eyes though told a different story. But Durukti was confident that Arjan could have taken Kali in a fight if only Kali hadn't ingested the Soma.The soldier stepped back as Arjan continued, "You are back, and that means you either have good news or bad news. But at least, you have news."

"I am fulfilling my promise." She was worried. Her hands were clammy, and for some reason her head felt heavy.

She began to think about Urvashi. She had vanished in the night and Durukti had no idea where she was. *Hopefully, Kali hasn't captured her . . . or has he?* But then, Durukti would have known. Perhaps Urvashi had left voluntarily. It was just messing with her mind.

After resting for an hour, she had come to meet Arjan. Giving the Soma to Arjan was her way of feeling a little less guilty for what she had done in Shambala.

"Can you release the others?"

"I can't do that. That would be stupid. It'll turn into a riot. I am giving you this." She handed him the pouch. "Use it well. I don't want you to kill Kali. Promise me that you won't."

"No, I won't." Arjan nodded, keeping the pouch. "You know how to ingest it?"

"I have no idea."

"I'll figure it out." He paused. "You seem worried."

"I am. Tomorrow you might actually win," she stifled a laugh, "and I am betraying my brother."

"No, you are betraying the king of this city."

Durukti knew Kali had to be stopped. Otherwise he would make things worse for everyone.

And that was when the bells began to ring and the trumpets were blown.

"Wait, what is going on?"

Arjan was confused and then a realization hit him. "Someone is escaping."

Arjan walked in front and peered out of the window. The window overlooked the field which was inside the prison. The field was filled with prisoners. They were jumping and beating the guards, escaping from there.

"Everyone has escaped. Did you do this?"

"No," Durukti was confused. "But how . . ."

"It doesn't matter. You should leave. You are Kali's sister. If they see you anywhere here, they will kill you. Thank you for the stones." He hugged Durukti.

"Are you escaping too?"

"It's wise to do so, right?" Arjan smiled as if he couldn't believe what was happening. He sprinted away into the dark.

Durukti stood motionless as Arjan ran away. She had stolen the Soma for nothing. There would be no fight now. This was a

disaster. She had no idea what was going on and hoped to god that Urvashi didn't have anything to do with it.

If so, Durukti was in big trouble.

27

Lord Kali was horrified—thinking about the red sea, the red world around him. He was paralyzed; his ears shut down so he couldn't hear anything. He walked the sands of the red earth, touching them slowly, realizing something was wrong with it. It was not sand. It was blood—the blood of his siblings.

And he turned when he felt someone touching the nape of his neck.

"You don't know the truth."

"What truth?" he blurted, angrily pushing and shoving the air as if it would help. There was no sound from the world he was in, but there were voices in his head.

"The truth about the fire."

"The fire?"

"That made you who you are."

Kali recalled the fire—back when he was at the village taking care of his siblings. Durukti had been young, but not as young as the others. And then the fire broke out and he tried to escape, but he couldn't save his siblings. Durukti had escaped with him. He had heard the infants crying. They had said it was the Tribals' conflict.

"You don't know anything."

"What is the truth?" He was panting now. Sweat trickled down his face.

"The conflict had nothing to do with the fire."

That's not what he remembered. What had really happened that night?

My subconscious is tricking me.

"No, I was." And there was a crackling laughter.

And then hands from the sand grabbed his feet and they began to pull him inside, down in the gutters of hell.

"WHO ARE YOU? WHO ARE YOU?" he kept screaming until his mouth was filled with blood and sand and he witnessed the oblivion, the inevitability.

He woke up.

Kali was sweating when he saw Koko and Vikoko by his bed. They would never dare to come in the room without his permission if it wasn't urgent.

"What happened?"

"My lord, the prisoners have escaped," said Koko.

"Escaped?"

Kali had dressed himself up. He was walking in the corridor, on his way to the prison. Koko and Vikoko trailed behind him.

"How many prisoners?"

"The count goes up to two hundred, my lord."

Two hundred! That's a disaster.

"Has everyone escaped?"

"Not all; some were stopped by the guards," said Vikoko.

"Kill the stupid prison guards. And there should be round-the-clock surveillance on the streets. Any person with a loincloth

around their groin should be shot by an arrow. Take the Yakshas if you want."

"Yes, my lord." Koko nodded.

Kali was about to reach the prison when he saw the horrible disaster from outside. Partially the prison was on fire, while the guards had grabbed some of the prisoners who had tried to escape. The prison had a rocky, bricked exterior with large poles and watchtowers. There were barbed wires, serrated fences, and grilled windows. It was a basilisk of a building.

"How does one escape this fortress?"

"They say the guards helped them escape."

"Helped?"

"We questioned them, but they say they don't remember anything."

Kali shook his head. "You mean to say they were hypnotized?"

Koko shrugged while Vikoko meekly nodded.

"What the hell is going on?"

And Kali went inside the prison.

Kali was passing down the cells—empty cells. And with each cell, his heart raced a bit more. He felt angrier as each cell represented his failure of not being able to handle this prison, these prisoners.

Now the people will hate me. They will say that I am worse than Vedanta.

Kali's soldiers were behind him. Koko and Vikoko were in front of him when Kali said, "Take out a petition saying that we are keeping everything under control, all right? How many soldiers do we have?"

"My lord, you have sent two thousand of your men to the Vanar captain and the rest of them are stationed at the villages to maintain order. Some of them have been stationed in other

cities. So we have a thousand men." Vikoko explained the entire situation.

Thousand?

"Call the ones who are stationed at the villages to come to the city. These prisoners must be captured. Who knows what atrocities they will commit in the city now that they are free." Kali scratched his head as he thoughtfully mused over the situation.

"But sir, the village people have been protesting against the rise in tax rates. The soldiers stationed there have been keeping these protests under control," said Koko.

Kali sighed. "Kill them then. Whoever is protesting, just kill them. In fact, even if one person protests, execute him. We don't want any revolts. We have a major crisis on our hands. Biggest criminals in the city roam the streets and right now, they could be slaughtering and raping the citizens, and according to me, that's what should be dealt with first."

He finally stopped when he realized that one of the cell doors, even though it was open, was not empty. Curious, he turned to see who was inside. The figure glowed in the shadow of the moonlight being emitted from the grilled window. It was a young boy. He was sitting cross-legged. He had his back to Kali, his wavy black hair glimmering.

Kali realized who it was. Turning around, Arjan cracked his knuckles, a smile dancing on his face. "Hi there, Kali."

"Why didn't you escape with your friends?"

"Because I promised you a fight tomorrow."

Damn! I forgot about that!

Kali nodded. "So you stayed? What a fool! I'll crush you like an ant," Kali said, confident.

Arjan stood up. He walked towards Kali and looking straight in his eyes, he softly said, "We'll see."

Kali was unnerved, though he didn't show it. There was something in his eyes; a glint, a fire. Kali ordered his guards to

close the cell doors, but he could see that Arjan hadn't stopped smiling.

And for some reason, Arjan reminded him of someone.

He reminded him of Kalki.

28

Urvashi knew she was in trouble when the criminals turned on her. The only person who was supporting her was a handsome, young man by the name of Rudra who was keeping them in control.

They had situated themselves in the armoury of Urvashi's old home. They had gone in, grabbed the guards, tied them up, and took all the heavy weapons for themselves.

For some reason, Urvashi did feel triumphant since she had taken her fort back, but it didn't mean things were all right. She had asked two prisoners to dress up as city guards and stand outside, making sure that no one suspected anything—that there were more than two hundred prisoners inside the fort.

And she was not sure if her father would have approved of the prisoners that she had kept inside, to be out here, on the same floor that he had walked on. But that didn't matter now.

Father is dead. And I'm here. And I have to take care of the bloody situation.

But that didn't mean that just because Urvashi had charmed her way in the prison, hypnotizing the guards to open the cells and promising each prisoner a better life, they would listen to her. Some of them had listened, some of them hadn't. And she had to prove that she was worthy of leading them, even though she was just a young girl.

They were in the common hall. As Urvashi stood at the pedestal quietly listening to Rudra, the sleek-haired man explained to the prisoners in detail. "Men! We are finally free from the tyranny of the wrestling and the pandering of Lord Kali. And now, we can do anything."

Everyone shouted in jubilation, hooting loudly.

"But we should not forget why this happened." Rudra looked at Urvashi. "She is the reason we are here."

Some of them grunted and some smiled at her.

"She's Vedanta's daughter! We should burn her!" someone called from the crowd.

"No!" Rudra cried out. "Vedanta had kept us in, but she let us out. We should not judge her for what her father did to us. And now we can go and do whatever we want to do."

People murmured to themselves when Urvashi whispered to Rudra, "I need to speak to you in private."

Rudra nodded, taking Urvashi aside while Harsha tried to handle the situation by making jokes.

"What happened?"

"I have not helped you all escape because I liked you all."

Rudra stopped smiling. "What do you want from us?"

"Fight and take the throne from Lord Kali. I want you to be my men-in-arms."

Rudra rolled his eyes. "Girl, all of these, they are not someone you can hire. They work on fear, not on money, and they will only work for someone they respect."

Urvashi clenched her jaw as Rudra went back to all the prisoners. "Lady Urvashi wants us to join her in the cause to fight and end Lord Kali's reign."

The prisoners laughed.

"I want to sleep and bed a wench and do a lot of things before I do that," someone else said.

"Yeah, true that, Rudra," said Harsha, scratching his beard.

Urvashi sighed as she came forward, trying to sound as womanly as she could. From the corner of her eye, she could see Shivani watching her intently. "I know I am not the ideal person to lead you all. I'm young. But I know one thing. I can give you a better life and I can give you riches and women if you work with me. Lord Kali is weak right now. We should attack him right now and we can take the throne."

"What about the soldiers? They'll turn on us," someone from the group cried.

"We just need to get rid of Lord Kali. Once we do that, we shall have the support of the soldiers. They follow him out of fear." And if needed, she will instil that fear in them when she ruled, she thought while clinging to her wooden doll.

"And why should we listen to someone who carries a doll?"

Urvashi shook her head as she walked down towards the man who had just spoken and plucked his hair. He groaned, grabbing her arm in the process, but Rudra told him to back off.

"What was that about?"

"I'll show you something," Urvashi said. She wrapped the coil of hair around the doll. "You must wonder how can a young girl like me enter and free two hundred of you. Think hard."

They all narrowed their gazes.

"Because I know something that you don't."

"Shut up, whore!" the man shouted, scratching his hair. "First you pluck my hair and now you say shit—"

And that is when Urvashi used her hairpin and stabbed the doll. Instantly the man looked down, seeing a wound opening up and spraying blood from his torso until he fell back and contorted in pain. Urvashi pulled the pin and cleaned it, wearing it back to tighten her hair. Everyone gasped.

"Guess what," Urvashi said glancing at the shocked faces of Rudra, Harsha, and even Shivani. "I know magic. Be on my good side and you shall have everything. Be on my bad side," she

signalled at the dying prisoner, "you shall die miserably. Do not underestimate me."

Everyone went silent.

And Urvashi liked it.

Oh yes, she did.

29

Kalki found himself in a strange world.

It didn't look like Illavarti. In fact, there was no land. It was only water and he was in the midst of it, swimming. His mouth opened and the water engulfed him. He grabbed the reefs as he struggled underwater, when something grabbed him. He looked down to see a huge boar who had his tusk around his body, carrying him upwards, swimming towards the surface, and finally Kalki was out, under the beating sun. He sighed in relief, his eyes red, clearly frightened at the ordeal.

Kalki turned to see the boar swim back inside.

"What are you doing here?" a voice called out from the back.

Kalki turned. The water was everywhere, covering every land. Only the long, dark trees remained, sprawled above the unending waters, almost touching the skies and the mountains. The hills were barely visible at this sea level. Otherwise, everything was in ruins.

"Where are you?" Kalki tried to float as much as he could, driving his feet.

"Down."

Kalki lowered his gaze and saw a strange figure underwater. He dove in again. This time, he was in control, and he looked at the figure who was speaking to him from beneath.

How is he speaking under water?

The figure was tall, daunting, dark-skinned, like the cloudy skies. He had a strange box-like helmet around him that was helping him breathe inside, and it was designed in such a way that it looked like a boar's head with conical tusks. A chakra hung from his neck and a mace clung to his belt. He was in a dhoti as well, but it was dark in colour. He was barefoot.

"You cannot speak under here. Let me take you to the lands." And with that, he began to swim upwards.

Perhaps he can speak under water because of the helmet. It prevents the water from getting inside, creating a breathing space for him. It didn't make sense though. He finally reached a boat which had a small mast. The man climbed over it and helped Kalki up.

And behind the man stood the boar that had helped Kalki out of the water. It jumped inside the boat, drying himself by shaking his bulbous body.

And then Kalki saw what had happened—the entire land was plunged in a tsunami-like situation and only the mountains and skies seemed to be safe. Not only that, he also saw boats of different shapes and sizes, far away from theirs. Some ships were there as well.

"What is this place?" he asked the figure who took out his helmet, revealing a dashing, young man with wavy hair that reached his waist.

"This, my friend, is Illavarti." He sighed, putting down the boar-shaped helmet as he patted his pet boar. "The question is, what are you doing here?"

Kalki realized he was Channelling. *Of course. That's why I'm in a different reality. And this figure, he's just a memory of the past.*

"You are Varaha," Kalki muttered to himself. "The third Avatar. But weren't you supposed to have a . . ." then he looked at the helmet, "of course."

"You have questions. Ask." Varaha wrapped his arms around his lean frame as he waited for Kalki to speak. His entire body

glistened under the sun and his hair was dripping water on his back. The boat rocked over the uneven stream of water.

"I have more questions about this world now."

"This is all because of Hiranyaksha and Hiriyakashipu. They led this world into this and now like a pirate, they have stolen my lady love Bhoomi, and have escaped through his ship."

Pirates? Oh god! It sounded bad.

"It's an apocalypse and I have to stop them and protect Illavarti from this disaster."

But how will one protect a world which is filled with water?

According to what Kalki had read, Varaha had used his big tusks to lift the earth from the clutches of the water and free it from its bondages.

"I am being aided by the snouty king of sea, Varuna."

Varuna? The god? He's a king. Of course, that's how it happens. Karma doesn't make you a god, your deeds do. Varaha, right now, is just another boatman with a boar, but later on when his journey finishes, he'll be termed a god.

Will I be too?

At that thought, Kalki was fascinated.

"We have found a way to get rid of this, but we have a lot to do. So tell me now, baby face, what is it you want?"

"I uh . . . baby face?"

"Yeah, come on, baby face."

This was the first time he was having an *informal* discussion with one of the Avatars. Lord Govind had been wracked with guilt, Lord Narshimha had seemed kind of aloof, Lord Raghav had been kind, but Lord Varaha seemed cool.

"I'm confused. I want to know how I can use my strength properly."

"The problem is that we often think strength comes from the muscles. No. It comes from here." He pointed at his head. "One receives the truest and purest strength from self-belief." He

stood up as the boar licked his legs, busy in his own world, making grunting noises. "You have stopped believing in yourself. You feel defeated. You feel hopeless. I see it in your eyes, lad."

Kalki nodded. "I do feel defeated. But it's not my fault. I was defeated. I lost everyone. I lost Bala . . . I lost my father . . . I lost Ratri . . . and . . . I lost Lakshmi. How can I be the saviour if I keep losing everyone I love?"

Varaha felt the pain that Kalki was going through. "What do you see around here?"

Kalki turned to see an endless amount of water. "Sea."

"This used to be a land, you know. This is my defeat." Varaha watched it like a warrior who had grown weary from personal loss. "Perhaps it is necessary for us to fail because it gives us the opportunity to succeed. Without failure, we will never learn and if we don't learn, we'll never succeed. Now I know how to defeat the two brothers who did this, but I didn't know better previously." He paused, looking at Kalki, straight in the eyes. "You are afraid of responsibility and I can see that. Because deep down, I was afraid too. Now as each waking moment goes by, I think of Bhoomi and what she would be doing with those monsters. I feel weak. I feel defeated, just like you. But you know what keeps me going?"

Kalki shook his head.

"The choice that I made."

"Of saving her?"

Lord Varaha smiled. "No, of doing the right thing. And in this world, if you constantly do the right thing, you'll be the strongest person alive." He grabbed Kalki's shoulders, tightening his hands around them. "Don't forget, your strength will come if you believe in it, so start believing in yourself because you'll be committing a crime if you don't."

Kalki nodded. "Also, how did the boar know that he had to save me?"

"Because I told him to."

Kalki laughed. "How is that possible?"

"We are capable of so much, you and me. We are. We stop believing, we lose hope, and we forget ourselves. You know who we are? We are Avatars, chosen by Lord Vishnu to roam the earth and finish evil. That's who we are and if we disappoint, what is the point of it all?" He winked at him.

And then his reality dissolved, and he opened his eyes to see himself in the same hut. Everyone was fast asleep. It was dark outside.

Kalki walked to the door where two Pisach were standing with their spears. Looking at him the Pisach got alarmed but Kalki held his arms up, trying to show them that he meant no harm.

We are capable of so much.

What is the point of it all?

I told him to do it.

Kalki recalled his conversation with Lord Varaha as he closed his eyes. He had forgotten about Shuko and he had no idea where he was now. And so, using all his powers, believing in himself, he let the energy surge inside him. Lord Vishnu has chosen him to serve this realm and it'll be a crime if he didn't follow it.

Shuko? Can you listen to me?

I can.

Damn.

Stop saying damn, boy. You left me all alone.

What? You were the who ran away when we were surrounded by the Simhas!

Well, no harm done. You are safe now. What's up, son?

Kalki couldn't believe he was talking to his parrot. In fact, he couldn't believe he had the capability of talking to him.

How am I talking to you?

Because you are trying to.

But how?

We are meant for each other, son. You think you found me in Shambala.

No, I found you. I waited for you. The prophecy states that the last Avatar shall ride with an eternal White Horse and a Parrot gifted by Lord Shiva.

How do you know all of this?

Because Lord Shiva taught me.

Lord Shiva talks to you?

He talks to all of us. We just choose to not listen to him, most of the time. And I did. And I know things.

There is a prophecy about me?

Of course. Shuko stifled a laugh. His voice was so human. *Though there are different versions of it and most of them don't make sense. We can talk about it later. Right now, figure out a way to escape this place.*

I'm still processing the fact that you are talking to me. Kalki's eyes were closed. He was concentrating on his trail of thoughts.

Well, process it later. Now listen, I stand at the tallest tree of their little place and I see no escape for you. There are guards who won't let you go out and even if you do, it is impossible for you to travel to the other side of the land since most of it is a swamp. You need to cross a bridge that goes through their leader's hut. Other than that, it's impossible for you to go out.

Can't you distract them?

Oh, I wish. It's quite the tough job, this one. And if they catch me, they eat me.

I understand. I can try to escape though.

Kalki stopped the trail of thought with Shuko and went back inside the hut. As he plopped down to sleep, he heard Padma murmur something in her sleep. She had been so brave today.

Perhaps she's not who I thought she was.

The morning dawned. He hadn't slept the night. The time had come as he could hear the loud hooting. He could also see Ratna practising with her weapons. Kripa and Padma had asked him to choose his own weapons.

Kalki looked forlorn. Even though he was nodding to most of what Kripa and Padma were speaking, he was thinking hard about what Lord Varaha had taught him, what Lord Narsimha had told him.

"Tell me more about the Pisach, Kripa," Kalki said.

"Ah well, mate, what do you want to know about them?"

"You said if a Pisach gets defeated, he has to kill himself and get eaten by the other Pisach, because it's dishonourable?"

Kripa nodded glumly. "It sounds pathetic, I know."

"Do they have a lot of ego?"

"In a way, yes."

"So they think they are superior to others, and if they lose, they don't get a second chance."

"You can say so, yeah."

Kalki nodded.

"So what weapon are you choosing?" Padma asked.

Kalki looked at her. And then he smiled without responding to her as he walked to Ratna who was sharpening her sword. She had really pretty eyes, wide and fish-like. Somehow, she reminded him of Lord Varaha. She had a full mouth, an acquiline nose, and a stern expression, as if she would kill Kalki at this moment.

"I don't want to fight you," he said to her.

Ratna was silent. Smrit on the other hand, stood up. "Well, you have to."

"We should work together and get out of here."

"Impossible! That'll be a coward's way! Are you afraid you will be defeated?" Smrit laughed.

Kalki could see the pain behind Ratna's face. There was something else. She was hiding something.

"Why isn't your friend . . ." he looked at Smrit, "responding to me?"

"Because she doesn't want to," Smrit grunted.

Ratna put an arm around Smrit to calm her down. "How do you plan to escape from here, kid?"

Kid? Kalki had assumed that Ratna was around his age, though a little wiser than he was.

"Make a run for it."

"Na, I would rather kill you and then stay safe."

"What'll be the point of it? Only one will survive in the end. It's better we escape first."

"Don't worry, we will find a way."

"Let's find a way together."

"Listen!" exclaimed Ratna, gritting her teeth. "You got us into this, so don't try making up to us by putting us in your plan. For all we know, you don't give a damn about us, kid. You only care about your friends who let a girl get eaten by these creatures."

"We didn't have a choice."

"Yes, you did. We could have fought—"

"And gotten killed."

Ratna was furious. "Don't forget you are responsible for all of us being here."

Kalki shook his head. He went back to Padma and Kripa, this time to select a weapon. *It's better to just kill the bald lady.*

Kalki was ready as he tried to maintain his balance over the net and in front of him stood Ratna Maru with her sword. They both had swords, for they were well versed in the art of swordfighting. The net dangled when they moved. Kalki made sure he wouldn't get his feet stuck like Padma.

He looked at Brahmaputraksh who was doing the same ritual again, announcing the fight, letting the duel happen, in his strange, exotic language.

We all have a choice.

Lord Varaha's words echoed in Kalki's mind as he looked intently at Brahmaputraksh.

Of doing the right thing.

As Brahmaputraksh was about to clap, Kalki yelled, "WAIT!"

The leader of the Pisach stopped speaking. All the Pisach looked at Kalki.

"What is it?"

Kalki raised his sword straightening towards Brahmaputraksh. "I CHALLENGE YOU FOR THE DUEL!"

30

Lord Kali was prepared.

He didn't know much about wrestling, but it didn't really matter. He would crush Arjan. As he wrapped bandages around his palms, made his dhoti tighter around the waist and wiped sweat from his face, he was visited by Lord Kuvera.

"What on seven heavens are you planning to do?" the fat man burst in Kali's office as Koko and Vikoko tried to push him out.

Kali waved his hand at Koko and Vikoko to stop.

"You are an idiot to do this," he continued.

Kali cracked his knuckles. "Do not worry about this." He went outside the room as Koko and Vikoko followed him with Kuvera at the back, trying to meet his pace. "I have it under control."

"People are in agony. I don't want the king of this city fighting a petty prisoner."

"They need to see who's in power," Kali grunted as they reached outside the fort, where his horse was waiting for him.

"They know already. What you should be doing is scouting the streets with your men and stopping the prisoners." Kuvera was turning red in anger.

Kali sat on the horse, ready to go to the wrestling field in the outskirts of the city. "I promised a fight and I shall deliver it." He looked at Koko. "How many have you gathered at the field?"

"Many, my lord. They are quite excited for the match. We have managed to contain the news about the prisoners' escape," Koko responded, sitting on his horse.

"I'm glad."

Kuvera shook his head. "You are being an idiot, my lord."

"You are afraid, aren't you?" Kali grinned. "That those prisoners might just come over to you at night and slit your throat. You are afraid for your life."

Kuvera didn't say anything but there was a flash of it—the fear that held him tight, grappled him hard. "You are being selfish right now. That's not how a king behaves. I let Vedanta die because I believed in your vision."

"No, you believed in taking Naagpuri."

"And will you deliver it when you can't even control your own city?"

Kali sighed as he stepped down from the horse and grabbed Kuvera by the throat, pulling his fat body up. "Don't think that just because you helped me with Vedanta you owe me something. You owe me nothing. I crack your skull today and the Yakshas will be mine. You are lucky I'm being nice but if you keep calling me incompetent, you'll meet Vedanta soon." And he pointed at the long spikes which were stuck and pierced to the ground with dead, impaled corpses that had flies brimming around it. "All right?"

Kuvera nodded.

Kali dropped Kuvera and he fell on the ground, coughing loudly. He mounted his horse and left for his fight.

31

Manasa knew what was going to happen. She was tied up in a rotten cell and she had no idea what was happening to Nanda. She wanted to cry but she had to be strong. The Naga prisons were ordinary, though they floated on the river and they were quite small in size. Outside, they had a stony path which floated over the water and that led to the main shoreline where Naagmandal was. There were individual prisons spread across the entire city and presumably Nanda was in the other floating cell.

She saw a shadow on the wall and realized it was none other than Kadru, in her battle gear—armour and knee pads, with a dangling sword. The Naga guard opened the door for her. She entered inside, her face impassive.

"How are you doing, cousin?" Kadru asked.

"Why are you here?" Manasa quietly said without looking at her. *You backstabber. How could you be idiotic enough to believe Jamun?*

"To bid you farewell, since you are being punished for treason."

"Treason? What have I done against the crown? You are the one who should be in for treason."

"You shouldn't have come." Kadru sighed. "I didn't want to kill you. After all, you are my cousin, my blood. And I should never hurt my blood—"

"You murdered Vasuki's children! At least you could have left them. I shall never forgive you for that."

Kadru nodded. "I don't want you to forgive me. I did what I did out of necessity."

"What necessity?"

Kadru twisted her lips thoughtfully. "Ah shit, you are about to die. What the hell?" She pulled out her arm gear to reveal deep-seated gashes over it that ran from her elbow to the wrist. "I've been hiding this from people."

"What is this?"

"I am dying. In fact, I will be dead in a few days if I don't find an antidote to this poison running in my veins."

Manasa understood the situation. "That's why you need Amrit. You need to save yourself."

"Yes," Kadru sighed. "I have to do it otherwise I'll die and you know how much I fear death."

Oh, how Manasa knew it. In her childhood, whenever Kadru thought about how she would have to die one day, she would curl up in Manasa's arms, crying. Manasa would pacify her, saying that they would go to Vaikuntha, the abode of Lord Vishnu and Lord Sheesha.

"But that doesn't justify you killing kids and families."

"Tarakshya wasn't ready for a peace treaty otherwise. He didn't get the satisfaction of killing Vasuki, so he went for the family."

And you let him.

Manasa sighed. "So your plan is to visit Tarakshya, learn about his city, take the Amrit that's scarcely there—"

"We know he has a lot of reserves. We have got inside sources. We just need a way in and once we get in, we take the Amrit for good."

"That's what my father tried to do and you know what happened to him?"

"Killed by his people for following this mad idea, I know." Kadru smiled. "That's why I have Jamun for that, to handle the ministers and the army. They are under control and they are ready for this. They are just angry that the Suparns are getting everything. It's time they share the good things with us. The problem with Vasuki was that he had been more interested in politics with Lord Kuvera, the Yakshas who were never really anything but thieves and idiots. He had been in constant conflict with Kuvera, but he had forgotten about Tarakshya. And that's what bugged Jamun. Tarakshya has far more intelligent and necessary resources. We need them for Naagpuri to survive the next thousand years."

"Suparns are a disciplined tribe while Nagas are famous for indulgence, my dear."

Kadru stood up, leaving for the grilled gate. "Oh, we have changed since those times. We know where to use the Amrit this time."

"Where? To your army? Make them strong and then raving madmen?"

"We know exactly how to use it and once I'm cured, we will conquer the entire Dakshini and then go for Udaiyas. I'm going to change the entire Illavarti with the plans I have. The Nagas will grow in number. They'll not be a little tribe in the outskirts anymore. They'll be supreme leaders of Illavarti. Bye, cousin. It was nice chatting with you. I'll be attending your execution."

And she left, leaving Manasa to wonder what Kadru was going to do with the Amrit.

32

Kalki realized it won't be wise to fight Brahmaputraksh when he stripped his clothes away, just wearing a loincloth. Kalki saw strange inked designs all over his body, strange and velvety, some of them glimmering in the sinister light. He jumped on the net and Kalki saw him tiptoeing his way around. He walked elegantly. And unlike the others, his feet didn't get stuck in the net.

Brahmaputraksh pulled out two Chakras and his hair fell. They were waist-long.

The Chakras acted like hairpins?

"You know what these are?" he asked, touching the inked designs.

"No."

"Karma. My deeds. All the crimes, the murders, everything I've done, it's there in the Pisachi language. And now, I will ink your name next. Once we are done, that is."

Good luck, Shuko spoke.

Kalki looked up as he saw Shuko sitting on one of the many branches. He grinned at him and then looked at the dangling Pisachs who were waiting for him to be defeated by Brahmaputraksh, almost licking their lips in anticipation.

Kalki pulled out his sword and waited for Brahmaputraksh to charge, but he didn't. He remained at his spot. "I never say no to

a challenge but no one challenges me. What makes you so special, *boy*?"

"I am the Avatar of Lord Vishnu, the soldier sent to Illavarti to end people like you."

"Are you serious?" He laughed, beating his chest. "I'm glad I'm fighting a soldier. Come on, then."

Kalki looked at the ropes that bound the net on which they were standing. And then he pulled out his sword and flung it right across Brahmaputraksh. Brahmaputraksh immediately turned, dodging it as the sword sliced the rope that bound the net.

"You missed." He laughed as he walked further.

"I was supposed to miss."

And he stopped at what Kalki just said when he realized the net was ripping apart from one end. The net broke as it toppled both Kalki and Brahmaputraksh from it.

Kalki grabbed on to it. So did Brahmaputraksh.

"Being smart? I like that!" Brahmaputraksh grinned. With the help of the Chakras, he began to climb the vertically inclined net now.

He came close to Kalki's legs and slashed his ankle. Kalki groaned loudly, losing his balance. With a sudden jerk, he leapt from the net and clutched one of the vines on which a Pisach was hanging. Kalki just punched him and tossed him in the swamp.

"You cannot keep running, boy."

And then Brahmaputraksh, like a monkey, jumped on the other vine. Now they both were on opposite vines, dangling mid-air. They glared at each other. Kalki, from the corner of his eye could see Padma and Kripa almost biting their nails in anticipation.

"I don't plan to."

"You don't have a weapon."

"I don't need one, boy!" Kalki grinned.

Brahmaputraksh snorted as the Pisach began to make hooting noises. He swung his vine towards Kalki with the Chakra in his

hand. Rather than hurting Kalki, he slashed his vine with the Chakra, toppling Kalki from it and making him fall down in the bog.

As Kalki felt the muddiness of the deep, dark swamp, his mouth and his vision began to blur, his feet went numb, and in the midst of all this he could hear the cries of Kripa and Padma.

Was this how he was going to die?

33

Lord Kali touched the red sand as the hooting increased.

The public was thouroughly enjoying it. The thrill of wrestling, the intoxication of wine, and bloodshed for entertainment. What was not to like?

And in front of the lord, stood his opponent.

Arjan glared at Kali. There was a certain air of confidence in him but Lord Kali didn't fear him. He swore to crush him. He saw Durukti sitting with Koko and Vikoko at her side at the front stage of the arena. The soldiers were standing at each exit and entrance, with spears and javelins, ready to strike if anything untoward happened.

Master Reddy came on the arena and clapped his hands to start the match. Kali expected Arjan to pounce at him, but he didn't. He remained afar.

"I haven't told you this, you know," Kali prompted him, jumping in the air to energize himself. "You will be happy to know that I have taken care of your friends."

Arjan was silent.

"I was thinking of keeping this a secret but this would be the perfect time to tell you."

The sun was harsh and the smell of sand engulfed their nostrils while the public cheered loudly.

"I burnt your friends down at Ratri's house. They all died, you know. Each one of them."

Arjan's eyes widened a fraction.

"You destroyed my court. They paid the price for it. And now you will."

"You killed Kalki?" he quietly spoke.

"Yep. He burnt just like all your friends. There were so many of them, so many bodies. In fact, that Ratri's friend . . . the big guy . . ." Kali scratched his head.

"Bala," Arjan sighed.

"Yeah, I broke his spine. Like I'll break yours today."

"You killed him?" Arjan looked up. "I thought I would take pity on you. But I've changed my mind."

"Pity? Me?" Kali stifled a laugh.

At that, Arjan ran towards Kali with full speed. Kali dodged him. Arjan turned and then with a swift mvement, grabbed Kali by the legs. Kali began to elbow him on the back, but none of it worked. None of his powers were working. Instead, Arjan pummelled him to the ground and with his mighty fists began to punch Kali on his face.

Slowly, Kali began to see spots of darkness. *What is going on?*

With a slick punch in the gut, Arjan fell back and Kali arose, blinking hard, trying to come to his senses.

"How's that possible?"

"Oh, you need more proof? Your end is now, Kali!"

The crowd cheered as Arjan ran towards Kali and lurched at him. He hit Kali with his elbow. The impact was so strong that Kali almost fainted. Arjan came forward and took a sly turn at the back, grabbing Kali by the waist. He somersaulted him in the air. Kali fell on the ground, hurting his spine.

The crowd started cheering uproariously. Arjan grabbed Kali's legs with one hand and with another, he grabbed his throat as he began to choke him.

Master Reddy came in between as Kali began to thump in surrender. But Arjan didn't stop. When Master Reddy tried to push Arjan, Arjan with his free leg kicked him in the groin, making him fall paces away.

"You . . . took . . . the . . . Somas . . ." That was the only thing that could've made Arjan this strong, Kali thought.

But no one can become so powerful even with Somas. It takes time; it's gradual. How was it possible in Arjan's case?

Kali could feel his bones splintering. He knew he was leaving this world. He saw Koko and Vikoko jumping in the arena. Durukti looked at the spectacle in horror. The crowd had stopped jeering.

And then Arjan stopped.

Kali breathed a sigh of relief as he was pulled away by Koko and Vikoko. He turned to see Arjan who seemed confused—and then Kali realized what had really happened. The crowd had stopped cheering because someone new had joined the stands.

The prisoners!

So many of them came in with weapons of all kinds. They started killing the guards, murdering them on the spot. And from the main entrance, with an army of her own, entered Urvashi.

And she had a smile on her face as pointed towards Kali.

"My lord!" Koko called, grabbing Kali by the arms. "We must leave right now."

No. No.

He was being pulled by his guards as he saw the undefeated Arjan standing frozen amidst the entire mayhem. The arena was filled with soldiers and prisoners fighting each other, as Kali was pulled away from all of it, with Lady Durukti in the centre. The people were trying to exit and most of them did, though the nobles were killed in the process. He didn't see Kuvera anywhere though.

Blood splashed and sprayed as Kali began to realize that his end had arrived and it had arrived for good.

34

Manasa was bound and gagged as she was taken to the execution river. Nagas had a different way of treating criminals—death by drowning. It would either be that or beheading. But for her and Nanda, as of now, it was drowning. She was being pushed towards the lake. She was to be drowned right here with her mouth gagged and her hands tied. Afterwards, she was to be given a burial. Her coffin would be thrown in this very lake.

They reached the shoreline where all the soldiers and nobles were standing. She saw Jamun standing in his multicoloured cloak covering his fat body. He was glaring at her. She glanced at Nanda. He looked apologetic.

Kadru stood in front of them, close to the lake. "In the name and holiness of Lord Sheesha who has created the beautiful land of Naagpuri, we sentence you to death."

Nanda's mouth was gagged and his hands were tied. Ropes had been tied to their legs so they could be pulled back up for the burial. A bag of stones would also be tied to their ankles to make them go to the deepest level of the lake.

And then they were told to stand close to the shoreline and for the first time, the lake looked scary and deep to Manasa. She used to come here with her father.

"I plan to never die, my child," he had said.

Manasa was ready for her execution. It had been a tough ride. She looked at Nanda again and blinked at him twice. *I love you.* She wanted to tell him this and at that moment, her eyes welled with tears. Her wish wouldn't come true now.

This is it.

Their gags were taken off. "We forgot there is a tradition we follow now. We would like to know if there are any last words," Kadru said.

Manasa watched Nanda. *Hopefully he would say something.* But he looked distracted. Manasa noticed that he was trying to cut his restraints.

How did he get a knife?

And then Manasa saw the man who was holding Nanda. *He is one of the mercenaries!* And the mercenary winked at her. *He must have given the dagger to him.*

Nanda had been smart enough to have some of the mercenaries dress up as the soldiers, to act from the inside. It made sense, since Nanda was always full of surprises.

"Yes, I would like to say something," Nanda began. "I love you, Manasa. And I wish we could have stayed together forever. But remember my gift." He looked at the pendant which was really a Shard of glass. It was tiny but sharp. "Always remember it." He winked.

And then his hands were free and with a single jerk, he flung the dagger at Kadru's eye. There was a sharp piercing sound as she cried in horror.

"JUMP!" he yelled at her.

"Not without you."

At that moment, the mercenary and Nanda began to fight the soldiers as much as they could, with one of them punching Nanda in the gut.

"You . . . need . . . to jump . . ."

Manasa realized the urgency. When one of the soldiers came to

grab her, she elbowed him. She immediately jumped in the lake. She saw Kadru yelling in pain, but she also saw Nanda being stabbed in the stomach again as the mercenary got beheaded by Jamun's men.

No. Please don't die.

She couldn't see what happened after that. Water engulfed her as she desperately tried to stay afloat. The current was strong and took her away from the shore. She had no idea where this lake would take her.

Remember my gift.

Manasa realized what Nanda had meant. She began to jerk harshly letting the locket flow out of her neck. Then she grabbed the string tight by the mouth. She put her arm next to the conical Shard of the locket and began to graze the ropes against the Shard until they ripped apart. Her hands free.

She now did the same with her feet. Once, they were done, she flapped her arms and came on the surface, panting in relief. She had come quite far from the shores of Naagpuri islands. She was now going towards a path she was unfamiliar with.

The ravine was takig her into the unknown.

As she swam in the lake, she recalled her husband's last words.

I love you too, Nanda. I always have.

35

Kalki grabbed on to something and pushed himself out of the bog. His entire face was covered in mud and grease which he wiped out. And he was able to stand clearly over the swamp. It had taken a toll on his strength, but he had been able to do it. He walked towards one of the tree trunks for support.

And finally, he saw Brahmaputraksh fall in the swamp as well, and he was easily standing over it too.

"To master the bog, one must be trained well. How did you do it?" he asked.

Walking slowly towards Kalki, his razor-sharp Chakra slashed across Kalki's chest. Another stinging pain coursed through his body. His ankle wound was also burning since all the bacteria and dirt had mixed in with the blood.

"You are a weaker kind of human. You are a Manav while we are . . ." and Brahmaputraksh went straight towards Kalki's chest.

Kalki stopped him.

His eyes opened as mud trickled from the corners of his forehead. He twisted Brahmaputraksh's arm as he groaned in pain.

"I'm not weak."

Kalki gave a swift smack on his torso. Brahmaputraksh staggered. And then he felt another smack on the head. Kalki grabbed him by the throat as Brahmaputraksh tried to attack

him with the second Chakra. Kalki let him stab his arm. Blood seeped from his skin, but it didn't hurt him. His focus was only on Brahmaputraksh as his fingers began to clasp him tighter and tighter, until he could feel the Pisach's larynx begin to break.

Kalki pulled Brahmaputraksh up from the bog. He rammed his fists into chest and shoved him inside the bog again. Brahmaputraksh struggled trying to push himself up, but Kalki didn't let him.

"It's over," Kalki growled. "It's over."

And then the protesting stopped for good. The hands stopped flaying and there was no guttery sound anymore.

He was gone for good.

Kalki sighed as he touched the blood on his skin. He began to walk forward, out of the heavy, deep bog that surrounded him, where there was a ladder. But before he could climb the ladder, he fell down, unconscious.

Kalki opened his eyes, gasping for breath when he realized he was watching his own shadow at the ceiling. He was in a dark room and his eyes searched and scanned for Padma and Kripa only to see candles around him. He was lying over a rocky slab and he realized his entire body was burning and stinging at the same time. His neck ached and his muscles did too. He felt extremely exhausted and weak.

God, this hurts!

Kalki sat up and saw that his chest was glinting. *What in the world?* He touched it. There was a strange symbol carved over it. It was a zigzag, maze-like symbol in the middle of his chest, shining as if it was powered by fire lights.

The door opened and he turned to see it was Padma. She was wearing a heavy fur-like coat around her body. She looked rested.

"You are awake." A glint of happiness was on her face. "I mean," she coughed, "you are awake." She normalized her voice.

"Where am I?"

"You saved us. The Pisach let us leave because you killed their master and that was one of the most honourable things to do according to them. They wanted you to be their next leader, but we kind of knew you didn't want to wear a necklace of skulls, right?" She smiled and Kalki realized that this was the first time that Padma had given him a genuine smile.

"Yeah, who does?" He looked outside the door. It was snowing.

"We are in the hills?"

"Oh yeah, come on. We have reached a cool place, by the way."

Cool place, eh?

Kalki walked to her and asked, "What is this?" He pointed at the symbol on his chest.

"I don't know. It appeared on your chest when you killed Brahmaputraksh."

"Like magic?"

"Oh yeah."

He stepped out and even though he was standing in the cold, he felt nice. The breeze was smooth and harsh at the same time. The mountains were large and capped with snow. The skies were sapphire-coloured. There was no sunlight. He took a deep breath in, letting the fresh air of freedom rest in.

"How many days have I slept for?"

"Three to four days. You kept waking up because of your fever so we fed you then."

"I don't remember anything."

"Yeah, because you were not completely conscious. But it's all right." She patted him on the back. "Don't you feel cold?"

"No, I don't."

"Of course, you don't. After all, you are the saviour of this world, right?" She winked.

She is cracking jokes now? "What really happened, Padma? Why are you being nice to me?"

"Because now I finally believe what Arjan told me. He believed you were the Avatar and I didn't believe it, not until I saw what you did back there, how you would've sacrificed yourself to fight the Pisach. You were fearless and you did it with ease, although I didn't expect an Avatar would collapse due to blood loss, heh." She grabbed his arm. "I believe in Lord Kalki."

Lord Kalki? I believe in him too, I guess.

For some reason, he could picture Lord Varaha grinning at this from afar, thinking that finally Kalki had done what he had been meant to do.

"And also, the folks here were quite happy to see that symbol on your chest. I mean, they wouldn't have rescued you if you didn't have that symbol."

"Folks here?"

Padma pointed to the side where there were more huts and cottages like the ones Kalki had just stepped out of. And then he saw there were furry civilians walking with coats and strange long dhotis, wearing shawls and what not. They had tufts of hair around their faces, bulbous noses, and big mouths. Some of them were using bamboo sticks to fight, while some were just meditating under trees. It was an entire town submerged in the snowy-capped hills with uneven, beauty slopes and the horizon that never seemed to end.

"Who are these people?"

"Vanars," Padma excitedly spoke. "I was always curious to see them and here I am."

"Vanars? We are in Dandak Hills?"

She nodded.

"They cured you. They had these crazy herbs."

"Wow."

"Yeah, but the good part is we are close to Mahendragiri

mountains." She pointed at the far hills which were visible from there.

"Should we leave then?"

"Oh no," she shook her head. "He wants to see you."

"Who?"

Padma licked her lips in anticipation. "He was quite curious to meet you, the leader of the Vanars." She paused. "Lord Bajrang."

"Lord Bajrang?"

"Yeah, you might know him from the books, the stories, the history of us. I can't believe he's real."

Of course he is.

"You know what the textbooks in my gurukul called him, right?" Kalki asked. "Where I used to study these myths."

"No."

Kalki smiled. "They called him Hanuman."

PART FOUR

THE DANDAK REBELLION

36

Kali had lost consciousness and by the time he woke up, he realized it was the first time in a long time that he hadn't had a nightmare.

He could feel that he was being transported somewhere—he could even see the figures that were carrying him. Koko and Vikoko were beside him. He could glimpse Durukti too. She looked concerned.

His body ached and his mind was fizzing. He could feel his temperature was high and in the background he could hear people shouting. Unable to understand what was happening, he fell asleep.

In and out of consciousness, he had wondered aloud, "Where am I?"

"You're safe." Durukti's voice had comforted him.

"What is happening?"

But then he dozed off again. It was quite evident why he was ill—he had been beaten to a pulp under the scorching heat of the sun. There were bruises all over his face and arms. Some of the sand had gotten in his mouth during the fight.

Finally, when he next woke up and saw his surroundings clearly, he realized he was in a small hut, with a concrete ceiling and fire lights around him. Right next to him, Durukti was sitting and looking at him intently while on the other side sat a strange old man with a grey beard and a crooked eye. He was wrapping

bandages around his arms and legs, and massaging a strangely scented ointment on his body. He could see shadows of Koko and Vikoko at the door, guarding him from harm.

"Are you better?" Durukti asked.

The room was far smaller than his quarters. Kali nodded to the question as he began to stand up but he was pushed down by the old man.

"Ssstay," he said with a wispy, snake-like tone to his voice. "You fell ill terribly."

Kali sighed as he looked at the man clearly. He recalled him from somewhere, as if he had seen him sometime back.

"You . . ." Kali's eyes widened. "I know you."

The old man nodded impassively as he went over to the other end of the room and brought something familiar to Kali's notice—it was Kali's crown which he had given to the old man.

"Gratitude reciprocates, I believe," the man said.

But somehow, the man looked different, strange. Now, he seemed more in charge and . . . dangerous, mysterious.

"He helped us take you in."

"What about the infirmary in the kingdom?"

"There's no kingdom." She lowered her gaze. "I am sorry, but it's been taken over by Urvashi. She killed all your loyalists and convinced the ministers to go against you since you got beaten up by a prisoner."

How did she do it?

"Did you get my pouch of Soma? That can help me."

She shook her head. "It got lost."

Someone stole it!

Kali was coming to his conclusions, but then his mind was going all over the place. "You mean to say, I've lost the very city I've been fighting for for so long?"

"Yes."

The old man didn't say anything. He kept himself busy tending to Kali.

Kali closed his eyes. He had been defeated. He rubbed his aching arm as he thought about all the things that had happened. "How did we escape?" he quietly asked Durukti.

"We were on a run, chased by the prisoners when Koko and Vikoko found a chariot in which we could travel out of the city and then we met Shukr." She pointed to the old man.

"Couldn't we just hide in the city?"

"Urvashi was hellbent on finding you. She wanted you out of the city and if we would have stayed there, gathering an army would have been a problem."

"We had Kuvera's allegiance."

"Kuvera allies with the powerful. And you are not it."

I'm a nobody again.

"Where are . . . where are we?"

"In the outskirts of Indragarh, one of the villages of Keekatpur," she sighed. "To be honest, it's not even a village, it's a farm."

Kali nodded. He tried to stand up, but couldn't. Feeling weak, he plopped down and fell asleep.

Kali walked out of the hut with a wooden cane. He leaned on it as he walked, looking at the mighty hills, the downward slope, and the local farm with sheeps and goats. There was also a small mill nearby. The pastures stretched wide and large. The skies didn't end where he stood and it somehow felt pleasant from where he used to be—in the oil drenched, smoke-infested city. This was cleaner.

Koko and Vikoko stood like diligent guards. Kali was proud to have them. They would never turn their backs to him because they had pledged a blood oath. No matter how much they hated Kali, they could never betray him.

He wondered how Urvashi had gotten the idea of releasing the prisoners. It seemed so far-fetched for a young girl to be able stage a coup. *There is more to her than meets the eye.*

He also thought about his pouch of Soma and how it had gone missing. And where had Arjan's strength come from? There was a connection that Kali was missing. There must be someone in the middle of it all. Someone had orchestrated Kali's downfall.

Though, whoever that person may be, he had been successful. Kali had been defeated and left out in the woods, in some farm that he had no idea about. With his cane, he limped forward to see a small, razor-like ravine flowing with crystal blue water, zigzagging and smashing against the rocks.

"How do you feel?" a sickly, troubled voice came from the back.

Kali turned to see Shukr who was slouching. He was wearing a long, dark robe. Walking over to the river, he came and stood beside Kali.

"Better."

"You came at the right time otherwise you would be dead right now. The river . . . it usssed to be bloody, you know."

"Bloody?"

"Red, scarlet . . . all red."

"When?"

"When Asurasss were alive." He opened his mouth and revealed his rotten teeth. Kali realized the man's eyes were golden. "Everything wasss in their order."

Kali arched his brows. "You are an Asura, aren't you?"

"Yesss." He smiled. "And so are you and so is your sissster."

"I thought we were the last ones."

"You don't know anything, foolish one." Shaking his head, Shukr continued. "You don't know what you are capable of. You don't know that your enemy is alive and is out there."

"Arjan," Kali nodded.

"No, no. Kalki."

Kali dismissively twisted his mouth. "He's dead."

"So you think, but he isn't and he's up there preparing to fight you," he pointed at the mountains.

"How do you know all of this?"

"I have seen everything." Shukr played with his beard.

"The crown . . . you didn't want money for your family or your daughter . . ."

"No. I wanted to see if you were generous or not, and you were. Good for you. You are sssupposed to be."

"Why?"

Shukr shrugged, leaving Kali to contemplate. He began walking further and Kali followed him. "Why? Why am I special? Why is Kalki my enemy?"

"The prophecy," Shukr mumbled.

"What prophecy?"

"The prophecy of every Age—of Dharm and Adharm, they shall come at the brink of people'sss troubles and shall fight, determining the fate of the world. You both will be trained in the arts of your expertise to have the last battle."

Kali clenched his fist. "Dharm and Adharm?"

"Yes. The good and the bad."

"So I'm Adharm?"

Shukr turned. "What do you think?"

"I must be. I have done awful things."

Shukr smiled.

"The Asurasss were the most majestic and the most powerful race. They ruled justifiably but history mocksss them."

"Asuras were evil. That's why our homeland Pataal suffered a witchhunt where Asuras were impaled and put to death. We were hunted by Manavs for we spread hate and did black magic."

Shukr sighed. "All liesss to apprehend us. We were good, justifiable." He said the word 'justifiable' as if it meant something to him. "The most beautiful race . . . proud and intelligent. Look

at usss now." He signalled at Kali's bald head and his loose skin. "You've made yourself worse, young one."

"It was the illness."

"I know. It was the Cursed One. He was behind it."

Should I believe what he is telling me? He seems a little crazy. But then there was one fact that Kali was supremely interested in and which he wanted to probe further. "You said Kalki is Dharm and I am Adharm. My training, what is it? How shall I be trained to fight him if you say he hasn't died?"

"You're wrong."

"About the training?

He shook his head, keeping his lanky fingers over Kali's shoulder. "*You* are Dharm."

37

Mayhem ensued.

Arjan had realized that this would happen. And it had. The entire city of Indragarh was in chaos after Urvashi had taken over the city. While the prisoners rejoiced, the council was furious over Urvashi who had promised them order in just a matter of few days. They had said to her that she can't control the public with a paramilitary force. Urvashi had been adamant though. She would rather have this army than trust the council. One of the noblemen who had been raging against her was Ramras. He advocated that it was unwise to let a young *girl* rule the city for which he started a motion for removing her, making him the interim ruler till they found someone suitable.

Urvashi denied the motion. She was the previous ruler's daughter. So she was queen by birthright.

The motions kept going back and forth while Arjan stood amidst the mayhem. He was given the task to cleanse the city, make sure there was no issue between the prisoners and the public. The public was retaliating while the prisoners supported her. Some prisoners had chosen to leave Urvashi after her purpose had been achieved but some of them, like Rudra and Harsha, had stayed back. Rudra had managed to convince Arjan to help Urvashi as well.

"You defeated Kali. You are special," she had said to Arjan.

But now as Arjan stood in her office, she looked worried. Her tutor was telling her everything about how the city had to be handled. Arjan stood there and watched in silence. She was asking her tutor about grains, transportations, trade with other cities, infrastructure designs, temple reorganizations, and donations by the nobles.

Beside him was Rudra who was now wearing decent, long robes with a tight waist belt. He looked extremely handsome and happy.

Urvashi's tutor scampered when she yelled at him for irritating her with all the problems. He left closing the door. She looked sheepishly at Arjan and Rudra.

"Don't tell me there's another revolt by the public."

"We are preventing them as much as possible." Arjan had noticed that Urvashi had a tempestuous nature. *I must remain calm when dealing with her.*

"But uh . . ." Rudra began, glancing at Arjan for permission. Arjan nodded. "The prisoners, they want freedom. They feel tied to you. They have grown afraid of you."

"I freed most of them!" She slammed her fist on the table, her eyes bulging out of her sockets. "The ones who stayed behind are getting their dues."

"I know and I'm trying to convince them. But they still want to leave."

"I cannot handle their drama, Rudra. Deal with them yourself and make sure you are successful." It sounded like a threat.

"My lady, since you are the queen—"

"Not for long!" She stood up as she showed the letter to Arjan. It was from the council who wanted a public hearing. "They want me to be elected just like any other ruler, prove my worth and let the public decide. They think it's the best way to end the processions that keep happening in the streets."

It does make sense.

"This might be a ploy from Ramras who wants to use this

opportunity to take the throne. But I don't believe it's a bad idea at all."

"If you have the correct agendas in place with the appropriate planning, you can show them that you are prepared and they won't take your age into account," Rudra said.

Arjan mulled over it. He had a few ideas he wanted to give. "What about taking help from Lord Kuvera?"

"The Yakshas?" She frowned. "My father hated them."

"But you need them, don't you? They bring in the money and that could facilitate the infrastructure, the trade. It could fund the reformation of the city."

Urvashi was silent for a moment, lost in thought.

"See, Ramras has control over the nobles and the nobles have the power of voting twice. Since right now you are the active ruler of the city, try to mend the problems so the public sees you in a better light and then at the day of the hearing, you would have good deeds backing your statements."

Urvashi nodded. "You are right."

"In return, you can ask what he wants. Once we have the helm, we push him back to his own kingdom."

"Sounds quite easy," Rudra added.

Arjan didn't like the comment laced with sarcasm, but then that was how Rudra was—he acted a lot like Kalki sometimes.

"Fine. Set up a meeting. We should go talk to him. I just hope he's not a Kali loyalist." She paused. "I just want Ramras to back off, so I can continue to do what my father wanted to do—build more temples around the city, especially rebuild the ones that have been demolished by Kali."

Arjan nodded. Ramras, a quiet, young noble had surprised them when he had spoken against Urvashi. They had later found out that the reason he didn't want Urvashi on the throne was because of her sex, not her age. It was all right for a cruel creature like Kali to be the ruler, but not a woman. Arjan didn't know how

capable Urvashi was, but she had managed to dethrone Kali. Arjan had helped significantly by breaking Kali's bones, but it had been Urvashi who had driven away his loyalists.

Speaking of breaking bones, Arjan had never felt so good in his life. His body was brimming with energy and his mind was moving at a fast pace. He felt great and he felt he could jump leagues away. It was amazing how the Soma could give him this kind of a power.

"Should we be worried that Kali might return?" Arjan asked.

"He has nowhere to go. If he comes, he'll come alone and we might just get the correct opportunity to kill him." She grinned at the thought.

"Let's hope we do this right," Urvashi said. "And let's hope we right the wrongs that Kali has committed in this city."

"Do not forget Raktapa. He's at Suryagarh as of now with his army. If he learns that Kali is not ruling Indragarh, he might make a move," Arjan said. He had been reading Kali's journals that mentioned all he had done for the kingdom till now. He had also learnt that a portion of his army had been sent to a certain individual called Taar for some reason. "There are a few Rakshas here, but I think most of them are now in hiding or have scampered off to Suryagarh to their leader. Martanja, their previous leader is dead, and then Pradm perished in a fight with your father. The Rakshas had no one to lead them. Kali's gone too, so they left. The ones who couldn't leave died at the prisoners' hands during the coup."

Urvashi ran her fingers in her hair. "What should I do about Raktapa?"

"Topple him as well," Rudra said.

"If you do that," Arjan eyed Rudra, dismissing his answer completely, "you might lose soldiers and right now you scarcely have them." He pulled out the journal of Kali and showed her the distribution of the army. "If you can appease the villagers telling them you are Vedanta's daughter, they might stop the revolts and

you can bring that army from the village to the city where they can be of use. Also, I would suggest you start building relationships with the rulers of Varungarh and Agnigarh. These cities are quite prosperous in different areas and the harvest in Indragarh is quite low."

Urvashi sighed. "Yes, teach me everything about it."

"I would suggest—"

"You are suggesting a lot," Rudra snapped in between.

Arjan frowned. "Because she told me to."

"I don't want any tension between you two. Both of you are the most stable people right now in my camp. So please, don't fight."

Arjan rolled his eyes and so did Rudra, but Arjan could see that Rudra was enjoying his moment.

"I would suggest that we give one of these cities to Lord Kuvera in return for funding Indragarh." Arjan went over to one side of the office where he opened the chart of Illavarti. "Agnigarh," he pointed in the middle, "has iron mills and manufactures most of the weapons for Udaiyas. We get it from here. Varungarh is popular for water tanks and conservation, especially rain harvesting. Agnigarh is more of a military city and you need someone capable to rule it. I would suggest you give Varungarh to Lord Kuvera, since it's not of any importance to us."

"Who's ruling Varungarh right now?"

"Some lieutenant of Kali. He can be dismissed. Also, when we get the funds, we can use them for soldier enlistments since our army has depleted majorly in comparison to Dakshini's army, and we clearly don't want Lord Vibhisana to see this as an opportunity to hit back at us," Arjan explained, pointing at Bhanmati where Lord Vibhisana lived.

Urvashi scratched her head, lost. "I'm so confused."

"It's all right." Arjan stifled a laugh.

"I feel like you have more knowledge about all of this. Why don't you just be the king?" she chuckled, glancing at Rudra.

"I'm a humble villager from Shambala." Arjan kept the chart back, rolling it up.

Urvashi nodded. "I know, I understand. Fine. I'll do whatever you just told me. And also, send out messengers to all the villages in Keekatpur to announce that Vedanta's heir will be handling the administration now. I should prepare a speech as well for the hearing."

Arjan could see that she was doubting herself. She had managed to take back the throne, but she had no experience, unlike Kali. He had waged a war and won the kingdom. But there was no questioning the fact that she was the legitimate ruler. All cards had been stacked against her. Her sex and her age bothered the council.

"There are people who want to meet you," Rudra said. "Some people have chosen to believe in their rightful queen."

"Don't they know I might just get deposed in the hearing?"

"They don't know about the hearing. It hasn't been announced officially," Rudra added. "Should I welcome them?"

Urvashi nodded. "I would love to see some supporters. It might change the heavy atmosphere."

Arjan and Rudra stood in the corner while they saw soldiers, labourers, villagers, and miners come and meet Urvashi. They kissed her hand, pledged their allegiance, and talked about their problems. Arjan noted most of the problems, so they could rectify them later. It was difficult being a ruler of a city. It was easy to depose one. But Arjan was glad everything was in order and he had convinced her to take help from Lord Kuvera. Otherwise they would have been left with no choice but to steal the money from Lord Kuvera's palace in Alakpur.

It always benefits to be nice.

One of the soldiers from Kali's regiment came to pledge his allegiance to her.

"Which post did you have?" she asked.

"I worked as his charioteer."

"Ah, not an issue. I understand. You can be the guardsman in this fort. I believe and trust you." She smiled at the man. Arjan had told her that it was important for her to treat her subjects kindly. He had heard from Rudra about Urvashi's black magic and had wasted no time in requesting her to refrain from doing any magic for the time being.

"I wanted you to know, my lady, I have news that might be beneficial for you."

She narrowed her gaze. "What is it?"

"I know who killed your father, the late great King Vedanta."

"I know it was Kali."

He shook his head. "Kali was the executioner, my lady. It was Lord Kuvera who had organized it."

At that moment, Arjan's blood froze. Urvashi took a sharp intake of her breath and shifted her gaze from the soldier to Arjan. Darkness glimmered behind her beady eyes.

Now, we are in an even bigger mess.

38

Manasa was fast asleep in the donkey cart when a heavy thud woke her up. She was huddled in the midst of strangers. She rubbed her eyes and stretched her legs. After a lot of swimming in the river, she had found a trader's market and decided to barter her precious earrings to reach Bhanmati. It was close by.

Now, she was in the trader's vehicle moving uphill to Bhanmati. And she had dozed off out of exhaustion. She had never felt so tired in her life. Manasa recalled her royal chariot. She would plop on the fluffy cushions while feasting on the fruits that were kept inside specially for her. *Now look at me.* A royal lady like her, travelling in a rickety cart full of commoners. This was the worst. And the creeping thought of Nanda being executed just made her stomach cringe and her heartbeat fast.

He can't die. I don't want to be alone again.

She touched the conical Shard of her locket. The travellers sitting opposite her in the cart ogled at her. She ignored them, frowning with distaste as she left the locket and opened the flap of her cart tent to see the road ladened with rocks and pebbles. She could see huge temples filled with people wearing bright-coloured clothes.

That's what she liked about Dakshini—everything was bright and beautiful here. People here were elegant while the Udaiyas people were more rugged. It was a turbulent city while Bhanmati wasn't.

Maybe because Bhanmati had a just ruler—the the citizens were happy. With ample sunlight and occasional rains, the crops growed and food was in abundance. Vibhisana was also a big advocate of humanism and liberal arts—the kingdom was rich in literature and paintings, with stunning architecture. Bhanmati initially was on the ground but later the main city had been shifted up on a slope, towering over every other city. It also had a military advantage. Guards stood on a watchtower to prevent any impending attacks.

Manasa looked out of the donkey cart and saw the rocky path divided into frames—on one side, the crops were being cultivated, cows were grazing on the fields and on the other side, the weeds and the flowers were growing in full bloom. The farmers were well dressed. As the cart moved upwards, the road down seemed to go on forever, with the hills and the little towns hiding deep down.

The cart stopped for a while so that the animals could rest. They had reached the city. Two guards came from the entrance gate and peered inside the cart. They glared at Manasa and then at the other travellers who were sitting inside. "Why is a Naga inside your tent?" one of the guards asked.

The trader and the guards discussed and the trader gave them some coins. They were allowed to pass.

Manasa got off from the donkey cart and left the trader to move towards the city centre while noticing the beauty around her. There were large conical towers made of sandstones and bricks, yellow grilled windows with trees at every corner, well organized roads, soldiers in green coloured pads and armour, and flag bearers were strutting around.

She had no idea how she would approach Vibhisana. But she did know that Nanda had sent him a letter that he hadn't responded to. And she wanted his help, and she would try to gain his trust and eventually his forces in helping her fight Kadru, by hook or by crook. For now, she just basked in the pleasant environment of a city she had never seen before. She would not mind eventually settling down here.

As she crossed the pathways and the roads, the street vendors, the astrologers, and the singers, she saw a small building in the corner—it was deep green in colour, with a little bit of teal splashed over. The smell of food and songs in the background with the brisk steps of the civilians gave a certain flavour to the place. The building, nonetheless, belonged to Lord Vibhisana. The people lived in simple homes here. Kings in Udaiyas believed in having castles and forts with well-guarded battlements but the Dakshini king was different. He had a cozy place, with soldiers walking around casually. Small buildings housing the ministers surrounded Lord Vibhishana's home.

She reached the guards and told them her name. "I am Lady Manasa, sister of late Lord Vasuki, from Naagpuri."

But before the guards could go inside and inform their king, someone from the window shouted, "Oi!"

Manasa looked up to see a burly old man. He was bald, had a freckled face, big beady eyes and a small mouth. He had a broad smile on his face. This man was Lord Vibhisana. He was wearing his usual green-coloured robes.

"Manasa? My dear!" he shouted. He was grinning and his cheeks turned red with excitement.

After a lot of hugs, Manasa was made to sit down. The comfortable royal chairs made her want to doze off again. But she shrugged the feeling off and concentrated on the man who was her childhood friend, her advisor.

He was the only Manav in Dakshini. Initially the Manavs had ruled over most of the regions and the tribes had been just nomadic settlements, taking a small region for themselves. But when the tribes grew demanding citizenship, a place in the politics, the Manavs refused. This led to a fight. The only Manav who had sided with the tribes was none other than Vibhisana. Avoiding a

war, he made sure that the land was equally divided between the Northerners and the Southerners.

Vibhisana ruled well, but the tribals didn't like a Manav ruling over them. They elected their own leaders, abandoning Vibhisana. Some tribals even attacked him. Vibhisana simply retreated, saying, "I won't harm you. Leave me with my duties and you can freely attend to your affairs." And since then, he hadn't interfered in the tribal matters until his hand was forced. He was now a king in name only. Though Manasa knew that he was innately afraid. He had always been afraid, just like his father. His older brother however had been different from him. Lord Dushasan, the head of Eelam, had converted himself into a Rakshas.

Lord Vibhishana had chosen not to join Kali's campaign against the tribals. He didn't want to associate himself with such a violent man. His age had caught up with him. Wrinkles lined his face, but his body was still plump.

"I'm so glad you are here."

Manasa sighed. Her body ached and she felt she would collapse at any moment, but she mustered up her spirit. "I think Nanda told you what has happened."

"I know! I know!" He got up from his chair. "It's absolutely absurd what is going on. Good heavens!" He took a handkerchief and wiped the sweat on his forehead. "What do you plan to do now?"

"The question is, what do you plan to do?"

"Nothing, my dear! I'm a humble ruler of this small place. You know, I do not interfere—"

"Well, you should. My husband is in danger. He's in Naagpuri and might be executed any moment. Kadru, the so-called cousin of mine is trying to steal Amrit from the Suparns."

"That is impossible. Have you seen that place? It's like a fortress. Lord Tarakshya has done some fine—"

"Tarakshya invited them."

"By heavens, why?" He gasped.

"He is being tricked. It's a long story." She wiped the sweat from her head. She was feeling a little down already. "What will you do?"

"A letter!" He stood up, his belly jiggling up and own. "I will send a letter, directed to Lady Kadru, asking her to leave Lord Tarakshya alone."

"She will come for you next if you do that."

"Then I shall tell Lord Tarakshya about what is happening around him."

"What makes you think he will trust you?"

He sat back in the chair, mulling it over.

"My dear," Manasa grabbed Vibhisana's hand. "We need to warn Lord Tarakshya of what is going to happen, but we should first save Nanda."

"Okay," he mumbled. Manasa could sense his reluctance. "But how did you escape?"

"I swam till I arrived at a market near Bhanmati. This locket proved instrumental in my escape." She showed it to Vibhisana.

Vibhishana was surprised and delighted. "Oh my goodness! Do you know what this is? Wait . . . I should call the librarian to make sure. . . no wait . . ." he stood up excitedly. "Where did you get this?"

Manasa was confused. "Nanda gave it to me."

"That cheery old man!" He laughed rubbing his paunch. "He has managed to get the diamond in the rough."

"What is it?"

Before Vibhisana could explain, the guard entered the room with a box in his hand and a sealed packet on top of it.

"Your highness, there is a parcel for you."

"Oh! A parcel?" Vibhisana took the parcel and set it down on the table. He rubbed his hands in anticipation, like a child about to open his present.

He decided to read the letter first. Manasa didn't hesitate to come forward and read it with him.

To the dearest king of Bhanmati,

I write to inform you that I am ready to accept your partnership if you step down from your throne and let us rule instead. We shall not harm you. We are already in the process of conquering every empire in the vicinity and plan to unite the Dakshinis and make our countrymen stronger than those in Udaiyas. It is time that the Dakshinis rule Illavarti in its entirety.

We are sending you a gift as a token of expressing how seriously we should be taken. The entire royal line who supported you—Vasuki, Manasa, and her fiendishly offbeat husband have been taken care of.

Vibhisana looked at Manasa.

"I'm not a ghost," said Manasa.

Vibhisana meekly nodded and continued reading.

We plan to use your city for betterment since it's the centre of power. We are waiting for your positive response. If there is no response in twenty days, you shall be taken down for good.

Regards,

Jamun

Vibhisana started shivering. He glanced at the box, hesitating to open it. Though that didn't stop Manasa. As soon as she opened it, a putrid smell spread in the room. She looked inside and instantly collapsed.

Nanda's dead eyes stared at them.

39

Kalki knew he was in heaven. At least it looked like heaven. As he walked to the snowy platform, he saw the world in front of him covered in white—there were wooden huts surrounded by willows and other trees, flakes had engulfed the wet leaves, the smell of organic fruits permeated the air, and the silence was soothing.

Dandak Forest—the place where the Vanars used to live, was now deserted. They had moved to Dandak Hills, high up in the forest when the winds and the cold came. The Vanars were one of the oldest tribes in Illavarti. They preferred to live in seclusion. Some said they live like the Suparns, but the difference between them was that the Vanars were a peaceful tribe. The last time they had waged a war was the time they had assisted Lord Raghav.

Kalki walked past the Vanars. They bowed to him. And then, he realized it was the symbol on his chest that they were noticing. He crossed the huts and walked down the slope along with Padma who took him to the hut where Ratna and Smrit were staying.

"How are you feeling?" asked Smrit. They had worn fur around their body to cover themselves up.

"Great."

"You don't feel cold?"

Kalki shook his head. He felt *nice* instead of cold.

"Where do you plan to go?" Kalki asked.

"We plan to stay." Ratna gave Smrit a mischievous smirk.

"Why?"

"We can talk about that later. For now, let's just say that I like to know the people I surround myself with." She looked at Kalki's symbol. "Good luck," she said and left with Smrit. Kalki realized she was carrying a double-edged sword.

"She's weird," said Padma. "You know she's the one who brought us here."

"Really?"

"Yeah. She's going to aid in the war."

"War?"

"There's a war brewing in this kingdom."

Weren't Vanars supposed to be peace-loving?

"Half of the population is out there at the Frontier trying to defend what you see here."

Kalki pursed his lips. "Where's Kripa?"

"Everyone hates him around here so he decided to do the one thing that does not irritate anyone."

"What?"

"Sleep."

Kalki stifled a laugh. He walked away from the hut and moved towards the cherry blossom trees. There was a cluster of these trees at some distance from the huts. A light breeze blew towards him as the orange sun began to dip, the rays beaming at him and deflecting from his chest. Kalki and Padma looked at the symbol on his chest. It was glimmering in the sunlight.

"I am sorry for . . . everything. I misjudged you." Padma's voice was almost a whisper.

"I am sorry as well," Kalki nodded, walking towards the cherry trees. "I blamed you for Arjan's death. It was not your fault."

"I believe he's not dead."

"I hope not."

Padma sighed. "He told me you are the saviour; he believed in

you. I didn't. But I realized something. The world will believe in you if you believe in yourself. And that's what you did."

"I uh . . . you are right. We fought for so long, I felt it was pointless. I realized while I was dreaming and while I was close to my death that in life, you meet certain people and they might not be ideal for you, but they are there for you. And sometimes, being there is what matters than being perfect."

"I have not really seen a lot of good people in this world, Kalki. It kind of made me realize there aren't many." Padma patted him on his back.

"My father used to say that there is goodness in the world, but there's no ability to realize it within you and the few that do, they become quite prosperous."

"Your father is a wise man."

"I guess. Speaking of wise men, he is waiting." She pointed to the edge of the plateau where close to the cherry trees someone was hanging from the branch, upside down, looking at the sun.

"Lord Bajrang?" Kalki had goosebumps.

Padma nodded.

Kalki, without any hesitation, began to walk towards the plateau as he saw Lord Bajrang. He was clad in a simple grey dhoti with a golden belt around his waist. His chest had been painted red. He had folded his hands and closed his eyes. Kalki also noticed that unlike what people said about them, Vanars didn't have tails at the back. They were furry, and resembled monkeys, but they were hairy Manavs.

Kalki didn't say anything to Lord Bajrang. For a few seconds he just stood there, awestruck.

The sun began to set, turning the sky orange. A cool breeze made the leaves of the trees dance. Kalki listened to the rustling of the leaves, thinking of what to say to the legend that stood in front of him.

"She's cute and I know you are wondering if I have a tail or not."

Having heard innumerable stories about the might of the great Lord Bajrang, Kalki hadn't expected him to say that.

"I have so many questions."

"Everyone does. But only few know the answer." He had a heavy voice, tinged with honeycomb sweetness, but also seeped with the rigidity of a commander. "And I am one of the few." And with a slight adjustment, he leapt from the branch, somersaulting in the air, letting himself fall on the ground. His arms held on to the snow and then he stood up on his feet.

"You are Endowed, aren't you? You are going to live forever."

Lord Bajrang turned to Kalki. His face was impassive—almond-coloured eyes, brown fur across his cheeks, and a warm face. "Indeed. By my very good friend, Lord Raghav, who thought it would be better if I live for a long time."

"You are not what I expected."

"You thought I was some wise sage? Or some king? I am not any of them. And all of them. You see, when you are Endowed, you must hide from the world, letting no one suspect that you will live forever since it would be considered magic and magic is something only few believe in. But word spread and my myth increased. I am the person who saved Lady Sita, who assisted Lord Raghav. I am so many things. But slowly those myths died and I just became like any other ruler, ruling his tribe. I live in peace with my people now."

He was muscular with thick thighs, a tight chest, and burly arms. Walking towards another tree, he jumped on the branch again, but this time to pull out a red fruit. He handed it to Kalki.

"You should have it."

"What is it?"

"Something that makes us healthy and strong."

"Like Soma?"

He laughed. "You don't know anything about that plant."

"I know enough."

"That's the thing. You and the others think it's Soma that

makes you go mad. But it's not true. Lord Raghav consumed a copious amount of Soma and he never fell ill. Never."

Kalki had believed Lord Raghav to be moral and righteous. It was impossible to corrupt someone who was so pious. "But he was Dharm, right?"

"Ah! The prophecy of Dharm and Adharm? You really believe it?"

Kalki nodded.

"Let me tell you something. There's no Dharm and Adharm. The concepts are bogus. Lord Raghav and Dushasan took Somas as well, but they used it for what they thought was best. Somas are not evil or good. It's the person. Somas just make you strong. It is up to you to choose your own path. And you know what paths define, right?"

Kalki shook his head. It was all new to him.

"Paths are defined by the choices you make as a person. Lord Raghav chose the right path while Dushasan chose the violent one. It was not because of Somas. Believe me."

There's no Dharm and Adharm? Then what am I supposed to be?

"We live in a world of contradictions. But don't worry, you shall understand everything in time." He patted his shoulder as Kalki ate the ripened fruit which turned out to be extremely sweet, filling his mouth with juiciness.

Then Lord Bajrang looked at his symbol. "You know what it is?"

"What?"

"A symbol of Lord Vishnu. He has given you the permission to be his warrior of Dharm. You are finally chosen by him."

"Wait, I wasn't chosen till now?" Kalki narrowed his eyes.

"No, you weren't."

"But . . . but . . ." Kalki's world spiralled. All this time, he had thought he had been chosen to fight for the world. "But how is this possible? Kripa told me that I was Dharm and I was destined to go to Mahendragiri mountains to learn the ways of an Avatar,

but now you are saying anyone could have been Dharm and I was not chosen?"

Lord Bajrang had a smile on his face. "Kripa was a liar. He made you *think* you were Dharm and that made you want to *do* things as Dharm. It was the power of belief which he used. The good part is, you are chosen now. Also, yes, Kripa is not someone one can trust. He betrayed his own brother-in-law to help the opposing faction causing his sister and his brother-in-law to die. You have no idea what he has done."

Kalki couldn't believe what he was hearing. He had had his suspicions about Kripa since he believed he had brought the Mlecchas who had killed Vishnuyath, Kalki's father.

"But I've never had Soma in my life . . . it was my mother who drank it and that made me be the Dharm. I don't understand. I thought I had been chosen. How am I so strong then?"

Lord Bajrang smiled. "Who told you about your mother?"

"Kripa."

And then it dawned on him. It was all a lie.

"Is there someone who can teach me the ways of an Avatar or is that a lie as well?"

"There might be some. I don't know about it much. But Kripa has been lying to you ever since you joined him in this cause. And it's all right. It was a necessary lie since he believed that you had the potential to be Dharm. You really believed in the idea that Soma had been passed down to you from your mother? It doesn't work like that. You need to take it directly. Perhaps Kripa slipped you some when you were young."

But then, how come Father knew Kripa?

"You have a lot of questions to ask him. Honestly, I don't trust him. But he brought you here, so he really believes in whatever is up there in the hills. So, you go for it." Lord Bajrang began to walk away from Kalki. "And be quick, because we don't have much time."

"Why?"

"There's a rebellion brewing in my tribe and tomorrow we go to war." Lord Bajrang left Kalki with more questions and less answers.

40

The stars mingled in the nightfall as Kali looked up at the sky, wondering who he was now that he had lost his city. He got up and walked towards the ravine. It was mirroring the sky above. He let his hand feel the current of the bristling water. It was tickling and itching at the same time. He turned when he heard footsteps. Durukti came and stood beside him.

"How's your leg?" she asked.

"Better." Kali was still using the cane.

She was silent for a while as if she was thinking of what to say. "I . . . uh . . ."

"Do you think I am a good man?" Kali interrupted her.

"A good man?" She fidgeted. "Uh, no."

Kali sighed. He wasn't angry. In fact, he had not been feeling a lot of things for a while now. Perhaps because he had no throne to make him feel proud and greedy and . . . omnipotent. Now he was just a man with a broken leg.

"Why?"

"You have done horrible things."

"So have you."

"But I feel remorse."

"I do too. But you are right, I'm not a good man. I have done things I shouldn't be proud of."

"Why are you asking me this?"

"Because of the voices."

"Can you hear them now?"

He shook his head. Surprisingly, they had vanished as if he had been stripped of his powers. He touched his scalp and realized that his hair was starting to grow. "Well, I guess my baldness is cured." He chuckled. "Have I been cured somehow?"

"What did the voices tell you to do?"

"I was never ruthless, but I was ambitious. A part of me wanted to be a good king, but the voices wanted me to lord over my people, instil fear in them, because fear rules the strongest."

"And you were proven wrong once you fell from the throne."

"Yes."

"Could it be . . . that the voices were only a product of your imagination that stemmed from your fear of losing your throne? And now that you've lost and you are here, that imagination is satiated from the conclusion."

Perhaps she was right. Perhaps, he was meant to fall down to rise up again. Shukr had said that he was Dharm. But then who was Adharm? Kalki. He was out there, readying himself to kill Kali's but Kali wouldn't let it happen. He will prepare himself, recover from his injuries, and build his strength.

"I have always believed you would be a good king. That's why I'm here with you even though you have done things I am not happy about. There's a spark in you, a spark of hope."

Kali blinked. He couldn't believe his sister was being so honest, and outspoken. Back in Indragarh, she mostly kept to herself. This was what she was like in the early days when Kali had been with a king and she used to teach him little things in life to overcome oddities.

"Thank you."

"What do you plan to do now?"

"To become a better person, of course." He paused, thinking

of all those horrendous dreams he had been having, about his siblings crying out from the bloody rivers and the sands, calling his name out, telling him to find his legacy, his heritage, his past. "But first, I must do something that I should have done a while back."

And with that, he turned around and walked away.

Kali had entered the shack where Shukr was lying down, but he couldn't hear any snores. He dismissed Koko and Vikoko who had been standing behind him. He knelt next to Shukr as Shukr opened his eyes.

"What isss it?" he said, hissing.

"I know it was you." Kali gazed at him. "You were the one, weren't you? The one who came in my dreams, who wanted me to find out about my heritage." Kali had realized that Shukr's voice and the voices in his nightmares were the same. Durukti had been wrong. It wasn't just his imagination.

Shukr smiled. "You have a good memory."

"Why did you do that?"

"O the last of the Asuras," he sighed, "I have no strength to defeat Adharm, but you do. For that you had to be trained. You also need to know about your heritage. You are destined to rule not just Udaiyas, but Dakshini as well."

"So, you made me fall down from the throne?"

"Yes. Initially, I tried to send messages through dreams, but you didn't listen. So I made those dreams more lucid and they started affecting you."

"But all of it, killing Ratri, that lover of hers, Vedanta, and troubling Arjan, it was all me. They were *my* decisions. And now you say you made me do it."

Shukr paused, patting him on the shoulder. "The decisions were yours. But I *influenced* them. I made you reach the tipping point

and let you fall yourself. So no, directly I didn't make you fall from the throne. I was just there, whispering in the corner, applauding you for what you were doing and in that sense, you thought you were doing the right thing."

"I thought my illness was the reason behind these visions."

"Your illness made it easier for me, of course, to penetrate your psyche."

"You influenced Urvashi to take me down?"

He shook his head. "You influenced her by killing her father. I just gave her the necessary tools to take you down."

"Tools?"

"I was her guru," he said. "Back when she was a little child. I taught her a lot of things."

"How did you know she would take me down one day?"

"Because I had the Eye of Brahma initially." He shook his head apologetically. "Before the Cursed One took it from me. He travelled to the land of Asuras to get it from me. This was during the Breaking, after the Mahayudh."

"The Cursed One?"

"He's the reason behind your illness, behind everything. He is orchestrating everything, to become who he is, and to do what he wants to do."

There were so many things Kali wanted to know, but he couldn't understand. "You are a Vidhyadhara?"

"I'm a lot of things, but I'm an Acharya foremost, an Endowed one, who has seen Asura kings rise and fall. And I wouldn't let the last one fall as well." He touched Kali's forehead. "I wanted you to be stripped down enough from your pride as a king so you'll come with me."

"Where?"

"Pataal."

Kali had heard about the island. People said that Pataal was hidden in smog and mist, a small place which had been home to the

Asuras—the earlier ones, before they migrated to Illavarti. It was believed that the Asuras still had their temples there, to hold their secrets, hieroglyphs, mysteries that shrouded their grand history.

"But isn't that mythical?"

"Oh it's real, and it will teach you about your heritage, the one I wanted you to know about."

"Why? What is so important about my heritage? Why do we have to travel to Pataal?"

"Because the Cursed One managed to take three Shards of the Eye of Brahma." He smiled. "But he forgot the first one. And the First Shard, it's there in Pataal. I will show you something that will change your life forever. Will you or will you not come?"

Kali looked into the dark eyes of Shukracharya and then slowly nodded.

Perhaps the burning questions will finally be answered.

"Also, do not blame me entirely for your downfall. It was not just me who did it. I only made Urvashi capable but she made your opponent stronger." He signalled at the door where Durukti was standing with her back to them, looking at the scenery ahead of her.

"My sister? But why?"

"All will be told in time," Shukr whispered. A chill ran down Kali's spine.

41

Arjan didn't know what she was going to do next.

He was in his room when a soldier came and informed him that Urvashi had called a meeting with Lord Kuvera, and Arjan and Rudra's presence was requested. Something was amiss.

Why didn't Urvashi ask me or Rudra to fetch Lord Kuvera?

Urvashi now knew that Lord Kuvera had been responsible for her father's death. This was going to be a big problem.

And Arjan hoped she could let bygones be bygones and find clarity in her mission. She *needed* Lord Kuvera more than he needed her.

"She's just thirteen," Rudra said. He was lying next to Arjan on the bed.

After the battle, Arjan had professed his attraction towards Rudra. And it was reciprocated, though that was no surprise. In fact, Rudra had said, "It took you so long, love." And it was funny because Arjan was in fact a *slow* individual in matters of love. And a little bit embarrassed and awkward too.

Arjan sighed. "I know. And that is kind of going against her. Should we . . . tell her to step down? Perhaps Ramras can be the one to lead the city."

"He's a wimp!" Rudra frowned. "Believe me, he does only what his father tells him to do. He's just a pretty face."

"And how do you know that?"

"Because he's the nobleman I was talking about."

"The one you were together with? Who didn't take the fall and made you go to prison?"

Rudra nodded, rubbing his forehead. "I didn't want to say anything to Urvashi about it . . ."

"No, don't. Don't tell her about us either." Arjan pursed his lips. "It can backfire. We will let her know eventually."

Rudra nodded. "What should we do then?"

"Convince her not to kill Lord Kuevra. She won't do anything today in her fort. So we have some time. We just need to remind her of what he can offer her."

"Fine, I think we should go then." Rudra got off the bed.

Arjan did too as he ran his fingers through his hair.

"How are you feeling?"

"I'm okay. Why do you ask?"

"You seem different since your fight with Kali."

"Different? In what sense?"

Rudra smiled. "You seem confident. And that's a trait pre-battle Arjan didn't have. Now, I wonder what really helped you in the end."

Arjan thought about it. *Was it the Soma? Was it turning him into something he was not?* No one knew how the Somas really worked. No one had tested its potential and people who had, had died years ago with their studies done and dusted.

Arjan scanned the room for his clothes. Sometimes he couldn't believe that he was living in a fort. The room was gigantic, ornamented with tapestry and elegantly-designed carpets. Urvashi was having the entire fort renovated to her liking. The fort housed the guards, Urvashi's loyalists, and the prisoners who had chosen to remain after the coup. Rudra had been charged with handling them.

Arjan got ready and walked down the halls with Rudra. The corridor was lit with fire lights. They walked past the *charbagh.*

Guards had been stationed around the garden. They reached the main hall and saw Urvashi and Lord Kuvera sitting inside. *That's odd. This is where she invites the people she likes.* Arjan and Rudra looked at each other, confused.

Arjan and Rudra walked inside the hall. A red carpet had been sprawled at the entrance to welcome the guest. Urvashi sat on the couch in the centre with two guards behind her. They were armed with crossbows, ready to strike if anything untoward happened. Opposite her sat Lord Kuvera with three of his Yaksha archers behind him.

You could cut the tension with a knife.

Urvashi greeted Arjan and Rudra with a warm, charming smile as she introduced them to Kuvera. "If not for them, I wouldn't be sitting here right now." She was not in a mood to fight, it seemed.

Lord Kuvera was sipping wine. "Indeed, they look fine, my dear. And also," he looked at Arjan, "I heard it was you, the little fighting prodigy, who defeated Kali. Didn't you?"

Arjan nodded glumly.

"How dear! What an accomplishment. I despised that wretched creature. He had no sense how to rule or how to be just *nice.*" Kuvera frowned. "But nonetheless, the dark days are gone and you are here." He turned his attention to Urvashi who was beaming.

"You two are late. We were just discussing how Lord Kuvera will be an integral part of the kingdom of Udaiyas. I seek to do what my father didn't—give a helping hand to the Dakshinis. That way we can all be happy."

"We can!" Kuvera clapped.

"My lord, I have some ideas." Urvashi leaned forward.

"Of course! I would love to hear them." Kuvera winked. "You might not know this but your father and I were allies before Kali decided to overthrow him. He even threatened me. But now that you have taken him out, I'm in your debt."

Urvashi looked at Arjan and gave him a genuine smile.

Arjan heaved a sigh of relief. Urvashi was being mature.

"I would love it if you can sanction some money to us so we could do enlistments in our army, grow our agrarian sectors, and sort other little issues. I need to appease the nobles—"

"To keep the crown, I know. But to give you such a huge amount . . ."

"What do you want in return?" Urvashi asked simply.

Kuvera was taken aback. He hadn't expected her to be so blunt.

"I can give you a city to rule," she said nonchalantly.

That's my idea.

Arjan smiled to himself.

"Which one?"

"Varungarh."

"You will let a Dakshini, a tribal rule a northern city? Do you believe the nobles will be okay with this?"

"They can go to hell." She laughed and so did Lord Kuvera. Arjan and Rudra chuckled nervously. "They won't, of course. They will have to understand that things change with time. You'll be integral to my reign, so I would love to give it to you."

Lord Kuvera put his palms on his cheeks and thoughtfully mused. "Seems interesting. What of Raktapa? He can be a problem once he finds out that Kali isn't ruling Indragarh anymore."

"I plan to have a peace treaty with him as well. After all, we are working towards a single goal, right?"

"What if you lose to Ramras?"

"Not a chance. Also, I heard that you have been sending messengers outside the city."

His face went red. "Oh well, I'm just waiting for my son to come here."

"Son?"

"Yes. You see after Kali died, I thought you would have me killed, so I called for backup. Now I'll just tell him when he reaches here that his journey was in vain."

Lord Kuvera always had a backup plan to ensure his safety. And if there was a chance that he could rule, he would never hesitate to take it.

"You wanted to take the crown for yourself?" She laughed.

"No, no, it was just insurance for me to be escorted back to Alak."

Urvashi nodded, showing him that she understood his predicament. "Don't leave now. You are the last Tribal left in Indragarh. We need an objective eye in the council, right?"

"Yes, you do, indeed." The fat man clapped, keeping the wine glass on the side. "Well I should leave. I will send you the scroll sanctioning the money and you in return give me the rights to Varungarh. I also would love your support in future against the Nagas," he quietly added.

Urvashi said, "Don't worry. I don't like the Nagas as well."

Urvashi and Kuvera began to shake hands. Arjan glanced at Rudra. *Everything went well.*

And then it happened.

It happened in a fraction of a second. Blood was spraying from Kuvera's neck as Urvashi sliced a knife in his throat. He fell down on the ground, all red and purple. The Yakshas instantly readied their bows but before that, Urvashi's men shot their arrows. They fell down on the ground, dead.

Arjan was horrified, stunned, frozen. His fingers were numb and his heart was racing. The King of Yakshas murdered by a little girl. Now they will have to go war with the entire Yaksha tribe.

This girl never stops surprising me.

Urvashi came to Arjan with the bloody knife in hand. Kuvera's blood was smeared over her face, but she didn't wipe it off. "Dispose the knife."

"Why?' Arjan could only muster this word in return. "Why did you give him hope if you were going to kill him?"

"Because that's what he did to my father."

Urvashi went outside, leaving Arjan and Rudra in the hall. They would have to deal with the corpses as well. Arjan sighed, looking at the blood-smeared carpet.

We are doomed now.

42

It was the next day. Kalki waited impatiently in his hut, thinking. Should he confront Kripa or should he not? Lord Bajrang had planted a seed of doubt in his mind. Even Arjan had warned him against Kripa.

It made him recall that Arjan had been an instinctive person. He knew when something was amiss.

Kalki wondered whether Arjan was dead or alive. *Would I ever see him again? Or my mother?* She was in fact in Lord Bajrang's temple right now, while Kalki had spoken to Lord Bajrang yesterday. *If she knew, I bet she'd smile.* He decided to find his brother and meet his mother after everything was over.

He peeked at the symbol on his chest. The Vanars had been staring at it, so he had wrapped a shawl around it. *You are not born an Avatar. Your deeds make you one.* That's what Lord Bajrang had told him.

He thought about his symbol as he walked down the Dandak Hills. The snow-capped hills ended at Vanarvata, a forest. Inside it was a big waterfall where seven rivers merged—crystal clear, they rammed each other. The place was breathtaking. Kara, the doctor in the camp, had told him about how the Vanar kingdom, Kishkinda, used to be in Dakshini. But the Vanars had chosen to migrate to Udaiyas to avoid the war politics of the place. Now, the kingdom

was divided into two factions—Lord Taar's and Lord Bajrang's. Lord Taar wanted the Vanars to expand the kingdom, and wage wars if needed. But Lord Bajrang stated that they had seen enough bloodshed during their battle with Lord Dushasana.

Opposing ideologies from the same race had ended up in a rebellion which was a common thing to hear, even for Kalki. Even back in Indragarh, there had been infighting because of this. It only made him realize how the world operates and progresses—on conflicts. And if there are no conflicts, there is nothing. Every place will be peaceful, but does peace really bring about fruitful change? Seems not. Lord Taar had rebelled. Many Vanars had sided with him. And today, Lord Bajrang's supporters were to fight and kill people of their own tribe.

Kalki walked around the Dandak Hills, amidst the scattered nomadic huts of Vanars. Deep down in the horizon where the slopes descended and the sun was brimming high, he noticed Lord Bajrang leading a dozen soldiers to the Frontier—the no man's land where Dandak Forest and General Taar's camp met. It was a battleground. As of now, they were at a stalemate. Both sides were losing men and both were trying to recruit more men. Unfortunately, Lord Bajrang's forces were depleting. He had been forced to recruit older people and even kids to join his cause against General Taar.

"I have never seen him so worried," Kara told Kalki. "Imagine being in a secluded world and then letting your entire world be destroyed by your own men. One of the reasons he has allowed outsiders to live with the Vanars is mainly because we are short on men. Especially you, Kalki. You look like you can take someone in a fight. The reason why we situated ourselves at such a place was because we wanted to avoid any contact with the rest of the world, but conflict can never be avoided it seems."

Kalki was in the middle of this conversation when he saw Ratna walking up towards him. He was sitting on a stony slab near

Vanarvata—their cherry blossom forest that was at some distance from the Frontier on which General Taar's camp was stationed. One had to cross Vanarvata to reach there and one could even go by the bridge, which Lord Bajrang had used to travel a while ago. The Vanarvata on the outer edges had been barricaded from the Frontier's end to prevent infiltration.

"What have you been up to?" Ratna asked.

"Thinking."

"About what?"

She sat down next to Kalki and began to sharpen her sword.

"What are you?" Kalki asked, frowning. Ratna suppressed a laugh. "No, seriously. I mean you seem like a Manav . . ."

"I was once a Manav before I was shipped off to be an Apsara. Apsaras, as you know, are prescribed Tribals. You are not born an Apsara, you can become one if you pass certain examinations."

"And you passed them?"

She nodded, her bald head bobbing. Kalki had a hard time believing this.

"You think I don't look like an Apsara, but . . ."

Kalki nodded in affirmation to her statement.

"Indeed, I don't." She announced proudly. "Because I don't plan to put Apsaras into a certain criteria of beauty standards. I don't want them to be whoring around. I want them to be women of power, of valour, and of hope. Women, before the Breaking, were powerful individuals, more so than men. Now look at us. We are forced into prostitution. What a waste!"

"And you cut your hair to make a statement?"

She shook her head. "I didn't like them. I couldn't fight properly because of them."

"What does an Apsara fight for?" Like many others, he had the same pre-conceived notions about Apsaras. They existed only for pleasuring men, and sometimes women. Just like Rakshas were supposed to be evil, Nagas elitists, and Manavs normal.

"To free other Apsaras. The Apsara that the Pisach killed . . . she was a free woman, and I had aided in her escape."

"I'm sorry for what happened."

"That's all right. She died a free woman. I am proud of that."

Ratna was a tough individual and Kalki liked that about her.

"So why are you here? You told me you were the one who brought us here. Why?"

Ratna sighed, looking at Vanarvata. "I had heard that Taar was holding Apsaras for his pleasure. I want to free them. He has an entire harem to himself." She glanced at Kalki. "Why are you worried?"

"I am thinking whether I should confront someone about my feelings."

"You should tell her you like her."

Kalki arched his brows. "Who her?"

"Padma. You fancy her, don't you?" She slapped him on the shoulder.

Kalki nervously chuckled. "Oh no, please."

"Stop it. I see the way you look at each other."

"How do we look at each other?" Kalki was puzzled.

"Like you believe in each other." She smiled. "I used to look at someone like that."

"What happened?"

She put the sword on the ground. "He died, what else?"

"How?"

She gave him a look. "You ask too many questions. All I can say is life is a journey with a lot of tripping in between. Just admit to the fact that you have to keep standing up and going forward."

"That's what you did after he died?"

She glumly nodded. "And that's what you should do about the person you want to confront. Don't wait." And with that, she left.

Kalki nodded, thinking she was right. He looked up and saw Kripa walking towards Vanarvata with Padma by his side.

And he decided to follow them.

Vanarvata was the prettiest of all in the entire Dandak—a vast, canvassing, beautiful canopy of cherry trees engulfed in snow. The path was partially clear. The flakes were melting on the ground so Kalki felt like he was stepping on something wet. The branches were thick and wide, the trunks were long, and the trees were almost fifteen feet tall. An exotic smell permeated the air in the forest as Kalki walked behind them.

"Vanarvata is what they say is built on the ashes of Lord Raghav. His ashes led to the growth of such wide variety, colourful flowers and shrubs and trees, lass." Kripa explained, no more in the sluggish, drunkard manner. He had sobered up.

"This is amazing."

"Oh yeah, it is."

"Also, Kripa, I just wanted to tell you how grateful I am you made those astras for me back in Indragarh. But weren't you worried that I might blow up the city with them?"

"I knew you won't use them," Kripa said.

Kalki could hear everything as he silently tiptoed a few paces behind them.

"How did you know?"

"Ah, well, you can kind of predict someone's actions by observing their behaviour, lass. And I have been observing people for a long time."

"How old are you?"

"I am more or less your age."

She shook her head in defiance. "You never share—"

"I am an Ancient, if that's what you want to know."

"An Ancient?" She gulped. "I never expected an Ancient to be a bumbling old man, to be honest."

"I didn't either. But it's not about how we look; it's what we have gone through. You see, people think Ancients are just individuals who can live forever, but they are more than that—they are the keepers of knowledge, they know the truth and history. In fact, there are only ten Ancients who are alive and I know three of them quite well. And the reason they survived was because they had been Endowed with the gift of immortality."

Padma nodded. "You remind me of my father."

"You never talked about your father, lass."

Kalki was surprised how easily Padma and Kripa were talking to each other. This made him jealous since they never talked about their personal lives in front of him. Perhaps they were hiding something from him. Though he won't blame them for being close to each other. They had been instrumental in saving Kalki together—they must have bonded during that time.

"My father is a bumbling fool, too. But he doesn't behave like you, you know. I mean, he lives in harmony and peace when the world is going to the dogs. He didn't do anything when my brothers were killed."

"Who is your father, lass?" He stopped walking. "Is he . . ." and then his head turned to see Kalki standing behind him. "Oh well, look who's spying at us. What are you up to, mate?"

Kalki blushed as he casually walked over to them. He glanced at Padma who looked confused and angry—perhaps because she had realized that Kalki had been eavesdropping on their conversation. "I wanted to speak to you," he mumbled.

"About? About this?" He signalled at Vanarvata. "I believe it is a good learning exercise for us to see the Vanars upfront for they teach us a lot, you know."

"Why aren't we just going to Mahendragiri? I don't want to be here anymore."

Kripa furrowed his brows. "Ah, well you seem worried."

“I am not. I am just . . . I think I should go by myself to the hills now. You can show me the way and I’ll go there.”

“I thought you wanted rest, mate, after that fight with the big fiend.”

Kalki shook his head. “Not anymore. I’m fine.”

“And alone?” Padma squeaked, frustrated. “We fought our way here to help you reach the hills and you want to shake us off.”

“You will be fine here. And it will be really cold in the mountains.”

“Colder than this?” Kripa looked incredulous. “Are you trying to get rid of us?”

Kalki sternly glanced at Kripa, his jaw clenching. “I . . . I want to know why you lied to me about being an Avatar.”

“But you are! The symbol—”

“But I wasn’t before. You said I was predestined to be the Chosen One, but I was not. You just got tired of searching for the One so you just made the strongest man in the village into the One.” Kalki had raised his voice. “Tell me something honestly. How did my father know you?”

“Did Bajrang corrupt your mind? Oh, I shall have a piece of him . . .” Kripa began to leave but Kalki held him back, grabbing his arm.

“You are not going anywhere before you tell me.”

Kripa watched Kalki for a moment. He was shivering with anger.

“Did you bring Mlecchas to the village, old man?” Kalki asked, gritting his teeth.

“What is he talking about?” Padma interfered.

“Did you?” Kalki asked, his hands tightening around Kripa and he could see Kripa was hurting, but he didn’t care.

Kripa bowed his head. The playfulness in his attitude had vanished and he simply nodded. “Yes, I did. Yes.”

Kalki released him. “You killed my father?”

“That was never part of the deal. I didn’t want them to kill your

father. I specifically told Keshav to just kidnap your brother so you could rescue him, mate. I didn't know you would bring an army against them. I didn't know . . ."

But Kalki had lost it. He came dangerously close to Kripa. "Didn't know? So much for being an Ancient."

He took a deep breath and stepped back. "I'm leaving. And I don't want to see you." He didn't want to say goodbye to Padma like this, but he just couldn't control his anger.

And that was when it happened.

He heard the trudging of heavy footsteps and as he turned, a bustling crowd of tall-footed, dark-skinned, oily haired men appeared with shafts and cleavers. They were wearing *rudraksh* necklaces and dhotis around their waist with battle armours.

Rakshas!

At that instant, the Rakshas leapt on to Kripa and Padma while Kalki tossed his shawl in the corner and lurched at one of them, grabbing the cleaver from him and smashing it over his skull. He could see from the corner of his eye that even though Kripa and Padma didn't have weapons, they were dodging the attacks. They had managed to take the opponents' weapons and were using them against the attackers.

Kalki also didn't have weapons, but he had to fight. He grabbed the fallen spear from the ground and flung it at the one of the Rakshas. The blade pierced his eye and he fell on the ground.

"NO!" He heard Padma's shriek as she was grabbed by the Rakshas. Kripa let out a groan as he was punched in his gut and taken away.

They didn't want to kill. They wanted hostages.

But how did the Rakshas turn up here in the first place?

And that was when three Rakshas came and grabbed Kalki. They jumped on top of him, dragging him away but Kalki was more powerful than them. Ten more were charging at him but he flung them away with a single movement, yelling in rage as his muscles

tightened. They all lay unconscious in the corner, and some of them managed to scramble away from Kalki.

He needed help from Kara, from Lord Bajrang, ANYONE!

He hoped Padma and Kripa were all right. Despite how much he hated their guts, he wanted them to be safe.

He had failed, yet again.

They were nowhere to be seen.

43

Manasa couldn't sleep for the next few days. Nanda's severed head kept flashing in her mind. She couldn't believe Nanda was dead. She had cried her eyes out that day. The next day, she had been in denial, and the day after that she had felt numb. It had been four days now, and Manasa had decided to break out from her stupor and do something.

She didn't feel like speaking to Vibhisana these days. Every day, he would bang on her door and ask if she was okay. She wanted to shout that she was not okay. *I am staying with a wimp!* But he was so nice that Manasa couldn't even think of harming him and assuming his throne. People weren't money-minded here. They followed their hearts. People believed in Lord Vibhishana. Even if he died, they'll still be his soldiers, and will do what's necessary and would never bow to another ruler.

I'm so desperate, I'm thinking of killing my own friend.

Manasa laughed at her predicament, fighting back tears. She left her room and walked outside. Reaching the dinner hall, she stood near a window. The hall was filled with bowls of fruits and dishes decorated the platters. A chandelier hung on the ceiling with a golden chain. The window had beautiful drapes and a red carpet covered the floor.

Vibhisana swivelled his head to see her and he beamed. "You are a sight for sore eyes, my dear!"

Manasa didn't greet him. She looked out the window and saw the colourful city of Bhanmati bustling with energy and music. People had worn colourful robes and dhotis. The women were bedecked with beautiful jewellery. It was serene to see such a peaceful city. But then, war only occurs when there is something to fight for. Bhanmati offered nothing but land and beauty.

"You never told me about what my locket does," she quietly said.

"Because you never let me!" He stood up, wiping his mouth with a handkerchief.

He walked to her and then touched the locket which was a Shard of broken glass inside a circular, gold membrane. "Oh dear, this is beautiful." His eyes glistened. "I have only heard stories about this. Never thought I would actually get to see it."

"How do you know about this?"

"My father, Vibhisana the First told me about it. He is an Ancient."

Lord Vibhishana had been given his father's name. This practice was common in Naagpuri as well. There, people believed in rebirth and christened children with the names of their ancestors.

"Ancient?" She had heard bogus stories about Immortals, people who could live forever. "There's no such thing as Ancients."

"Just because your beliefs don't match mine, doesn't mean they're not true." He made her take off the locket. "It had been with his brother's advisor."

"His brother?"

"You might know him as Dushasan." He rolled his eyes. "I'm related to one of the evilest men in the world, but well, not anymore!"

"How did your father die?"

"Oh, he didn't. He just left the material world, thought people would find out about his immortality and question things. I gave him a gurukul to stay in and he teaches children now. Can you imagine a Rakshas teaching children? Sort of ironical since Rakshas don't believe in textbook training but hardcore, combative learning. He is a learned man, my father."

"How did he become an Ancient?"

"Lord Raghav had blessed him with the power of Endowment."

Slowly and softly, Vibhisana began to rub the locket's exterior, but nothing happened and he frowned. He then struggled to pull the golden membrane out. It was protecting the Shard. Once he did that, the Shard came out. It looked beautiful and had a nice sheen. On both sides, it had a mirror-like quality.

"What is this?"

"The Eye of Brahma, or at least part of it," he said. "Let's see which part." He didn't explain any further. Looking at the Shard, he said, "Show me the future."

Nothing happened.

"The future?" Manasa squeaked. After such tumultuous days, she wanted to laugh at the absurdity of the situation.

"Show me the past!" he yelled.

Nothing happened yet again.

"Let's stop," said Manasa.

Vibhisana shook his head. "You give it a try. I want you to really picture what you want to see."

"What do you mean?"

"I think this is the Fourth Shard. Try to think of what will happen if you stay here for the rest of your life."

She held the Shard in her hand and asked the question that he wanted her to ask. She closed her eyes and let it happen—the energy zoomed from her chest to her arms and she could feel the Shard was slowly burning. It was glowing now. As Manasa opened her eyes, she had a vision. She saw the fortress of Suparns—large iron, basilisk-like building and then from inside, it showed chaos, fire. In the midst of the fire was Kadru, her eyes blazing. Jamun stood beside her.

And she held Lord Tarakshya's severed head in her hand.

Then in another image, she could see large vessels made of iron and bronze attached with Amrit. They were lit up. These vessels zoomed in the sky and exploded in the streets.

And then the images stopped and she came back to reality.

"Did you see anything?" Vibhisana asked, worried. "Oh dear! You are bleeding!"

"You didn't?" She could almost feel her voice gasping for breath, as she wiped the blood that came from her nose. "But how is that possible?"

"Your Chakras mixed with the Chakras of the object, but mine didn't, so only you could see it." He took the Shard from her and fitted it back into the membrane. "What did you see?"

"Kadru had won." She sighed. "And she destroyed the Suparns. And I saw fire."

Vibhisana was quiet.

"And I saw Amrit being used in weapons. She wants to make nuclear weapons out of it. That is why she's so sure she could take over Bhanmati. That's why she said to me 'it's going to be different this time'. She realized Amrit was not good for humans but it's good for objects." She blinked hard. "Is this the future? Have we lost?"

Vibhisana shook his head. "It's a possibility, dear, it's not the future." He sat down on the chair, sweating profusely. "Oh dear, oh dear, oh dear, I cannot let this happen. She's making astras out of Amrit. That means she could possibly start the next Breaking. My father told me stories—there had been lepers, cannibalism, the sane went mad. It was a bad, bad time."

Manasa knelt. "This would happen if I don't do anything and I stay here."

"What will you do?"

"Can I see it again? I'll see the possibility of what will happen if I go there."

Vibhisana disagreed. "You bled. If you use it more often, you might lose your sanity. This is a dangerous object."

"Then let me do something about it. Maybe I should go warn Tarakshya."

"Warn? You want to send him a letter?"

Manasa shook her head. "I want some of your men, only a dozen or so, to go to Suparnika before Kadru attacks him."

"What if he doesn't believe you?"

Manasa thought about it. He had gotten Vasuki's family murdered. *He might try to kill me.*

"How valuable is this?" she asked, looking at the Eye of Brahma. "I mean, it showed me something spectacular, it must be pretty damn valuable."

"You can't give this to him. Are you planning to?"

Manasa sighed. "Is this valuable or not?"

"A lot!" he exclaimed. "But you cannot give it to someone like Lord Tarakshya. Oh dear! Oh dear! We are living in bad, bad times. Oh no! They were lost. I-I . . . they were supposed to be lost."

"What is the history behind it?"

"I need to check my father's accounts for that. I'm not sure."

Manasa could understand why he was panicking. But she knew what she had to do. "Give me one chance. Let this be a way for us to reach out and stop Kadru. I promise you, I will do everything in my power not to give this Shard away. I promise you, I will stop her. Just believe in me and give me your best men. I will warn Tarakshya. He might not believe me. He may even try to kill me. But if there is even a small possibility that he will listen, I am ready to take a chance. Suparns and Nagas have had a long, bitter rivalry. It's time we put an end to it."

Vibhisana looked at her for a moment, his eyes meeting hers. "If I don't give you my men, you'll end up taking them yourself one way or the other."

"What do you mean?" Manasa could feel her chest pumping with excitement.

Vibhisana smiled. "You have my support."

44

Kali had been travelling for a while now. He didn't know how far they had come. They had taken a donkey cart for themselves. He and Durukti had covered their heads with shawls so no one would recognize them. Shukr was their guide.

Sitting inside the cart, Kali saw Koko and Vikoko. Their hands were clutching their swords. Durukti looked exhausted. But no matter what, Kali couldn't help but wonder why Durukti had betrayed him. Shukr hadn't given him all the details. *She was my ally. My only sister. And she stabbed me in the back.*

Kali thought about how he was led up to this moment. He had been a true friend and a noble advisor to his dear friend Parikshit before he went mad and started to burn down his own kingdom. Kali had had to stop him.

Kali decided to confront Durukti about this later. Right now, he was simply curious about the place they were headed to.

Pataal.

They had left Keekatpur a few hours ago. Kali opened the flaps of the cart and saw that they were close to the shores of Illavarti now. The great wide ocean stretched in front of them. There were a few dimly-lit farms that canvassed further regions.

"We are at the shore," Shukr called out from the front.

Durukti looked up. "Where are we going, brother?"

Kali sighed. "Where we were born."

"My lord, may I speak?" Vikoko asked nervously.

"You don't have to call me a lord, Vikoko. I'm just a peasant now." He gritted his teeth in frustration. "But yes, please speak up."

"Why are we going to Pataal?"

"What's wrong with it?"

"Don't you know what happened to it?" Vikoko asked. It was common knowledge.

Before Kali could answer her, the carriage stopped. Kali got out and saw a cottage. Instead of sheeps or goats grazing in the field, he saw hyenas—three of them tearing the flesh of a goat . . . or perhaps a human.

Kali walked towards the ocean, leaving behind Durukti and his guards. It reminded him of the beach in the western part of Suryagarh where he had fought King Janmejaya. He saw the dark and decadent ocean stretching ahead. Maybe it was because of the lack of sunlight, but the water looked almost black.

"The Black Ocean," called out Shukr from behind as he walked towards Kali, his hands behind his back. "The Ocean of Asuras, in other words. The entire ocean is drenched in the blood of Asura children, women, and men."

Asuras had come from a different land and conquered the beautiful Illavarti. People said that when they came, they were bright, beautiful, lovely, and had charming accents. They were so strong that they could defeat anyone. They were foreigners who had conquered Illavarti—the nomads as well as their animals had been hunted down or driven away. The rest of the population was backward, different from Asuras. Only the Manavs were dusky, but they were not as fair as the beautiful Asuras and then slowly the Asuras took over them and became their kings. The fearless and strong Asura people had easily defeated the Manavs and taken over the entire Illavarti.

"One of the mightiest times in our history was when Lord Vritra ruled the Seven Seas in Illavarti."

They called him the Dragon—he had been the strongest Asura at the time. He had fought against Lord Indra, eventually getting beheaded. Shukr told Kali how the myths about Lord Indra were not true. He had always been just a madman who believed in science and inventions and cutting down those who opposed his strict rules. Like the Asuras, he too was a foreigner, coming from the land of Swarg, the islands of North, far beyond Illavarti. They had stationed themselves at Mount Meru where stood the Temple of Shiva. With his brothers, he had come and destroyed everything. Half of Illavarti had been plunged into invasions by foreigners from all ends.

"Indra is considered a god, but it wasss Lord Vritra who challenged his tyranny. Now, he'sss just called a demon while Indra is revered as a majestic hero," sighed Shukr.

"What's the next plan? Am I going to be entertained by these history lessons?"

"At least you are being entertained." Shukr smirked and Kali noticed that he was missing a few teeth. "We gather supplies and leave for the ocean."

"Ocean?"

Kali shook his head in confusion.

"And I would like you to meet someone as well."

Kali followed Shukr. The old man staggered towards the cottage that they had spotted earlier. A large boat made of wood had been tied to a pillar. It had a long mast, a cabin inside, and underneath it was a paper thin jib and a hull that was made of iron. The figurehead in the front was of a strange, growling figure—a demon, one could say.

Kali saw the hyenas inside the barricades. Bamboo enclosures had been used to contain the hyenas so they won't jump outside. When they saw Kali, they growled. But Kali passed them, trying

not to show any fear. He finally reached the entrance to the cottage with Shukr. Shukr knocked on the door. It was opened by a pale woman, who glanced first at Shukr and then at Kali.

But Kali instantly noticed something about her. She had golden eyes.

An Asura!

"You seem shocked," Shukra said. "Come in."

Kali entered. He found himself in a small space with two rooms.

"I welcome you to Alakshmi's house," Shukr said.

Kali turned to see that Durukti, Koko, and Vikoko were standing outside.

"Alakshmi?" Kali mused as he glanced at the Asura girl. She was beautiful. "It's nice to meet you."

"She will be our guide in the Black Ocean," Shukr added. "That's her boat out there and I know you have questionsss. How is an Asura alive like this? Well, aren't you alive?"

Kali sighed. "I am alive because they thought my golden eyes was just a genetic trick and not because I am an Asura. No one believes that Asuras are still alive."

"There are only a few left," Shukr said. "And we need to protect ourselves. Also, golden eyes are not the only indication that you are an Asura. In fact, some of the Devas who came from Swarg were themselves golden-eyed, and some Asuras were brown and black-eyed."

Kali looked at Alakshmi again. There was something off about her. But he got distracted when he realized there was an awful smell in the house. He looked at the draped room. "Has someone died in here?"

"I need to feed my babies," added Alakshmi. She had a sleek, razor-like voice.

Ugh. There are carcasses in the house.

Kali was disgusted. He frowned as he said, "We should leave." He went out hoping to take a breath of fresh air when he heard

a whistle from Alakshmi. At that moment, the hyenas from the barricade jumped over and reached for Kali, growling.

At that moment Koko and Vikoko came forward to defend Kali and stood between him and the hyenas, ready to slice the animals if they harmed their lord.

The hyenas jumped over Koko and Vikoko and went for Kali.

Kali was shielding himself with his arms when he heard another whistle. He had closed his eyes in fear but when he opened them, he saw that the hyenas were sitting on top of him, calmly licking their paws. Their skin was soft and they had round, black eyes. Some of them had scars on their bodies.

Kali turned to see Alakshmi who came towards him with a sinister smirk over her face. "That's for being rude."

A woman who can control animals. Interesting.

Durukti came to Kali and asked if he was all right, but Kali ignored her. He kept watching Alakshmi. She walked towards the boat and the hyenas followed her. Koko and Vikoko just stood there, unsure of what to do next.

These animals have been trained to do her bidding.

"Who the hell is this woman?" Kali heard Durukti saying that to Shukr.

"None of your businesss, woman," Shukr said in response.

"Shush, Durukti," Kali chided her, patting her on the shoulder.

"I don't know what is going on and why we have come here, to this island."

"What choice do we have?" Kali snapped at her. "If you hadn't betrayed me, we wouldn't have had to come here."

"You know?"

"Of course, I know." Kali sighed, trying to calm himself down.

"I'm sorry."

Kali simply walked away. He took Shukr to the other side, walking down with him towards the boat, ignoring Durukti as much as he could. His eyes were fixed on Alakshmi who was preparing

the boat. She was tying up some of the hyenas inside the boat. Compared to other land animals, they were quite large.

"How did she do that?"

"When you are born into the world with these animalsss, you learn to speak their language."

Alakshmi glanced at Kali and her stare was poisonous, but at the same time, sensual. She had a full mouth and her eyes, they spoke a thousand words.

"Who is she? How is she still alive?"

"I made sure she did," Shukr said. "For you."

"For me?"

"Yes." He walked forward as Kali remained frozen. "She's going to be your wife."

45

They were in the middle of the ocean.

Kali couldn't believe Shukr wanted him to marry Alakshmi. Sure, he wasn't opposed to it, but then it was an absurd idea for now. He had no kingdom, he had no power, and Shukr, who was acting like Kali's father and mentor, wanted him to be wedded to a mysterious woman who controlled hyenas.

The boat moved slowly and Kali looked at the ocean. It wasn't black as it seemed from a distance. It had a crystal blue hue. But in the darkness of the night with only the burning fire lights that hung on the boat, it did look black.

He sighed as he moved to see Durukti in the corner. She had been watching him, avoiding his gaze. But Kali couldn't care less about her. Durukti had crossed a line and Kali felt cheated. He was now looking at Alakshmi. She was steering the boat, surrounded by her hyenas.

Shukr came and stood beside Kali.

"Does she know?" Kali asked.

"Does she know what?"

"That you want her to marry me."

"Yesss, she does. But you have not made a good first impression."

Kali stifled a laugh. "Why do you want me to marry her?"

"The bloodline of Asuras shall not be tainted." He coughed. "Marry a woman from your tribe and keep it pure. You are one of the last males in the Asura clan."

"What about Koko?" Koko and Vikoko were Asuras as well. Kali had kept their identity a secret.

"They celebrate celibacy." He shook his head. "You are an alpha male and she isss an alpha female. You both shall birth the purest of Asuras and the lineage shall continue. The bloodline shall be strong." Shukr smiled to himself, as if his plan had finally come to fruition.

"What about Durukti?"

"What about her?"

"Asuras married their own sisters," Kali nervously added. "Aren't they the purest breed?"

"Ah," Shukr smirked. "You want to bed your sister?"

Kali flustered. "Oh by the hells and mighty, no. It was just a question."

"Yesss, they do bed their sisters and mothers. In fact, you can bed both of them. The more the merrier." Shukr laughed. Kali tried to hide his embarassment.

"Why haven't you bed Alakshmi? You are an Asura too."

"I'm a priest. I cannot reproduce. But I want the Asuras to rule Illavarti, make them formidable again, just like our forefathers wanted."

Kali nodded. He had never thought about his bloodline this much until Shukr had made him realize its importance. The ocean began to swirl rapidly and Alakshmi looked over at Shukr who nodded back at her.

"We are here."

"We are where?" Kali looked at the ocean again. He could see nothing but the water. The moon overhead was turning red.

"Pataal."

But there is nothing here!

He stood up and then glanced at the water. "I am sorry, but I don't see it."

"Because it's plunged inside," Shukr said, signalling at the water. "Don't worry, I'm not going to tell you to swim. I want you to do something for me, all right?"

Kali nodded.

"The island dissolved with the First Shard of the Eye of Brahma and the the land wasss no more. To retrieve it, the Chakras of the Eye of Brahma have to be mixed with the Chakras of the water," Shukr explained. Durukti and Kali's guards were listening as well.

Kali had heard about the Chakras—energy atoms that are everywhere and can be used according to the person's will. That's how Vidhyadharas use elemental magic by mixing body energies with energies of certain objects.

"I want you to really look into the past of everything, of you, of the Asuras, of our people, and of the island. I want you to deepen yourself into the memory of our ancestors and of yourself, and learn the truth."

The truth? What is this so-called truth?

"How should I do it?" Kali asked, peering at Durukti and sharing a worried glance with her. She was surely anxious about all of this and her eyes spoke volumes—she didn't trust Shukr. But that didn't matter because Kali did.

"Feel the Chakras."

Kali nodded as he slipped his hand in the water. The water was cold but he could feel the waves slowly touching his fingertips, tickling him. And he thought about it—about all the things Shukr had just told him. The water began to burn and he realized the coldness was now inside him, and the water was now a part of him. The pain and pleasure began to topple him, his consciousness faded, and he opened his eyes to find himself alone on the boat. The water had turned completely black. And from then on, the

blood red skies danced around him. It was just like the visions he had had, but this time he felt like he was in control of his visions.

And just around him, like magic, he saw images made of tiny little lights forming into individuals and creatures—he saw the Dragon standing over the water, he saw Hiriyankshipu and Hiriyanksha. He saw his father and his mother. And he saw his siblings. They were all made of lights and they were all dancing over the water, shimmering under the red sky.

He saw the other Asuras and then out of thin air, he was in Pataal. The boat came on the surface and Kali saw that the island was smaller than Illavarti. He could see tall iron buildings in the distance. The island was unlike any other he had ever seen.

And it was all surreal.

I want to see my past.

And just like that, he was pushed back. The images evaporated, coalescing to show Kali a forest.

He saw a lanky, tall man with long braided hair. His crown was tilted and he was wearing a long robe. He had soldiers around him. Holding a bow and an arrow, he pointed it towards Kali.

And Kali recognized him. He could recognize this man anywhere.

In front of him stood King Parikshit.

46

Kalki had almost forgotten about Shuko until he appeared in front of him. He flapped his wings and squawked at the snow as if it was something to eat.

I never liked the cold.

Kalki looked at the Vanars. They were repairing the ruptures in the barricades they had erected in Vanarvata. Lord Bajrang was instructing them. Ratna and Smrit were helping as much as they could.

Where were you for so long? Kalki asked. It was still very awkward for him to be communicating with Shuko telepathically.

Oh please, you didn't miss me, the parrot squawked.

Kalki rolled his eyes. Shuko fluttered his wings and sat on Kalki's shoulder. He was quiet as he played with the snowflakes when a shadow appeared before him. He found Lord Bajrang towering over him. His golden ornaments glinted in the light.

"Are you sure they were Rakshas?" Lord Bajrang asked.

"I've battled plenty of them. So yes, I am sure."

Kalki sighed. Padma and Kripa had been abducted in front of his eyes. He was shaking in anger. But then, Kalki was furious at Kripa for what he had done to his father. He wanted to bash his head for it. Padma had to be saved but he would leave Kripa in Taar's camp.

He can plunge to his death for all I care.

"We have a problem. My men say they saw some Manavs as well. Taar must have made a truce with the Manavs and the Rakshas," Lord Bajrang mumbled. "Don't stress. We shall find them."

"How do you plan to do that?" Kalki stood up, irritated. He faced Lord Bajrang and said, "You don't have enough men. Do you plan to grow in size and save the day?" He was referring to a myth. It was believed that Lord Bajrang had once grown to the size of a mountain.

Lord Bajrang remained calm. "I know you are angry but never forget that your tongue can be sharper than your sword when anger takes over it. And it can leave scars that one might not be able to heal."

Kalki looked away, annoyed. But he understood what Lord Bajrang was trying to say.

"But that doesn't mean I can grow tall, young boy!" He let out a hearty laugh. "We have a lot to do. The point is, do you want to help or sulk with your funny parrot?" He winked at Shuko.

He knows me, Shuko told Kalki.

Kalki wondered how, but he didn't prod further.

"All right. I'm in."

I am coming, Padma.

"You don't believe in our cause, do you?" Lord Bajrang asked as he leaned forward, entering a dark pathway, engulfed in snow and large glaciers.

Kalki had no idea where Lord Bajrang was taking him. "No, I don't. I don't see the point of the Vanars fighting each other at all."

"Vanars by nature are animalistic, like most tribes. We had been gifted by Lord Shiva to Illavarti to act as peacekeepers, guardians, helpers to the world. But none of the inhabitants of Illavarti wanted

our protection. We were peace-loving, so they thought we were weak. So the Vanars decided to live in seclusion until Lord Raghav and King Sugriva signed a pact with us."

King Sugriva? He had been Lord Bajrang's ally. Some people even claimed that he had been like a brother to him.

"You made that pact happen?"

Lord Bajrang proudly nodded. They had now entered a strange rock-like structure and started ascending the uneven staircase.

"I thought living in seclusion would be for the best."

"What happened then?"

"Lord Raghav left us and so did King Sugriva. People say the Endowed are blessed because they can live forever. I don't believe so. It is painful to see everyone you love perish in front of you."

They had reached the top. Kalki slipped on the step but Lord Bajrang grabbed his fist and pulled him up. Kalki grinned as he stood in front of the seven rivers. The sight was truly magnificent. He had seen it earlier, but from a distance. Here the seven rivers merged into each other.

"Wow."

"Oh yeah." Bajrang grinned.

"I have heard that you stopped waging wars after the incident with Lord Raghav."

"Oh yes, I did. I have lived for a long time. I realized that wars—they might be good to solve a small conflict, but they have major repercussions later on. And that's what Taar doesn't understand. He thinks war is necessary to survive." He sighed. "So here we are, doing exactly what he wanted—fighting. War never solves anything, Kalki."

Kalki nodded. He remembered the corpses of the people of Shambala. He had those people up to fight against Durukti. That fight had led to the killing of the people he had loved.

Oh Lakshmi! Please forgive me.

"Do you think you'll be able to stop him?"

Lord Bajrang looked at Kalki for a moment and grinned. "I can lift a mountain. What do you think?"

"Did it really happen?"

"Not really," he shrugged his shoulders, "but I brought every herb on that mountain for brother Lakshman who was quite ill and wounded."

Lakshman was Lord Raghav's brother.

"What about you burning Dushasan's—"

Bajrang lifted his hand. "You are a very curious child."

Kalki laughed.

"Why are we here?"

Lord Bajrang turned serious. "Have you heard of the Eye of Brahma?"

"I know a bit. The teachers at my gurukul told me about it."

Bajrang explained about the Four Shards and then he said, "I have the Second Shard."

"Where is it?"

"Right in front of you."

Kalki was stunned. "Wait, no . . . You? How is it you?"

"The Eye of Brahma is made of Chakras. One can dissolve those Chakras and join it with his own Chakra. There's a reason why I am considered invincible. I know what Taar is doing right now. Unfortunately, I was busy at the Frontier and couldn't foresee the infiltration by the Rakshas."

"What is the history of the Eye?"

"Dushasan had given it to his advisor. The advisor ran away with it. Some say he was an Asura and left for Pataal. It then came into the hands of a good friend of mine. He had stolen it from someone. Giving me the Second Shard, he had said that it was an important object that would serve me well."

"Your friend?"

Bajrang nodded. "You might know him. He has a scar on his

head. We weren't initially on good terms but he was kind enough to do give me the Shard."

"Where does he live?"

"Where you plan to go—Mahendragiri."

Kalki looked at the mountains. Bhargav Ram was waiting for him there.

"Close your eyes, boy. There's something you need to see."

Kalki hesitated a little, but closed his eyes. Bajrang held his hand.

For a while nothing happened until Kalki realized his hand was burning. Soon, he could feel his body moving like gel and withering away. He opened his eyes to find himself in the snow again. He was in a camp. Around him were large tents, roasted beefs, fires, Vanars in dark fur combating each other. Some were having their supper, some were sleeping, and some were teasing the dancing Apsaras. Lord Bajrang and Kalki stood in a corner and watched.

"Don't worry," Bajrang said, patting Kalki on the shoulder. "No one can see us."

This is unbelievable.

Bajrang and Kalki walked around the tents. In the distance they could see a frozen river. Some of General Taar's men were looking at the barricades that Bajrang's men had put up on the other side of this river. Now, they reached the largest tent of the camp, inside which stood a tall Vanar. His fur was as dark as coal, he had big eyes and a big mouth. The Vanar was pacing inside his tent, worried. Manavs and Rakshas surrounded him.

The big, dark-skinned Vanar spoke to another brown-skinned Vanar, "Aruna, where are the captives?"

"Should I bring them to you, General?

"Yes."

He is General Taar! He looked devious. Soon, Kalki saw Padma and Kripa come out from one of the tents, looking haggard. Their faces and arms had bruises.

Taar walked and stood close to Kripa, his thick, bushy brows arching. "What are Manavs doing in Bajrang's camp?"

Kripa didn't say anything. Taar flared his nostrils in anger.

"Who is the man who injured so many of my men?"

He was referring to Kalki.

Kripa glared at Taar, and then he smirked. Taar howled and punched his gut. "We don't have time for this. ARUNA!"

His right hand man came forward in a hurry. "Yes, my lord?"

"What the hell am I supposed to do with an old man and a girl? Go find out something useful about what's going on in Bajrang's camp."

Taar was being impractical again. Gently, Aruna reminded him that they had to battle with Bajrang's army in a few hours. "It would be wise to let the men prepare for battle right now." Kalki's heart skipped a beat and he could feel Bajrang's heart leaping as well.

"Don't tell me what to do, you idiot." Taar sat down and looked at the people around him. He had a devious smile on his face. "What are we waiting for? Let's attack now."

"What should we do about the prisoners?" asked Aruna.

Taar turned around, looking at the docile faces of Kripa and Padma. "Rape her and kill him. What else?"

Kalki flared his nostrils. He moved to hit Taar but Bajrang stopped him. "He cannot see you and you cannot touch him."

"We should go back and prepare ourselves."

"Are we at war?"

Bajrang nodded. "Unfortunately, yes."

47

This won't end well. We'll have to constantly watch our backs.

It had been announced to the public that Lord Ḳuvera, the king of Yakshas had been killed by Lady Urvashi in self defence. But the Yakshas suspected foul play. They were protesting. Some had even tried to assassinate Urvashi.

She had created a mess, and Arjan was trying to clean it up.

But for Arjan, the worst was yet to come.

How long will I have to guide this unpredictable, dangerous queen? I only stayed because Rudra asked me to.

"We should leave." Arjan clasped Rudra's cheeks, carefully gazing at him. "We are not safe here."

Rudra shook his head. "I know what she did was wrong but I cannot let her be defeated by Ramras. Believe me, he's worse than her.

Ramras was proving to be a bigger problem than Arjan had anticipated. He was a despicable man who drank and whored, but his influence in the council had grown tremendously. He, like the other rich people, had been happy serving Kali. Though Kali had tried to help his citizens, his reign had only seen the rich getting richer and the poor perishing even more. When Urvashi had taken the city, the nobles as well as the citizens had grown afraid, uncertain about how this little girl would rule their city. This fear had been

fanned by Ramras who never stopped reminding the ministers that she had murdered the King of Yakshas in broad daylight.

"And if we leave now, we will be considered fugitives. We have pledged ourselves to the crown."

"There's no crown. There's a just a whiny girl who does what she wants without thinking."

In order to stop the protests, and save her life, Urvashi had passed a law. Now, it was illegal for Yakshas to live in Indragarh. The Yaksha minister in the council, Gumukha had voiced his outrage at this.

"There will be consequences to what you did! You shall be punished! The Yakshas shall retort," Gumukha shouted at the top of his voice, pointing his cane at Urvashi.

Ramras patted him on his shoulder to calm him down. He then looked at Urvashi. "Lady Urvashi, you shouldn't have done that. The Yakshas are creating problems in the city."

"He killed my father. He deserved it."

"You could have taken him to the court," Ramras protested. "Why did you take the law in your own hands?"

"I am the law and justice. I am your queen."

"Yes, you have the authority to do what you want," Ramras turned to leave. "Until you are the queen," he added under his breath. Gumukha followed Ramras outside. Just as they were about to turn the corner, Ramras stopped. He looked at Urvashi and said, "The Yakshas are a proud tribe and they feel slighted. We should discuss what is to be done about them in our next council meeting."

"I didn't mean to send them away. I have no qualms with the Yakshas as people. I had passed the law to stop the riots. If you promise me there won't be any riots, I'll withdraw it, until the council votes for the ruler."

With a pleasant smile, Ramras glanced at Gumukha. Gumukha didn't say anything, but just nodded meekly.

Arjan knew what Ramras had been hinting at. He will defeat Urvashi and bring back the Yakshas in the city. It was the day of

the council meeting. Councilmen were going to decide who was fit to rule Indragarh.

Urvashi, Arjan, and Rudra stepped inside the council chamber. There was a huge round table surrounded by wooden chairs occupied by the councilmen. Windows were lined on one side of the room but the drapes had been closed. Manav guards had been stationed at the entrance. Gumukha sat at the back beside other Yaksha noblemen. He and Ramras were glancing at each other.

Urvashi sat opposite Ramras. "Let's begin. Lord Ramras can speak first."

Ramras stood up. Rudra fidgeted nervously in his seat, but Arjan clasped his hand in his. They both smiled.

"I know you hate him. But you've got me now," Arjan whispered.

"Many of you might not know me well. Unlike Lady Urvashi, I'm not royalty. But I plan to herald this place and its people into better, stronger times. I will set up more temples. Tax rate will be lowered. More gurukuls will be set up. Women will receive equal pay in the government. And I also plan to increase Indragarh's export and import business with other cities."

"And how do you plan to do that?" a minister asked.

"I plan to change Agnigarh from a living settlement to a working area. And all the civilians will shift to Indragarh. To tackle population control, Manavs shall be employed to build houses. And in my plan, the Yakshas headed by Gumukha will play a major role. In fact, as we speak, the son of Lord Kuvera, the heir of Alakpur, Nalakuvera is on his way to Indragarh and we shall have a treaty with him so we could use the Yaksha workforce. We all know the Tribals are faster when it comes to menial jobs."

Arjan remembered that Lord Kuvera had mentioned that his son was coming to Indragarh. Though he hadn't anticipated that Ramras would have already gotten in touch with him.

Ramras' speech is filled with empty promises. And if he is going to employ

Manavs, why would the Yakshas play a key role? He is just doing this to please Gumukha.

"We have already talked to him. He has been kind enough to forgive us for his father's murder."

I get it now. He plans to please the Yakshas by bringing Lord Kuvera's son in the city.

"But he wants me to be the king. If I am elected, he will come to us in peace."

Urvashi coughed. And with a smile, she asked, "And what if I become the queen? What shall he do?"

Ramras sighed. "He'll attack the city."

Everyone gasped in horror. Urvashi looked bored, as if it didn't matter to her if the city was attacked.

"This is outrageous! Then, we have no choice but to make you the king or face the wrath of the Yaksha prince," one of the councilmen said.

"What is the point of this discussion if it has been decided already?"

Everyone started shouting. *So there are people who believe Urvashi should rule.* Ramras awkwardly sat back in his chair and Urvashi stood up to speak.

"We won't scamper. We are not cowards. If Nalakuvera wants war, we shall give him war." She directed his attention to Gumukha. "I might be a little young to rule. Not the most favourable contender here. But I am royalty. I defeated Kali. While the rich became richer during his reign, the poor were plagued by problems. He wasn't a perfect ruler and I wouldn't be as well. But I know one thing. I have plans that could make this city great again." She paused, glancing at Arjan. "I really can. We shouldn't give in to Yakshas' threats. I will follow every rule that my father followed and soon, we will witness the Golden Age of Indragarh, OUR DAYS OF GLORY! But I won't run away from the Tribals. I'll lend my support to them, but if they don't cooperate I shall not hesitate to cut them."

"All the rules by Vedanta?" one minister said, nodding his head. "They were good!"

"Yes, all rules and regulations followed by my father shall be implemented except the Tribal program. I have no issues with including them with us, if they don't create any problems. And if they do, we'll deal with them then."

"You let the prisoners out. There were many who had been thrown in because of sodomy. What will you do about that? Sodomy brings ugliness and unhealthiness to the society," a minister added.

Arjan held his breath. *This is not happening.*

Urvashi sighed. "I know and I agree. Those who practise sodomy shall be imprisoned."

And Arjan's blood ran cold as he shared a worried glance with Rudra.

The ministers though were satisfied in bringing back these conservative laws. Urvashi had officially won over all the noblemen and the ministers.

"And if we select you," Gumukha asked, "what would you do about Nalakuvera who stands outside the city doors?"

"I will extend a hand in friendship."

"And if he doesn't take it?"

Urvashi grinned. "I shall let him know then that every Yaksha that is there in this city shall be cut open till he surrenders. And I'll start with you, Lord Gumukha."

Flabbergasted, Gumukha stood up from his seat. He was about to head towards Urvashi but his fellow ministers stopped him. Unlike Kali, who had tried to keep the Tribals happy, Urvashi was keeping the Tribals in check, though not disqualifying them totally.

Urvashi sat back and and looked at Arjan. Arjan hesitatingly gave her a thumbs up. The voting started as Urvashi bit her nails, nervous. Arjan and Rudra didn't want Urvashi to win.

Urvashi came and stood beside Arjan.

"How was it?"

"You promised something about recapturing the prisoners," Rudra said.

"Only a few of them. How does it matter?"

"But they helped you—"

"And now I'll have the guards of the crown to help me, the army on my side. The prisoners were a temporary solution. But do not worry, you two won't be going anywhere since both of you are my thinktank." She winked and then seated herself comfortably on her chair.

Rudra and Arjan clasped their hands in each other's.

The spokesperson had completed counting the paper stashes given by each member of the council. He stood at the pedestal to announce the results. Arjan was trying to study his expression. Both Ramras and Urvashi were inexperienced rulers, but at least Ramras won't put Arjan and Rudra in prison.

"Going by the results . . ."

Don't be Urvashi.

Don't be Urvashi.

Arjan's eyes were shut and he could feel the sweat in his palms, the hair at the back of his neck standing up.

"The new ruler of Indragarh, the capital of Udaiyas, the sole power of Keekatpur is Queen Urvashi, the youngest queen in the history of this country."

And with that, Arjan could picture his doom.

Damn.

48

Kali had just travelled back in time.

Or at least, his consciousness had.

He was standing in the midst of the jungle with King Parikshit aiming an arrow at him before a guard stepped up to him and told him to put it down.

"He's just a boy," the guard said.

But I've grown.

Kali turned and realized that King Parikshit and his guards weren't looking at him. In fact, they didn't even know the older Kali was standing there. Instead he saw his younger version on the ground, clutching his small, cherub-faced sister, Durukti. He felt goosebumps. It was eerie watching himself—fair-skinned, with golden eyes and long wavy hair.

"But he is an Asura! Look at his eyes," commented Parikshit. "They should be burned down. They spread curses."

Kali realized this was the time when Asuras were said to be a stinking, horrifying race who were despicable to look at. They were being pulled and pushed down, killed and beheaded for being who they were. Kali recalled how it had all started after the Breaking. Rumours about the Asuras had started spreading. People said that Asuras had caused the Breaking through their magic. Obviously, Kali knew that Asuras didn't dabble in magic

extensively, not more so than Vidhyadharas, but people had chosen to believe the rumours. As a result, Asuras in Illavarti had been taken down, raped, and murdered. It didn't matter to Manavs what their gender or age was. And then the killings stopped for a while when Parikshit became king. He was a benevolent king, heir to the throne of Udaiyas. He had controlled the Northern cities from Indragarh.

"Fine." Parikshit nodded. "Make use of him somehow."

The guard nodded. He was a young man and looked fierce though recognizable. Kali looked at the guard as he helped the younger Kali and Durukti up and took them back to the kingdom.

Kali realized why he was recognizable. He didn't have the grey beard he had now, but was young and captivating—he was none other than Koko.

Earlier, the majority of the provinces in North were ruled by Parikshit in the Kuru Kingdom. The country had not been divided like the present time.

The scene changed. The present scene dissolved and Kali was standing in the street. Parikshit was walking in front of Kali with his guards. Younger Kali stood beside him. He was carrying a sword and a shield.

Kali remembered how he used to be Parikshit's squire, his aid. Parikshit would ask Kali to do menial jobs. Along with Parikshit, stood his son Janmejaya, a teenager. Parikshit was showing him around the city. The people were nodding at Parikshit, bowing to him.

And then out of nowhere an assassin appeared with a sword to attack Parikshit. Before Koko could do anything, younger Kali jumped in front deflecting the attack from the Naga assassin and then stabbed him. Parikshit looked at his aid and was surprised. Their relations with the Nagas had turned sour. It was not the first time that an assassination attempt had been made at the king.

Kali remembered how this was one of his proudest moments

since he had saved the king. Parikshit went the younger Kali—who was growing with a strong, muscular body—and said, "I owe you one, Kali."

Koko was embarrassed but the younger Kali patted him on the back. "Big brother, I hope you don't mind that I did your job," he said. Parikshit and Janmejaya began walking ahead.

The scene ended.

Now, Kali was in the king's court. These scenes were just marking the important details of his past.

He saw Janmejaya, now a bit older than he was in the previous scene. He looked scrawny. Standing close to the throne, he was yelling at his father. Parikshit, who now looked old and weak, sat on his throne.

"You cannot let Kali lead. An Asura shouldn't be allowed to lead the army, Father!"

"How does it matter? He's a good boy." The old man coughed.

Kali had no idea about this conversation. He always thought Janmejaya hadn't liked Kali because he had been like a son to Parikshit and there was this inherent jealousy emanating from him. Kali had thought that Janmejaya had just wanted his father's attention. But Janmejaya had hated Kali because he had believed him to be a stereotypical Asura.

"We are losing to Nagas—"

"We are losing to Nagas because we did not employ Kali's intellect till now. He has a sharp mind and he's a genius. He has studied all the ancient ways of war tactics."

"That Asura has blinded you!" he yelled. "He has used some magic on you and it's making you trust him."

Parikshit laughed at the idiosyncratic objection made by Janmejaya. "You are weak, child, and you are stubborn. I'm having second doubts about whether I should make you my heir or not to the Kuru . . ."

The scene instantly changed to a room that belonged to Parikshit.

A small goblet had been kept beside the bed. Kali watched Janmejaya sneaking in. He poured some liquid inside the goblet of wine.

No.

Kali couldn't believe what he was seeing. He began to shout at Janmejaya. "Don't you dare!"

The scene changed and showed Kali a painful memory. Parikshit was on his deathbed and Kali was sitting next to him.

"My dear friend, you have been like my own son," the coughing, dying king said. "It was a privilege knowing you."

"It was an honour serving you, your highness."

"You shall be a great man but you must be careful. There's a thin line between . . ." he coughed again.

Kali saw how weak and frail Parikshit looked. His eyes had shrunken and his face had lost all colour.

"There's a thin line between good and evil. Always make sure to do good, for life is too . . . too short to be evil."

That moment, the younger Kali had lost the man who had been like a father to him. Parikshit's eyes were closed forever. Kali now felt sick. If only the Eye of Brahma had the power to not just show him the past but let him alter it, Kali would not hesitate to murder Janmejaya.

Kali already knew what the next scene would be. He clearly remembered.

Now he saw Janmejaya with the crown over his head. Younger Kali and Durukti were had been tied up as Janmejaya ordered their execution.

"My father never had the courage to do so. But I would. Kill them both! They poisoned my father! We know you are working with the Nagas and I shall burn all of them after I deal with you. You and your sister are evil."

Younger Kali and Durukti were taken into a cell where they would be killed quietly for Kali was getting a lot of support from the people. But the executioner was none other than Koko and his

sister Vikoko who were Janmejaya's guards now that Parikshit was dead. Koko and Vikoko cut off their restraints and told them that the cell opened up to the sewers which would lead Kali and Durukti out of the kingdom.

"Why are you doing this?" asked Kali.

"Because he's killing you for being an Asura, my lord. And we are Asuras too."

"You are an Asura?" young Kali shrieked.

Koko and Vikoko nodded.

Young Kali had wondered why they didn't have golden eyes—the usual Asura trademark. But then, not every Asura had golden eyes. Only the pure ones did. Kali's father had been of pure breed. He had been a nobleman while his mother had been a slave, both of them from the Asura race. Thus, Kali and Durukti were purebloods while some of his siblings weren't.

"Thank you, my friend," young Kali patted him on the shoulder.

"Let us come with you. Janmejaya is a tyrant. We do not wish to work for him anymore," said Vikoko.

"Are you sure?"

"Without a doubt," Koko said.

And the voice trailed off as the scene dissolved. Kali realized now that the warmth, the burning sensation in his hand had stopped and he woke up. He was sweating profusely as he watched the water where his hand was. Swallowing a lump in his throat, he sat upright on the boat, wiping his sweat. He was back in the present and Durukti was watching him intently while Alakshmi was still at the wheel. He looked at Koko and Vikoko who looked worried. Kali stared at Koko. He looked so old now with his wrinkly skin, his grey beard covering his face, and his white hair.

The past seemed so real to him, as if it had just happened.

Kali looked at his hand which was wet. He wiped it off on his dhoti. Shukr came and sat beside him. "What did you see?"

Kali told him.

"Yes. The Eye of Brahma doesn't just let you see the past from your eyes but from every perspective. You had no idea about Janmejaya, did you?"

Kali shook his head. "I didn't know he had poisoned his own father."

"We do some crazy thingsss for power and the crown." Shukr sniggered. "You have blood on your nose?"

Kali hadn't realized that. He wiped it away. "This is horrible." He shook his head. "I just don't understand how—"

"You left the kingdom, made peace with the Nagas, led an expedition against Janmejaya and killed him." Shukr narrated the rest of the story that Kali hadn't seen through the Eye, but he knew. "You helped Koko and Vikoko conceal their identities and gave them a new life. Thus, they swore a blood oath to protect you sssince in the original Asura culture, we protect the almighty one," Shukr hissed, signalling at Koko and Vikoko. They were now old and battered, but still the same, strong individuals that they used to be.

Kali recalled how he had defeated Janmejaya. It had taken years for him to come in the inner circle of the Nagas before joining their ranks and fighting Janmejaya. But by then, the Kuru empire had been dissolved and broken into scattered provinces by Janmejaya. He had then assigned these provinces to the kings of his choice, one of them being Vedanta's domain. Janmejaya had been in Varungarh when he had been attacked.

Kali had come with his ships and cannons and blown Janmejaya's gigantic castle that was situated on the sea. As the battle came to shore, he had used the technique of Mandala Vyuha. It was a defensive position—cavalry in the front while the Commander-in-Chief, Kali at the back. Once his men had started killing Janmejaya's men, he had raced ahead to fight Janmejaya, who had been waiting for him on his chariot.

Kali had lurched from his chariot to Janmejaya's. They had

tried to slice each other apart. Janmejaya's chariot had been moving at a breakneck speed. The horses had trudged and collapsed when the chariot had jerked. Janmejaya had been flung into the sea. Kali had also fallen. Standing up, he had walked towards Janmejaya as Janmejaya had tried to find his sword in the water.

Kali had no need for a weapon then. He had punched Janmejaya and plunged him deep inside the water, drowning him until Janmejaya's body stopped resisting. He had won. Varunagarh had been his. The Nagas had cheered for their leader.

All this was coming back to him and for a moment, Kali felt proud for who he was and what he had achieved. Though now he had fallen and had lost everything.

"You saw the wrong part, though," Shukr quietly added.

"What do you mean?"

"You saw what you wanted to see. But you must now go back and see what you don't want to see."

"Why? I have learned my lesson. And I am proud of what I did." Kali paused, thinking. "I am one of the last Asuras and I conquered half of this country. If that's not damn well impressive, I don't know what is."

"That's true. But there is still something you don't know about yourself. You are, after all, just beginning your journey to fight the Adharm. And you are preparing yourself. But first, you must know the truth."

Kali narrowed his gaze. "What truth? That Janmejaya poisoned his own father?"

Shukr shook his head. "It is about the memory you have blocked. Remember the night your siblings died in the fire?"

Kali nodded.

"Now go back to that time and see for yourself."

"Who should I see in particular?" Kali asked.

"Your brother."

Kali recalled the image of a baby boy—the only male in his entire lot of siblings.

"What truth? He died in the fire like the rest. End of story!" Kali spat.

"No, he didn't," whispered Shukr.

Kali's blood ran cold. "What do you mean?"

"Your brother is alive. He lives in Illavarti and has grown into a fine, strong man. And it is time you know who he isss."

49

Kadru was getting bored.

She had been waiting in the meadows for a while with her men and Jamun. They had accepted the invitation and were here in Suparnika—the land of Suparns. Far off, across the sea, she saw a large dome-like fortress as huge as the entire Naagpuri. That marked the entrance to Suparnbhoomi. Around it was a long-winded bridge. Trees lined both the sides of the fortress.

Suparnbhoomi stood above sea level with long, strong pillars that held the entire city. Little caves had been built on the sea where the actual Amrit could be found. The wheels of her mind were turning.

How can I steal the Amrit?

She glanced at her wound. It had filled with pus. She needed the bloody Amrit to save her life. She felt weaker every day. Jamun had noticed that too. But then, the political leader didn't care much about Kadru's well-being. He was glad to be here, standing in the meadow close to Suparnabhoomi.

People said that Suparnbhoomi is a well-nourished, well-supplemented city belonging to one of the brightest and the most technologically advanced Tribals. But then there had been a massive war, the Breaking had happened, the Mahayudh had caused the Suparns to be more cautious and reserve their resources. They had already been extensively using their abundant supplies.

I hate them.

She didn't like the Suparns—selfish creatures that were hoarding the Amrit. But she was going to take it. She had a plan, of course. Go inside, bond with them well, make her way to the caves, steal the Amrit and escape. Though the stealing part was going to be tricky. She will have to create a diversion and she had a plan for that as well.

She couldn't see partially. That bloody Nanda had stabbed her eye. The recovery had taken time, which is why it had taken them so many days to accept Tarakshya's invitation. The eye had been covered with a patch. She was in a cloak that covered her battle armour, her short skirt made of linen, and a bronze plate on her chest.

Jamun was in traditional Naga robes.

"They take too much time," he rasped under his breath.

And perhaps it was a coincidence but at that moment, Kadru saw something in the air. She looked up and saw three winged chariots appear. They were flying, shooting blue remnants of the Amrit from the back.

Finally, they landed in the meadows and from one of them came out Maruda, chewing something in his mouth. "Ah well, lookie!" He grinned.

"What took you so long?" Kadru asked, trying hard not to cuss at him.

"Chill down, snake." Maruda chuckled. "On board now."

Kadru nodded. She didn't expect she would get to sit in one of these thingies, though this way she might be able to observe the mechanics of the chariot.

"We aren't using the main gate?" Kadru asked as she sat with Jamun. Maruda sat opposite them.

The Naga soldiers climbed in other chariots that Maruda had brought with him.

"We aren't Tribals, my dear," he grinned before he asked the driver to ignite the Amrit and manoeuver the chariot.

The feast had begun. Tables had been filled with all kinds of delicacies. Some people were eating, and some were dancing with Apsaras.

But even with the festivities around, Kadru couldn't help but think about Manasa. She was worried that Manasa might return. She had jumped in the lake that merged with the river Sheshnad. This river joined another river in Bhanmati. *Hopefully she hasn't reached the bloody kingdom of Vibhishana.* She could only hope.

There was a lot of distraction. Lord Tarakshya, seated in the centre, was caressing the cheek of an Apsara sitting on the arm of his chair. The Suparns were joyously celebrating the treaty between the Nagas and Suparns. Kadru's men were thoroughly enjoying themselves as well. She had brought fifteen of her trusted ministers. Tarakshya had had one condition—no soldiers, only the people in Kadru's inner circle could attend the feast.

Kadru noticed how Suparns looked quite similar to Manavs. The only difference was that they were strangely obsessed with the colour yellow and golden. They would dress themselves in that colour, paint the buildings in that colour, and even preferred to eat things of that colour.

The feast was happening in the open. Guards had been placed around the premises. The tall, bronze statue of Garuda towered over the place. All the guards had strange, small wings clasped at their backs and Amrit in their pockets to fly off when needed. Some people laughed as the clown entertained them, while the others were ogling at the dancers.

At least the Nagas don't treat women like objects.

Jamun was drinking a delicious gold wine. He even nudged Kadru, told her to have some fun, but her mind was on other

things. She was observing the little entrances and exits that were in the crevices of Suparnbhoomi, the city.

Unfortunately, the feast was happening outside the main domain of Lord Tarakshya and it was evident that that was where lay the reserves of Amrit. Kadru saw one of her guards that she had sent to scout the city while everyone enjoyed the celebration. The Naga guard came to her and whispered in Kadru's ears. "There's a trolley that goes down to the caves. Usually many guards are stationed there, but today some of them missed their duty to come and watch the feast."

Kadru nodded. She knew what she had to do. She hadn't come here to wine and dine. She glanced at Lord Tarakshya. He was seven feet tall, had kohl in his eyes, and his waist-long hair had been oiled. He was busy drinking and dancing.

Time to go.

The trolley was close to Lord Tarakshya's palace in a small citadel that was hidden in the shadows. Kadru was traversing through dark lanes, lit by fire lamps. She, with two of her guards, entered the lane and grabbed one of the fire lamps. Two armed Suparn guards were standing next to a grilled door.

"Who is this?" one of them called.

Kadru wasn't afraid. She pulled her sword out of the sheath and without wasting any time, she stabbed one of them in the throat and with a quick reflex, beheaded the other one. She had been so fast, the guards hadn't seen it coming. She looked at the grilled door as she began to bash it open, as much as she could, finally breaking the lock and coming inside a small platform that had a rope and a pulley. Her guards pushed the pulley and the trolley moved downwards. As the cement in the corners began to wash off, she saw she was leaving the floating city that was held up by the pillars.

The city finally revealed to be hollow from within, made of iron just like the entire façade. The pillars were intertwined with vines and shrubs. She looked down to see the rushing sea as she saw a small shore of sand and marshes that led to the deep, glimmering caves made of charcoal black stone. The trolley finally reached the platform. The smell of seaweed and oysters wafted in the air as she stepped out of the trolley. There were rocks of black and brown texture, humongous in size, that glinted in the light.

She walked to the caves and saw what she desired—Somalata plants were spread across the entire cave. The caves were incredibly huge. They seemed to go on forever.

Suparns can conquer the world with this. And yet they don't, impervious to what they have.

Some Tribals just didn't have foresight like Kadru did. She wanted to conquer Illavarti and make it the land ruled by Nagas. And she would be able to achieve it only through the use of Amrit. She plucked out one of the plants and crushed it over her wound. Her guards questionably watched her as she began to rub the paste. It didn't soothe her initially but rather burnt her.

But it'll be fine after a while.

"Gather as much as you can in the sack."

The guards nodded, pulling out cotton sacks that they had kept inside their breastplates. Kadru also pulled out the sack from under her clothes and kept the fire lamp on the ground. As she began to tear out the plants, dropping them inside, she heard a familiar voice.

"Whatcha doin', snake?"

Kadru turned, so did her guards. They dropped their sacks, pointing their swords at the figure. But Kadru signalled them to lower their weapons.

Standing in front of her was Maruda with a devious grin over his face. He was alone.

"I'm quite shaken by your betrayal. But then, I did expect this

from a snake. I was quite curious as to why there were two dead guards at the entrance of the trolley. Now, it makes sense."

Kadru just smiled. *He is an idiot to come alone to face me.*

"Why are you alone?" she asked.

"Because honestly," he pulled out his sword, "I can defeat you all by myself. Imagine my reward when I tell Lord Tarakshya about how I stopped you from stealing his treasure."

Kadru sighed. There had to be some complication. Before Maruda could come forward, Kadru lurched forward with her own sword. Maruda instantly deflected it.

"You thought you can be spontaneous. Naw, snake. I'm better!" And then he clanged his weapon against hers. She deflected it again.

"Why do you never use these against armies?"

"Because unlike snakes, we respect our tribe and other people."

He pushed her towards the back of the cave. The fire lamp broke apart and the fire spread and reached the oil that was around the Amrit.

The cave was on fire.

Kadru saw her guards leaving with their sacks out of the cave to be safe, while she and Maruda watched the burning caves going up in ashes.

"You fool! You don't bring a fire lamp inside! The plants give out oil from their roots. It's combustible."

And with that, he bashed his sword against her sword. She dodged, rolling around as she saw the flames burst open and there was a crackling noise. The crackles grew louder, a strange light emanated, blinding both Kadru and Maruda.

The cave had exploded.

Kadru was flung outside from the impact. She yelled in pain. Her body was burning and she jumped in the water to douse the flames. She had no idea where her sword was. Four hands gripped her and pulled her up.

Maruda came out of the cave slowly. His back was burnt. He

staggered towards Kadru trying to attack her with his sword, but by the time he reached her, he was dead.

They climbed in the trolley as Kadru staggered and sighed. She was panting, carrying the heavy sacks of the remaining Somalata plants.

As she came out of the palace, she felt tremors in the ground. Kadru told the guards to hide the sacks while she went to fetch Jamun. She had to escape. As she reached the area of the feast, she saw Jamun enjoying the show. He was in the same spot, but Tarakshya wasn't there, nor were his guards.

Kadru walked up to him, trying to act naturally as she sat down. Jamun's smile vanished as he turned to Kadru and said, "We have a problem."

"And I solved that problem. I got the plants, but I kind of . . . destroyed the stock."

Jamun widened his eyes in horror. "What should we do now?" He was drunk, but was trying to retain his wits as he bit his tongue.

"Find a flying chariot and escape the hell out of here." She paused, recalling something Jamun had said earlier. "What was the problem you just referred to?"

He shook his head irritably. "She's here. She demanded Tarakshya's presence immediately."

"Who?" Kadru arched her brows.

"Manasa."

50

Nala was never the 'revenge' sort of a person.

In fact, the only reason he was coming all the way from Alak was because he had started feeling constricted there. The sand dunes, the ugly hot weather—he was sick of that place. He had been on his way to Indragarh with his army only to learn midway that his father had been killed by a young girl.

A girl!

Nala spat at the idea, but then he knew his father was not an intelligent man. Now Nala was stranded in the middle of nowhere, waiting outside the gates of Indragarh with his men.

He was resting on a cushion, sipping his wine, next to his naked Apsara wife, Rambha. Her emerald necklace gleamed in the light.

"Kill her," the voice said in his head.

Nala was not the sanest person. Since he was a child, he could hear his dead mother's voice in his head. His father had murdered her after she had borne the kids. After all, women had no importance in the Yaksha tribe. That's why they often slept with Apsaras, who could be easily disposed. But Nala had been exceptionally close to his mother and losing her made him lose his mind. He didn't do anything about it, didn't take his father's life out of spite. All he wanted was to hear her voice, in any form.

Nala wasn't the ideal Yaksha. Tha Yakshas were bald and ugly, but he was handsome, tall, and firm. His ripped body, silky hair, dusky eyes, and deep voice made the women turn around to look at him. Everything about him exhibited a sense of royalty, especially when he wore his golden-laced overcoat with a dhoti, open in the front showing his rippling muscles. He had a goatee.

"Was it the right thing to do? Letting Gumukha appoint Ramras as the king?" the voice asked.

"I don't care," he whispered to himself so Rambha won't hear him. "I would kill Ramras too. I just want . . . I just want to go inside and burn the place."

"That won't be wise, my child. If you have Indragarh, you have the entire North."

"But I have never thought about ruling Indragarh."

"You are talking like your dead brother now, my child," the voice chided. "Remember, there's no progress in remaining the prince of Yakshas. Now with your father dead, you have no one stopping you. You are the heir to Alak and you can be the heir to Indragarh."

The thought rolled around in his mind. His father always told him to never be too ambitious but his mother wanted him to chase his dreams. It was the only way to survive.

It was not so bad.

"First, give them what they want and then infiltrate and rob them," the voice of his mother spoke to him softly. "And you can only do it if you dream bigger."

"I don't have a big army. Manavs still outnumber us."

"You can buy the mercenaries. Money is something we are never short of."

Nala thought for a moment. His wife grazed the back of his coat.

"My dear, who are you mumbling to?" she asked.

Nala ignored her.

"Kill her," his mother said. "She has stayed too long and cannot even bear you an heir. Kill her."

Nala shook his head. He was wild and impulsive, but he didn't want to kill the only person who cared for him—Rambha. She was always there for him. She let him bed other girls, but didn't sleep with other men. That was what Nala loved about her—she let him own her without making him feel restricted. Nala turned to see Rambha. *She is perfect.* Intoxicated by her green eyes and her broad smile, he leaned forward and kissed her on the neck. She giggled. He then kissed her on the cheeks and then on her lips.

"Erm, my lord?"

Nala grunted. He hated being disturbed when he was in bed. Standing close to the tent flaps was a young Yaksha soldier.

"My lord, Lady Urvashi has sent her messenger. She demands your presence."

"Ah." Nala smiled looking at Rambha who patted him proudly.

Nala walked to the guard and asked, "What did Gumukha say?"

"I haven't received any news from him."

Ramras lost.

That was not a problem. Gumukha's plan had been flimsy. He nodded to himself as the voice in his head spoke again, "Do not be hasty. Do not kill the girl. Perhaps she could be used for later."

Nala nodded to himself. The Yaksha guard looked at him, confused. Nala said to him, "Tell the messenger that we can have a meeting here in the centre of the camp. I shall not go inside . . ." *because I don't trust that girl.*

"Aren't we going to war, my lord? Wasn't that the original plan?"

Nala had an amused look on his face. "Plans change, my friend. Plans change all the time. Just tell the messenger, all right?"

The guard nodded and left. Nala turned to see his lavish, luxurious tent with candles and fire lamps, grapes and wine. In the centre was a bed on which were plush cushions and smooth cotton

blankets. Rambha casually opened her hair as she asked, "What do you plan to do?"

Nala thought for a moment.

"Kill her," said the voice again. "She has no reason to stay alive anymore."

Nala sighed. "I don't know," he responded, ignoring his mother's voice. "I just don't know. But for some reason, I'm excited to see what happens next."

Things are finally getting interesting.

An open tent had been set up for Urvashi's welcome. Some food and drinks had been placed inside it but Nala made sure that his guards had been armed, ready to strike if the need arose. Unfortunately, Yakshas weren't the strongest and the fittest when it came to battle like the Rakshas, but they could take someone in a fight. They were quite sharp.

Lady Urvashi arrived. Nala stood up from his chair.

Urvashi had an oval-shaped face. Her braids stirred and her long robe rustled as she walked. Two bannermen stood at her sides and fifteen guards marched behind her.

The roads were dusty and sandy. Some trees and bushes had grown at the sides. Nalakuvera had had most of the trees around the tent removed.

Nala also noticed that just like he had brought Rambha, she had brought two men—one short with wavy hair with a scar on his face and one black-haired hunk who looked like a wrestler. Nala's heart raced in excitement at the sight of these handsome men. He liked men as well as women.

Urvashi didn't take a seat. She was being formal.

"Let's cut to the chase. I harmed your father, so I'm here to make a proposition."

"Harmed?" His eyes brightened. "You killed my father."

Urvashi remained impassive.

"Mind to sit down with me?" Nala asked.

She shook her head. "I'm here to make a proposition. If you won't listen, I shall return. I don't plan on dining with blackmailers."

"I'm not a blackmailer," he softly added. "I'm just a . . . well . . . I'm just a boy who wants to have his father's corpse so I could give him a proper Yaksha burial."

"That could be arranged."

"And Gumukha said you were unreasonable!" he exclaimed with a laugh. "Why did you kill my father? I mean, he's not the most pleasant man, I know, but why?"

She looked in his eyes and said, "He killed my father."

"Karma," he nodded. "You sure you don't want anything to eat?"

She shook her head. "Ramras told me you plan to attack my city if I become the queen." Nala was keenly observing Urvashi. *Her eyes are so expressive. There is wisdom beyond her years in those irises.* "Would you do that?"

"It depends on how reasonable you are. I mean, I thought my involvement would make Ramras the king. But I'm surprised they chose you. You must have offered something really enticing for them to be interested."

"Yes, I convinced them." She paused as the scarred boy leaned down and whispered something in her ear. She nodded and then said, "I come in peace. If you accept my friendship, you and your army can situate yourself in the quarters and fort that once belonged to Lord Kuvera, and you can give him a proper burial there. I wish you no harm and I hope we can let bygones be bygones."

She's good.

"It's convenient for you, isn't it? That she has killed your father. Although I guess he deserved it," the voice said. "She can be useful. She holds the North. Marry her!"

Nala didn't hate the idea. It did make sense, but then he had Rambha who he was lawfully wedded to. The only other problem was Urvashi was quite young for Nala, though there was no age barrier in marriage for Yakshas.

Nala stood up and walked towards Urvashi. Urvashi did the same as Nala extended his hand. "I accept your partnership. Let's hope this benefits both of us."

Urvashi had a sly smile on her face. "It would." And she shook his hand.

Urvashi began to leave. Nala watched her party retreat. He stood watching them for a few moments and then Rambha came and stood beside him. She was wearing nothing but a transparent robe, her bushy hair cascading down her back. She whispered in Nala's ears, "You are really letting your father's killer leave unscathed?"

Nala knew what she meant. Where they lived, the Yakshas pretty much considered Kuvera a god. They used to touch his feet, wipe his hands, kiss him palms. For them, all the other gods meant nothing. And when you kill a god, there's no knowing what his followers would do.

Nala turned to face the Yakshas who were standing behind him in a line. They looked disappointed. And then Nala realized something—since his father and elder brother were dead, he was their god now.

"For now," Nala said and kissed his wife passionately, as he thought about a plan that might just work in his favour. "But I'm seeing the bigger picture."

51

The plans were being discussed in the biggest hut in Dandak.

Kalki stood in the corner, cross-armed. He was listening to the conversation between the quarrelling Vanars. At times, they would begin to squeal and croak arguing with Lord Bajrang. Even though he was revered like a god all across Illavarti, his people didn't hesitate to voice their apprehension. Lord Bajrang often glanced at Kalki, worried.

Shuko was sitting on Kalki's shoulder. He was getting bored. Ratna and Smrit had joined the planning council, but neither was speaking much. Kalki knew they were much more interested in freeing the Apsaras that Kalki had seen in Taar's camp.

Plan for them, Shuko said.

I'm not Arjan. Arjan was a planner, I am more of an executioner.

Well, Arjan is not here. So, I would like you to plan.

Kalki sighed. *Where did you go for so long? You kept vanishing in between.*

If you plan, I will tell.

That's . . . all right. Kalki smiled to himself. Shuko would often disappear for days only to be seen later on. *This parrot comes and goes as he pleases.*

Kalki came forward and stood near the table. A map had been spread on it. There were scribbles all over it. He could see the

location where Taar was stationed along with his men. He was in the hills near a valley and in front of the hills, was the frozen lake where the battle might happen. It was not an ideal battleground. The ice was thin. One misstep, and they would plunge to their deaths.

"One needs to cross this frozen lake to reach us." Bajrang sighed. "And from the back, there's a steep way, but it should be well-guarded. There's another path that Taar might take to come here . . ." he showed the flimsy design of the bridge that reached Bajrang's camp. "What I suggest is block all paths and stand in defence. The moment they arrive, we go in."

"But my lord," one of the Vanars said, "you can stop them single-handedly. Please, stop them."

Lord Bajrang looked up. There was pain in his eyes. "You know I promised Lord Raghav that I shall not involve myself in battles after the one we had with Dushasan. And I mean to keep that promise."

Kalki didn't know about this. Lord Bajrang was revered for keeping his word. And it was true—Lord Bajrang was so strong that he could beat an army, but he won't, because he was a man of his word.

"But what if we lose?"

"Then we lose," sighed Bajrang. "But I shall not fight. That's why we are planning our defence. I'll be always there to help you . . . methodically, but not physically. I cannot do that."

That's a bad plan, Shuko said.

Shut up. You are a just parrot. Don't act like you know everything about battle plans.

Kalki raised his hand as if he was in gurukul. Bajrang looked at him and smiled. "What is it?"

"What about my frien . . . I mean what about Padma? If we are not attacking, that means my friends are going to die."

Bajrang looked puzzled. Kalki realized Bajrang had not

anticipated this. He had not thought about Kalki's friends at all. But Kalki had.

"I, uh . . ."

"What about the Apsaras?" asked Ratna, gritting her teeth. "I explicitly told you I'm here with my friend just so that I can liberate them. I am not interested in joining your pointless Vanar politics."

Bajrang didn't take offense at that. He listened to Ratna with patience.

"All right. I have another plan." He cheekily grinned, trying to diminish the tension with his lovable nature. "You and you," he pointed at Kalki and Ratna, "go from here," he said, pointing towards the back of Taar's camp which snaked through the valley. "Sneak in, find your friends and comrades, get them out and leave. You don't have to join our cause. But I cannot give you any of my men because they'll be blocking these two entrances . . ." he pointed at the frozen river, which was near the Frontier, and the bridge.

"Seems fair," Ratna nodded and left the hut with Smrit.

What? Kalki was confused. Did Ratna just agree to having no backup? Did she really think she could defeat so many bloodthirsty Vanars? He had seen them. They had looked dangerous. He had seen their sturdy armour and sharp axes. It was not wise to attack them mindlessly. Plus, Vanars' hearing was sharp. The slightest of sound, and they will be caught. *They cannot be taken by surprise.*

"Is it fine with you?" Bajrang asked, concerned.

Kalki reluctantly nodded.

"Good." He smiled. "I'll show you what you'll be riding now." He muttered something to his Vanar general to execute the plan into motion, informing him of the men who were to be stationed at various locations in the camp, and of the men who were to remain inside for backup.

Kalki followed Bajrang out of the hut and into the thick crust of snow that lay on the field. As he walked, Kalki tried to catch up to Bajrang. "I didn't know you had renounced violence."

"I had to. It was the only way to stop it."

"Stop what?"

"Stop violence."

They were coming close to a wide range of red tents where horses had been lined up in a stable, tied to wooden barks.

"Just because you have stopped violence, doesn't mean the world will," Kalki said grimly. The idea seemed foolish and kind of suicidal. Bajrang's and Taar's men were about to slaughter each other. "It'll not make a difference and there will still be evil at bay. At least if you fight, you have a chance of winning."

Bajrang responded. "There might be. But then when will it stop? The problem is we think one man can't make a difference. If your morality is in the right place and you have a strong will, then all you need is one man to make a difference. You ask how? Because he ends up inspiring the world to follow these morals." He winked.

"You are preaching to be peaceful but the world is ending. That's idealistic. You should be practical."

"I'm an idealist through and through."

Kalki laughed as he reached the stable, but then he saw the Vanars sitting on the horses. They were taking them away.

"You need a ride," Bajrang said. There were only mules and donkeys left in the stable now. "But my men have already taken the best stallions for themselves."

"Monkeys on horses?" Kalki chuckled.

Bajrang smiled back at Kalki. He was not offended and Kalki had immediately regretted saying it. "Vanars are actually not monkeys, they are just worshippers of monkeys. You do realize that, don't you? The word *vana* means jungle and *nar* means man. That means we are men of the jungle, but since we have to migrate in the winters, I don't know what we are." He shrugged, his muscles flexing in the process.

"Kripa drinks so much because he is tired of being an Immortal. How are you so content with your life?"

They reached the end of the stable where Kalki saw a white stallion.

"I think it's about the attitude towards the problem."

Kalki nodded. Bajrang was philosophizing again but he had a point. *Would Bhargav Ram mentor me like Lord Bajrang?*

Bhargav Ram was the sixth Avatar of Lord Vishnu. *He must know so much.*

"Who's this?" Kalki asked about the white horse. The horse grunted at Kalki.

"This is someone who no one rides because no one can ride him," Bajrang said and patted the horse.

The horse looked regal. His fur was white but had a golden tinge to it. The hair on his mane were dense and silky. They flowed freely in the breeze.

"I tried as well. We found him in the forest, drinking from the stream nearby. But we couldn't domesticate him."

"And no one could ride him?"

Bajrang shook his head. "Do you know how to ride horses?"

"Oh, I wish."

Kalki came inside the den where the white horse stood. He patted him on the head and brushed his skin. With a quick jerk, the horse used its back limbs to kick him. Kalki landed at the other end of the stable, as Shuko leapt from Kalki's shoulder to save himself. Bajrang helped him up.

"He's feisty." Kalki panted.

"I told you," Bajrang said. "I think I can give you my horse."

"No," Kalki shook his head as Shuko perched on his shoulder again. "I shall ride him. I think we can come to an understanding."

The horse grunted in response.

"Or not."

Bajrang laughed. "You are a funny man, Kalki." Then he turned serious. Listen, you must leave as soon as you get your friends."

"You don't need my help?"

"Come on," Bajrang smiled. "You don't want to help me. You are healed and you are done here. I thought I would change your mind, but you are destined to do better things than solving and fighting Vanar wars. Wars will be waged, and people will move on. You must move on. Your destiny awaits you. I will stay here and help my people. They are my family."

"What if you lose?"

He lowered his gaze. "See, I cannot be killed, but if it comes to the worst scenario, I'll make a deal with him."

"You will sacrifice yourself for your people?"

He shrugged. "It's all right. I don't mind doing it as long as my people are safe. Taar needs me."

"Why?"

"Remember the Eye of Brahma? He thinks I have one of the Shards. What he doesn't know is that I have it inside me. I won't tell him, but I will use it as leverage to work out a deal with him. I'll say I'll let him use the the Shard of the Eye of Brahma in return for the safety of my people."

"He could become invincible. And the power might end up corrupting him."

Bajrang nodded. "And it will corrupt him, I know. But that's a problem for another day."

Kalki couldn't understand why Lord Bajrang couldn't just end the war by picking up his *gadha* and using it to massacre Taar's army.

"You don't get it, do you?" Bajrang understood his confusion as he studied Kalki's face. "You don't get why I don't fight."

Kalki nodded.

"When Lord Raghav won the war against Dushasan, he and my brother Sugriva were supposed to leave for Mount Meru in Swarg, the original homeland of Lord Raghav, in the far north, out of Illavarti. I was supposed to follow them. I had been their friend and a supporter of their cause. But I didn't. You know why?"

Kalki shook his head.

"Because I'm a Dakshini. Sugriva was too, but he didn't care about that. I was a Dakshini, a Southerner whose life was in Illavarti, in this homeland, to protect and guard my tribe. And I've lived with Vanars for so long. I've seen the old perish and the young grow up. I remember Taar used to be a rebel even during his gurukul days. I had been like an uncle to him. Even then he had been ambitious. He hadn't cared about the plans I had had for Kishkindha. He always talked about how we ought to conquer the world." Bajrang sighed thinking of the problems he had had to deal with for decades. "And I don't blame him for that. He wanted to conquer it because he knew what we were capable of. He knew we were advanced in comparison to other Tribals. We are wiser, more agile. But he forgot one thing. I've lived for hundreds of years. I know a lot of things and I've seen a lot of things. And it doesn't matter how much you can conquer. I believe if you can conquer someone's heart, then that's enough. We live long enough to fight, but not long enough to love. And I knew there's no satisfaction in colonizing the tribes as much as it is important to develop your own tribe, to nurture them and help them."

Kalki was mulling it over when Bajrang put his heavy arm around Kalki's shoulder. "What are you thinking?" he asked Kalki.

"That I can never be like you."

"You don't have to be. My war is over. Yours has started and perhaps you will have to fight. But remember one thing, just because you are non-violent doesn't mean you are weak."

Kalki nodded. "That's why you didn't do anything during the Mahayudh, during the time of Lord Govind?"

"Of course. Govind was a dear friend, but he understood. Our wars were different, our times were different. He had to resort to violence by associating with people like Arjuna, Yuddhisthira, and the others. I didn't. And that's all right. Though I did manage to enthrall Bheema when he tried to pick me up." He laughed.

Kalki smiled back. As Bajrang left him, whispering 'good luck'

for his mission, he looked at the horse again. Even in the dark, he was gleaming with pure white angelic beauty.

Kalki sat beside the horse. "You know, you are like a person I knew—stubborn." This time when Kalki patted him, the horse didn't jerk him away. He kicked the den doors open and let the horse knock the hooves up as they brushed the snow, coming out of the stable. Shuko fluttered his wings and sat on Kalki's shoulder.

Isn't Bajrang too much of a melodrama?

Shut up.

Genius, where is your weapon?

Kalki shook his head in confusion. He had prepared himself, but had forgotten to take a weapon.

I'll get it.

Shuko flew away towards the armoury while Kalki balanced himself on the horse. He didn't make the horse wear any saddle since it might end up irritating the beast. Shuko returned clutching a short sword in his talons and dropped it in Kalki's hand.

How did you manage to hold such a heavy sword?

Because I'm special. Like you.

Oh please. Also, where were you till now?

Shuko squawked. *I went to see Arjan back in Indragarh.*

WHAT?

Yeah. I thought of checking up on him, to make sure he's alive or not.

And is he?

Very much so.

Kalki beamed. He was ecstatic. *Thank god. I will go see him as soon as possible. I missed him terribly.*

You were being unnecessarily harsh on that assassin girl, Padma.

Kalki nodded. *You're right.* Though he had sorted out his differences with her, there was still enmity between them. Before she was kidnapped, Kalki had angrily proclaimed that he would venture into Mahendragiri without her.

And what will you do with Kripa?

I have no idea.

He saw Ratna and Smrit mounting their horses, moving towards the path which led to the valley. Ratna turned and signalled Kalki to follow her.

Kalki patted the horse and then rode forward.

Let's see what Taar's men are capable of.

52

Kali was afraid of putting his hand inside the water again. He wanted to be strong. He *had* to be strong emotionally before he could take the leap of faith and believe that his brother was alive! All this time, he had thought that all his siblings had died in the fire, the last one being his only brother. He lamented each death and held himself responsible for them. And now he had learnt that one of them was safe and was here, in this world.

Who can it be?

What is he like?

Kali wanted to hug his brother if he ever had the chance of meeting him, but then Shukr had said to Kali that it would change everything. Kali didn't understand how it could change anything. He wanted to share this news with Durukti, but he refrained. He was still angry at her.

Kali saw Shukr standing at the edge of the the boat. He was watching the sunrise. The sky had turned orange and the sun looked like a fruit from afar. Kali walked to the Asura priest and stood next to him.

"You still haven't seen your past," Shukr sighed.

"How will it change everything?"

Shukr pursed his lips. "I shouldn't have told you."

"Well, you have and you should explain how everything will change."

"Do you know the prophecy of Kalyug?"

Kali arched his brows. "I've heard of it—Kalyug will be the last Yug of Illavarti where the Dharm and Adharm will fight to determine the fate of the world."

"Yesss." He nodded. "There are two main versions of the prophecy, the Manav version and the Asura one. The Manav prophecy saysss that the the Dharm is a Manav and Adharm is an Asura. The Asura's prophecy states the opposite. There are other versions of the prophecy too, but all of them say that the last war in Kalyug shall be between Dharm and Adharm. And the prophecy even explicitly states that the Asura will be the last of his kind when he will fight in Kalyug. He will be a male though it is not clear whether he will be pure-blooded or not. The problem is if your brother is alive, he can also be the Asura who'll be the Dharm to fight the Adharm."

"What about Koko?"

"Do you really think he could be the Dharm?" Shukr asked.

I guess not.

Kali swallowed a lump in his throat. *I thought I was special.* "If you knew who my brother was, why didn't you call him here?"

"Because I believe in you, not him. He's not fit to be the Dharm."

Kali nodded.

"If you have got your answer, you should go back and see who your brother is. We have other work to do."

"What other work?"

Shukr was watching the ocean. It was moving, and the waves were strong. "I have a plan that will help you get back your throne."

Kali was appalled and excited at the same time. He turned to see Durukti approaching him. She was looked worried as she tried to slowly hold Kali's hands, kneeling down next to him.

"You don't look well, Kali. You need to stop doing what you are doing." Kali huffed in irritation and took her hands off him. Durukti's eyes started welling up.

"I shouldn't have done what I did to you. I'm sorry. Please accept my apology, like I once did, remember?"

Kali remembered. He had hit her once because of Kalki. Unsure of what to do, Kali ran his hand on his scalp. Hair had started growing on his head. "Well, what do you know? I'm not ill anymore. I am feeling much better now."

"Kali, please pay attention! I don't know where we are, what we are doing. And the woman with her beasts, she scares me."

She's going to be my wife.

Kali sighed. Durukti was getting on his nerves, but he had to keep her fears at bay and just make her understand. He cupped her pretty face in his hand and looked straight at her. "I'm trying to go back in time to see what happened to our brother."

"What are you talking about?"

"I think it's time I go back and see the truth for myself."

Durukti was confused, but chose to believe him. "The Eye of Brahma . . ." she whispered. "Where is it?"

"How do you know about it?"

She shook her head. "Where is it?"

"The First Shard is in the ocean."

"The sea?" She arched her brows. "And why do you want to see our brother?"

Kali paused for a moment and then told her. "He's alive." Durukti's breath hitched. "That's why we have come here. Shukr wants me to see him."

"I don't believe it. Our brother has been alive all this time. All right, you go see him." She smiled at Kali. "But please, let's leave this place after you've seen our brother."

"We will."

As Durukti walked towards the cottage, one of the hyenas

started growling at her. Alakshmi whistled and the hyena fell silent. She went inside and sat with Koko and Vikoko.

Kali put his hands in the water. It felt chilly for a while. The water caressed his skin before he could feel things again. The current turned hot, humid, and he felt his hands were burning again, but the water was lukewarm. He concentrated on one single memory—when the fire had started.

And then the present scene dissolved in front of him. A new scene, part by part, was emerging in front of his eyes until he saw the same, small village he used to live in. He saw there were a few Tribals getting drunk close to the tavern of the village but he didn't care for that. He walked around the place until he found his own hut, in which he saw younger Kali and Durukti sleeping. It was a starry night. Kali walked towards the last room of their hut where the babies were sleeping. He looked at his siblings and smiled, tears brimming in his eyes. He never thought he would be able to see them again.

Kali wiped the tears. He longed to touch them, hold them in his arms, but he knew he couldn't interact with any of them. He cursed himself for what was going to happen. He walked towards his brother now. Kali had named him Bali after the great king Mahabali who had ruled Illavarti a long time back. Mahabali had been overthrown by the Vishnu Avatar Vaman, and had been eventually thrown back in Pataal. Mahabali's time and reign was considered the golden age of Illavarti because it had been perfect—utopian, one could say, until the tyrant Vaman snatched away his throne from him.

Bali, Kali's brother, had small brown eyes. *He had such promise.* His mind got distracted when he heard noises. They were coming from outside. Perhaps the fight between the Tribals had already started.

This was how it began.

Kali came out instantly to see the fight. He was living through

the worst night of his life again. At that moment, the fight escalated. They had started punching each other. It was a Rakshas and a Naga. It was a strange combination. Both were strangers in this part of the land. The Manavs were trying to stop them, but one of them got punched in the process. It was pandemonium. Kali was watching the fight unfolding before him, when he saw a strange figure holding a pot in the shadows. The figure started spilling black liquid on the floor, all around Kali's hut and other huts as well. No one noticed this figure. Everyone was busy watching the fight.

The figure took the fire lamp that was hung on the throes of each hut, and was about to spill the fire lamp over it when Kali yelled, "NO!"

The figure stopped, confused. He looked around him at that moment. He turned in Kali's direction, but Kali knew the figure will not be able to see him. The shadows cleared and Kali noticed a strange mark on his forehead.

Who the hell is he?

And then he broke the lamp on the floor over the kerosene. The fire crackled and slowly began to engulf the huts. Kali wanted to run towards that figure, but he was more concerned about his own hut. He saw other huts being burnt as people ran, scampering and staggering, trying to escape.

Kali came inside his hut where his younger version had woken up and was shaking Durukti, trying to wake her up. Fire had engulfed their hut now and they were hastening to move to the room where their siblings were.

Kali was trying to fight back tears. He would have to watch as his siblings burned in the fire.

His younger self entered the room where his siblings were crying out. He picked up his brother and gently tossed him out the window. Before he could save the others, the hut exploded. Durukti had managed to drag Kali out at that moment. They both saw their hut crumble before them. He could hear the wails of his siblings.

I had saved my brother. Why didn't I remember it?

He saw his younger self and Durukti gazing at the burning hut. His siblings' wails were so loud. They were being burnt alive and young Kali could do nothing to help. His younger self fainted.

"Our brother is there! GET HIM!" Kali shouted but Durukti couldn't listen to him.

Kali now realized why he didn't remember any of this. The trauma had made him repress his memory.

Kali wiped his tears. He moved to where he had thrown his brother out. He saw right there, in the midst of the fire and the smoke, a middle-aged man had picked his brother up and tucked him safely in his cart. He grabbed the cart and walked ahead.

Kali followed the middle-aged man who had reached the end of the village, away from the burning grounds. The man kissed his brother's forehead.

"You have nothing to fear, my boy. I will treat you like my own son."

Who are you?

Kali wanted to speak to the man but before he could say anything, the scene changed—and he was in a different village, bigger, greener than the last one. It had a lot of tropical trees and mud huts. Children were playing outside. Kali walked around till he saw the same man talking to a kid. It was Bali, now a little grown up. Kali held back tears. *He really is alive.*

The man told Bali, "You must always use your strength from here." He pointed at his head.

Bali nodded.

The scene changed and Kali saw a teenage Bali. His hair had grown. Kali furrowed his brows in concentration. *He looks familiar.* Another boy was sitting with Bali, who also seemed familiar. They were training to fight using wooden sticks. Bali was losing to the older boy.

"You are weak," the older boy said. "Be strong."

Who the hell are you?

"I'm strong." Bali attacked only to lose again.

"Charming, brother, charming," the older boy said.

And then the scene changed. Kali's head was spinning now and he thought he was going to get sick. The Eye of Brahma was really affecting him, but he had to see the complete truth.

And now he saw another field—next to the hills and jungles where the cows had been slaughtered and a young boy sat in the bloody land, weeping to himself. He was hiding his face. Kali went and sat opposite to Bali when he moved his palms away to reveal his face, a face that Kali recognized.

Kali gasped in horror.

He was always there in front of me.

Kali's blood ran cold. A chill ran down his spine. He fingers were numb as he slightly traced Bali's weeping face who didn't take notice of him.

It can't be.

Bali was no more Bali. He had a new name. And Kali, surprisingly, knew that name.

Arjan.

53

Kalki fell thrice from the horse.

"Haven't you had enough, you little beast!"

Ratna and Smrit chuckled at the sight.

They were at the valley near the frozen river. A few trees lined their snowy path. The were walking inside a dense forest that would lead them to the back of Taar's camp.

Kalki stood up as he trudged on the partially-frozen leaves, frowning at the horse. The horse neighed angrily.

What is wrong with him?

Try talking to him, Shuko said.

What do you mean?

Try talking to him like you talk to me.

I thought that was only possible for us.

No, it's not. All of this, whatever is happening, these are blessings bestowed by Lord Shiva. Me. This horse. These are gifts by Lord Shiva.

You are a gift? Gods, what kind of a gift are you?

Genius, stop being a wimp and do it. Your friends are in danger.

'Padma' is in danger, Kalki corrected. He tried to concentrate on the horse.

Come on. Come on.

Kalki tried to concentrate hard when Ratna called out to him. "Can you stop scrounging your face and start moving? We don't have much time."

He sighed. They really didn't have much time.

Kalki tried to climb up the horse and as he did, the horse didn't fidget much. They began to walk on the path as Kalki wondered about how he had been able to communicate telepathically so easily. *Lord Shiva gifted me all of this?*

Lord Shiva was revered as a god who loved animals. He had left certain animals for people—for those who could take care of them. It was a myth that people believed in.

As they reached the path and crossed the jungle, they finally came upon the shadier, darker part of the forest. They could peer at Taar's camp from there. Hundreds of tents were lined up across the landscape till the frozen river. The black and furry Vanars could be seen strutting about with axes and spears. They weren't exactly big like the Rakshas, but they looked quite threatening with their protruding faces and their big, fish-like eyes.

"What's the plan?" Kalki asked Ratna.

Ratna glanced at him. "Well, I'm glad you asked me."

"Why?"

"We live in a patriarchal world. I thought you would not bother to ask my opinion because I am a woman."

"Well, I don't think like that."

"The plan is to barge our way in and attack," she said.

"Umm . . ." Kalki gulped. "That sounds—"

"Dangerous? Of course, it is. Do you have a better idea?"

"I want to save my friend, but I don't want to die."

"Is this friend close?"

Meh.

"Yeah, sort of."

"Then you should—"

Kalki shook his head. "No. Let's do one thing. I'll distract them while you sneak in from there . . ." he pointed towards a small bamboo gate that had been dug inside the ground a few paces away from where they were standing. The gate led to a small, shallow

opening. "Put your horses at the back so they think we're alone, all right?"

Ratna smiled. "All right. How will you distract them?"

"Oh, I have a plan."

Ratna and Smrit had gone to the side where the opening was while Kalki instructed Shuko to come when he whistled. Though his whistling skills were not great. He tied his white horse in the corner, away from the tents.

Kalki came forward to the gates where the two Vanars stood with their spears.

Here goes nothing.

Ratna and Smrit's faces collapsed. They had realized what Kalki intended to do. He was going for a straight-up encounter. No tactics.

Kalki reached the gates. The Vanar guards immediately pointed their spears at him.

Think. What would Arjan do?

Kalki threw his sword on the ground and raised his hands in surrender.

Play the enemy.

"What do you want?" one Vanar asked, poking his chest.

Kalki wasn't hurt, but he was surely annoyed. He just smiled and said, "I want to meet General Taar. I have come from Lord Bajrang's camp and I have some news for him."

Kalki was bound and gagged, punched and kicked before he was taken to General Taar. He didn't mind all the hassle because he knew that Ratna and Smrit were making their way inside right

then. Taar's tent, as Kalki had seen through the First Shard of the Eye of Brahma, was huge. It was purple in colour. A stable was close to it where his finest stallions had been kept. Kalki realized how vast Taar's army was. The lithe, scary Vanars in the tent alone were uncountable. *This could be a problem.* Lord Bajrang's army didn't have much men now. And he could even see some Rakshas and Manavs within the consolidated army as they carried out their business of sharpening weapons or gossiped in the corner. The impending war was keeping the people alert. Their respective generals were informing them about several attacking positions and battle strategies.

As Kalki entered the camp, he saw Taar in the centre. He was wearing a single breastplate. Multiple weapons were hanging on his belt. He didn't notice Kalki for a while until the guards who had brought him bowed in respect. Taar looked up and studied Kalki as he came forward from his table where they were strategizing.

"Who are you?" The voice was gruff. Kalki had to look up to see Taar's face. He was gigantic, almost twice the size of a Rakshas and Rakshas were pretty huge themselves. He was even taller than Lord Bajrang.

"My identity doesn't matter. What matters is, I have some information regarding the Eye of Brahma."

"The Eye of Brahma?" His eyes lit up. He glanced at another Vanar. Kalki remembered he was called Aruna. He had seen him through the First Shard of the Eye. "And . . . what sort of information would that be?"

"It's not with Bajrang."

"Of course, it is," he hoarsely added, putting pressure to his words.

Kalki shook his head.

"How do you know?"

"Because he told me."

"And you want to tell us . . . out of the goodness of your heart?" He had a playful smile on his face.

"I wish I was that good," Kalki shrugged, "but I want to free my friend."

"Who?"

"The girl you have."

"What about the old man?"

"Uh, you can keep him."

Taar narrowed his gaze as if he couldn't understand what Kalki was up to. In fact, Kalki himself didn't know what he was up to. He was just making up things as he went along.

"All right. What's the information on the Eye of Brahma?"

"Bajrang had sent it out with a messenger . . ." and before Kalki could lie any further, Taar began to laugh, so did Aruna and then the other Vanars joined them.

What the hell is going on?

"Do you think we don't know?"

"Know what?" Kalki gulped.

"That you are trying to be smart." Taar squared his shoulders fiercely in front of him. "I know the Eye of Brahma is not around Bajrang; it is inside him."

How does he know?

"I lived in that village for quite a while. I was under Bajrang's command. I was close to him. I have seen things that he doesn't know. And you know how we plan to use Bajrang? Not kill him, nah, that'll be too nice for a cruel man like him. We are going to torture him, keep him alive, and use his powers against our enemies. So, if you think you can make a fool out of us," he slowly traced his thick, black fingers across Kalki's neck, "you are wrong."

"He's not cruel." Kalki got serious as he knew this was going to end badly. Taar was not an idiot. In fact, he had turned out to be a genius.

Taar again glanced at Aruna and laughed. His laugh was hoarse,

thick, and full of life. It was as if he was cherishing this moment, trying to prove Kalki wrong.

"I really don't care about what you all are fighting about, but I know Lord Bajrang is not a bad man. He's a good man who has done good deeds."

"You seem old but you act like a kid. What foolish things has he stuffed in your mind? You don't know anything about our culture. You are an outsider, and yet you speak for us. A Northerner cannot understand what we suffered in the Southern lands." Taar came dangerously close to Kalki. He could feel Taar's breath on his face. Taar resumed in a threatening tone. "Did he tell you that the reason I'm waging a war against him is because of our differing ideologies?"

Kalki stared at Taar. *How does he know?*

"Ah, of course. He believes that's the truth, but that's not it. I mean, surely I would love to spread the Vanar culture more in the North and South, unlike him who is content in being in one place all his life. But there are things he has done, things he shouldn't be proud of, and yet he is."

Kalki waited as Taar breathed. The fierce General looked vulnerable. His voice shook a little as he continued his story. "We have been in awe of the so-called Lord Bajrang since we were children—the greatest Vanar who ever lived. We all strived to be strong like him. But I was born during the Breaking, when the world was on the brink of collapse—leprosy was spreading, thousands were dying in war every day—and we all looked up to Bajrang, hoping he would save us. When the war happened with the Manavs and the other tribes, Bajrang didn't do anything. He let it happen. He planned things . . ." his voice rose in anger, "but he didn't do anything. You do realize Bajrang was, and still is, more powerful than anyone else and yet he chose not to do anything. He let his people die when he was *capable* of saving them." Taar showed his hairy arm where Kalki noticed a claw-

shaped scar that had torn part of his skin. "This was when my mother was clutching me, trying to hold on to me before she was taken away by some Rakshas soldiers. She was kidnapped and I asked Bajrang to help me save my mother. But our great lord, the man I worshipped said to me 'I cannot save her but I will send some people who will'. And they went and they died and my mother died as well."

He sighed. He was holding back tears as he recalled his past.

"And you employed the same Rakshas?"

"Because these are not the same Rakshas who did terrible things to my mother. There is good and evil in every tribe. You just need to recognize them, son." Taar was treating Kalki like a kid who didn't understand things. Kalki, oblivious to it, furrowed his brows in confusion.

"He kept his word . . ." Kalki protested.

"To a dead man. While people who were alive, died every day because of a promise. What good is a promise if it kills your own race?" He paused, a sad smile spread on his face. "So, I pondered over things and we all devised a plan. Perhaps Bajrang doesn't help us because he doesn't care for us. There's a reason why there are so many Vanars supporting me. It's not because of my idea to open the Vanar community to the world, it's because they all have lost their own families, their livelihood because of Bajrang's inaction and they want their revenge. And they are willing to do anything to get it. Bajrang just stood by when our people were raped and murdered, so I shall do the same with his supporters. I shall kill and rape and pillage every single one of them and I don't care if it's a child or a woman or a man. He will face my wrath, so that my people can fulfil what they have ached for all this time—revenge." He flared his nostrils and added, "And people like you interfere with those plans, so I hope . . ." he grabbed Kalki by the throat, "I don't see you again."

And then Taar tried to pick him up. But even with his incredible

strength, he was unsuccessful. Kalki remained on the ground no matter how much Taar tried. Taar looked at Kalki, puzzled.

"How are you doing this?"

"I'm so sorry." Kalki looked at Taar. "I had no idea about what you went through."

Taar was incredulously watching Kalki.

"I was judging the situation from one perspective, but wars . . . they must be seen from both perspectives. And you know what?" He clenched his jaw. "You both are wrong and this war, this battle is worthless."

"I thought you didn't care about the war."

I don't!

Kalki was confused. He cared, but he didn't. It was like a dichotomy that danced in his mind. And his thought process broke up when he saw a Vanar entering from the tent, exclaiming, "General! There are two women killing our men. They have just let the Apsaras escape."

Taar looked at Kalki and Kalki knew what he had to do.

We are capable of so much . . .

He had repeated Lord Varaha's words to himself so much.

I am capable of so much.

Kalki clenched his teeth and broke the ropes binding him. With the power of self-belief entrenched in him, he could feel his strength surging. Taar could sense Kalki's power. He punched Kalki in the chest. Kalki backed a little, and it did hurt him. Kalki hurtled himself towards Taar, toppling him over the table, crashing it in the process.

Kalki turned over as Taar tried to get up. The Vanars leapt at Kalki. He grabbed the nearest splinter of wood from the cracked table and stabbed one Vanar on his foot. As the screams ensued and they caught the other Vanars' attention, Kalki scuttled towards the main door where another Vanar was waiting with a sword. He charged towards Kalki.

And right then, Kalki saw the silhouette of a man behind the Vanar. The man sliced his throat.

"Come on, mate."

It was Kripa.

Damn.

Kalki followed Kripa out of the tent. Accompanying him were Padma, Ratna, Smrit, and her three Apsaras whom she had rescued from the camp.

Manavs, Rakshas, and Vanars were pursuing them. Kripa asked them to hurry towards the frozen river.

Kalki was the first one to sprint. His comrades followed behind him. As soon as a Vanar jumped in front of him, Kalki used his elbow to push and toss him in the corner. And then three Vanars appeared in front of him, stopping them in their tracks. Behind these Vanars was the frozen river. The Vanars were steadily moving towards them, pointing their sharp spears. At that moment, Kalki whistled. Shuko flew towards the Vanars. He flapped his wings and poked their faces with his talons. The Vanars covered their faces to protect themselves and their spears tilted away from Kalki. He grabbed one, jutted it at the Vanar's chest, and pummelled him to the ground. Padma handled the other Vanar by jumping over him and stabbing his face. Ratna handled the last one with a swift stab in the abdomen.

They had now reached the bright frozen river. They traversed it carefully but slipped and tripped on their way. The Vanars were now using fiery arrows to shoot them down.

Some of the arrows missed them and collided on the forest ground. Soon the forest was set ablaze. And if the fire reached the river, they would have nowhere to escape.

One arrow was about to hit Padma, but Kalki grabbed it and threw it away. He burned his hand in the process.

"Thanks." She smiled.

Kalki managed to smile back, though he was in a lot of pain.

Ratna, Smrit, and the other Apsaras were the first ones to reach the other side which was the Frontier, where Bajrang's troops were waiting. They helped Ratna to get Kripa and Padma out of the lake.

As Kalki was close to the Frontier, a fire arrow hit him on the back. Collapsing on the ground with lacerating pain, he pulled the arrow out and tossed it away. But due to the weight of his fall, a crack appeared on the floor and his feet got stuck in the cold river. The coldness was unbearable. His legs were still healing from all the cuts made by the Pisach. As he struggled to gain his balance, Padma, Kripa, and the others tried to come to his rescue. Padma was about to jump but Kripa stopped her.

"Don't!" Kripa pulled back Padma. "One has to be very light or very fast while stepping on it. Otherwise, the ice will break and Kalki will drown."

Kalki was feeling helpless as he turned to see Taar standing on the other end of the frozen river, glaring at Kalki with all the venomous hatred he could muster.

"But how will we save him then?" Padma was frantic.

Kripa looked confused. But there was something else in his expression. He looked like he was in pain. And then Kalki saw it—a huge slash across his chest made by a dagger, perhaps. He was severely wounded. Bleeding had turned his upper body a shade of deep red. He was turning pale, and it looked like he was about to faint.

Why didn't I notice this earlier?

Everything had happened so fast. Perhaps that's why Kalki had failed to notice what had happened to Kripa. But now his eyes were focused on every individual in front of him. Ratna was bruised too; so was Padma with a scar across her forehead. Everything was so clear as he looked at them closely.

He tried to pull his feet up but it was to no avail. The fiery arrows began to descend faster on Kalki, as he tried to dodge each one of them as much as he could. The Vanars on Kalki's side used

their arrows to shoot back at Taar's archers, but they weren't as effective as the fiery ones.

With the Vanars down, Shuko came towards Kalki. Fluttering his wings, he tried to clutch Kalki's rudraksh, struggling to pull him out with his beak, but the childish effort was in vain.

Kalki's feet were slowly turning into dead weights and that was when he heard the voice.

Need my help?

The voice was very godly, almost angelic. And then he realized who it was. He turned to see Taar's side again and from there, he saw Vanars scattering from their formation. Taar had turned around to find a huge white horse galloping towards them. He was so fast that they just ran away from the horse's way. The white horse leapt on the frozen river, moving at an unnatural speed. It reached Kalki in seconds.

But the horse didn't stop galloping. When it reached Kalki, he hurriedly grabbed the horse's leg. As the horse sped towards the Frontier, Kalki was pulled out.

He groaned in pain. Busy massaging his feet, he didn't notice Padma running towards him. She hugged him tightly.

Kalki forgot how much pain he was in for that brief moment.

Realizing what she was doing, Padma stopped embracing him.

"You have a good horse," Ratna grinned.

"He reminds me of someone . . . who helped me when I was in danger."

Devadatta!

Kalki's thoughts were interrupted when he saw Kripa sluggishly walking towards him. "G-Great job, lad, but I suppose . . . I need . . . uh . . . I need some help."

And with that, he fell on the ground.

54

Kalki would be lying if he said he wasn't worried.

He was watching the feverish, hot face of Kripa with concern. Kripa was shivering like a leaf. The Vanar nurses were tending to him—cleaning the blood, stitching it all up—but he had already lost a lot of blood. The gash had been very deep. And the cold was not helping his fever. He was freezing.

Kara, who was tending to Kripa, looked over at Kalki and shook her head before leaving to meet Lord Bajrang. She had been their guide, their medical expert, and she had been the one who had nursed Kalki back to health.

But she couldn't cure Kripa.

Kalki sat there in the corner of the room, hard-faced. Padma was worried sick. Ratna and Smrit were there in the room too. They had come to pay their respects. Kalki sighed as he came forward to look at Kripa. "Hey, old man," he softly said.

Kripa was quiet. He seemed to be at peace. "Tell your lass to stop worrying about me." He patted Padma who was tearing up, trying not to make a scene.

"She's not anyone's lass." Kalki clenched his fist, touching the burn he had received while shielding Padma from the attack.

In his peaceful days at Shambala, he had never thought he would be facing so much turmoil in the time to come. He had

never imagined that he would be battered with burns and scars and bruises, only to end up losing the people he truly loved . . . and hated.

"You got that right, mate." Kripa coughed. He was growing weak by the second.

"How can an Endowed die?" Kalki asked. "They are Immortals, right?"

"I wish I knew, mate. This has never happened to an Immortal. I had heard something about them dying if their heads were cut off. But death just by bloodloss? Maybe there was something in their arrows . . . I guess I'll never know. Maybe you should ask Bhargav Ram when you see him. He is older than me . . . He might know something."

He gave a sad smile to Kalki. Kalki just looked away.

"I know you are angry with me. We couldn't complete the conversation we were having earlier in the forest."

"That's all right. I know enough."

Kalki tried hard not to show that he resented Kripa for killing his father. After all, Kripa was on his deathbed.

"No you don't, mate. You think you do, but you don't. Avatars often are full of themselves; believe me, I've seen one before you. You think you know the world, but you have only experienced a speck of it."

"What do I not know?"

"Uh . . . I know it was my mistake for the Mleccha thing. Hiring them. I specifically told them not to hurt anyone but . . ." he shook his head, "Mate, it's more complicated. I had to test you."

"Of course, you had to," Kalki responded in a sarcastic tone.

Kripa blinked slowly. "I know you think I chose you as an Avatar because I was tired of waiting for one to come up. Not really. That is not true. As I have told you, I tried to stop the coming of this new Age before it even began. As was instructed by Lord Govind, I tried to close up the caves and burn the Somas as much

as I could, but I failed miserably. And after my repeated failings, I stayed in your village, Shambala. I thought there was no other way to stop the Age. And then I learnt about you. Your mother was sick during pregnancy. Your father was worried. He had heard about the legend of Somas from someone and went to the caves—"

"And he got it, I know."

Kripa shook his head. "No, he didn't. I kind of lied to you before. I told you he got it before I stopped him. But he couldn't because I stopped him from taking it. At the time, I didn't know why he had wanted to take it. I was safeguarding that cave. He got angry and left. He even fought with me, though I beat him to a pulp, mate." He sniggered. "The point is, a few days after you were born, you were weak, frail. You were too small for a baby and too thin. Your father realized you won't live for long . . . so he . . ."

"What did he do?" A shiver ran down his spine.

"He left you in the jungle." Kripa sighed. "I saw it happen. I had wandered into the jungle after a drunken brawl I had had. You looked emaciated. Such a small, fish-eyed infant you were."

My father left me?

"What did you do then?"

"What any man would do, mate," he smiled, "I tried to save you, took you to the shamans, but they said you couldn't be helped. And I knew I had to help you in some way or the other, so I did what Lord Govind specifically told me not to do. I gave you the Somas. You were small and gulped it right away. And you regained your strength slowly. I then gave you back to your father and told him about the consequences of my actions."

Kalki could feel his eyes stinging.

"So no, I didn't choose you as an Avatar because I had no choice. You didn't become an Avatar because of destiny."

I became an Avatar because of an old, drunken, and a . . . caring man?

Kalki was dumbstruck. He wiped the onslaught of tears from

his eyes. He couldn't help it. Kripa tried to sit up a little, and groaned in pain. It was too much to bear, and he was sweating profusely.

"So Bajrang is wrong, just so you know."

"Why did you do it? You, in a way, started this Age . . ."

"Out of a simple act of kindness?" He nodded. "Yeah, I did. But at that time, when you were an infant, I didn't see it that way. I saw a baby who was about to die."

Kalki glanced at Padma. She was as surprised as Kalki was. And with that, she walked out of the room, unable to bear it. Kalki had been wrong all this time about Kripa. He might have been a strange old man but he had been like a father to Kalki. He had been watching over him since he was a baby. And his real father had left him to die.

"Why didn't you tell me this? Why did you lie to me?"

"And let you despise your father? Jeez no, mate. That's not me." He paused, shaking his head. "I must tell you though that I did give you the Soma to make you powerful, to keep you alive, but remember that an Avatar is made of the deeds he commits, either good or bad; that is what defines him as a hero," he said, pointing at the symbol on Kalki's chest. "Well, you were just a young boy from Shambala who thought he was an Avatar. But this brands you with absolute confidence that not only should we believe in you, but the gods do too. You are the only one capable of becoming this Age's saviour."

"But *you* believed in me before Lord Vishnu did? That's why you followed me when I grew up, you saw me, you checked if I had the traits to become an Avatar, to become Dharm."

He nodded weakly. "I . . . uh . . . I thought you had it in you, when you and Bala saved a girl from the tavern, and you helped her . . . I don't know if you remember, but I was there. I saw how frantically you were searching for a house for her, asking around who she was, where she belonged. You helped the girl as if she was

your own. That day I understood that you are a kind man. And a Dharm is not just made of strength, but of kindness as well."

"You said I was Lord Vishnu himself but . . . I mean an incarnation. I'm only a foot soldier, destined to do his bidding."

"Mate, there are multiple versions of this prophecy. I had forgotten some of them. Some said Lord Vishnu shall take birth again in their Avatar's body, others said Lord Vishnu shall choose his finest warrior and make him an Avatar and that this Avatar would be a soldier who Lord Vishnu believes in. There are so many theories about it, but it doesn't matter, you know. What matters is, you are here, and you are strong, and you have the symbol of Srivatsa on your chest."

He always believed in me.

"I might sound contradictory in what I say now and what I had said before, but everything that I just said is true." He chuckled and took deep breaths. "I'm a confused man, after all. I'm a drunkard, yes. I've done horrible things in this world, I've become a . . . a . . . I lost my brother-in-law and my sister during the Mahayudh."

"What happened to them?"

"You are better off not knowing, mate," he winked, "but I do know one thing. I am sorry that I lied to you. After seeing this symbol," he placed his hand on Kalki's chest, "I thought, mate, that . . . that Soma can only work on Dharm and Adharm and it'll make other normal people mad. But then again, you were a regular person too, at one point."

"This symbol means that Lord Vishnu has chosen me as an Avatar. But if I wasn't the Avatar till now, how was I able to Channel and speak to other Avatars?"

"It was the power of your belief, mate. You were completely convinced that you were an Avatar. That kind of confidence is extremely potent. That, coupled with the power of the Somas, enabled you to connect with the others."

Kripa coughed violently. Speaking so much was taking a toll on his already diminished strength. But he still went on.

"I think Somas give you the capacity of strength, of enormity, of invincibility but your deeds shape their nature, their purpose and that makes you Dharm or Adharm. I wanted to travel with you till th-the . . ." His hand turned cold even before it left the warmth of Kalki's chest. He had closed his eyes as his laborious breathing finally stopped, after an age of agony.

And he was no more.

Believe in yourself.

Kalki looked away, batting his eyelids to stop himself from crying again. He glanced at Ratna and Smrit who didn't shed a tear, but patted Kalki on the back with a sign of respect. Kalki couldn't believe Kripa was gone.

"Old man, may you drink suras in the heavens too." Kalki smiled faintly, brushing his fingers through the frail, white hair of his guru, his friend, and his father till the end.

Padma was standing near Vanarvata when Kalki walked towards her. The cherry leaves withered and descended, floating in the sky. The white flakes were moving and there was light snowfall. It was a beautiful day for a man to have breathed his last. Kalki's heart felt heavy after the revelations.

He was still in denial.

Kalki stood behind Padma, hoping to ask her how Kripa had gotten his wound, but Padma wrapped her arms around him. She hugged him tightly and said, "A Vanar was taking me into a tent but Kripa came in between to stop him, and that is when he got slashed."

She turned, finally letting Kalki see her face soaked with tears. "Is he gone?"

Kalki nodded.

She burst out sobbing as she embraced Kalki. He was dumbstruck. But he too wrapped his arms around her waist.

"I'm sorry."

"Thank you for saving me that time."

"Don't mention it."

"You are warm," she said, nuzzling his neck.

"Thank you." Kalki blushed.

"I'm sorry about Arjan, Kalki."

Kalki shook his head, patting her head, running his fingers in her hair. "Don't be. He's alive."

"What?" Her excitement shot out.

"Yep." He smiled back. "And I'm sorry I blamed you for Arjan's disappearance."

"I'm sorry I ever doubted that you were not the Avatar."

Kalki remembered how he had fought with Padma and Kripa in the forest. He was so guilt-ridden. The woman who cares for him and the man who had watched out for him . . . And he had been so rude.

"Are you leaving then?" Padma moved back, wiping the tears.

Kalki thought for a moment as he swivelled his head to see the frantic Vanars. He looked at the women calming down their babies. He saw the men gearing for battle. All these people might be killed by the tyrant General Taar—a monster created by Lord Bajrang himself. He even saw Kara bidding farewell to her eight-year-old. All these Vanars, they believed in Lord Bajrang and now because of that, they might die. Lord Bajrang, no matter what, will not fight in this war, will not be part of this crusade, will not fight for his people.

"I always thought," Kalki began thoughtfully musing as he saw the sunset in the horizon, beyond the terrains of Vanarvata, "that being Dharm or an Avatar is about having strength. My goal was always about fighting the big bad evil Kali and abdicating him from his throne."

"Isn't that your destiny? To bring order to these lands?"

He shook his head. Looking at the Vanar huts, he wondered what would happen if Taar conquered them all. "Being a Dharm is a choice."

"A choice for what?" she asked.

"A choice to be a better person," he sighed. "I don't think I am leaving, Padma. I'm staying right here."

55

The eagle was bigger than any winged creature she had ever seen.

But then, it wasn't an eagle. Manasa knew it was Tarakshya's vehicle. Unlike the flying chariots she had seen till then, Manasa could see that Tarakshya's vehicle was different. It was huge. Instead of having wings on the sides, a golden eagle had been fashioned in the front and with its wings the chariot soared in the air. Tarakshya's servants stood in the corners. At the back of the chariot was a huge tail from where the Somas were being burnt and crackled, igniting it to launch it in the air.

Manasa was standing in the meadows. Tarakshya landed his bird on the ground and stepped out of the chariot graciously. Tarakshya hadn't changed much since the last time Manasa had seen him. His eyes were still smeared with kohl, his thin face was absurdly white because of the powder he had used, and he still had a long, conical beard. His golden skin glimmered in the sunlight. Though she knew he had painted himself to look golden.

With his head held high, he came down from the chariot and walked towards Manasa. He was wearing a flowing robe which was being carried by his men. Guards, majestic like him, surrounded him as soon as he stepped on the ground.

"What is it?" he spoke dryly. "Manasa, we have known each other for a while. Your brother wasn't the friendly kind. You have

some nerve coming up here . . . meeting me." He sighed at the end as if he was already exhausted.

Tarakshya was exactly what one might call a spoilt, rich king, but he was also disciplined and knew how to utilize his kingly power.

"Your kingdom is in danger."

"Hmmm . . ." Tarakshya starting humming a melody. "And what makes you say that? Am I in danger from your troupes?" he said, signalling at the guards standing behind Manasa, only a handful of them.

"No, Kadru is planning to do something sinister that would affect your kingdom."

"Kadru? When one snake enters, the other bites. What's with the Nagas and their politics? I didn't even know till now that you were alive. I thought you had been eaten by the fishes of the North. But no! You are very much . . ." he sighed, panting. "You are very much alive, I can see. Now tell me, why should I believe Vasuki's sister?"

"Because I'm telling the truth. You must not let them enter."

"Enter? They are already inside."

Manasa gritted her teeth, lightly stamping her foot on the ground.

"And you think my kingdom is in grave danger? I have entertained you for long enough because I pity you. But now I must leave and fend for my guests. This is a glorious day," he panted, "to be happy that we are all a single community."

"She's going to betray you."

Manasa wanted to show off the Shard from the Eye of Brahma, but she refrained. Tarakshya was someone who lived in excess and if he got hold of the Shard when he already had Amrit, who knows what he will do. But then, what choice did she have?

"All right, let me talk to them, I can prove it to—"

He shook his head.

Manasa was getting desperate. She tried to make another

attempt to convince Tarakshya but before she could say anything, she felt a tremor!

The ground shook.

Manasa's gaze shot up to see the bridge and the colossal iron-barricaded castle standing over multiple solid pillars. But there was one problem—from underneath the pillars, Manasa could see smoke emanating. And the next moment, the pillars were enveloped in fire.

The castle is falling!

Tarakshya gasped. "What in the name of flying Garuda is happening?"

"My lord!" A guard approached Tarakshya and said, "Someone must have brought inflammables to the cave."

"Oh dear," Tarakshya moaned. "Oh dear," he said, shaking his head.

Manasa took this opportunity to convince Tarakshya again. "Lord Tarakshya! This is Kadru's work. Let me stop her. I want to be the one who catches her red-handed. She's doing this because she doesn't want any partnership with the Suparns. All she cares about are the Somas and now she has the plants. Don't you understand? I'm trying to save you."

Tarakshaya matched Manasa's gaze. "Why are you trying to help me? You know I killed your brother's family."

"Because I believe that the past doesn't matter. What matters is *now*. And I want to forge good relations with you, unlike my brother. I promise you that, and I can prove my worth to you by stopping Kadru before she destroys your people and your kingdom."

Tarakshya thought for a moment, humming to himself. Manasa grunted, leaving the king of Suparns and moving towards the vehicle and jumping on it.

"What do you think you are doing?"

"Your people are going to die. We need to act now. Are you coming with me or not? Either way, I won't let thousands of Suparns die just because you take too much time to think."

Tarakshya sighed, sitting inside the vehicle. "I better hope you don't betray me, snake."

"Don't worry. I won't, my dear." She cheekily grinned. "I know who are my enemies and who are not."

56

They had to leave.

When Urvashi had reintroduced the sodomy law, Arjan had realized that he and Rudra were not welcome anymore. After Urvashi had invited Nala to be a part of her council and help her with the treasury, Arjan and Rudra had been sidelined from the administration council. It was evident that Urvashi had realized that there was something going on between Arjan and Rudra. They were always together and she had begun to hear rumours. Once at dinner, Urvashi had suggested that Arjan should have a girl in his life. Arjan had brushed her off saying he didn't need a girl to make him happy.

But Arjan could feel the paranoia seeping inside his skin. And he didn't want to lose Rudra like he had lost his brother, his father . . . the thought just gave him goosebumps. It frightened him to the core.

Nala had begun to be a bigger part of Indragarh. Unlike his father, he was in every council meeting and even raised himself to become a councilman. He didn't need sponsors for elections because he had enough money of his own. And according to the rules of the state, Nala had full right to contest politically and be in Urvashi's inner council. He didn't care about what Urvashi had done to his father. He didn't mind it at all.

All the policies Urvashi had come up with were being enforced stringently. Due to the sodomy law, lots of free prisoners had been thrown back in. In fact, Urvashi had made sure that this act was well-implemented. She had even created the Execution Force to handle the execution of all the policies she had administered upon her people. The Force had fished out a lot of homosexuals—from the cabinet, the council, the mining colonies, and the labour class. In fact, even Ramras had been imprisoned because of it. Urvashi hadn't bended the rule for a nobleman either. There were other policies as well—stringency on the labour force, heavy taxes, splurging money on the creation of temples and idols—that were keeping the nobles happy but the condition of the civilians was worsening day by day. There was no rebellion because any rebellion would be crushed, not by imprisoning, but killing the rebels. Public execution had been thankfully cancelled, but all the law and power was under Urvashi and if she wanted to kill a man, no one could stop her.

At least with Kali, it hadn't been this bad.

Even if he had bent the system, he had had his humane moments. He had, at times, shown compassion towards the citizens and had devised proper ways to hold power over his councilmen. Urvashi seemed like she might just kill anyone who spoke against her. There was harmony in the city. It was quiet out there, like the silence before a storm.

She is going to be the death of me.

"We have to leave," Arjan said, grabbing the sack, trying to put in as many of his belongings as he could.

"Calm down. What happened?" Rudra sat next to Arjan, letting his hands run across his hair. "Don't worry. Nothing will happen to us. Ramras is in prison because of Urvashi. If she wanted us in prison, we would be in it right now. She likes us, love." Rudra kissed Arjan on the cheek to calm him down.

"I understand," said Arjan.

His gut was telling him to leave with Rudra right there and then.

"She needs you to advise her. She likes you more than me."

It wasn't just the ban on homosexuality that was bothering Arjan, but also Nala's growing influence in the court. He just gave Arjan the creeps. Arjan had often noticed Nala speaking to himself.

Arjan took a deep breath. "You like me, right?"

"I love you."

Arjan smiled. Even though he was stressed, Rudra made him smile. "God, I love you too. But listen to my gut feeling. Please trust me. I know when something is wrong. And I can feel it's in the air."

"Where do we go?"

"To my mother. She's at Lord Bajrang's temple. We get her and we go to a village, toil all our lives to hide ourselves, and perhaps we would be able to live the way we want to."

"It will be treason if we escape. This paranoia will be with us everywhere we go, Arjan. Are you sure living in obscurity would be good for us?"

"I don't care," Arjan quietly responded. "But at least we'll be happy."

"I'm happy here. I don't think Urvashi would do anything . . ."

And then there was a knock on the door.

Arjan looked at Rudra, uneasy. Rudra went to the door and opened it. Three guards were standing outside.

"Yes?" Rudra asked.

They were still at Urvashi's fort and her guards occasionally came to escort them to meetings.

"Lady Urvashi demands your presence."

Demands? It was always 'requests' your presence.

Arjan shook his head at Rudra. Rudra smiled at him, mouthing that it was okay.

"Is she in her chambers?"

The guard nodded.

"Tell her we are coming in five minutes."

The guard shook his head. "You need to come with us now."

Arjan was perspiring, dreading what was to come. Rudra just shrugged his shoulders, showing there was no need to worry. He wore his overcoat and began to walk outside, with Arjan striding behind him. His eyes wandered around the place. The guards were watching them with suspicion.

Arjan swallowed a lump in his throat as he made way to Urvashi's private chambers. It was guarded by two men. Their breastplates had the symbol of the City Guard—the national security for the premier king. The guard signalled Arjan and Rudra to enter.

Arjan entered first. He saw the magnificent room of the youngest queen of the capital of Udaiyas. She was looking out of the iron-grilled windows, her earrings sparkling in the light.

The door closed behind Arjan with a loud bang.

Without turning back to look at them, Urvashi spoke in a mellow tone. "You know why I've summoned you here?" She was fragrant. Arjan caught a whiff of lavender in the air. Her long gown was exquisite and richly-woven. Ever since she had been crowned, she seemed more confident. Like she knew exactly what she had to do and when she had to do it. Close to her sidetable, Arjan saw her dolls carved specifically for each council member. If they ever did anything problematic, she would not hesitate to use them.

Black magic. No wonder the people have started calling her the Mad Queen.

Mad or not, Urvashi should not be queen, thought Arjan. Kali had been a better ruler.

"No." Arjan was the first one to respond.

"Ramras is making accusations, Arjan, about your friend. I threw him in jail after the Force found him playing around with male prostitutes. He is shouting that people like Rudra should be thrown in as well."

Urvashi finally turned to look at them with her cold, kohl-

smeared eyes. She quietly walked towards Arjan and Rudra. She was petite, yet she looked menacing, devious. "He's telling the nobility about you two." She shook her head, disappointed.

"We were meaning to tell you," Rudra came forward and admitted.

You honourable idiot! We could have lied!

"You didn't have to. I knew it already. But I was keeping quiet to save you both."

"What?" Arjan realized Rudra had been right about her. She did like them.

"I didn't want my two favourite men to be jailed as well. But Ramras is making noise . . . too much noise for the other councilmen to become suspicious of my . . . well . . . what should I call it? Bias? Ramras' father plans to bring this issue up in the next meeting. I cannot protect you like always."

"What do you want from us?" spoke Rudra. Arjan was now thinking of how they could escape at that moment.

Urvashi glanced at Rudra and then casually walked to her bed, wearing her sandals. "I would like you, Rudra, to take the fall and return to prison again."

57

Kali didn't know what to do with this kind of information. This was just so *weird.* He had been hurting his baby brother for so long. He had been torturing him, pressurizing him.

And now he had the Soma too.

Kali bit his teeth as he thought about all this. Arjan could be capable of being Dharm. And that wouldn't be so bad. Arjan and Kali, ruling side by side, reviving the Asura name. The thought made Kali giddy with excitement.

Or Arjan is the Dharm and Kali will have to rule along with him.

Arjan has been adopted by Kalki's family. They are not related. He is my blood.

That Shambala native had corrupted Arjan, made him . . . weird. It was exactly what Kali didn't want.

I shall change him and show him our ways.

Kali looked at Durukti as their boat moved towards the centre of the sea. Darkness had enveloped the sky. He could smell the saltwater. The silence was often broken by the noise of the birds screeching in the sky. Durukti was quiet and she seemed distraught. Kali had forgiven her though he hadn't told her this. The thought of his brother being alive had made everything else forgivable.

Kali smiled at her.

He began to move towards Durukti when Shukr came in between, his hands at the back. "I know what you are going to do," he said softly.

"What?"

"You are going to inform her, the betrayer."

"She's my sister."

"She also betrayed you for someone else." Shukr shook his head. "In the ancient Asura culture, a sister and a brother are so close that their souls are supposed to be glued together till the time they leave this world. She doesn't deserve to be your sister anymore."

Kali sighed. "All right." He tried to divert the subject. "So you think Arjan is not Dharm?"

"No, he'sss not. He's inexperienced, but he can be a good ally if you use him to your benefit. He can adapt. The little I have seen of him tells me that he has a fire in him. You have to use it when you return."

"How will I return to an already conquered city of mine?"

Shukr gave Kali a devious smile. "You shall. I have a plan." He guided Kali to the sea where Alakshmi had brought them. Here especially, the ocean was raging, waving with terror. "During the Mahayudh, there was an astra that had been buried in Pataal. This had caused the islands to collapse. They were submerged, never to be seen again."

"The islands?"

"Yes, they are right here, underneath this boat, in many pieces."

Kali widened his gaze, trying to see through the black water. He nodded. "So what can we do?"

"Have you heard about Danavs?"

"Yes, of course." Kali had heard stories. Danavs were the ancient brothers of Asuras. They were the ones who had fought Lord Indra when he was in Illavarti. Danavs were huge, fifteen to fifty feet giants, whose steps would shake the ground when they

walked. People were so afraid of them that the Asuras out of fear of not being able to control them, made them sleep forever on the land and buried them in the ground. Nobody had seen them ever since and no one knew where they were buried. But it was said that if they woke up, they had the power to end this world.

"They . . . are right here where we float upon."

"THAT'S IMPOSSIBLE."

"It is true." He nodded. "And according to the prophecy, only the Dharm can wake them up with the blood of his own."

"Blood of his own?" Kali hadn't heard this version of the prophecy.

"An Asura." Shukr nodded.

Kali gulped. This was not going according to what he had expected. "What if I'm not Dharm? What if I'm unable to wake them up?"

"Then this will be a disappointing crusade of mine and I shall not do anything. But I know you are the one, the saviour of the Asura people, the one who shall return our race back to greatness." He grabbed Kali, looking straight in his eyes. "My son, it's time to realize what you are worth."

Kali nodded.

"Good. With the army of Danavs, you shall be able to control your fate and control the entire Illavarti."

"But wouldn't it destroy many livelihoods in the process?"

"For a greater cause, casualties are a must."

Kali didn't understand this concept. Ever since he was child, he knew that whatever he had done, he had done it because it was the right thing. He had done things for the people. He hadn't wanted to be the king that ruled over people, but one that ruled with them.

"And I shall ensure that you fulfil your destiny."

"How will the Danavs rise? They had been put to sleep many years ago. They must be dead by now."

"They were wrapped in honey and special Asura paper and

put in limestone boxesss, wrapped up so their bodies won't be decomposed. And you now have the power to wake them up and induct them into your crusade—for Asuras, for Illavarti."

Kali was afraid. He was so afraid, but the confidence in Shukr's eyes, as if anything else didn't matter to him much, strengthened his resolve. Shukr was here to see Kali do what he had dreamt of doing his entire life.

"You have no idea how long I have waited for thisss." He hissed under his breath. "I have seen so much and I know thisss is it."

"Then, you had seen the future through the Eye of Brahma? The Danavs will rise again?"

"Yesss, I had." He nodded. "That's why I'm telling you to do it."

"Was I the Dharm in the future?"

Shukr looked puzzled. "The identity of Dharm and Adharm, both were shrouded in mystery. They were never absolute. I could only see the events being played out around you. I only know what's going to happen."

Kali only wondered if he really was the Dharm. But this was a great way of proving it. "How did you get your hands on the Eye of Brahma?"

"How doesss it matter?" Shukr was getting annoyed.

"It matters," Kali squared his shoulders, "because I want to know."

"When I travelled from the land of Pataal to Illavarti, I heard stories about the Eye of Brahma. I had to have it. I went on a crusade and found its Shards in the unlikeliest of placesss since there were myths about its location, but only few had the power to sniff it out. I worked half my life to find it. No one knew where it had come from. Stories were bizarre and unreliable. I finally combined them and took the Eye with me until I started serving Lord Dushasan. When he died by Raghav's hands, I escaped and then I joined the crusade of Duryodhan. He also died even though I had shown him

everything he was supposed to know. I knew Govind and Arjun were in power. They were slowly vanquishing the Asuras in Illavarti so I had to escape from there. I had the Eye of Brahma and I was trying to use it in the best manner possible. But it was not enough. When the Mahayudh happened and the Breaking occurred, I wandered aimlessly. I was lost, seeing the future, the past, and the present. Only the hope that the next Dharm will arrive soon kept me going. By then, everything happened as it should . . . until . . ."

Kali narrowed his gaze. "Wasn't Pataal destroyed during the Breaking?"

"The Breaking only occurred in Illavarti. Not in Pataal or Swarg. These were two lands away from the mainland of Illavarti. You must realize, I came back to Pataal when the Manavsss were leading an expedition against the Asuras, to burn the islands after they had learnt that Duryodhan had Asura blood. They got paranoid proclaiming that the Asuras will lead Illavarti to damnation. After all, Asuras were foreigners. Arjun was at the height of his power. I wasss afraid. But before Arjun could even step in and destroy the Eye of Brahma, it was stolen. Except one Shard . . ." he pointed at the ocean. "The only one."

"Who stole it?"

"The man with the scar."

The man with the scar. From Kali's dreams, the man who had burnt down his village. *Why had he wanted Kali's siblings to die?*

"I know him. I saw him in the past."

"I know you saw him. I did too."

"Who is he?"

"A Chiranjeev, someone who has lived for a long, long time."

"Why did he kill my siblings?"

"That I do not know. I wish I did." He gritted his teeth. "But do not worry. We shall find him. For now, you must concentrate—"

"Hold on," Kali snapped. "There's something wrong with your story."

Arching his brows, Shukr backed off. "I have told you everything now. What is wrong?"

"You have lived from the time of Raghav's reign in the North to Govind's reign to finally this age? That's more than a hundred years." Kali advanced towards Shukr. "And I know that Asura priests cannot live for so long." His eyes narrowed into slits as he asked Shukr, "Who are you?"

Shukr looked at Kali, unperturbed.

"You are not a priest. You are someone else. Who are you?"

"An Asura . . ." he coughed. "Just like you."

"Which Asura?"

At that moment, Alakshmi whistled letting the hyenas roar at Kali to break the confrontation. But Kali was not interested in the beasts. He just shushed them by putting a finger on his lips and directing them to sit. The hyenas obediently and surprisingly listened. Kali peered at Alakshmi who was smitten after observing his forced control over the animals. Honestly, Kali had no idea how he had done it, but he had read somewhere that hyenas responded to power in a person and they would eat the prey who reeked of fear.

"My name is . . . Bali. You might have heard of me."

Kali smiled.

Of course I have.

He had named his brother after him.

"Mahabali, the man who lost to a dwarf," Kali said and smiled, as the last piece in the puzzle unravelled itself.

58

Kalki geared himself up.

He knew he had to prepare himself for the battle against Taar and his forces. He went to the armoury, gathered supplies, wore his breastplate, tightened a belt, dangling two of his best swords in it. He even had a dagger wrapped around his ankle. He held up a shield, which was not too heavy nor too light. He could see Padma getting ready as well. She didn't want to lose an opportunity to fight for the Vanars. Kalki liked that.

It was a choice to be a better person. And he was being one. He could just feel it. It was not about being casual about the world affairs. It was about lives, human lives that needed saving, regardless of them being a Manav or a Tribal. It didn't matter who was what.

Kalki came out of the armoury, packed with everything he needed when he saw his white horse straddled in the stable. Kalki came and stood in front of him. It started nudging him to pat him. Kalki did.

Thanks for saving me out there, buddy.

You needed help.

But I had tied you to a tree.

Hah! As if a piece of rope has ever stopped me, man!

Kalki grinned. Shuko fluttered and flapped his wings, sitting on Kalki's shoulder.

What should I do now, boss?

Kalki handed Shuko a piece of rolled-up parchment.

Give this to Arjan, back in Indragarh.

What is it?

This will tell him that I'm alive. It says that I am safe and he need not worry about me.

But I want to be a part of this war!

You are an integral part of this war. You are helping me, friend.

The parrot squawked in anger. He grabbed the parchment and fluttered away.

Part of war? Pffft! He's just a parrot, hope he knows that.

You are a lot like a person I used to know.

Who?

A stubborn, old beast who helped me in the nick of time. He was called Devadatta.

Eh? I like that name.

Kalki smiled. *I will call you Devadatta from now on.* Though he did feel that the human Devadatta would not have been impressed to know that a beast had been named after him. He saw Padma leaving the armoury and mounting her horse. She was ready, and so was Kalki. They were standing in the midst of the thick snowy land as the Vanars crossed them, armed with swords, wearing heavy armours. Kalki could even see a slight blizzard coming as the winds had gotten strong.

From the edge, he saw Kara. Kalki had told her that he'll be joining the war and will fight alongside them. She was going towards the frozen river where Kalki had been standing a while ago. Some of the army was being positioned at the bridge and the rest had been instructed to go towards the valley where they began to create bamboo pillars so they could block that pathway. Whatever the Vanars did, they did for defending themselves.

And that's what is going to kill them?

"Where do you think you are off to, kid?" Kalki heard a familiar voice. "I hope you haven't forgotten about me, eh?"

Kalki turned to see Ratna Maru standing with Smrit. They were both geared up as well. Ratna was cheekily grinning at Padma and Kalki as she came forward.

"I thought you had done your job of saving your kind and wanted to leave," Kalki responded.

"I did. But after hearing Kripa, I felt I should follow you, at least for this mission. You must be really special." She winked.

"I don't know about that, but thanks." Kalki smiled.

"I'm sorry I didn't complete my story. I didn't trust you all that much, so I didn't share it with you." She put her hand on his shoulder. "But that was before."

"The story where your husband . . ."

"Yes." She sadly nodded. "He was a kind man, a good man. Just like you. You remind me of him—brave and honourable. But don't be a fool by getting yourself killed like him. You see, now that I look back, it was his tragedy that set me on this path—to free all the Apsaras. His death became the salvation of my race. I know you are sad, but try to see this tragedy as an opportunity to become stronger. And you shall be."

Kalki held her hand and nodded. "Thank you."

And as Ratna was moving with Smrit towards the frozen river, Kalki asked her, "Who was your husband?"

"He was the Prince of Alakpur, Manigriva. He was killed by his own brother, Nalakuvera." She clenched her jaw as she went ahead, not realizing she had raised Kalki's spirits.

There was no way that he was going to lose this battle.

Before heading to fight, Kalki had to visit the man himself.

He was standing where Kalki had seen him for the first time, hanging from the cherry tree, looking at the sun. But this time, the wind was blowing fiercely and the sun was just an orange dot in the

faraway horizon. The snowflakes brushed Kalki's face, though he ignored them.

Kalki walked forward, hoping to intercept Lord Bajrang, but before he could do anything Bajrang spoke up.

"You do realize I am praying, don't you?" Bajrang asked without turning his head. His bobbing ears had let him hear Kalki's footsteps.

But Kalki didn't care. He was furious at Lord Bajrang—he was not fighting for his people. It was stupid of him to just be there, praying to the sun.

"I hope you know I'm fighting for your cause."

"I thought you didn't care."

"I started caring after I learnt you are doing nothing about it."

At that, Bajrang leapt from the tree and faced Kalki. He was not smiling anymore. "I have told you the reason."

"I know." Kalki sarcastically smiled. "Lord Bajrang, you are a revered god. People worship you. I have sent my mother to your temple so she could be safe under your protection. But I guess I was wrong. My mother is not safe with you because you can't even save your own kind."

"There's a reason, son, why my idols exist till date, because I keep my promises, my words. I have honoured my word to Lord Raghav. He didn't want any violence and wanted me to start with it."

"Perhaps Lord Raghav was right. Perhaps he didn't want violence anymore, that's why he told you to follow the path of non-violence and spread peace and harmony in this world. But have you ever thought that if Lord Raghav was alive right now, would he not break his word to protect his people?"

Bajrang shook his head. "He would never do that. He had asked Lady Sita to stay away from the kingdom because his people wanted so. He was faithful to his kind. He kept his word. They hadn't trusted Lady Sita even though she was the most pious woman

to walk on this earth. And Lord Raghav adhered to it, because he was not just a king . . . he was a god."

"I know that." Kalki had heard what had happened to Lady Sita. He had heard about the *agnipareeksha.* "He was a king, not just a husband. He trusted his wife and yet he allowed other people to influence his decisions. And Lady Sita died alone and he still kept his word to his people."

Bajrang nodded. There was no doubt in his mind as he said, "He kept his word and that shows what a true god he was."

"I know that. He was the perfect man, that's what my gurukul taught me, the perfect man who did perfect things and strived to create a perfect society. But what is so great about perfection?" Kalki stood close to Bajrang, meeting his eyes. "I would break every word, every oath if it means I could save a single soul. I would break it without thinking twice. I don't care if I am thrown in hell and I'm considered disrespectful because of it. That's the difference between you and me. You are right. We all have our battles to fight. And unfortunately, I'm fighting your battle. But it's all right because if you can't do it, I will. Taar is a monster created by you. Now he's someone I have to kill."

Kalki turned to leave and Bajrang stood frozen to the ground, his face impassive.

Sitting on Devadutta with his head held high, Kalki tightly wrapped the warm fur that covered his body. He was at the Frontier near the frozen river. Kara stood close to the shore, ready to pounce and attack. He saw Ratna and Smrit taking their battle stances. Most Vanars here were on foot, some were on horseback, and the smaller Vanars were on mules.

Kalki waited for Kara's order, who was leading the army. He dismounted from the horse and looked across the lake where Taar

was with his army. Aruna was standing next to him with many of his ferocious, scarred Vanars along with him.

"We cannot move further," Kalki said to Kara. "The ice is thin and it might break if there's an army fighting on it."

Kara nodded. "But they don't know that, right?"

Kalki smiled. "Then start the mocking."

Kara smiled back and then ordered in her Vanar language to spew abuses and vulgar words at Taar and his men. Taar initially didn't do anything but then he glanced at Aruna, and with two of his thick burly fingers, he signalled his army to move further. Taar and Aruna stayed in the same spot.

They did what Kalki and Kara had anticipated. They were walking on the ice, but Kalki noticed something—the ice wasn't shattering. They were tiptoeing on the ice, and didn't have any heavy weapons or armour to increase their weight. They were nimble-footed and their steps were unhurried. Slowly and steadily, they were advancing towards Bajrang's camp.

"If they continue like this, we might have to jump on the frozen lake as well," Padma suggested.

Kalki shook his head as he took off his fur. He walked and stood close to the frozen lake, though a little bit away from the actual ice. Looking at his reflection in the lake, he knelt down.

"What are you doing, boy?" asked Ratna in her high-pitched voice.

Kalki didn't respond.

It's better to do than to say.

He pulled up his arm, flexing his muscles as he saw Taar's army approach them. Almost a hundred of them were trudging over the ice.

And then, curling his strong fingers into a fist, he punched the frozen lake.

"What!" Kara exclaimed. "You cannot break it! It's too hard."

Kalki didn't listen. He punched the ice again. The army was

getting close. His fist was bleeding and the blood was seeping into the ice. And then the ice turned white and black at the same time—a crack appeared.

It was happening.

Kalki delivered one final blow on the lake. The cracks started widening and slowly reached the entire facet of the river, making way towards the army who just looked at it, unsure of what to do next.

And then the ice smashed.

The entire army was plunged inside the cold, harsh water, fighting for their breaths. He looked up to see the Vanars, trying to reach the shore, but getting drowned in the chaotic waters. He also saw Taar's face. He was petrified but furious. Flaring his nostrils in anger, he left the scene.

"I think we surprised him."

Kalki could hear applause from everyone until a panting, restless Vanar came towards them, running from the bridge.

"What happened?" Kara asked, trying to calm him down.

"Madam, Taar's army . . . they are crossing the bridge. They are about to attack our men!"

Kalki gritted his teeth.

He knew what he had to do next!

59

Manasa saw chaos.

As she entered the once glorious kingdom of Suparnika, she saw chaos. And it was not Tarakshya's fault. It was Kadru's. Things were blowing up. Fire had engulfed everything. People were running around here and there. As the flying eagle stopped and landed, Manasa lurched from it.

People were running, trying to find some sort of refuge while others jumped on their own *vimanas*—the flying Amrit or Soma induced vehicles—trying to escape. They looked similar to the one she had seen Padma riding back in Indragarh, albeit with a few modifications. Here the vimanas were crafted better, with light metal to hold them higher in the sky and to take sharp turns with strong wings.

Manasa knew that the ground was shaking and the city would crumble any second, because the pillars had started to collapse and it was destabilizing the entire order of the place.

"Listen," she called out to Tarakshya and her guards, "get as many as you can on this vehicle of yours and other vimanas. We do not have time. We need to help everyone escape. How long can the pillars sustain this city?"

"Not for long." Tarakshya was shivering as if he had seen a ghost.

"Do you know how this could have happened?"

"The Somalata plans, they are infused with an oil which is very combustible but the Somas themselves are not. That's why whenever we fly in the sky, we do not let the oil touch the fire when we ignite it. We bind the Somas from one edge of a cloth when we . . . uh . . . from where the oil comes out, so it doesn't come out when we bind it, I mean. In that way, the flying is not harmful or dangerous to the passengers."

"I don't want to know the physics of your bloody vehicle! For all I know, they are made of stupid magical contraptions." She cursed. "I want to know how this happened. Why are the pillars weak?"

"Uh . . . everything is connected to the oil from the Somalata plants. There are vines that are attached to the pillar which push out the oil. Someone must have brought combustible material inside the caves, which is strictly prohibited, igniting the plants. This may be why it has spread like wildfire."

Manasa understood the situation. Kadru must have burnt down the Somalata plants or at least ignited the oil, causing it to spread. This fire was eating away the strong pillars, and with every minute, it was devastating the foundation of the city.

"Get the biggest vimanas, the biggest ships, and get the people out of this city and down to the bridge or the meadow, where they could be safe! DO YOU UNDERSTAND?"

Tarakshya nervously nodded.

"What are you going to do?" asked Tarakshya.

"Stop Kadru!"

From there Manasa walked forward, with a sword dangling on her waistbelt, encased in a sheath. She walked as the frantic public ran around aimlessly. She finally saw the remnants of the feast, but there was so much screaming in the streets that were being engulfed by the unrestrained fire, that she could make neither head nor tail of the situation. Worse, the city was quaking every few seconds. It was getting hard for her to maintain her balance.

There she is.

Her eyes caught a glimpse of Kadru and Jamun racing towards one of the vimanas at the flying station. The guards didn't care to stop them. They were busy running away from the fire. Manasa walked towards Kadru and Jamun, pulling out her sword from the sheath, keeping her limp hand close to her chest.

"KADRU!"

Kadru turned and Manasa realized how different she looked with a one-eyed patch. Her other eye was twitching in hellish rage.

"Oh god!" exclaimed Kadru as she hopped on to the vimana, hastily positioning herself on the seat along with two sacks that she kept on it carefully.

They must be the plants to be used for the astras. I have to retrieve them from her.

Manasa moved forward. She saw Kadru pushing Jamun aside. He was trying to get himself up on the vimana, but was finding it difficult to climb in because of his weight.

"I don't have time for this," Kadru yelled.

Jamun was shocked by Kadru's betrayal as the vimana flew up in the air, leaving him behind. Manasa cursed at her. Jamun saw Manasa coming close to him, screaming for vengeance. He instantly dropped down on his knees, begging for his life.

Manasa didn't take much time. She knew what she had to do.

She plunged the sword inside Jamun's throat and pulled it out, letting the blood spray on her gown as he fell on the ground, lifeless.

"This is for Nanda, my dear," Manasa spat at the corpse of Jamun.

She had to act fast. She went for the nearest vimana regulated by a Suparn guard. Manasa knocked and elbowed him out of the way as she started to pilot the vimana. She could see a lot of buttons and switches. Unable to figure out how it worked, she started to panic. And then she saw a lever.

She had no idea what it would do. And still, she pulled it.

As soon as it was pulled, heat started emanating from the end of the vimana which was shaped like a tail. The heat hit the Amrit that was inside. The fire crackled and with a blast of smoke, Manasa was up in the air.

Manasa thought about how she would one day like to sit down and understand the machinations of the vimana. *But not today!* The only purpose in her mind right now was to kill the bitch.

The vimana suspended her in the air as the wind grew harsh. There was a small explosion in the city, but Manasa's face was locked on to Kadru. She could see Kadru flying away into the distance, out of her reach.

Manasa looked at the mechanism now. There were a few other levers that she could see. She began to pull them one by one, and with each pull something or the other was happening. The vimana was tilting, turning upside down, and changing positions. Manasa was getting agitated when at last, she pulled a lever that speeded up the vehicle. The heat was maximized now, as she could feel the heat wave emanating from her seat. But she didn't care. She had to catch up to Kadru. She had to reach her before the fuel ran out. She had to stop her.

Her vimana had now caught up to Kadru's vimana. They were positioned parallel to each other. Manasa used the wheel in front of her to manoeuver her vimana and rammed it against Kadru's vehicle, causing the right wing of her vehicle to blast. The wing was now scorched and her vimana started to spiral.

And then Manasa realized that the speed was depleting the fuel. The vehicle's movements were getting slower, and the vimana was losing altitude.

She had to do something.

And she did the unthinkable. They were above fifty feet, in the midst of clouds where the breeze was strong.

She had come to Suparnika to talk to Tarakshya. Here she was

now, standing in mid-air, about to do something she had never done before.

Here goes nothing.

She jumped.

She jumped from one vimana to another, grabbing onto the edges as she came inside the space where Kadru stood. At that moment, Kadru attacked her with her sword. Manasa parried it with her own sword, climbing inside the vimana in the process.

"It's over, Kadru. STOP."

"I'll only stop if you kill me. But today is not the day I die."

The clanging of their swords went on for some time. Kadru managed to wound Manasa's shoulder. Manasa howled in pain, letting her sword fall. She was standing near the edge. Kadru came forward pointing her sword at Manasa. And with a quick and a final strike, Kadru charged at her with tremendous might.

In an instant, Manasa lowered her stance and grabbed Kadru by the waist, taking her by surprise. It happened in a flash as she pinned her against the edge and toppled her from the vimana. Kadru managed to grip the edge, but her sword fell from the skies, never to be seen again.

"Please . . . please . . . sister, grab me," she pleaded, her hand outstretched.

And for a moment, Manasa saw the cousin she had always loved and mentored.

She had waited for this moment. She wanted to revel in it. But all she felt was deep-seated sadness.

"I would have, but Nanda, Vasuki's children . . . There is no place for you even in the deepest reaches of hell. I fare you well, sister." And Manasa picked up her sword, stabbing her in the arm. She plunged the steel as deeply as she could. Kadru screamed and howled in agony, as she dangled from the edge, unable to die.

Kadru knew the look on Manasa's face. It was pity.

Manasa pulled the sword out.

And she fell . . .

Down . . .

And down . . .

And down . . .

Kadru became a dot and then disappeared altogether. Manasa sighed. She had fulfilled her mission.

At that moment, she sent a silent prayer for the souls she had loved, those who had left her too soon.

60

They were on the run.

Arjan had asked Urvashi for some time off with Rudra before he left for prison. She had asked Rudra to leave without a fuss, so that she wouldn't face any political brunt. But Arjan didn't care. As soon as they got their private time in the room, Arjan packed his sack and asked Rudra to run away with him.

Rudra agreed. He was afraid of going back into that hellhole where he had had to spend most of his life. Never again. Ramras' attempts to incriminate him would be in vain. Today was the day he would be truly free.

They silently crept out of their door. A guard was standing outside. Just when he saw them, Arjan elbowed him hard, making a dent in his armour. Arjan was glad that the effects of Soma were still active, and it was not hindering his mind into doing evil things, or mad things. In fact, he was now able to control his strength. Perhaps the stories of people going mad after taking Soma were just fanciful tales or perhaps it depended on the person who had ingested the Soma—whether he used it for good or bad.

And Arjan was clearly using it for good. That was what he had been taught since his childhood, to be good to others.

The sun was bright as Arjan and Rudra casually rushed out towards the main hall, sprinting towards the meadow where the gate

was. There was no extra protection at the gates which meant that Urvashi must have not informed her guards to be on the lookout.

As they moved towards the gate, the guards turned on them with pointed spears. They even closed the gate, locking it from the inside.

"ARJAN!"

He heard the familiar, childlike voice of the Mad Queen—Urvashi. She was with twenty or so of her guards, who were standing by her side.

"If you leave, you go to prison too."

"Then I shall," he said, holding Rudra's hand. "I won't leave him."

"Fine by me," she shrugged. "Grab them!"

Arjan and Rudra took out their swords. They stood back to back as they tried to defend themselves from the guards.

"You cannot defeat an army, Arjan. Do you truly think you can take my forces down?" Urvashi was in the corner, where the fountain was, far away from the main gates. "I will let this pass. But I demand your cooperation. I promise you Rudra would be free after serving some time, once I have discussed it with my councilmen."

"You are just trying to save your crown," Arjan responded, his eyes and feet still alerted at the guards who had surrounded them. "You don't have the intention of saving Rudra. In fact, you think of us as expendable men. You are stuck to your father's ideals. You are repeating history, and despite of what you claim, you are a TYRANT!"

Urvashi sighed. "This wasn't how it should have been. I liked you, you know. We could have gotten married. You are quite handsome, but you had to like a man. I wanted you by my side. But not anymore. Kill them," she said in such a casual manner that Arjan was taken aback.

Urvashi liked me? Of course! That's why she always favoured me.

Now, he wondered whether there were any councilmen who

had objected to Rudra's sexuality. He thought about whether Ramras had been the one behind it all. Perhaps it had been Urvashi all along, trying to get rid of Rudra, so she could take Arjan for herself.

Or Arjan could be wrong.

"Before this happens," Rudra called out as loud as he could, "I just want to say . . . Arjan, I love you. Thank you for being in my life."

Arjan smiled. *He will always be the melodramatic kind.*

As soon the guards came forward with the spears towards Arjan, he deflected the attacks. He was stabbed from his blind side, but it didn't hurt him much.

"Are you even . . ."

And he heard a loud thud. Someone had collapsed.

Arjan turned to see Rudra bleeding profusely. He had been stabbed. He was turning pale, his eyes bulging in shock.

No! I survived because of the Soma. But Rudra . . .

Arjan knelt down as the guards backed off, realizing they had accomplished their objective. Arjan grabbed Rudra, whose eyes were desperately trying to search for Arjan. As Arjan caressed him, Rudra's weak eyes flickered around, and he whispered, "It's going to be fine, love."

Rudra shook his head weakly as he struggled to speak, "Be . . . yourself . . ." He sighed before closing his eyes and breathing his last in the arms of the person he loved.

Arjan was stunned. He didn't want to believe that Rudra was no more.

Wait. Wait. This can't happen.

He tried to shake Rudra. He did it again.

One of the guards came forward, ready to stab Arjan. He plunged the blade through his arm, but Arjan didn't care. He kept shaking Rudra.

"Come on, wake up. Come on."

Another guard stabbed his shoulder.

And then another one, until twenty blades had been rammed inside Arjan as he mourned for his love. Blood gushed out from his body but he felt no pain. All that was left was an empty numbness.

"This is impossible." Arjan could hear Urvashi gasping in dread. He was sobbing hysterically. He hadn't realized that his body had been repeatedly pierced by spears and swords.

His eyes were red and his blood flowed free in crimson.

"You are a wonder, Arjan," Urvashi said, smiling. "How are you still alive?"

Arjan lowered his head as he left Rudra on the ground. He wiped his tears and with clean movements, he pulled out the swords, one by one, as he wailed in pain. He was hurting. The guards backed off, wary of the beast that stood in front of them. Arjan stood up. His face was impassive as he wiped the blood from his chest. He was bleeding, but it didn't matter now.

What had mattered was Rudra.

And he was gone.

Urvashi signalled a few archers, who were standing far behind, to shoot him down. Her smile had vanished. She wanted to see the end of the beast. The archers shot a volley of arrows at him. Arjan grabbed few of the arrows in mid-air and he dodged the rest. It was a cakewalk.

"All right. Calm down, Arjan. We can discuss this."

A guard appeared in front with a sword. Arjan grabbed his sword and then jabbed him by the hilt, exploding his ribcage. He held the same blade, twirled it around, and whenever a guard appeared, he swiftly slashed their throats without batting an eyelid. By the time he was done, he was standing in a pool of corpses.

Never in his life had he thought that he would like it when he killed someone.

The archers stopped shooting as Arjan came forward, looking down at Urvashi.

"You don't have your dolls right now," he whispered, as his

fingers wrapped themselves around her throat. "Then again, I never gave you my hair, did I?" he mumbled.

"You . . . shouldn't . . . kill . . . you are . . . you are not this person."

"*You* have made me this."

Arjan recalled the conversation he had had with Padma—one should be forgiving. But now he realized that he wasn't practicing what he had preached. He was fulfilling her vendetta, letting his fuel for revenge cloud his judgment.

But did it matter?

No. Not anymore.

Rudra was dead. Kalki was dead. Padma for all he knew was dead too.

Arjan had no one. He was too tired to care anymore.

With one quick snap, he broke Urvashi's neck, not even giving her a chance to say her last words. It happened in an instant. Arjan tossed her body towards the pool of bodies, her lifeless eyes reeking of desperation.

He looked at the archers, sighing. They had backed off. The guards he hadn't killed and who were inside the fort had also backed off. In fact, they had opened the gates for him so he could leave.

Arjan nodded to himself as he walked towards Rudra's corpse, picking him up.

And he walked away from the chaos he had just orchestrated.

There had been a time when he had vowed to never to look back again. A lot had changed since then, but even now, he never looked back again.

61

Durukti couldn't believe that Shukr was none other than Lord Mahabali. She had read a lot about Mahabali—the great, wise, benevolent Asura king who had brought about the golden age of Illavarti. The king had been tall, strong, and handsome. And yet Shukr here seemed like a poor imitation of all the tall tales that had been told to people about Mahabali.

They had been on the ocean for quite some time. Durukti was feeling weird. She didn't like this and Kali's hatred was bothering her. But then, she didn't feel bad about it. She knew she had done the right thing by betraying Kali. And after that, she had also helped him recover. Though being here, isolated from all the mayhem in the city, Kali seemed better, kinder. He was angry but not cold or distant, not like before.

Alakshmi on the other hand was just creepy.

She didn't speak or she chose to not speak. Her dangerous beasts were always prancing around her. Durukti was always nervous around her, wondering when those hyenas would just pounce, but they didn't. They wouldn't unless Alakshmi wanted them to.

Durukti looked at Kali and Shukr. They were having an argument.

"You should have told me," Kali said. "But you chose not to. Why?"

"Because I'm ashamed of myself. What more? I was once a great king and look at me now—an old man adrift, in the middle of the ocean."

"I don't even know if I can trust you."

"You can, Lord Kali. You are Dharm. I believe in you. My past doesn't matter. With my support, you shall rise and conquer the world like the Asuras always do."

Dharm . . . Adharm . . . it was just too much for Durukti. She hadn't meant to eavesdrop on their conversation, but it was quiet out there. Even their whispers seemed loud.

"You stripped me of my glory. I am just a madman on a boat right now," Kali said, furious. Durukti could glimpse his earnestness that she had seen in the beginning, at the time he had fought against the mad Janmejaya.

"You need to sacrifice your own blood in the ocean for your enemiesss to fear the wrath of Asuras. You need to . . . wake up the mummified Danavs."

Danavs? That is not a good idea at all.

She had heard stories about them. And all of them told tales about how no one had been able to control the them. Danavs had killed thousands in their time. She wanted to stop Kali but just like Koko and Vikoko, she was frozen to her spot. This was clearly between Shukr and Kali.

Kali clenched his jaw. "All right, I will."

Durukti narrowed her gaze. *This is not happening.*

Shukr smiled as he called Durukti. "Come, child."

Durukti stood up and walked towards Shukr, puzzled.

"Are you ready, Kali?"

"Ready for what?" Durukti asked.

Kali was confused as well. "I thought it was Alakshmi I had to—"

"No, it has to be your sister. Alakshmi's role is to be your wife. She must be kept alive. Durukti, on the other hand, is the one who betrayed you."

At that moment, Durukti turned to punch Shukr but Koko and Vikoko stood up and grabbed her. Durukti realized that they had done it on Kali's orders. They took her to the edge of the boat. She peered at Alakshmi who was grinning at the situation, her pale skin and her golden eyes glimmering with sadistic pleasure.

"Kali! You can't do this. I'm your sister." She turned to Koko and Vikoko. "You are family. You have known me since I was a child. You cannot do this to me."

"We have sworn a blood oath to Lord Kali. And we do what he demands," Koko said with sad, mournful eyes.

Durukti was close to sobbing now as she saw the conflicted Kali walking towards her. He touched her skin, her cheeks, her collarbone.

"She's my sister," he whispered. "She betrayed me, but she's my sister."

Walking close to Kali, whispering in his ear, Shukr added, "Yes, she betrayed you. She had thought of leaving you for a boy from a village. She loved that boy when she should have loved only you. What a cruel wench! Dispose her; she wouldn't bring any luck to you. With her death, a life shall be given to the Danavs and they shall be in your control. They shall do what you want them to do. Imagine how easy it would be to win wars then."

Durukti glanced at Kali. He was troubled. He was frowning. He would have to just push her down and she would be gone forever.

What is he thinking? What's he going to do?

Only if she knew . . .

She didn't want to die. She didn't.

Please. I beg of you.

Her eyes begged him.

But in return, she saw no mercy.

She recalled the time they had been young. She had asked him what kind of a king he would grow up to be. She had always looked up to him. And she recalled other things—from her time with Kalki

to the things she had been through with Kali. He was not a bad man. He was just a very conflicted man.

"Her death will be good for you. Finish her off, Kali, and we will resurrect the Asura Empire from the ashesss and rule the kingdom you always wanted to rule. Destroy the North, the South, and everything, and BRING THEM TOGETHER! Fulfil the dream I could not," Shukr pleaded, trying to convince him.

Durukti looked straight in Kali's eyes as she said, sighing, "Now that's not a kingdom I would like to be in, Kali."

And at that moment his eyes widened, as if he had realized the importance of her words. With a swift movement, he grabbed Shukr by his throat and pushed him over the boat. His wails filled the air around them. The hyenas roared as Alakshmi looked at the drowning Shukr, aghast. She glared at Kali.

Koko and Vikoko hauled Durukti back into the boat as they saw that Kali had made his decision. Durukti gasped and looked at the Black Ocean. Shukr was nowhere to be seen.

Durukti instantly came forward, hugging Kali. Kali hugged her back. She didn't care about the hyenas or the startled Alakshmi. She cared about her brother.

"After everything I did. Why?"

"What king would I be if I can't forgive people," he said and tightened his embrace.

"You shouldn't have done that!" exclaimed Alakshmi in a raspy, thin voice. "He would have been a great mentor to you."

Kali turned to Alakshmi. "Consider yourself lucky that I didn't throw you off."

Alakshmi was speechless.

He pulled back as the boat began to rock. Kali looked at Alakshmi who was as surprised as they were.

What's happening?

"They are rising," Alakshmi gasped. "At least something good came out of it."

Durukti looked at the ocean. The waves had grown stronger. The clouds had covered the sky completely. Their boat was rocking. The last of the Asuras on the boat watched the ocean, expecting gargantuans of the past to come out.

And they did.

Their saw their heads—large in size, almost as big as the boat's size. Durukti gasped, her hands covering her mouth. *This can't be it.* She turned to her brother. Kali was beaming. Durukti was confused. Until now, she had thought that the old Kali was back, but it was clear now that he had wanted the giants to be with him. And as Alakshmi came close to Kali, glancing at the Danavs with him, Durukti realized something else.

He was, nevertheless, going to follow the path he was supposed to.

In the midst of giant heads rising from the ocean, with Danavs towering over the tiny boat with their twenty feet high frames, Durukti heard Alakshmi commenting, "One thing is clear, Kali. You are Dharm. And my waiting for you has not been in vain."

Kali just proudly looked at his new army.

Here I come, Illavarti.

62

The army had already trespassed the bridge.

Kalki saw Taar's men assaulting their forces as they entered the bridge in a straight line, with their swords and spears in front. The bridge was wooden, made of planks tied together with thick ropes. It was between two snowy hills, at a height of fifty feet. If anyone fell from it, they would die.

Kalki had to do something about Taar's men.

Kara had left for protecting the valley side.

Kalki was accompanied by a few Vanars, with Ratna, Smrit, and Padma beside him. And he marched forward, trying to stop the Vanars that had come through the bridge, cutting through their formation, slaughtering the Vanar guards, anyone who displayed the insignia of Taar. Kalki didn't care about anything else.

He was fighting, but they needed a strategy to stop the onslaught of Taar's forces.

Kalki swung his sword from one end to the other as he stabbed, pummelled, and plunged his blade through the raging Vanars. Blood sprayed and splattered on the snow. He saw Padma, with her agile and flexible frame, lurching at the Vanars' shoulders, slashing their throats, and taking refuge by climbing the trees. Ratna and Smrit on the other hand were using their horses to fight the Vanars, throwing their spears to pin them down.

Taar's innumerable men were crowding the bridge. Kalki knew he had to do something. Amidst the roaring and and other battle sounds that were drowned in screams and shrieks, Kalki came forward grabbing a shield from a fallen Vanar.

He protected himself with the shield, blocking and dodging the attacks as he fought back, swinging his sword. The Vanars were quick and sprung around like monkeys. One even managed to jump on Kalki but lost his balance and fell down.

Another Vanar attacked him. He threw his spear at Kalki but Kalki lunged to his side, dodging it. Racing ahead to swing his axe at the Vanar, Kalki raced towards him. But the Vanar's reflexes were quick. He immediately crouched down and toppled Kalki. But instead of killing him, he snatched Kalki's axe and ran away.

Kalki stood up, and made his way to the bridge. He could see Lord Bajrang's army being depleted. So many Vanars lay on the ground, lifeless. Even Padma was panting and was close to losing consciousness.

Ratna and Smrit had lost their horses and were fighting on foot now.

It was chaos.

And then he saw Aruna moving through the bridge, showering arrows at Bajrang's men. The right-hand man of Taar, Aruna came with just two men behind him. He smiled as his arrows pierced the people. He had a crossbow in his hand unlike other Vanars who had single blades. A sword clung to his belt as well.

"You cannot stop us, boy," he said gruffly. "We are more powerful than you. You are outnumbered. The Rakshas and Manavs in the valley have broken through the bamboo barriers that you had created. Your army will perish. They won't stand for long."

"How did you get this?" Kalki asked as he looked closely at Aruna's sword. It looked familiar.

"Lord Kali helped us."

Damn! That man won't leave me alone.

"Do you know who Kali is? Better not deal with him. He might backstab you the moment you have served his purpose."

Aruna shrugged. "How does it matter to me? Isn't that what Bajrang did to us?"

"You shouldn't be harming the children and the women. These are your own people."

"They are NOT OUR PEOPLE! For those who support Bajrang, shall also carry his sins."

And with that, he shot an arrow at Kalki. Kalki deflected it with his shield.

"FOR TAAR!" Aruna screamed as he aimed at Kalki again.

And that was when a figure leapt from the trees, grabbing Aruna and stabbing him in the back. Aruna coughed up blood. Before he could turn around and see who had attacked him, Padma appeared in front of him. She was bruised all over but gathered her strength and tore his spine in half. She jerked the corpse upwards, flinging the dead Vanar at Kalki's feet.

"Thanks," Kalki said, smiling at her.

Padma smiled back. "You saved me, I saved you. He talked too much. I couldn't take it anymore."

"I know."

Kalki shrugged. He saw more of Taar's men appearing at the entrance of the bridge. With the shield in his hand, he walked towards it. He kept the shield in front, with all his force behind it. As the guards jumped at him and retaliated, Kalki held them off. It was tough but he tried not to let them go any further. The Vanars tried to jab Kalki, but he only got scratches.

And with one step and one push at a time, he kept toppling them to the side from whence they came. Kalki peered from behind his shield. He kept pushing to the point that all the Vanars who had gathered on the bridge were thrown on the other side.

Kalki was in the middle of the bridge by now as he panted. Pushing out more than thirty Vanars with just a shield as a weapon

had been difficult, but he had done it. A horn resounded as the Vanars stood transfixed with shock.

Kalki turned to see who was blowing the horn. He saw Taar on a horse, above the cliffs from his side of the bridge as he descended slowly. The Vanars stopped fighting. Everything was at a standstill. Taar dismounted from the horse and took off his golden robe.

Kalki stood there dumbstruck, unable to comprehend what Taar was trying to do.

And when Taar wore his gauntlets and armed himself with small spikes of bronze and gold, Kalki realized that he was being challenged for a one-on-one match with him.

Taar walked to the bridge, adjusting his gauntlets. His tall figure was intimidating. The bridge shuddered a little when he walked upon it, as if his steps were too heavy for it.

Kalki knew he could defeat Taar, but not with those spikes. They looked sharp enough to sear right through Kalki's skin and puncture his vital organs. They might harm and bruise and perhaps even internally bleed him out. Kalki knew he was not ready to fight the monster approaching him.

Standing a few paces away from Kalki who had a shield for a weapon, Taar said, "It's you and me then. You surprised me with your strength. But then I noticed that symbol on your chest and then, I remembered. I've read about this symbol in the scriptures of Udaiyas. That Lord Vishnu reincarnates in every Age to fight evil, and this . . . this is his mark."

"You must have read the flimsy version then. You see, I was not born with this symbol. I earned it."

Taar shook his head as he began to run towards Kalki. Kalki sprinted too, holding the shield in front for defending himself.

That instant, Taar somersaulted up in the air. Kalki looked up at him, confused. Suddenly, he felt sharp blades tearing through his back. The pain was unbearable. He was on his knees.

Kalki realized that he was bleeding as he struggled to stand up.

"These spikes, they are made of obsidian. They are the sharpest weapons of all. I suppose this spiritual symbol you've earned wouldn't make much of a difference in front of this."

Kalki gritted his teeth as Taar paced himself. He punched and punched like a rabid animal, but Kalki deflected each blow with his shield. Taar was quite powerful. Kalki's shield was cracked now.

Taar leapt from his place, throwing the spikes with force. He raced towards Kalki and punched the shield right in the middle, shattering it completely.

Kalki now held a tiny part of the shiled as Taar smiled with confidence.

"You are nothing but words, son."

Taar punched Kalki on the face and before Kalki could gather his wits, he punched Kalki on the abdomen. It was so fast and sharp that Kalki was met with immense pain and surprise with each blow. And with a final punch on Kalki's chin, Taar tossed him aside. Kalki spat volumes of blood, panting for help.

Kalki could see Padma and Ratna standing on the cliff, close to the entrance of the bridge, worried. Padma wanted to help him, but this was Taar and Kalki's fight.

She could not interfere.

This was only between him and the Vanar general.

"Where is Bajrang now? Has he left you, son?" He grabbed Kalki's throat and dangled him in the air. Kalki gasped for air. "Just like he left us. He served one incarnation of Lord Vishnu, right? Why isn't he serving the other? Bias, you say? That's what I hate. You know, now I wonder if Bajrang has the powers that our legends spoke of. Flying? Controlling his size? They are tall tales made by men who worshipped him. They are not true. At the end of the day, he is a weak man who can't do anything, just like you are a weak boy who thinks he can defeat me."

He grabbed Kalki and carried him towards the edge of the

bridge. "I wanted to choke you till I could see the light leave your eyes, but it's better if your friends don't find your body."

And he released his grip.

Kalki was glad that Taar had released him. He could breathe now. But the breeze was harsh as it whipped it across his face. And then it him.

The rocks would batter his body. He was plunging to his death.

And then something picked him up.

Right when he was about to touch the ground, he was grabbed by something. Kalki was elevated in the air for a few moments, and then he felt himself rising.

He could hear the gasps from the people close to the bridge.

And then Kalki saw who it was.

Kalki was being held up by Lord Bajrang. He was flying.

He looked at the Vanar King's face and saw something that he had never seen on his face—anger.

Flying.

The sight was awe-inspiring and comical at the same time. Bajrang was in the air, cradling Kalki like a baby.

Kalki was placed back on the bridge. Bajrang was suspended in the air. Finally, he landed and stood beside Kalki. He had his big, famous gadha dangling from his belt as he patted on Kalki's back.

"I'm sorry I was late," Bajrang said.

"You came to save me." Kalki smiled as he realized that Taar was staring at Bajrang with his mouth open. He was horrified and afraid.

"Taar was beating you senseless and it was kind of selfish of me to not interfere. I won't kill anyone, but at least I can aid you in the battle, right? I fought in my war ages ago. This is your war. And this is your chance to be who you are." He kept his hand on Kalki's head and said, "And you have my word. I'll be there to pick you up when you fall, and I'll be there to aid all my fellowmen, my tribe in moments of darkness. They will never be alone."

Kalki nodded. "That's what your tribe needs right now. Thank you."

"Have this." Bajrang gave him his gadha, unhooking it from his belt.

"Really?"

"Yes. For now, of course. But I want it back, boy." He winked at him.

Kalki nodded.

"HOW DID YOU FLY, BAJRANG?" shouted Taar with his hoarse voice. "Was it one of your magic tricks? You only interfere when there's a Vishnu Avatar involved but when it comes to your people, you back off?"

Bajrang flared his nostrils. Kalki could see he wanted to break Taar's neck, but he refrained and remained patient. "Taar, I apologize for not helping our people in the past. But when have I ever left them alone? It's fine if you besmirch my name, but if you drag my people to the ground, then you shall face my wrath. I will protect them."

"You've come to your senses too late. They don't need a saviour. They need someone who can lead them and fight with them in the battles to come." He crushed both the gauntlets together to unite his fists in his rage.

Kalki knew this was the time.

Holding the gadha in his hands, he sprinted towards Taar. Taar sprang towards Kalki, raging like a beast.

And at that moment, Kalki stopped. Taar was surprised but didn't stop sprinting. Kalki used all his strength, swung the gadha, and waited.

He waited for the right moment.

The resounding blow landed on Taar, smacking his face and crushing his teeth. Blood poured out of his mouth and his nose as he reeled back with the impact. Taar wanted to swing his sword, but before he could muster the strength to do so, Kalki was upon him.

Kalki rose high up in the air, swung the gadha with full force and hit Taar's spine. Taar tried to shield himself with his gauntlets, but his hands couldn't reach his back. There was a loud cracking sound as Taar's spine broke.

Kalki swung the gadha again and smacked Taar's arms. The gauntlets cracked open. One gauntlet fell off as Taar looked on in horror.

But there was no stopping Kalki's wrath.

He stepped on Taar's arm, crushing it. Taar howled in pain as Kalki hit his wrist with the gadha, where the remaining gauntlet was. It shattered.

"NO!" Taar screamed.

Kalki stomped on Taar's arm. He swung his gadha aiming for the already defeated Taar's head, ready to smash it to a pulp.

"KALKI!" A voice boomed over the battlefield.

Kalki lowered the gadha. He kept his foot away from the shivering, rebellious Vanar as he looked at Bajrang. He was walking towards them.

Bajrang wasn't angry anymore and looked at Taar with compassion.

"Don't kill him."

"Why? He might strike again."

"He might, but he's a monster I created. He is my responsibility to bear. Let me rehabilitate him."

"He killed your people. Are you sure about that?"

"Of course." Bajrang smiled, patting Kalki on the shoulder. "Being a hero, Kalki, doesn't mean defeating the enemy. It's also about giving them second chances." He paused. "I shall help all those who had supported Taar in his conquest."

Kalki was not sure if Bajrang's decision was a wise one. But his faith in him outweighed any other emotion he was feeling. He nodded and handed the gadha back to Bajrang. At that moment, he saw Ratna and Padma approach the bridge with the surviving

Vanars. Padma hugged Kalki tightly and Kalki hugged her back. Bajrang's men grabbed Taar and took him. He looked forlorn.

The war had ended.

Bajrang left to address Taar's men, making them understand the pointlessness of the rebellion that they had participated in.

Kalki felt a rush of gratitude and respect for the Vanar King, the Pawanputr. But he had another question. "How did you fly, Lord Bajrang? I thought you said they were tall tales."

Bajrang looked back at Padma and Kalki.

And he smirked.

"Not all stories are tall tales. Sometimes, all you have to do is believe."

63

Manasa was standing close to Vasuki's family's pur. It was being rebuilt.

She had ordered her men to build it again as a shrine for Vasuki—in his remembrance. As the Naga labourers worked hard, she looked at it and recalled all that had happened in the past few days—she had been defeated, wrecked, almost killed, and declared dead. She had lost her lover. She had lost her brother.

No more.

No more it shall be.

Manasa smiled as she turned to see that each mini-island that crowded Naagpuri didn't only have Nagas, but Suparns as well. She was smart enough to not isolate the Suparns anymore—not after the entire Suparnabhoomi had been destroyed. The city had crumbled when all the pillars had collapsed. She was lending a hand to Tarakshya and as was promised, she was keeping the Suparns in Naagpuri till the Bhoomi was rebuilt.

Tarakshya had been reluctant about sending his people to Naagpuri, but he had no choice but to agree. Manasa had demanded a small price in return—every vimana that he had, she wanted them for her own cause.

"What do you plan to do now?" A familiar voice emerged from the back.

Manasa turned her head to see Vibhisana—bumbling and wiping his sweat on his double chin. He had come from Bhanmati to visit Manasa and congratulate her. She had achieved the impossible. There was a truce between the Suparns and the Nagas after so many years.

"I plan to restore peace to our empire. Naagmandal is still under crisis as our people do not like the idea of their rivals sharing the same space."

"I presume that'll be cleared soon . . . oh dear." He wiped the sweat. "It's too hot here!"

"That's Naagpuri." She clutched the Shard of glass her husband had gifted her. "Thank you for helping me."

"No, you helped yourself, Manasa. I was just being a coward." He sighed. "Because of you, we finally have a truce. You've set things right."

Manasa nodded. She was happy. After such a long time of turmoil and defeat, she had won. "My dear friend," she hugged Vibhisana, "I'm just glad I'm rebuilding the ruins that welcomed me when I first came here." She glanced at the half-built pur.

"I'm glad too. So I have a few plans in mind. I want to extend the truce towards the Dandak as well . . ."

Manasa shook her head. "No. No more truces."

"What do you mean?" He arched his thin brows.

"My dear, I have done all of this to do one thing—to take revenge on Kali for what he did to my brother, to my men, and to myself. I handled Kadru. The coast is clear. Now, I shall do what I came here for. Leave Kali to me," she said, determined.

"You are sailing towards Udaiyas then?"

Manasa nodded. "Not sailing."

"Then?"

Manasa smiled. "Flying towards it, my dear. Flying towards it."

64

Arjan stood next to the funeral pyre.

He scratched his scrawny beard as he looked at the fire burning over a bunch of logs. The heat hurt his eyes, but he watched the fire without blinking. A light breeze was blowing and the trees were sighing. He wrapped his arms around himself. His face was tear-stained, clenched in grief. And he looked at himself in the fire—it reminded him of something from the past.

He was in a small village close to Illavarti where he had taken refuge. He had gone to the closest shaman and gotten his wounds treated—he had been bandaged, and treated with healthy ointments. The power of invincibility had vanished when he had killed Urvashi. He had realized that the Soma worked on emotions—the stronger your emotions are, the stronger you become. And when Rudra had died, Arjan's anger and grief had made him invincible.

As the fire blazed in front of him, he held the small-rolled up parchment and decided to read it again.

To my dearest brother,

I am safe and sound. I'm at Dandak now and will be leaving for Mahendragiri soon. I have heard that you are safe too and I'm glad. I'll be returning soon and I hope everything will be fine till then. I miss you,

brother, and I remember how we sat and talked in the fields of our village. Hope we do it again once everything is over. You were right about Padma. She is as good as you. You both have good hearts. And I hope you both stay like that.

Till we see each other again,

Kalki

Arjan stopped reading. Shuko had given him the letter and left. Initially Arjan had been glad to receive it—at least, he knew for sure now that his brother was alive, but when he read about him having a 'good heart', he grew depressed. He felt guilty.

No. I don't have a good heart anymore.

I killed a young girl with my bare hands.

Arjan sighed, unable to accept that he had committed a murder. He hadn't been able to control his anger. He just had to . . . *end her.* And even though he should be regretting it, if he got another chance to do it, he would. Any day.

Rudra was dead because of her.

"They told me you'll be here." A voice came from the back. It was royal, majestic, but papery.

Arjan turned away from the pyre and saw a tall man. He was wearing an overcoat with gold linings on his garments. He had all sorts of jewellery while Arjan, on the other hand, was wearing a scorched dhoti.

Nala was standing with twenty or so Yakshas and some Manavs as well. The villagers were watching the spectacle with curiosity. People were surprised that a man from the royal court had to come to meet a civilian. He walked in front, leaving his men behind. "I apologize for what happened to you. Urvashi was kind of an idiot, right?"

Arjan didn't dignify this statement with a response. Nala's empty words were irritating him.

"All I want to say is, Arjan, I've heard what you did. You slaughtered an army by yourself. And yet, you stand here, denouncing your divinity." Nala smiled, the shadows of the fire hitting him, with half his face darkened.

The sun was dipping in the horizon. Scarlet threads sprawled across the sky.

"The thing with gods is, they need people to worship them," Nala added. "To feed on their ego. I know that because in my culture, I'm a god. But in front of you, I'm nobody. I can be killed, while you can't."

Arjan whispered, "I'm not a god."

"That is exactly what a god would say." Nala chuckled. "You must understand, Arjan. We live in a world where men are not capable of ruling themselves. They don't need a king. They need a god to rule them. That's why the Yaksha society thrives while the Manavs fail because kings . . . they are humane—weak and fragile. They need someone to look up to, otherwise men like Rudra . . . die and perish. Imagine how many people like Rudra you can help if you assume that pedestal."

Arjan's gaze widened. He understood what Nala was implying. "What do you want?"

"I have a lot of money, Arjan. Initially I thought of using that money for myself, to sponsor myself and be the king. But then it would be just another one of my selfish desires. I don't think I am suitable for the throne. What I want is to support someone I believe in . . . and that's you. I want you to be the king. My mother . . ." he twitched at the thought, "She feels I'll be protected if I partner with you, associate myself with you because she sees great, grand visions for your campaign against the dark forces of Illavarti."

"Me? A king?"

Nala nodded as he knelt down on one foot. So did the other

Yakshas and the Manavs. Upon seeing them, the villagers knelt as well, out of respect. And Arjan stood there, his arms crossed, horrified. This was what it had come to. This was what his one act against Urvashi had led to.

It had created fear in the heart of the Yaksha king, and his people.

Does fear truly control people then?

Arjan recalled how Lord Indra had not been just a scientist but a ruler who had controlled his subjects by fanning their fear.

Perhaps that's the best way to go.

"My lord," Nala said, "I would love to sponsor you for the next elections, to be our king and to rule Illavarti the way you want to rule. I hope you accept this partnership."

Arjan didn't know what game he was playing, but Nala seemed honest. He was afraid and he didn't want someone like Arjan to be angry with him.

Nala offered Arjan his hand.

Arjan looked at it, conflicted.

You both have good hearts.

Arjan grasped the Yaksha king's hand.

It was a new beginning for him.

65

Kalki was standing at the same hill that he had stood on with Lord Bajrang.

It had been a month since the day Taar had been defeated. And he was still here, perhaps wondering if another rebellion would rise. But none did. As Bajrang had promised, he had rehabilitated the rebels, supported them, listened to their problems, and won them over to his side.

Kalki was met by Shuko who had told him that Arjan had sent no letter in response, but he had delivered Kalki's letter to him. Arjan had been standing close to a funeral pyre when Shuko had met him. Kalki was worried. *Why was he close to a pyre?* He was afraid for him and decided to eventually go back to his brother. In time.

"KALKI!" A voice came from below the mountain.

He turned his gaze away from the setting sun and looked down to see Padma, who was waving at him. He smiled and descended quickly to meet her.

"What happened?"

"What should we do now?" she asked.

"I don't know. I must complete my journey." Kalki sighed. "Listen," he looked up at Padma, "I told you before. Arjan is alive! So, I have a favour to ask."

"Yes?"

"I want you to guide him. I am sensing that he is in the wrong company. Maybe he has lost too much and death is the only thing that he sees around him."

"How do you know all of this?"

"I don't know." He crossed his arms thoughtfully. "I want you to go back and guide him back to the right path. Will you?"

"You want me to leave you?"

Kalki nodded, his breath getting heavier by the second.

"Why?" She clenched her jaw. "You come with me too."

"My journey isn't complete, Padma. I have to go to Mahendragiri and meet Bhargav Ram. I shall meet you once I'm back." He clutched her hands. Padma looked at him, surprised. "I . . . uh . . . I li—"

And he was stopped mid-sentence when he heard someone approaching them. Kalki turned to see Lord Bajrang. He was wearing a white dhoti. Kalki noticed a rudraksh on his neck.

"I hope I didn't disturb you both."

"Not at all." Padma smiled.

Kalki glumly nodded.

In a way, you did.

He brushed the thought away.

"What happened?" Kalki asked.

"I want to show you something. I think this information might come in handy to you two."

Kalki and Padma were puzzled, but decided to follow Bajrang.

They had entered a cave.

It seemed like a cave, but it was different from the one Darooda Simha had led them to. It was wider and denser, with fire lamps carefully adjusted on the walls. The walls inside the cave were gleaming brightly.

Bajrang walked deeper into the cave as the path turned rocky

and hard. Kalki and Padma had had enough practice walking through different terrains. There was no snow inside, though it was chilly. They finally came to the middle part of the cave, where it opened up to a sealed clearing, with the outline of a dome. It was centred in the middle and around it, there was a pathway for one to look at the dome from all angles.

Kalki noticed instantly that this dome wasn't ordinary—it had intricate designs carved on it of figures, buildings, weapons, and whatnot. As Kalki studied these designs, Bajrang began to speak.

"These two designs," he showed a red and a blue figure, "represent the Asuras and the Devas. Blue represents the Devas from the North where Swarg was, a foreign land where their abode Mount Meru stood. On the other hand, the ones in red depicts Asuras who came from Pataal. Both were foreigners who came to our land," and then he led his finger to the battle between these figures. They had strangely shaped spears in their hands. "They were in constant battle over the territory before the Devas and the Asuras decided to establish a treaty. They decided to divide the unconquered lands—Udaiyas and Dakshini, North and South. The North was ruled by the Devas and the South was ruled by Asuras. The problem was that the Asuras were quite the barbarians while the Devas were agriculturists, inventors, innovators. Indra, one of the best scientists of Devas, invented the Somas. And the Asuras wanted it. They kept fighting over it for centuries. Indra realized that the Somas were always going to be the bone of contention, so he spread it across the lands, hoping the worthy would receive it."

"I thought he had made the Somas to help Manavs."

"He did, that's why he left most of the reserves in Suparnika which was home to a majority of the Manavs."

Kalki knew most of this history, but he had never seen it depicted graphically. The figures carved on the cave portrayed everything that had happened between the Devas and the Asuras.

"One should know their past to set their future," Bajrang explained when Kalki seemed confused at this discussion.

Kalki pointed at one of the figures in blue who stood in front, while others stood behind him. The same was the case with the red figure, who towered over the others standing behind him.

"What is this?"

"Ah," Bajrang grinned, "the so-called prophecy of good and evil, the Dharm and Adharm. The blue one is Dharm who stands at the front while the red one is Adharm."

"I don't understand one thing." Kalki arched his brows. "Who are these people behind Dharm and Adharm?"

"The supporters of their cause, boy. I thought Kripa must have told you that. But alas! That man hardly knew anything." Bajrang continued, "As an Avatar, Dharm is a soldier of Lord Vishnu, and all the people behind him are his supporters who will walk with him to fight the Adharm. Adharm will also be followed by his own army. You as Dharm will be in the front, leading your people, but there are others too as important as you who are going to assist you in this battle. They will decide the fate of this world."

Kalki sighed. "But Lord Govind . . . Lord Raghav, they alone . . ."

Bajrang raised his bushy brows. "Lord Raghav was alone?"

Of course not!

"You were part of his army, the soldier of Lord Raghav."

"Yes, and so was Lakshman and numerous others. Lord Govind had all the Pandavs with him to support his cause. The battle of Dharm and Adharm, it is not between just two men." He paused. "It's between two armies fighting for their beliefs to save the world. A clash of two beliefs."

Bajrang looked pensive as he said, "I hope you find your army soon, kid."

Kalki stood at the exit of Dandak Hills, from where the slopes ascended to Mahendragiri. He was with Devadatta and Shuko. Padma had pursed her lips, disappointedly watching Kalki fading into the distance.

"Don't leave," she said.

"I have to. This is my destiny."

She shook her head. "You were going to say something to me?"

"I like you." Kalki smiled at Padma. "I hope you like me as well."

She narrowed her eyes. "Look at you, you overconfident buffoon."

"I'm a buffoon? I just beat a Vanar with a gadha. You should hug me in appreciation."

"Shut up, you."

There was an awkward pause.

"I should leave then."

"Hold on."

She came close to him and planted a soft kiss on his cheek.

"Yeah, now leave," she said.

"A kiss on the cheek? That's it?" Kalki said, disappointed.

"You do realize that I am not an expressive girl . . ."

Kalki grabbed Padma by the waist, not waiting for a single second as he kissed her—as hard as he could, letting her hair open from the bun in the process. And when he left her, she was flustered.

Regaining her breath, all she could manage to say was 'Wow'.

"I have been waiting for too long. I didn't want to wait anymore."

She kissed him back. They were wrapped in a close embrace for a while, until she said, "I'll go to Arjan, all right?"

"Thank you."

They parted and Kalki felt weird leaving her, but he had to. He mounted Devadatta who nudged his head while Shuko squawked.

He gets a kiss and I get to carry him on my back. What luck? Devadatta cursed.

Kalki just laughed at it. He looked back at Padma who was waving at Kalki.

"When I return, I want to know who you are, where you are from. I know so little about you."

"If our fates allow, I suppose you will end up seeing my father when you return."

Kalki was curious, but with a final goodbye he straddled forward, his horse going towards the depths and the paths that would eventually lead him to Mahendragiri Mountains. He looked back. Padma was now a dot in the scenery. The thought of leaving her behind, leaving everyone behind and going alone . . .

It scared him.

And he knew it was supposed to scare him.

But he would be okay.

He was ready.

66

He waited.

He had been waiting for a long time now. And he didn't mind. He liked it. The patience, it gave him the energy and the drive to do what he intended to when Kalki reached here.

And he was here. He was quite close to his goal.

He had seen it from the Third Shard—Kalki was about to reach—that meant he was on his way to meet Bhargav Ram.

And once he meets Bhargav, he shall be disappointed. Poor boy.

He would like to see the look on Kalki's face when he comes to know the harsh truth.

He walked from the throne, casually strolling in the ancient Temple of Shiva—the once revered abode of Lord Shiva himself, where everything was made of bronze and granite. There was a thirty feet tall idol of him as well, but no one to worship his image.

He walked out where he saw the snow, the pillars, the wide clearing in front, and long spears plunged into the ground. And near the spears, stood cloaked men.

Sunyavadis.

He knew that Kalki will be afraid of them, but he didn't mind. He liked the Sunyavadis—the worshippers of the void, the true keepers of the ancient prophecy. People in Illavarti had circulated all sorts of different prophecies about the great old evil, but none

knew the true one, the one that held secrets and mysteries. Only the Sunyavadis did and they were here, joining his cause.

They wanted to be a part of what I was doing. Orchestrating everything, so that everything falls into place . . . by seeing from the Third Shard of the Eye of Brahma.

He had lied to Symrin about the Eye of Brahma being lost. A Vidyadhara like Symrin was just a pawn in his game. She didn't need to know the truth.

He hadn't lost the Eye of Brahma. After the Mahayudh was over, he was alone and weak. He wanted to do something. And he went across the country, passing the seas and reaching Pataal to find the Eye of Brahma, eventually stealing it from Shukracharya.

After he got it, he tried to use it only to realize that the Eye of Brahma was useless to him without the Third Shard which showed the future. With that, he could control all outcomes since he would already know what was going to happen. But the Third Shard was difficult to use. It could be used only after long periods of time.

He hadn't brought the First Shard with him, and he had given the Second Shard to Bajrang to build relations with the Vanar king. Bajrang was a good man and he wouldn't use it for his advantage. It would be harmless under his protection. That way, no one would be able take it for themselves. He had kept the Third Shard for himself, and the Fourth Shard he had given to Nanda, so that it eventually reached Manasa. He had seen what Manasa would do with it in the future, how she would use it for her own cause.

And that is exactly what I want.

As he waited, he could feel the scent of Kalki reaching him, ready to free him from the treacheries of the curse that he had received.

After ages, he would finally be free.

He ruffled his wavy hair with his fingers, pulling it back to touch his scar where his *mani* used to be—in the middle of his forehead.

Kalki would come and break his chains.

Kalki was his saviour.

An ironic twist, he mused. The man who had suffered because of him would be the one to save him. He was the man who had orchestrated the entire Kalyug. The Age was a bookend to his long life.

He was the Cursed man.

He was the Scarred Man.

He was Ashwatthama.

THE END

TO BE CONTINUED…

TRIBES

RAKSHAS – Intelligent humanoids, born in the South on the island of Eelam, are strong in combat and have tougher skin compared to other Tribals. Their average height goes above six feet. They have a patriarchal system and their culture, regardless of their furiousness, is quite backward. Most of them worship Lord Shiva, but are often considered by others as atheists. They have black skin and oiled hair.

NAGAS – Royalty and aristocrats living in the city of Naagpuri which floats on a lake. Nagas worship Lord Shesh Naag and Lord Vishnu. Nagas are diplomats more than warriors, but have grown their military system over a period of time. Women are respected in their culture. They are said to have blue eyes and fair skin.

YAKSHAS – Short in height and mischievous. They are considered the least threatening, but are very good in finances. They worship only their king and not any god. They lack military and political skills. Yakshinis, the female counterpart of the Yakshas, are rare. They live in Alakpur which is in the midst of a desert. Their Tribe is considered the richest of all.

ASURAS – Extinct race. Not much is known about this Tribe. They were considered to be the reason behind all the evil in this world. There was a great hunt of this Tribe where many Asura children, women, and men were slaughtered and hanged due to the

superstitions about them. Some survived and have been wandering. They are atheists.

DANAVS – Brothers of Asuras, they are supposedly as tall as trees and as huge as mountains. They were the arch-enemies of the gods and had been put to sleep for their walks could create tremors. They are grandly fantasized during bedtime stories and many have not seen them since the Breaking.

PISACHAS – Cannibals. Live over swamps in Daldal Lands. They worship the 'the fittest'. They believe in karma and they ink their bodies with each crime they have committed. They are considered to be mentally unstable and only a fool would cross their lands.

VANAR – They live in Dandak Hills. They are considered to be vastly knowledgeable. They have hairy bodies which are sometimes ridiculed as being defected. They have gone underground and they choose not to be friendly towards visitors. They worship their protector Lord Bajrang who is considered an immortal and their king.

NOTE: There are other tribes that are not in the list. They are yet to be researched and documented.

– Ved Vyas.

ACKNOWLEDGMENTS

First of all, I would like to thank my parents, Leslie Missal and Jyotsna Missal. They have been my pillars of support in this journey and guided me when I strayed.

I would like to thank my agent, Mr. Anuj Bahri who's helped me get the Kalki series to the right people.

I would like to express my gratitude to the people at Fingerprint! Publishing. Gaurav Sabharwal and Shikha Sabharwal are unlike any other publisher out there. People of Prakash Books, such as Surendra Dangwal, Rajaram Rawool, Nataraj sir, Gururaj sir, Nihar sir, Neeraj sir, Mahesh ji have constantly supported me in this venture. My thanks to Garima Shukla for deftly editing my book and also loving it.

Thanks to Bijit Sinha, my personal editor, who helped with the first edits.

I would like to thank Ayush Dogra for his beautiful rap on Kalki, and Shubham Ghatge for composing the rap.

Thanks to Sana Shekh for handling my interviews and reviews, Ajitabha Bose for creating wonderful posters and banners, and Anuj Kumar who helped me start this journey. Thanks bro!

The other names as follows: Seema Saxena, Gagan bro, Manpreet Kaur (for supporting the book always), Helly Chatterjee.

I would like to thank my two brothers—Shrey Singh and Ryan Mario Cardoza. You know why you are here.

Most of all, thanks a lot my readers. You have been patiently waiting for this part. Hope you enjoy it!

KEVIN MISSAL is a twenty-two-year-old graduate of St. Stephen's College. He released the first book of the Kalki Trilogy, *Dharmayoddha Kalki: Avatar of Vishnu*, in 2017. It has been praised by many reputed newspapers, such as *Millennium Post* and *Sunday Guardian*, that termed it '2017's mythological phenomenon'.

Kevin loves reading, watching films, and building stories in his mind. He lives in New Delhi and can be contacted at kevin.s.missal@gmail.com.